More praise for Lan Samantha Chang and *Inheritance*

"Rich, complex, historically resonant, and beautifully told, *Inheritance* illuminates a crucial time in China's history through the passions of a remarkable family."

— Andrea Barrett, author of *Servants of the Map*

"In this vivid and haunting novel of people caught up in love and war, Chang creates characters with such passionate understanding, they remain with us permanently."

— Patricia Powell, author of *The Pagoda*

"A wonderful story—both unique and universal, it moves through time and history as intricately as it travels the troubled roads of the human heart."   — Elizabeth Strout, author of *Amy and Isabelle*

"In this absorbing story of two sisters whose lives are shaped by the battles within their family and their country, Lan Samantha Chang once again displays her remarkable gift for creating characters whom the reader will want to follow anywhere. *Inheritance* is a wonderful, passionate novel."

— Margot Livesey, author of *Eva Moves the Furniture*

"In *Inheritance*, Chang has done much more than create a dragon lady and counterpose her to a quietly heroic sister. Junan's steely will is a carapace that presses on and imprisons her beating heart. . . . Junan's younger sister is also searingly portrayed, but as much through absence, silence and annunciation as through action."

— Richard Eder, *New York Times Book Review*

"History and family are two pillars in Lan Samantha Chang's novel *Inheritance*, which follows two sisters from China to the United States.

But the book's strength is its characters, who are driven by love, crafty relatives, and a hunger to know the past. Most striking are Junan, the older sister, and her efforts to control those within her emotional reach. In other novels, she might merely be a sketch of meanness. Here she inspires a mix of disapproval, respect, and affection." —*Boston Globe*

"Chang . . . tells a polished story, smooth as stone. It is most poignant as it delves into the follies that make us human."

—Ana Cabán, *Milwaukee Journal Sentinel*

"Like eating a meal that you've enjoyed before, you come back to [*Inheritance*] gladly ready to satisfy yourself again."

—Anhoni Patel, *San Francisco Chronicle*

"The sense of long family histories both spoken and unspoken is powerful, and the restrained conclusion has the force of Ishiguro's *The Remains of the Day*." —*Publishers Weekly*

"Readers who enjoy the works of strong writers like Amy Tan, Gail Tsukiyama, and Hong Ying will relish this novel."

—*Library Journal*

"The skill with which this novel is written is magical."

—*Historical Novels Review*

"Chang's debut novel is filled with complex characters and intricate details about their troubled lives." —*Asian Week*

Inheritance

ALSO BY LAN SAMANTHA CHANG

Hunger: A Novella and Stories

W. W. NORTON & COMPANY

NEW YORK | LONDON

LAN SAMANTHA CHANG

Inheritance

Although many of the political and military figures mentioned

in this novel did exist in Republican China (1911–49),

the narrator, her friends, and her family are imaginary.

Copyright © 2004 by Lan Samantha Chang

For information about permission to reproduce selections from this book, write to Permissions, W. W. Norton & Company, Inc., 500 Fifth Avenue, New York, NY 10110

Portions of this book have appeared previously in *Harvard Review* and *Ploughshares*.

Grateful acknowledgment is made to W. W. Norton & Company, Inc., for permission to reprint "*Classic of Poetry* LXXXI: I Went Along the Broad Road," from *An Anthology of Chinese Literature: Beginnings to 1911* by Stephen Owen, editor and translator. Copyright © 1996 by Stephen Owen and The Council for Cultural Planning and Development of the Executive Yuan of China. Used by permission of W. W. Norton & Company, Inc.

Manufacturing by R.R. Donnelley, Harrisonburg
Book design by Barbara Bachman
Production manager: Amanda Morrison

Library of Congress Cataloging-in-Publication Data
Chang, Lan Samantha.
    Inheritance / by Lan Samantha Chang.—1st ed.
        p. cm.
    ISBN 0-393-05919-7 (hardcover)
1. Sisters—Fiction. 2. Betrayal—Fiction. 3. Women—China—Fiction. 4. Women immigrants—Fiction. 5. Military spouses—Fiction. 6. Arranged marriage—Fiction. 7. Mothers and daughters—Fiction. 8. Chinese American women—Fiction. I. Title.
    PS3553.H2724I54 2004
    813'.54—dc22   2004006203

ISBN 0-393-32711-6 pbk.

W. W. Norton & Company, Inc.
500 Fifth Avenue, New York, N.Y. 10110
www.wwnorton.com

W. W. Norton & Company Ltd.
Castle House, 75/76 Wells Street, London W1T 3QT

2 3 4 5 6 7 8 9 0

For my sisters

Inheritance

Prologue

Hangzhou 1925

WHEN SHE WAS THIRTY-FOUR, NO LONGER A YOUNG WOMAN, my grandmother Chanyi crossed West Lake to see a fortune-teller. She didn't tell my grandfather; she wished to keep her fate a secret. Perhaps her years of married life had deepened her need for privacy.

"You come along, Junan," she told my mother. "She'll predict your husband." At twelve, my mother had no interest in a husband, but she welcomed every chance to see the world. She took her sister by the hand and together they followed Chanyi to the waiting cab.

Soon it would be summer. Warm rains had rinsed the coal dust off the gray house walls, forming puddles in the streets where insects bred. The cabbie pedaled slowly, cursing as his front wheel dipped and sloshed the mud over his feet. His three passengers paid scant attention. Chanyi sat lost in thought. Little Yinan gave the man one frightened, curious glance and looked away. My mother maintained the cool poise that she would have throughout her life. As usual, she kept her questions to herself. Why weren't they taking their own horse and cart? Why was the trip a secret? They had never been out alone before. She didn't let herself relax until they reached the famous lake, where the sweet air and tranquil beauty soothed her. Deep clouds suffused the lake and sky with violet tones, making a vivid backdrop for the crumbled Thunder Peak Pagoda.

"Look over there," she said to Yinan. "The old pagoda's fallen."

"Is it dead?"

"No, silly, it's made of stone."

Yinan covered her eyes. Certain objects frightened her and she wouldn't go near them. She refused to touch the carved goose handle on an old water bucket. She claimed the rose on a silk cushion had made a face at her.

Junan appealed to their mother. "Mama, see how silly she is."

But Chanyi didn't respond. She sat clutching a package with the fortune-teller's payment, her eyes bright with resolve and fear.

Junan turned her gaze back to the fallen tower. Not even her mother's mood could lessen her interest in the pagoda, which she had read about in a history book. The structure dated back a thousand years to when Hangzhou had been the capital of China and poets had praised the city in their songs. It had been standing when Marco Polo declared Hangzhou the most beautiful city in the world: a city built around a lake deep and serene, a city of holy places marked with palaces and temples. The pagoda had stood through the fall of the last emperor. Junan could remember it, mysterious and beckoning across the lake. But now it had crumbled. There was just the ruined stub fringed with weeds, nested by swallows.

Sometimes, when Junan looked at an object that had frightened Yinan, she would try to imagine what her sister had seen. She rarely could. But as she studied the pagoda, she believed she knew. Like every child, Yinan had heard the legend of the pagoda. There was a female spirit trapped in the hillock underneath as punishment for her excessive love. Perhaps Yinan imagined the spirit, blackened and battered after centuries' exposure to the water and stones, still loving and still trapped. This was the punishment of a wife who tried to hold on to a wandering man. It would be the fate of any wife who resorted to tricks or magic. There was only one way to keep a man: to give birth to his son.

Riding the ferry to the temple where the fortune-teller lived, Junan kept her gaze trained on the remains of the pagoda. This curious errand had led her to understand that she would someday be a wife. In only a few years, she would leave her mother behind and go to live with strangers. She kept her face impassive, helping Chanyi to the dock. Chanyi moved slowly. She had spent six years in binding cloths before the fashion ended. Her feet had taken on the spiral shape of shells, with the big toe pointed forward and the small toes curled beneath. She leaned on Junan, wavering. Yinan reached for Chanyi's other hand.

THE FIGURE AT the temple door could have been either a man or a woman dressed in a thick, brown wool robe and cloth sandals. The clipped gray hair was barely visible on the ivory scalp. But when Junan peered again, she recognized a woman's face: hidden and dark, folded into herself over the years.

"Shitai," said Chanyi, bobbing her head, using the most respectable form of address. She gestured with the package in her hands. "I am Wang Taitai. I have—brought a gift for the temple."

The woman bowed and led them through the door.

In the courtyard, they could smell the scent of thawed earth. The camphor trees were sprayed with green, and the vegetable garden along the side displayed a few lines of pale green points. In the tiny cottage wall, one shaded window closed its eye upon the garden.

Chanyi said, "Your garden has come up."

"It is in a shambles," the old woman answered properly.

Junan knew her mother was encouraged by this show of manners. "This is my older daughter," Chanyi said. "And my younger daughter."

The woman nodded.

"My older daughter was born the year after the Revolution, and her meimei was born in the sixth year." This time the nun did not reply. To her, it seemed, the Revolution did not matter.

Inside, the floor was soft underfoot, covered in layers of matting. There were two more windows shaded with rice paper, and the resulting still air and lack of sunlight made a damp smell as if the cottage had been built over water. There was nothing in the room except a bowl and chopsticks on a shelf and a blanket on the bed. But Junan could sense a shadow somewhere in the room. She felt a sudden desire to turn and leave. She reached for Yinan, who hung behind. The door closed and the light vanished.

Yinan whispered, "Why is it so dark?"

"Hush," Chanyi said.

The woman answered easily enough. "It is better for my eyes," she said. Her voice was pleasant, but Yinan held fast to Junan's elbow. "Two girls. The tall one is first. You come here."

Junan had no shame about her height; she knew the worth of her beauty. She stood straight and still, defiant as the dim eyes studied each part of her face: the shape of her brow, her jaw, her forehead.

"Hold out your left hand." The nun took Junan's hand in her two old, dry ones. For a long moment she peered at Junan's hand, and then she let it go.

"Strong," she said. "A strong, fierce girl."

Junan was pleased by the words. She turned to her mother and saw written on her face a dull relief. "Her marriage?" Chanyi asked.

"She will marry a soldier."

"That's impossible."

The woman shrugged.

"But she'll have a generous dowry. And look at her," Chanyi protested. "Surely she's worth more."

"She will decide herself. She will let him in."

"What do you mean?"

For a brief moment the nun caught Junan's gaze. "We are entering a new time," she said. "A new world with its own ideas of love and power."

Junan wished to ask the woman what she meant. But Chanyi shook her head. "There is Yinan," she insisted. "You haven't spoken of her."

"But the meimei does not want me to speak of her."

They all turned to the girl, who had bowed her head to hide her face behind her shining hair. Gently, Chanyi touched her cheek. "Meimei, go to the woman and let her tell your fortune."

Yinan didn't budge.

The nun examined Yinan, but she didn't soften at the sight of her face, as Chanyi had. She watched impassively, as if she weren't looking at a child.

"Meimei," Chanyi repeated, "don't you want to know whom you will marry?"

Yinan whispered, "I don't want to marry."

Chanyi looked down. "Maybe it's better that way." Then she straightened as if gathering her courage. "She is young for her age. Now I need to talk to the shitai alone. Go, children—go outside and wait for me."

Junan hesitated. The urge to stay was strong. She had begun, years earlier, to protect her mother from situations that might threaten her vulnerable heart. But in this case it would only make things worse to disobey. She took Yinan's hand and left the room. Outside the cottage, she immediately took off her shoes. Yinan, puzzled, did the same. Junan led her barefoot around the cottage, to the window on the other side. Standing in the soft earth of the fortune-teller's garden, the sisters watched and listened as their mother faced the fortune-teller and began to speak.

CHANYI WAS NO longer the lovely woman she had once been. She had kept her delicate bones and long, deep eyes, but her face had worn away like sand, sharpening the nose and leaving hollows at the mouth. Now the dim light cast deep shadows under her eyes. Her lips closed in a rueful line, as if at her unluckiness. Other women in their thirties grew full-breasted and contented. But she had reached her beauty in her youth and now she dwindled.

"For years," she said, "since Yinan, I have not been with child. I have tried all the usual methods. There is one thing I haven't tried. A drug from an apothecary." She paused, and swallowed hard. "I'm no longer a young woman," she said. "I turn thirty-five at the new year. But others my age have not yet finished bearing children. I want you to tell me—if I will have a son."

"You are afraid that your husband will take another wife." The nun spoke judiciously, each dry word like a doctor's hand examining a wound. "But there is a reason you need to know. A more important reason."

Chanyi closed her eyes.

"You have something of an illness," the old voice said. "I can see it in the lines around your mouth. You lie awake at night. You lie awake because you want to know what will happen. Let me tell you something

I have learned. There is no point in knowing what will happen. Do you understand?"

The voice floated like a dry leaf. There was detachment in the voice; it carried no resonance or weight, and Junan knew that this disinterest showed she spoke the truth. She felt her body flinch as if the nape of her neck had been stroked by a bony finger. "Please," her mother whispered. "I will pay you." She reached toward her purse. "Silver dollars. One hundred dollars."

"Some women, Taitai, have only daughters."

"One thousand dollars."

"I have taken a vow against untruths."

"Anything," Chanyi whispered. "Anything."

"Other women learn to share their men, Taitai."

Chanyi cried out as if she had been struck. She wrapped her arms around the package and turned, dragging her feet like stones toward the door.

Junan stepped out of the garden. She wiped her feet in the wet grass and told Yinan to do the same.

"No, we have to hurry!"

"Wipe your feet," Junan insisted. She thought their mother wouldn't get far. But panic had brought urgency into Chanyi's stride. In her effort to move quickly she surrendered every particle of grace, and by the time the girls had caught up with her she'd almost reached the lake.

"Mama," Yinan called.

Chanyi didn't seem to hear. She stood facing the water as if searching its depths.

YEARS LATER, JUNAN would let herself remember the trip across the lake. She would see the pagoda, fallen on the low hill scattered with the bruised petals of fruit tree blossoms. She would think of the old woman who predicted she would marry a soldier, and she would remember that Yinan said she didn't want to marry. Finally, Junan would envision Chanyi's slender figure outlined against the clouds, and she would try to imagine what her mother had been thinking.

Perhaps Chanyi had been remembering an afternoon when she and her young husband had visited that very shore and sat with blithe and careless happiness under the falling flower petals. They had hired a boat and drifted on the surface of the lake, sharing their hopes and wishes for a family, for sons.

Or perhaps Chanyi had been looking into the future. It was surprising how bad news could make things clear. If she went on without a son, she would have to learn to live as one who'd fallen out of favor. Sharing a man, sharing his house, she would twist toward survival as so many others did. She knew the stories. Her desires and motives would grow crippled and deformed, and she would learn to hate this other, younger wife. As she became skimpy and gray, she would learn to speak with hidden knives, keeping things off-balance. She would fight ruthlessly for small concessions. When the younger woman finally triumphed and gave birth to a son, Chanyi would learn to hate that child, try to stunt it, thwart it, ruin it.

She knew that it was possible to live through this grief and shame. Anything was possible. But did she want to be the woman who would emerge at the end of it? A woman without hope? Chanyi stood before the vast, indifferent beauty of the lake. She watched the world reflected on its surface: a promenade, a temple, and mountains in the distance. For one long moment all else faded from her vision. Her eyes found the lake as deep and promising as rest.

Marriage

MY FAMILY STORY IS LIKE A STONE. I OFTEN THINK ABOUT ITS true dimensions, weight, and shape. Many years ago, it was pitched into deep water, pulling after it a spout of air, leaving only ripples.

BAD LUCK STRUCK us long before my grandmother's death by drowning. This much I know from Hu Mudan, our former house-keeper, who said the trouble began before my mother was born. One autumn night in 1911, a group of men entered the family's unlocked front door. Inside, they lit fire to the house, then hurried out to report what they had done to the Revolutionary Alliance. At the last minute one man, thinking of the people inside, turned back and knocked once, twice, thrice. But his knocking was muffled by the shadow wall, which had been built inside the door to repel unhealthy influences. The fires spread steadily and brightly in the autumn air, and by the time the household was aware of what had happened, it had become impossible to stop the conflagration.

Only one person inside heard the soldier's knocks. Hu Mudan was then fourteen, fifteen in Chinese years. She wasn't yet our housekeeper or even a maid. She was a hungry girl, a stray, who had stolen into the house to lie with the errand boy in his small side room near the door. Like many hungry people, Hu Mudan did not sleep well. And she knew something was the matter; she had an ear for trouble. That is how she described her memory of the Revolution: the sound of trouble, three loud knocks on the heavy wooden door, waking her in the middle of the night.

Bang. Bang. Bang.

Hu Mudan remembered the fire's quick consummation in images of extraordinary lightness and weight. The gold light flickered up the rice-paper windows, illuminating them in brief screens of blaze that quickly settled into ash. The rows of glazed green roof tiles glittered like serpents' scales. She saw a man stagger into the courtyard, carrying an armful of ledgers. He should have hurried to escape, but instead he stood, a small, gray-bearded figure, staring at the scene as if he were not part of it. A falling beam, heavy with tiles, struck him on the forehead, and he dropped like a puppet whose strings had been cut.

Hu Mudan couldn't reach the man; the blazing beam lay between them. She turned away from the fire, hoping to find the back door and disappear. But then something made her stop in her tracks. On the left side of the house, a young woman hovered on the rail of a balcony. The stairway was ablaze, and her robe of pale green silk was lit up in reflections of the flames.

Their eyes met, the woman's beseeching. Hu Mudan couldn't look away. She couldn't leave behind this woman staring down into the courtyard as if it were the maw of death. She must take the woman with her. She must become her safety net.

She gestured with her arms. "Jump, jump!" she shouted. But the rough roaring voice of the fire rose higher.

"Jump! I will help you!"

The green figure hurtled into smoke. The woman fell to the ground, bringing Hu Mudan down with her.

Hu Mudan could hear her own cry, faint against the roaring flames, but she heard no sound from the woman next to her. This silence worried her. She pulled herself to a poised, defensive crouch. She took the woman's shoulders in her hands and turned them over. They were the slender, almost sharp-boned shoulders of a young wife. Her eyes were half closed and her eyeballs had slid back; her parted lips exposed a few even, white teeth. Her face, which was serene and smooth, was lit up in unearthly shadows from the glow of the fire. Hu Mudan studied the sensuous flare of her upper lip, her curved cheekbones, her high oval forehead and shadowed, deep-set eyes. The eyelids flickered.

"Up, up," Hu Mudan gasped in the heat. "Hurry." She pulled the green silk robe, warm and smooth against her fingertips.

The woman, coughing, pointed toward the back of the house. She had difficulty walking and leaned heavily on Hu Mudan. Step by step, they struggled.

Behind the house there was a smaller courtyard that had been built to house a temple and had fallen into disrepair. A small pond lay in its center. The water was low at this time of year, but still it made a firebreak. When they had hobbled around the pond, they couldn't go another step. They collapsed to the grass, leaning on each other, watching the fire. The young woman wept. Hu Mudan stared dazed into the flames. The glowing house reflected in the pond recalled a fireworks spectacle that she had once glimpsed over the river.

Finally the woman raised her head and told Hu Mudan her name was Chanyi. "Who are you?" she asked, in her curious, gentle way. "Are you new in the house?"

"No."

"Where do you come from?"

Hu Mudan shook her head.

"Please stay here with us," Chanyi said, and closed her eyes.

Hu Mudan stayed there, in the garden, breathing the smell of autumn chrysanthemums and the sweet, worn scent of roses faint amid the odor of burning. The woman's heavy head dropped into her lap. A thick braid slid against her calf, but otherwise she lay still, the head flung back over Hu Mudan's knees. A jade pendant lay in the hollow of her throat, and the pockets of her robe were embroidered with dragons. Examining the pale green robe that washed and flickered in the flames, Hu Mudan noticed the slight bulge of the belly beneath, and understood that the robe was a gift from someone who very much desired this daughter-in-law to give birth to a boy.

The fire burned. All over China, houses were flaming up in a splendid light before they settled ghostlike into embers and ashes. Hu Mudan

sat in the garden with the young daughter-in-law from the Wang family. She felt a sense of peace and determination rise through her like an
answering flame. She had found someone on whom to focus her care.
She had been with many men, but she had never felt trust before, and
now she instinctively knew that to trust someone meant to be responsible for that person. Hu Mudan tipped her palm to the marbled glow of
the fire, and she saw the path of her life run before her, like lightning
branching in her hand.

SHE HAD BEEN HUNGRY. She had been alone. In that time of trouble,
Chanyi had made room for her. Hu Mudan believed in the old loyalties,
and she immediately began to serve as Chanyi's maid. Only she knew
how to comb Chanyi's knee-length hair, beginning at the ends and
moving gently to her scalp. Only she understood how to keep her mistress safe from the despondency that haunted her. After Chanyi bore
two daughters and her hair grew light and thin, Hu Mudan did not comment but continued to comb carefully, gently. When it became apparent
that Chanyi had lost her beauty, Hu Mudan did not offer flattery or false
hope. For this, her mistress loved her more. She gave Hu Mudan her
pendant of green jade. She begged Hu Mudan to take care of her
daughters if anything might happen to her.

When Chanyi died, Hu Mudan vowed never to marry. Instead, she
would watch over the two girls.

For more than five years afterward, Hu Mudan immersed herself in
the household whose master had stolen Chanyi's beauty, serving the
mother-in-law who had broken Chanyi's spirit. She sat old Mma on her
chamber pot and helped to pull her up. She watched over my grandfather and tried, with limited success, to keep him out of the paigao
games. Most importantly, she looked after my mother and aunt. She
watched the girls as tenderly as she had watched Chanyi. She monitored
their manners, appetite, and growth. She checked their stools, fingernails, their palms, the scent of their breath, all with a dry, clear expression, as if she waited for the worst but would not flinch from it.

She worried that they would suffer from the melancholia that had overtaken their mother. But the sisters showed no sign of it. Junan had faith in justice and in the order of things. She read Confucius, with his strict hierarchy of obedience within family walls: wife to husband, daughter to father, younger to elder. According to these laws, she was responsible for Yinan, and Yinan must obey her. She would in turn obey her father, who would in turn respect and cherish old Mma. This system guaranteed that when she grew old, her own grandchildren would tend to her.

Two more different sisters could not have been imagined. While Junan's white skin and studied calm foretold her beauty and poise, Yinan's narrow face and tadpole eyes predicted nothing. While Junan held her temper, showing only cool propriety, Yinan had no propriety to speak of. She favored roots and secrets, buried treasures. She liked to dig in the earth, arranging mud and stones into imaginary courtyards. When told to come indoors, she sat for hours in the kitchen, drinking rice porridge mixed with sugar and listening to the cook's outlandish stories. She listened carefully and rarely laughed. It was as if she sensed that veil, thin as rice paper, which divided the living world from what had passed away.

And yet, with all their differences, the sisters loved each other with a ferocity that soothed Hu Mudan. It comforted and haunted her to see the way they loved each other. The two girls had always been close, but after Chanyi's death, they grew inseparable. They did everything together and they never fought. In the afternoons, when Junan studied her characters, Yinan sat drawing at her side. On some nights when Hu Mudan could not sleep, she left the pallet in her room behind the kitchen and crossed the courtyard to the sisters' quarters. She often found them together, in one of their bedrooms, with their dark heads close and their hair strewn across the pillows like lines of ink.

MY GRANDFATHER HAD indeed taken a mistress, although not a mortal woman. He had always had a thirst for games, and in the time Hu Mudan had known him he'd gradually become insatiable for paigao. All other pastimes grew pedestrian and dull. Cards could be counted and chess strategized. Only in paigao did he find what he desired: the dedication to uncertainty, the fellow players who shared his own need to extinguish themselves in the wild and bitter hopefulness of chance.

He explained to Hu Mudan that she must keep the household expenses to a minimum. Only his daughters and old Mma must be spared. "Don't say anything to anyone," he said. "The trouble won't last for long." But the trouble lingered and of course the servants were the first to notice. The cook remarked upon the poor quality of the vegetables; the errand boy was not happy with the smaller pot of rice. Hu Mudan ate less. By day, she monitored the gossip of the neighborhood servants—the most reliable way to learn how much my grandfather had lost. On the nights when he played host, she would convince the girls that he was only having fun; after they had gone to bed, she would eavesdrop on the front room. She learned which players were cowards and cheats and which were bluffers.

Toward midsummer, the doorman took to wandering off for hours at a time. My grandfather didn't notice and so Hu Mudan herself stood at the front doors, waiting. The mud from the spring rains had dried into a cracked visage. She stood shivering in the slanting sun. Something hung over the house, a shadow with black wings.

FROM HER POSITION at the doors, Hu Mudan could detect the smell of horse mixed with the closer odor of ammonia. On her left, she could plainly hear the spattering sound of the errand boy relieving himself. From the kitchen came the sounds of china spoons scraping on china bowls.

For a half hour, nothing happened. Then she heard someone coming up the road. She peered between the doors and saw a man walking up the Haizi Street from the center of town. Clearly a countryman, a stranger, and no friend of the family. Despite the heat, he wore a bulky cotton jacket that made it impossible to see the shape of his body. But he seemed familiar to Hu Mudan. Perhaps it was his walk. She watched as he approached until she could almost make out the features under the brim of his straw hat: strong and sun-stained features with eyes hidden in shadow. It was the chicken seller from the neighborhood market. She knew little about him except that he came in twice a week from a large farm owned by his wife's family outside the city.

Hu Mudan possessed a hunger unforgivable in a respectable house-keeper. The hunger showed in her small almond eyes, slanted a bit too high, and unusually bright; it showed in her shrewd mouth, which could soften into an enticing pout. She had a smooth neck and high breasts, neat arms and legs, and unblemished skin the color of sand. Moreover, she had never been pregnant. Long ago, she had suspected she was barren, and this brought her a freedom that lasted into her thirties.

She had noticed him earlier that morning, a warm morning when even sounds took on the vividness of impending summer. The sun already burned upon the merchants and their goods, brightening the flock of chickens and strengthening their smell. Hu Mudan recalled bet-ter times, not long past, when Mma had ordered a bird slaughtered for a single pot of soup. It was while contemplating this that Hu Mudan became aware of the man watching her.

He was a strong man, with ruddy cheeks and muscled shoulders, whose vitality stood out in each gesture. He saw that she was looking. He revealed a line of strong, white teeth. Then he produced a long reed flute and raised it to his mouth. His generous lips puckered around the flute. A cascade of small, bright notes flew out, not put together in the way of any tune that Hu Mudan could recognize. The chickens strutted toward him and gathered at his feet.

For a moment Hu Mudan stood captivated by the gathering birds, by the chicken man's music, by his quick, long-fingered hands. But when he stopped and smiled at her, she remembered the family. Since Chanyi's death, she had been like a nun, watching over her two charges, afraid to let them out of her sight. She had no money to buy chickens and no energy to deal with his entreaties. She turned and walked away, considering it ended.

Now as she peered between the doors, she realized that he had found her house. He stood outside the doors, bashfully, his hands hidden inside his coat. She felt herself redden with this flattering surprise. She knew that he could see her peering through the hole. Slowly he brought out his hands and held up an offering: a plump brown cochin hen, with pretty black spots and a little green hood tied over her eyes to prevent her from fussing.

Hu Mudan cracked open the doors.

She first defended herself. She pointed out that she was in charge of the two daughters since her master had lost his wife. As their caregiver, she should uphold the good values of the household. When he rebutted her with rumors—that her late mistress had killed herself and her master was a hopeless gambler—Hu Mudan said the stories were false. She placed value in the old ideal of xingyi: faithfulness and loyalty. Cheerfully, he heard her out. He replied that this was the kind of word the emperors had once used to control naïve and hopeful people. Meeting his eyes, she felt a sudden pounding in her chest, as if a stranger had spoken her childhood name.

For years she had sealed herself away from the delight of touch. And now, when she had forgotten herself in sorrow and worry, it came knocking at her door. Here was pleasure, as troubling and undeniable as the scent of summer. She had raised my mother and aunt with care, remembering what Chanyi would have wanted. But she suspected that dear, lost Chanyi, who had been her friend, would not have minded this one man.

"Go to the pump and wash," she said. "Then come around to the kitchen door."

She closed the door and leaned against it with the hen under her arm, her brown face blank in the sun.

If it hadn't been for the weather, so fragrant and so warm; if she hadn't stopped to listen to his bird-charming music; if he hadn't tied that little green scarf over the hen, would Hu Mudan have left the house untended and brought upon us the story that would define our lives? I wonder if there was anything she could have done to protect us from the fate that had been knocking, waiting for this small, unguarded moment to enter.

Hu Mudan and the chicken peddler entered her small room behind the pantry. It was swept absolutely clean. The shelf held only her straw hat and a glass jar with holes punched in the lid, where Yinan's pet silk-worms were growing fat upon the leaves from the mulberry tree. The two of them lay down together. The man looked into her with his strange eyes and gently touched her face. Hu Mudan felt her skin pull tight and her face began to glow, felt all of her—her fingertips, her nostrils, her pupils sensing light—grow charged with pleasure. She took a deep breath; she was acutely aware of the scent of the man, and her own scent rising to meet his. Very close to her face, he smiled. She smiled into his eyes, the wet color of earth on the bottom of a pond. She did not hear her master's evening guests entering the gate, did not hear them greeting him in their bright, expectant voices.

Later, in the courtyard, Junan called her name. "Hu Mudan?" She raised her voice. "Hu Mudan!" But Hu Mudan didn't hear a thing.

AT SEVENTEEN, JUNAN LET VERY LITTLE ESCAPE HER NOTICE.
She had seen the skimpy meals and had caught on to the way the pretty maid, Weiwei, eyed with anticipation what she and her sister left in the serving dishes. She had noted that the doorman wandered off. Of all these troubling changes, the most disturbing was the way her father had faded to a kind of daylight sleep, with his energies held back, waiting for the games, when he would leave the house for days or stay holed up in the front room with his friends.

He had big plans, her father did: only a few nights of lucky tiles must come his way, and he would realize them. He would finance an expansion to the north, using the Grand Canal to send cotton to a lucrative new market. She had overheard him describing this expansion to his cousin Baoding—omitting, of course, the necessity of the lucky tiles. But she knew the tiles' significance. She was his daughter and she understood, even approved of, his big plans. What made Junan uncomfortable were his plans for her. He had none. That is, she knew that when the subject of her marriage grew unavoidable, he would send her to the household of his friend and neighbor, Chen, as a suitable bride for young Chen Da-Huan.

There was nothing in Chen Da-Huan that Junan could object to. He was a quiet boy, idealistic and round-shouldered, who, whenever she saw him, looked right past her and into his vision for China's future. He would wave his soft hands and speak about the perils of imperialism, set forth his belief that China must be freed from the oppression of

all foreigners and returned to the glory of her past. He had such ideal-
ism because his family was rich, far removed from the worrying about
the yuan that could be made through dealing with foreigners.

Perhaps young Chen Da-Huan would be a decent husband. And yet,
whenever she spoke to him, she could not shake the sense that Chanyi
would have been saddened by the match. Her mother had never mentioned the subject, and yet she knew this. Whenever Junan considered
marrying him, her lips pressed tight against the thought.

Junan approached her father's office with her lips set in a line. She
could hear the scraping, banging sounds of men bringing more chairs
into the adjacent room. The lights were on, and Junan saw her father
gesture to the errand boy. As she stood listening and watching, the
sound of moving furniture grew so loud her bones hurt, so loud it
seemed the house would rattle apart.

"Where is Hu Mudan?" she asked. But in the kitchen they didn't
know. Perhaps she had run out on an errand.

Junan decided to sit near the door and wait. She knew she shouldn't be
seeking Hu Mudan as if the housekeeper were a blood relative, but no one
noticed. She sat on the stool where the cook sometimes snapped the beans.
The dusk thickened in the courtyard. From somewhere in the house came
the faint sound of a flute. Then she heard the slap of the white tablecloth
and the spilling of the little bone chips, followed by a brief silence and the
click of tiles, broken by shouts and laughter.

It was almost dark when Junan heard a knock. Could it be Hu
Mudan? She slid off her stool and went to open the door.

In front of her stood two young men. One wore a faded tunic and
the other an Army uniform short in the sleeves. They were too young
and poor to be her father's friends and yet she recognized, in the expression of the taller one, a familiar aura of anticipation. Parasite, she
thought. She noticed something careless in his face and did not like it.
He was handsome. The other was younger, tight-lipped and angular,
with bad posture and little round eyeglasses.

"We are here for Wang Daming," said the handsome one. He had a
country accent. "Will you let us in?"

"No," she said.

"Ah, come on," he said lightheartedly. "We won't eat you up." He glanced over her shoulder. They all could hear the men plainly, laughing in the office.

"Let's go, Li Ang," said the younger one. "She doesn't want us here."

"Let me handle this," said Li Ang.

"I'm leaving," said the other.

Li Ang set his jaw. In that moment Junan understood the visitors were brothers. Li Ang did not turn around. "You go home and read," he said, and shrugged. "In the morning, you'll see how much you've missed."

The younger brother vanished into the dusk.

Li Ang remained, expectantly. Junan thought of closing the doors in his face, but she did not. He took her silence as encouragement. "Well?" he asked.

She raised her eyes up briefly to his face and then down.

Although she had only flicked her eyelids, although she had barely glanced at him in the thickening dusk, she had taken him in as completely as a breath. She saw a young man, really a boy, dressed in a handed-down second lieutenant's uniform but with no hat, revealing stand-up hair and features stained from the outdoors. He was only a little older than she, long-legged and not quite grown. She sensed that he was hungry. She could also sense in him the effect she had on people, one of widening distance. She could already feel a vague hostility toward herself, a cool, pretty girl, indifferent to handsome strangers. This did not trouble her. She held herself as carefully as if her spine had been painted with a brushstroke, and traced her finger in a circle on the doorframe.

He took refuge in the personal. "Is Wang Daming your baba?" His voice was deep and surprisingly rich; his smallest phrases hinted melody. Such a voice could summon even a woman bent on coldness. She lifted up her gaze to him. His eyes were bright, remote. He stepped closer to her, close enough to touch her.

Junan watched him through her eyelashes. "My father's busy. You can't come in."

"I am here to play paigao, not to obey you." He smiled. What made him do this? How did he know, immediately, that teasing was the one thing that she could not bear?

It was something gentle in his voice that broke her control. She reached out and grabbed his sleeve. "I didn't say you could!"

They stared at one another. Her arm was long, her grip fierce. If he pulled away she would rip a piece out of his only uniform. Surely he must have been alarmed, faced with such fierce passion in a strange girl. Certainly he must have seen and been warned. How could he not have been aware of it? But he was not. He merely smiled again and waited for things to change. A long moment passed. Eventually he saw what he was waiting for, a softening of the brow, a yielding of the mouth. Her shoulders dropped. His smile had done its work. She did not invite him, did not lead him, but she allowed him to pass, to enter the room where the players had gathered.

LI ANG HAD A CONSTELLATION OF SCARS ON HIS BACK, CLUSTERED
from his left shoulder blade down to the center of his spine. He was a
dark young man, and the wounds had healed to lavender. When he was
overheated or emotional, he flushed all over his skin, and the scars
shone pale along his back, as marbled as burned flesh.

He had been wounded in Shanghai during a Japanese provocation.
As an errand boy, a volunteer, he'd spied a grenade aimed for the young
Corporal Sun Li-jen and had pushed the corporal out of the way.
Shrapnel had torn Li Ang's shoulder; a few pieces lodged near his spine.
But Sun had escaped, and in order to show his gratitude, the corporal
had sponsored Li Ang in military school.

Now that Li Ang was commissioned, he felt proud of his scars. He
often turned his shoulder to the mirror, craning to see them on his
smooth dark back. His father had been a small farmer, virtually a peasant, but he, the son, had now been marked and chosen for a nobler path.
He had bought this future with only a small sacrifice of flesh. He didn't
worry for his body. Indeed, there were times when he felt puzzled by his
body. Did it belong to him, or did it exist apart from him like the flickering images projected in a movie theater? This dappled shoulder—had
it stood in between the corporal and the enemy? Was it truly marked
with scars? Or did it still exist somewhere he didn't know, untouched,
as if none of this had happened? Typically he put such thoughts out of
his mind. They were as useless as the memories of his mother and
father, who had died when he was ten. They were only echoes in his

mind, shapes that lingered on the edge of sleep. The gentle sound of her voice, the depth of her soft-lidded eyes. His hand on the bottle of sorghum liquor, fingernails bitten down. Li Ang tried not to think of them, for they were gone.

THE WICKED PACE of paigao required a bone-deep recognition of the tile combinations and careful observation of the host. Li Ang had learned this from his uncle, who played all games. In the afternoons, Charlie's stationery shop was a hotbed for go and chess. Charlie could even bluff his way through duplicate bridge. He and his best friend had once won four hundred coppers from the Christian coffers by beating two ministers from the Hangzhou Methodist Church.

There were seven players, including a bald colonel whose brigade had overrun Nanjing in 1911. He nudged Li Ang. "Ha! Promoted!"

Charlie showed the gap in his teeth. "Let's see if you remembered how to have fun in the Army, nephew."

Li Ang wondered why his uncle liked to play paigao with this host. Wang Daming appeared moderate: not boisterous, not loud, not large or in any way obvious. Behind his silver spectacles, his eyes were watery and mild; he smelled healthy. Li Ang couldn't detect a gambler in him from his manners or his old, well-furnished house. But when Wang began to mix the tiles, Li Ang understood. The tiles clicked at a thrilling pace with absolute precision, and yet Wang's movements worked against this rhythmic exactitude. They were mystical and frantic: back bent, elbows wide, hands somehow dramatic. His fingers moved over and around the tiles, caressing them like prayer beads. Watching and listening, Li Ang knew that Wang was in the grip of a compulsion: he believed in magical thinking as a way to hold off some hidden pain. He would encourage large bets, which he would cover at all cost. Tonight something unusual might happen.

The baijiu shrank in the bottle; the heat rose into the room. The men grew boisterous. Li Ang thought that only Charlie and the old Colonel Jiang were truly enjoying themselves. One neighbor, Chen, had come only to placate Wang. He drank little, placed careful bets, and won and lost almost nothing. Some of the men drank too much and made sloppy bets. And Wang, that mystical, anxious man, was dissatisfied with them. Li Ang decided to impress Wang. He kept his face serious, as his uncle did.

Two bottles of baijiu, three bottles. Wang mixed the tiles. This time he bent over them as if he were trying to spark the game with the friction of the tiles against the table. Li Ang thought he heard someone knocking at the door. He turned, but there was no one. Then his attention was brought back to the table by what had been sent to him. A twelve and a red eight, the highest combination. It was time to make his move. He bet everything he had on that round, and the next round, which he won again, with a two and a red eight. Wang smiled and pushed over his chips, and it seemed to Li Ang that some of the tension had left his hands.

Charlie shrugged. "Young luck," he said. As if some unseen force had heeded his words, the wins turned away for a few rounds. But Li Ang played those with caution. He had begun to feel luck in the relentless, even clicking of the tiles, in Wang's wild and caressing hands. He could sense it coming little by little, like a rising wind.

The tiles lay arranged under the light: long, black bars encrypted with red and white patterns of dots. The ten-dot tile like an arrangement of white flowers. The two-dot tile like an open face. Together, in combinations, the dots could spell out victory, riches, luck; or they could spell defeat. Around this bright table crowded the men with their greedy eyes; also the house; also the great black night; and somewhere in that night, there lay the shadow of all that had ever taken place along with consequences, good and bad. Li Ang held himself apart from this; it was the only way to see it. It was in such a moment that he had seen the man with the grenade aimed for the corporal.

Now he found the twelve-eight again, and then the intricate pairs. Li Ang made larger bets. He had reached that place apart, where he could play untouched. Another bottle was opened. Smoke rose to the ceiling. Li Ang missed rounds, now and then, but the largest stakes kept coming to him. His pile of chips grew enormous, until he had to reach around it. His uncle sat at ease, his face polite and calm. But Li Ang could see the man was listening. Li Ang sat still. There it was, a soundless rushing. The table seemed far away. The bets dropped neatly out of his mouth as if he were simply relaying messages. They used up all the chips. They tallied up, then divided the chips and started over again. After some time, he realized that the tiles no longer gave off shadows on the tablecloth. The lamps had also dimmed; it was close to dawn. The game was ending.

He was suddenly exhausted. Before him sat the enormous pile of chips and pieces of paper on which various sums had been written. The table before the host was empty.

WANG DAMING HAD the heavy safe brought in and he opened it. There, stacked right in front, were tall, neat piles of various banknotes. Wang counted nineteen stacks of bills: eleven hundred from the Central Bank itself, two hundred in notes issued by the Bank of Communications. Then there were six hundred in different notes issued by British, French, and Japanese banks.

After Wang had counted out this money he paused for a moment. He leaned back into the safe. Carelessly he hauled out bags of silver coins and began to count them into piles. "Our president," he said, and held aloft a Yüan Shi-k'ai dollar, coined years ago at the hopeful inception of the Republic.

"A better dollar, more revered," joked Charlie, picking up another coin, an older, silver Sun Yat-sen that had been minted at the Revolution. Li Ang stood watching the money. Three of those coins would have kept him well fed for a month. Ten would have kept him and his brother living like princes, with plenty for books and tobacco. Soon the coins would be his. As Wang counted, the occasional sound of two coins struck together rang out with a high, shimmering, almost mystical beauty. Occasionally, he paused and laughed. He counted into neat piles of twenty each: three hundred coins for Colonel Jiang, a hundred for Old Chen.

He was nearing the bottom of the fourth bag. There were only three hundred and sixty-two of the fifty-eight hundred owed his uncle, and Wang had not even begun to pay Li Ang.

When he finished counting out the fourth bag, Wang turned to his uncle. "For the rest of this, and for your nephew, in the morning I'll make a trip to town."

"All right."

His uncle and Wang Daming shook hands, Western-style.

The men stood to leave. Colonel Jiang, who had drunk heavily, stumbled out the door. Neighbor Chen shook Li Ang's hand and bade a polite goodbye to everyone present. As he was saying goodbye to Wang, Charlie struggled for an unusually long time with the sleeve of his jacket. "Nephew," he said. "Help your old uncle here." Li Ang had no choice but to stand behind him and help him fit his arm into his sleeve.

"See you again," Wang called to Chen, who was nearly out the door.

"See you again." The door slammed. They were alone with Wang Daming.

"My apologies for the delay in payment," Wang said. He stood before them, tired and diminished but somehow finally at ease.

"Of course, of course. What's a little money between us?" Li Ang felt the pressure of his uncle's arm, resisting the jacket. From the collar of his uncle's shirt a scent escaped, the smell of sweat and cunning. He was saying, "A little money is nothing. But a drink, now, how about a drink?"

The bottle was brought in by a sleepy maid.

Wang Daming poured three shots. "To your winnings. Ganbei!" The delicious liquor scalded Li Ang's throat.

"To you." Charlie raised a glass at Wang. "It's you who permitted us to win. Only a powerful man could afford to be so generous. You're a good host. Ganbei!"

Again, they drank.

"Still," said his uncle, considering his glass until Wang took the hint and poured another round, "four thousand yuan: that is quite a lot of money for even the most generous host to pay."

Wang shrugged. "My apologies! I'll have it tomorrow."

"Still, since you are a dynamic man, you must not have so much idle at the bank."

"As a matter of fact, most of what I have left is tied up in investments."

"So you might be open to another form of payment?"

Wang's eyes flickered to meet Charlie's. Li Ang held still, puzzled. Charlie continued thoughtfully. "My nephew is too young for such a fortune. On his behalf, as his uncle, I will ask if you might do the kindness of granting him, instead of money, something else: say, one of your properties."

Wang smiled. "I didn't know your family was interested in the cotton business."

Charlie said, "For myself, no. But for my nephew: you do have a property that my nephew is interested in."

"And what would that be?"

"Your older daughter, Junan."

Li Ang's mouth opened, and he shut it. The two older men were looking at one another as if he weren't in the room. Then Wang Daming slapped the air and laughed. "Ha! That's a good one, my daughter. My daughter."

Charlie tilted his head back and laughed along. "She's of age and she is not yet matched."

"I have no intention of marrying off my daughter."

Charlie shrugged. "You could do worse," he said, gesturing at Li Ang. "He's young, he's healthy, as you see, and he's just been promoted. And he'll be promoted again." He paused. "With all of the changes due to come, it may be wise to have a shield in the Party."

Li Ang frowned. He was a member of the Army—not the Party.

"You might also consider it repayment of a family debt," said Charlie.

The smoke from Wang's cigarette seemed to stop in the air.

"If you agree to marry your daughter to my nephew, we'll wipe out not only what you owe my nephew here but everything you owe to me. I'll consider tonight's four thousand yuan my contribution to the wedding."

Through a haze of baijiu, weariness, and surprise, Li Ang admired his uncle's mind for details: he could not afford to pay for a wedding, and now he wouldn't have to.

His uncle was saying, ". . . a few minutes to think about it?"

Wang cleared his throat. "To think about it."

"It's not yet dawn. We'll wait," said Charlie. "Why don't we have another drink?"

He leaned forward and tilted the bottle into Li Ang's cup and then Wang Daming's. "To thinking," he said. "Ganbei!"

"Ganbei!"

After another round, Wang Daming excused himself.

For several minutes after the door closed behind their host, Li Ang and his uncle sat and waited, saying little. Li Ang searched his mind. He longed to feel once more that sliding, soundless wind of luck. But he was so tired he could barely think; his mind was empty. He looked up for guidance, but Charlie sat expressionless. Then, suddenly noticing his nephew, he jauntily poured another round.

"To thinking," he said.

"To thinking."

Charlie had filled the host's cup, and after he downed his own, he reached for it as well. Li Ang picked up the bottle and raised it to his lips. His uncle wagged a finger at him. "The toast!"

"The toast."

"To marriage," Charlie said.

"To marriage," Li Ang said. He was floating a finger's width above the chair; he could barely sense the weight of the bottle in his hands. He closed his eyes and drank. The morning sun glowed red against his lids; his ears were ringing. Only the sting of liquor anchored him. "But Uncle Charlie," he said, letting go of each word carefully as if it were a paper boat in the sea, "I don't know if I want a wife."

"That decision has been taken out of your hands." He showed Li Ang his gap-toothed smile as if some problem had been solved. How long had he wanted Li Ang married? This was a complicated and startling question. Li Ang vowed to think about it later. Then the room turned neatly, twice. He rested his head in his hands.

He tried to remember the face of the girl. He could recall only an impression of her height, her graceful coolness, and her fierce hand on his sleeve.

Someone opened the door.

"He's just tired," Li Ang heard his uncle say. "Did you decide?"

MY AUNT YINAN HAD SEASHELL EARLOBES, THIN AND SMALL, A sign of an unfortunate life. Her ears were delicate and sensitive to touch. As a child, she feared the ivory wand, narrow as a straw-stem, which was inserted now and then to scrape the wax. Only Junan could wield this instrument without causing pain. While Hu Mudan held up a lamp, Junan would peer into the twisting tunnel of Yinan's translucent, rosy ear. Junan's hands were steady and her vision accurate. Years later, Hu Mudan would claim the sisters grew up in such intimacy that Junan had memorized the twists and turns of Yinan's ear canal. The story was offered as proof that they had been inseparable.

It was the morning of Junan's wedding day. As Junan bent over Yinan's ear, she and Hu Mudan went over the final list of things to do. The red qipao must be checked for loosening beads. Junan would wear this dress to bow before the ancestors. Then she would change into a fashionable white gown for the hotel ceremony and banquet. The two separate gowns and ceremonies were a last-minute compromise for the traditional Mma, who, although she had grown almost blind, was able to see the difference between red and white.

"Hold still, Meimei."

Yinan sighed.

"To be an elegant girl, you must be clean and have clean ears."

"But I don't want to be an elegant girl."

"Just for today," Junan said. Yinan submitted, and Junan felt some regret that she had insisted on the ear-cleaning. She didn't want to cause

Yinan unnecessary distress. Both sisters felt a dread of separation that roosted like a crow over the wedding plans. Junan had reassured Yinan that nothing would change. She would remain in the Wang house with Yinan. Li Ang, stationed nearby, would visit on his days off, and things would be the same as ever. But she knew better. Any change could lead to trouble. Like her sister, she distrusted any promise of safety. She knew that it could vanish like a stone thrown into a lake.

She tucked a wisp of hair behind her sister's ear. Yinan's hair, although not black or glossy enough to be considered beautiful, was thick and soft to the touch. Leaning closer, Junan noticed something on the scalp. She bent and parted the tender waves. There, at the roots, a large, red pimple had been scratched open.

"Meimei, what is this?"

"I don't know. It itches."

"You've broken the skin."

Junan noticed another spot. She pulled down the shirt to examine Yinan's neck. There were pimples on her back and chest.

Junan consulted Hu Mudan. The woman bent over Yinan and nodded briefly.

"Tell me what it is," Junan demanded. "What illness does she have?"

"She has the shuidou," Hu Mudan said matter-of-factly. "It is a normal childhood disease."

"Is there any way to cover her forehead? Everyone will see it."

Hu Mudan shook her head. "She can come with us to the hotel, but she should not attend the wedding. This pox is easy to catch. And it's dangerous for any pregnant woman or any adult who hasn't had it as a child."

"I'm sorry, Jiejie!" Yinan hung her head.

"She should be kept from scratching. She can be cooled with wet cloths. The pox has to run its course."

Junan thought quickly. "Tell them to pull one chair away from the banquet table. And Yinan. Stop looking like that. Let's go to your room."

"May I bring Guagua?" From the courtyard, they could hear the clucking of Hu Mudan's pet hen.

Junan shook her head. "Keep that chicken out of here. For all we know, you caught this illness from that filthy bird."

In Yinan's bedroom, Junan cut her sister's fingernails with the tiny scissors that had belonged to their mother. She had Weiwei bring a basin of water and soak cloths to press on Yinan's skin when she complained of itching. Hu Mudan had said that if the shuidou were scratched, they could leave scars or holes as big as rice grains.

Junan pressed her hand on Yinan's forehead, searching for fever, but she couldn't sense it; she felt feverish herself. She wasn't ill, but merely floating on the river of her plans into this day, her wedding day.

She recalled the moment when she had learned her fate. Sometime in the early morning, she had woken to find her father sitting on her bed. She smelled the alcohol on his breath. He was talking, almost to himself, repeating the name Li Ang. It was the young lieutenant she had let into the door. "We must move toward the future," her father had said. "In the modern world, a man's political connections matter more than his money or his family." Outside her window the low sun had cast a frail light into the room; she had gazed at this light and thought of the lieutenant.

Now Yinan asked, "Jiejie, is Lieutenant Li Ang a good person?"

"Of course he is, Meimei. Baba wouldn't marry me to a bad person. The lieutenant is working to make China strong."

Yinan was silent for a moment. Then she asked, "Jiejie, where do you think Mama has gone?"

"What do you mean?"

"I know where her ashes are. But where do you think the Mama part of her has gone?"

"She will be reborn. Do you remember the chant from the memorial services? The Mama part of her has left this world to go to a new life, and her body has been returned back to the physical world."

"I wish we'd had her longer."

"We had her for a certain amount of time, and now she is returned to the world."

"I wish we'd had her longer," Yinan repeated. She rolled onto her back and stared at the ceiling with bright eyes.

Junan herself had searched for Chanyi's ghost, eagerly, shame-fully. On the second night after her mother's death, she had thought that she might see her. She'd woken in the middle of the night to the smell of frost-cold air. Was it the sound of her own voice that had woken her? Could there have been a visitor? But there was nothing, not a sound. Now she remembered the Buddhist chant from the memorial service:

Se bu i kong
kong bu i se

Life does not differ from nothingness; nothingness does not differ from life.

Junan closed the shades against the violent sun, which burned against her eyes.

"If I were a boy," Yinan said suddenly.

"What are you talking about?"

"I know." Yinan turned her head toward the wall. "But if I were a boy she might not have killed herself."

Junan closed her eyes. Against the backdrop of her lids the image of the sun made a fierce blue spot. "Mama didn't kill herself."

"I heard Gu Taitai tell Weiwei that she did."

"Stop it!" Her voice, breaking shamefully, rang into the room.

After a long moment, Yinan said, "I'm sorry, Jiejie. Duibuqi."

"Don't ever speak of this again."

"Duibuqi!" Yinan's voice shook.

Junan pulled her arms into the sleeves of her jacket. She closed her eyes again and held herself stiffly against the back of her chair. Her own name, Junan, meant "like a son." Yinan's name meant "will bring forth sons."

After several moments, Yinan spoke, and she was sobbing. "Jiejie, are you angry at me?"

Junan couldn't speak.

"Please talk to me. Please don't leave me. Promise. Now that you'll be married."

Junan looked away. "No," she said into the room. "I won't ever leave you, Meimei."

Satisfied, Yinan closed her eyes. "And I won't ever leave you."

Some time later, the maid called Junan to Mma's room. After Junan had kowtowed properly, the old woman held out a drink that Junan didn't recognize: syrupy, sloe-purple, redolent of dates or prunes. Mma leaned close to watch her raise the glass. Over its rim Junan glimpsed the old woman's cloudy eyes, inquisitive and vengeful, and she suspected what the liquid was. She knew she might have gotten sympathy by clinging to her grandmother, confessing fear, or begging for advice, but she was no more able to reveal such weakness than she was able to refuse Mma's implicit challenge. She raised the fertility potion to her lips and drank.

SEVERAL HOURS LATER, LI ANG SAT WITH HIS BRIDE AT THE front table of their wedding banquet.

Junan had turned modestly away from him, revealing the long line of her neck, her high-bridged nose, the angle of her cheek. Her glittering white cap set off her large eyes and slanted brows. Earlier that day, in the traditional ceremony, she had worn a red dress and a long red veil to kneel to the ancestors. Now she was stunning in white. She was both stylishly modern and pure in her face—she held a virginal quality, perfect as the images of saints he recalled from his one visit to a cathedral. Everyone had stared when she walked into the room. Li Ang took pride in this; it compensated, somewhat, for the fact that almost none of the guests were his. Of the two hundred people at the banquet, Li Ang knew only eight. Aside from Charlie Kong, the bald Colonel Jiang, and the wealthy Mr. Chen, none of the paigao players had been invited. Li Ang's guests were only three: his mentor Sun Li-jen, his uncle, and his brother. Li Ang suspected that the meager Li connections had been remarked upon by everyone. He heard his mentor explaining that the groom and his brother had been orphaned in the influenza epidemic.

"I'm afraid I don't have many guests to add," Li Ang apologized to Wang Daming.

"It is fine with me," Daming replied. "They say it's bad luck to have too lavish a wedding."

At this, Li Bing raised his eyebrows. Li Ang could imagine his brother's disdain for the stylish celebration that had been deemed appropriate by his new in-laws. The banquet was being held at a remodeled mansion. The festivities were in the modern section, lit up with electric lights. The guests had come from as far away as Nanjing: distant relations, fellow merchants, and a variety of officials representing each of the thirteen separate guilds and offices to which Wang gave yearly bribes. They did not appear to be what Li Bing would call progressive thinkers. Li Bing was seated next to the young Chen Da-Huan, who wore a long mandarin robe. Chen was talking about restoring China's glorious cultural past.

"Western literature has corrupted us, this movement toward so-called 'progressive language' has destroyed the dignity and music of the written word . . ."

Li Bing fidgeted, rolling in his long fingers an imaginary cigarette. Li Ang knew his brother was currently engrossed in a "progressive" translation of H. G. Wells's *The Time Machine*. He knew Li Bing would rather be reading at that moment. But his brother would restrain his impatience, for his sake.

Li Ang stole glances at Junan as he ate, smiling at her now and then. She handled herself perfectly, always gracious and demure, although the day had been a long one. Li Ang had to admire her; he grew tired of sitting. One course followed another. His favorite was a local specialty, crispy fish from the lake itself. For a moment he assumed it had been chosen for him, but then he realized that no one knew the first thing about him. Other seafood had been brought by motorboat that morning: enormous shrimp with graceful whiskers, scallops, abalone. A course of chicken wrapped in lotus leaves, another local specialty, had been included for the guests from out of town. In honor of Li Ang's mentor, who was now a colonel, they ate pork intestines prepared by a cook from Anhui. Also there was the bride's favorite, quail eggs. But the tiny eggs were brought out too late for Junan to enjoy them. By then, she had already left the room to change out of her gown, remove her elaborate headpiece, and prepare for the wedding night. In the spirit of modernism, she said, she had refused the customary games around the bridal bed. Later, Li Ang would go alone to meet her in their room.

Li Ang found the egg course difficult. Since his promotion he had, on some occasions, eaten with ivory chopsticks rather than his usual bamboo, but the small, slender silver banquet chopsticks presented a new challenge. Earlier, he had dropped a slippery piece of abalone in his lap. Since that moment of shame, he had tried to ignore the irritation that arose whenever he brought a sliver of food to his mouth. He found the chopsticks impractical, trying, and pretentious. They were smaller than average, with pointed tips, making them more difficult to use, and, he decided, effeminate. This brought to mind a story he had read years ago, on some drowsy afternoon in his uncle's store. It was a story of the old days. The emperor's new wives were tested by being required to eat a meal of quail eggs with silver chopsticks. Perhaps the Wangs tested a son-in-law in the same way? Were they mocking him? Flushed, he stared at the tiny eggs for several minutes before beginning.

He lost his grip on the egg halfway to his mouth and lunged forward, trying in vain to save it as it bounced off the plate and disappeared. Li Ang stared straight ahead. When he dared look around, he met the eyes of Wang Baoding, Junan's uncle from Nanjing.

Baoding was an elegant man: thin, with long hair combed carefully back from a high forehead. He had eaten and drunk well, and although his face retained a clay-like pallor, his earlobes had turned pink. Now, acknowledging Li Ang for the first time, Baoding leaned back and spoke.

"My dear new nephew, let me apologize to you for this question I am about to ask," he began. He leaned back in his chair. "It's so seldom that I actually have the opportunity to speak candidly with men connected to the Army. So I must ask you: What on earth could your General Chiang Kai-shek have been thinking when he agreed to join forces and cooperate with the Communist Party? Does he know who those men are?"

Beneath the man's conspiratorial tone, Li Ang sensed the acid flavor of antagonism. "You presume too much of me, Uncle," he said. "I'm on the military side of things. I try to stay out of politics."

Charlie Kong shook his head. "He's not a thinker," he said cheerfully. "Indeed."

Li Ang saw his brother's lips twitch into a smile. Baoding did not appear to notice. "Let me ask you a question," Baoding said, turning to Li Ang. "Have you ever actually met a Communist?"

"I beg your pardon?"

"It's a simple question. Have you ever actually spoken with a Communist?"

"Come on, now," broke in Old Chen. "This isn't the time for a political discussion. We all know the country must unite against the aggression of the Japanese." Chen had served as the official elder witnessing the wedding. He clearly enjoyed his food; he'd worked his way through every course with splendid appetite, keeping his imported British suit jacket spotless. Now he raised a tiny egg in the air to emphasize his point.

Baoding leaned forward. His long, pale face was marbled with the faintest pink of wine. "Well. As a matter of fact, I have. I met him very early on in life."

"Really," said Charlie. "Was he a Russian?"

"No. A Han. His name was Wu Shao and he stole my lunch when we were in the fourth grade."

His long, shrewd eyes flickered over the others. He brought his cup to his lips.

"His grandfather had been a blacksmith and his father hauled ice. This was a boy with no decent family, no education, no property, and no money. He was rough and ignorant, with a thick accent. He had nothing for lunch that day and he was hungry."

Without even glancing down, Baoding reached to his plate with his chopsticks and deftly popped a quail egg into his mouth. Then he examined his listeners. Li Ang made himself look back.

"He left school after sixth grade and went to work at a factory. For years I didn't know what had happened to him. Now I read in the paper that he's a member of the Party! Not just any member, but a local leader, an organizer." He made a wheezing sound something like a laugh. "So, boy, perhaps in order to increase your professional acumen you might want to know who the Communists are and what they want. It's simple. The Communists are hungry men. They're poor men who want our money. They're men without business and property who resent those of us who have them. That's all they are, and no doctrine or claim they make will ever change that fact.

"You say you've never met a Communist? You have been to Shanghai.

You've seen the beggars in the streets. More and more poor farmers and peasants swarming the city, where there is nothing for them. Those are the Communists. Yes, those are the Communists. They are all around this hotel. They cleaned this room. They carried our water, collected these eggs, planted and harvested these vegetables. They beg from us. They steal from us. And they hate us. Why do they hate us? It's not personal. It's not complicated. They are hungry and we have what they do not. They watch us. They are waiting for us. They are waiting at the door. At night while we sleep, they don't sleep; they are plotting to overthrow us." He leaned so close that Li Ang could smell the sulfurous egg on his breath. "Young man. Do you know what makes me so curious about your Army's arrangements with the Communist Party? It's that you don't seem to know that as soon as the Japanese threat diminishes, the Communists will not hesitate to turn and stab you in the back."

Around them the talk had trailed to silence; half of the room had turned to listen. Old Chen straightened his silk cravat. Li Ang sat without speaking, smiling slightly, trying to downplay this spasm of words. He resented the way Baoding implied this all had something to do with him. He glanced at his brother, hoping for support. Li Bing was listening carefully, but his face held no expression.

LATER, LI ANG walked through the courtyard toward the bridal chamber. The night air cooled his cheeks, and he walked lightly, without caring where his feet landed. The rich dinner and sly, provocative talk had addled and disturbed him. Moreover he wanted to see, to claim and touch, his bride. All had stared as she had passed, with her coiled, glistening hair, and her slender body covered in white, luminescent with pearl beads. But as he passed out of earshot to the banquet room, as the drunken sounds faded away, his steps slowed. When they had stood together for the brief ceremony, the bride—his bride—had seemed so elegant and remote, like the fine woman riding in a palanquin he had once glimpsed as a child. And on her face, set off by braids and silk and flowers, he had seen nothing he could reach—no happiness or joy—but rather an expression of impenetrable privacy.

Today he and this woman had made a bond, a promise of a certain kind. What was she like? Would she be like the other women he had known? His thoughts wandered to a back room in Nanjing, a flapping bamboo shade on a rainy night, where he and several friends had taken turns visiting a round-limbed young woman with lips the color of pomegranate seeds who had moistened herself with the dregs from a glass of wine. Some time later, there had been another woman, no longer young, whose beautiful, supple white back shielded a belly crisscrossed with stretch marks—lines that had, for some reason, moved him.

He had often gone to chaweis with his friends but he had not chosen a single woman into whose eyes he would look for approval and worth. He had given himself selectively, not scattering himself, never falling to the power of the other sex. He had been involved, to some degree, but never enraptured. He supposed that his new wife was equally practical. She would not grow foolish over love; she was composed and contained, intelligent and proud. And she had accepted him; she must feel at least some partiality to him.

Li Ang spat on the ground. Partiality didn't matter; he was her husband. So what if he was the orphan of a father one step removed from a peasant? He may have been a nobody, but he was also a blank slate with the promise to reach far above these people.

The bridal suite was in the old courtyard, built around a garden with a footbridge and a rushing brook and precious stones arranged after the landscape paintings of the high Soong. There were two doors on the left, and as he walked down the long porch he couldn't remember if he was supposed to enter the first or second one. He stopped automatically at the first door. A faint light showed from underneath. How would he know if he had come to the right place? With a quick eye he examined the curtain window and noticed that the curtain didn't cover the corner. Perhaps Junan's young cousins from Nanjing, true to tradition, had prepared that spy hole for practical joking later on. Although he had in the past participated in such games, he frowned. Like Junan, he didn't appreciate the thought that his own wedding should include them. He noted his own seriousness and was mildly surprised by it. Why so involved? Why so excited at this moment? For despite the new law prohibiting multiple marriages, it was not as if his marriage would limit him to the company of this one woman. There were the chaweis; and the new laws didn't define concubines as wives. Indeed, they were considered appropriate among military men, or any men whose work required travel. He was surprised at his own damp palms and quick breathing, as he peered through the window for a first glimpse of his bride.

He saw a plain wall and an unadorned bed. The marriage room, he knew, would be decorated with wedding draperies of red and gold, embroidered in dragons and phoenixes. He had chosen the wrong window. But he found himself unwilling to move. His earlier glimpse of Junan's long, black eyes, the image of her glossy hair and dazzling dress, the heavy food, the red- and gold-draped banquet with its hidden, ominous quarrels, brought his mind to rest with some relief on this quiet space.

The bed curtains were open. Someone had positioned the lamp close to the bed, perhaps to read, and had left open the bed curtains to let in light. It was a girl, wearing pale and shapeless cotton pajamas, with wavy hair spilled loose. She lay face down on the draped bed with her head in her hands. A medicine bottle and spoon were on the bedside table. Her extreme youth was apparent in the shape of her slender, ivory hands, pressed into the dark hair. She was unhappy, terribly unhappy. He could see it in the way she held her head, the occasional shudder of her body. She cried without a sound.

Li Ang looked away. Once in a great while, more often as a child, he had experienced what he came to think of later as a memory of the senses. Surrounded by friends, or laughing at a joke, he would remember, very suddenly, the bright, soft blue of his mother's dress, the smooth cotton threads under his fingers as he clung to her. This happened very rarely, almost never since he had become a man. Now, as he stood before the window, he recalled a faint, sweet smell, the scent of his mother's cheek and the area between her neck and collarbone, where he had, many years before, buried his face. "Hush, hush," she had whispered. "It's not that bad. Nothing could be all that bad, now, could it?" Silently, his lips shaped the words.

For several minutes he stood before the quiet room, no longer seeing it. Then the wind shifted, bringing a gust of music from outside. Li Ang remembered the reason he had left the others. He collected himself and walked ahead. He reached his wedding chamber and knocked on the door.

Occupation

LATER THAT YEAR, ON A LEAF-SCENTED EVENING FOLLOWING the Harvest Festival, Hu Mudan entered the room that had been Chanyi's. The furniture had not been rearranged since Chanyi's death. In the weeks after the funeral, Weiwei and Gu Taitai had flipped a coin over the task of cleaning the haunted place. But their interest had soon faded; Hu Mudan had taken over. Now the air smelled pleasantly of wood oil. She made her way into the dark, reaching for the lacquered edge of a small bureau. In a corner of the bottom drawer she had hidden a satin pouch. Her swollen stomach made it difficult to kneel, but she found the pouch and closed her fist around it. Climbing down the stairs, she was forced to stop and catch her breath.

She had told no one she was pregnant, even when her belly revealed the truth to all, and she had confided in no one her expectations that this child would be a boy and that he would be unusual. Without Chanyi, there was nobody to tell.

She had paid a peddler to whet the kitchen shears. To sterilize the blades, she took a bottle of fiery sorghum liquor from Wang's office cabinet. She even found a chamber pot, remembering the way that women in labor moved their bowels. Clean rags waited in a willow basket. Everything was ready. She closed the door to her room and slipped the satin pouch under her mattress.

For hours she lay, and stood, and squatted, struggling not to shout although her body was being torn apart by a powerful and indifferent pair of hands. Between the bouts of pain, she raised the bamboo blind and watched the gibbous moon, a lemon kite, fly up over the garden. The pain returned, erased the moon. The room took on the smell of the sea, steaming sour with each breath. She believed she would not die, for recent dreams had shown her she would live to see her living child. But even if she died it might not be the end of things. She might learn what had happened to Chanyi. Perhaps she might even see Chanyi. Perhaps it was true what the Methodists believed, that there was a peaceful place where friends collected after life.

The hours passed; dawn cast the room in dazed, gray autumn light. Someone knocked on the door. "Come in!" Hu Mudan cried eagerly, thinking that it might be Chanyi. But the door swung open to the orders of a midwife.

Although her sight was almost gone, old Mma had not failed to note the changes in the sound of Hu Mudan's voice, which months ago had taken on the high pitch of pregnancy. She had consulted with Junan and ordered her to fetch some help. So in the end, Hu Mudan did not have to finish her task alone. The child was born during the noon meal, which Gu Taitai prepared so haphazardly that the doorman broke his molar on a stone in the rice. Loud infant cries rang through the courtyard. It was a boy, as Hu Mudan had guessed, dark-skinned and round-skulled as a northerner, with a cap of spiky hair and eyes the same color of earth at the bottom of a pond. Hu Mudan explained politely to the others that the hair predicted a lack of intelligence and the enormous head great stubbornness. The midwife cleaned the child and wrapped him tightly, saving his umbilical cord, since Hu Mudan had once heard a story in Sichuan about the importance of drying the cord and making an amulet to protect the child from trouble. Later Mma told Junan that Hu Mudan was being inappropriately cautious, as if her son were something more than an illegitimate child of a servant.

TO JUNAN, THE PREGNANCY and birth presented a problem in household management. Hu Mudan had given the boy her own surname, Hu. Where was the father? Junan and Mma went over the list of men who worked in or around the house and they decided Hu Mudan could not possibly have wanted them. She and the doorman had a long-running feud. Old Gu was indeed so old his gums had turned to sponges and he had to eat rice gruel. Gongdi, the errand boy, was young enough, but so backward that he could not have figured out how to mount a woman even with clear instructions. It must have been someone outside the house. Perhaps the man who sharpened knives? A rickshaw runner? The mystery might not be known until the child matured enough to reveal the father through his face or manner. Perhaps it would never be known. Meanwhile, this baby boy, this Hu Ran, was living in the house as if he had been brought there by a fairy. Junan believed Hu Mudan ought to be told to leave at once. But Mma refused. She didn't want anyone else, not even her granddaughter, to help her use the toilet. She wouldn't be persuaded by Junan or her father. And Junan knew better than to expect support from Yinan.

Yinan was another problem. Since the wedding she had become even more of a bookworm; her right hand was often stained with ink. She spent hours reading newspapers and had developed a fascination for the slender film star Ruan Lingyu. She persuaded Junan to see *New Woman*. Junan suffered through two hours in the smelly, noisy theater, holding her handkerchief to her nose, while Yinan sat enchanted by the melodramatic story of a beautiful and talented woman writer driven to prostitution in order to save a sick child. During the final scenes, as the dying woman heaved upon her hospital bed, Junan heard a choking sound from the seat next to her. Yinan had burst into tears. Junan found her another handkerchief—her sister never remembered them—and sat through the movie's end aghast.

One afternoon, Junan walked into Yinan's room and noticed an unusual scent of sugar and fruit.

"Meimei, what is that smell?"

Yinan's eyes widened. She darted a glance at the cushions on her bed. Junan went to the bed and tossed the cushions aside.

She discovered a smooth, flat box, decorated with red flowers and gold trim. She lifted the lid and found a mosaic of bright candies nestled in fluted paper, some shaped like striped ribbons, some flat disks with a bloom of color in the center. She turned from the gaudy box to

Yinan's frightened face—eyes round, lips pursed, still sucking guiltily at the sweet stone in her mouth.

"Where did you get this box of candy, Meimei?"

Yinan shook her head.

"Meimei?" Threatening now.

"I promised I wouldn't tell."

"You know I'll find out anyway."

Still, Yinan resisted. After half an hour of badgering and threatening her with no results, Junan was forced to give up. She left the bedroom frustrated, carrying the candy box, knowing no more about her sister's suitor than she could guess.

The fact that Yinan had an admirer troubled Junan. The extravagant gift was disturbing, but more disturbing was Yinan's refusal to give away the boy's identity. To whom did she owe such loyalty except to her family? How had she met him when she rarely left the house?

Junan was forced to consult Hu Mudan. She found her in the courtyard working on a bundle of blue cotton. Hu Mudan made her own cloth shoes and was very particular about the soles. Next to her, Hu Ran lay in an enameled wash pan, watching everything that happened. His very presence posed a question she couldn't answer. Ignoring him, she went right to the point and asked Hu Mudan if she knew anything of an admirer.

Hu Mudan answered mildly that she had no idea who the man might be. She hadn't known of any admirer, but a few days ago, when Deng Xiansheng came through the gate, she had seen something colorful— red and gold—tucked between his books and papers.

Junan couldn't conceal her surprise. Deng Xiansheng was Yinan's calligraphy and writing tutor. He was in his forties, with pouches under his eyes and thinning hair over a high, round forehead. He came to the house three times a week wearing respectable but shabby clothes; his tutoring was strict and very serious. If he'd been born three decades earlier, he would have been the kind of man who studied for more than half his life to pass the jinshi exam. Now, at a time when the studious life had lost its power and significance, he had no fulfillment but from what could be found within the purity of a line, or an intelligent, forceful turn of the brush.

"Surely you're joking," Junan said. Yinan wasn't even a good calligrapher. Her writing was artistic, but it lacked ambition. It was typical woman's work.

"Most people become attached to someone. Why not Deng Xiansheng?"

"It's too absurd—has he no shame? He's almost three times older than she is."

Hu Mudan said, "Older isn't always bad. Someday she will need a man to take care of her."

"I know. But she's so backward that I wonder. And who would put up with her, and who would know what she was up to, and how to manage her?"

"There's more to her than meets the eye. About a match, your father might have ideas."

Junan frowned at Hu Mudan, but the woman sat pulling her thread through the sole of her shoe, mild and uninvolved. From the wash pan, Hu Ran watched and made no sound.

"My father's connections aren't what they used to be." She thought for a moment. "But this box of candy is an insult. It is an insult to us that Deng Xiansheng could have thought we would even tolerate this attachment, even though she's backward for her age, and not beautiful."

Junan watched Hu Mudan's thimble ring push the big needle back through the layers of cloth. "And so much of it is her fault. How could anyone have assumed we cared what she was up to, when she won't wear any of the new clothes I took the trouble to have made for her? And she won't take care of her things. They're all wilted and wrinkled. She looks like a salted lettuce."

"She doesn't like to wear starched clothes," said Hu Mudan.

"She is getting more and more strange."

"No," said Hu Mudan evenly, "she's the same."

"She won't wear her new clothes until they've been sitting in the drawer for six months. She won't learn to run a house or do embroidery or behave. All she does is read and write and talk to that pet chicken." This was not precisely true, but true enough. Yinan snuck the chicken indoors, and sometimes, when she passed by her sister's room, Junan could hear Yinan confiding in Guagua or asking if she wanted a drink of water. Junan felt a wave of irritation with Yinan, whose behavior had only amused her in the past. She could no longer defend her sister if she was old enough to entertain admirers.

She hurried into Yinan's room.

"Sooner or later," she said, "you're going to be married. In the meantime, you can't go around accepting miscellaneous gifts from slippery-headed and impoverished men."

Yinan didn't answer.

"I'm going to speak to Baba about your marriage. You are almost sixteen years old."

As she waited for Yinan to speak, Junan observed once again that her sister hadn't learned the importance of concealing her feelings from the people that she loved. Now she appeared both curious and frightened. "I don't want to marry," Yinan said.

Although it was considered proper for girls to feign reluctance, Junan could see that Yinan wasn't pretending. She didn't have enough sense to pretend anything. Junan frowned to hide her own confusion. As she looked at her sister's bent head and glossy braids, she felt that she was trying to hold a conversation with a stranger.

"You need to learn how to be a woman," she said.

"What does a woman do?"

Junan considered this question. "She is patient," she explained. "She is canny, and above all, she is careful, *xiaoxin*. I like to think of what the characters mean: small heart." Yinan sat very still.

"That means you must be cautious. You must not make inappropriate friendships with men."

"But how will I find someone?"

"Are you telling me you want to make a love match?"

Yinan did not reply.

"You've been watching too many movies." Junan left the room.

As she went back upstairs, she put the mystery of Deng Xiansheng aside. *Xiaoxin*. She must have a small heart. Junan had read in the newspaper about young Chinese women reading Marx, joining the Communist underground, and practicing free love. Still others were illiterate, struggling to raise a bleak and ancient living from the earth. In the eye of this storm of change, Junan planned her way. She embarked upon her marriage with a personal agenda: she did not expect to love her husband, nor ever to lean on him for happiness or money.

When seen in this light, her own marriage was promising. Li Ang's lack of family brought advantages. Since Li Ang was an orphan, she could live with her own family. Unlike other wives, she would not have to kowtow to a demanding mother-in-law. She could create her own, more modern marriage, free of the vicious treatment and terrible isolation of being a new daughter-in-law in a big house. Li Ang's job was dangerous, but the threat of civil war had diminished now that the Communists and Nationalists had reached a truce. She would certainly be able to persuade him to take a safer job as a staff officer.

She assured herself that Li Ang was inferior to her. He was clever enough, but unrefined. Oh, she saw his handsome face, his height and strength, his ability to please people; she knew he would become somebody. But now he was a soldier and his family was nothing. They had just the uncle's broken-down shop. She assumed that Li Ang knew he was inferior and would therefore be more open to her guidance. She clung to this advantage: that marrying Li Ang had made her safe, that his family was of such low stature it would be impossible for her to truly fall in love with him. This would save her from the fate that had overcome her mother. No, she would be careful. She knew how dangerous it was to get overly attached, how treacherous it might be if she grew to want devotion from the man she married.

THE IDEA OF LETTING Yinan find someone herself was out of the question. Yinan had no experience with men; she was unusually shy. Moreover, Junan didn't trust her judgment. She might be inclined to marry a man because she had taken pity on him, or for some other foolish reason. Junan didn't want to see Yinan sentenced to poverty as the result of a sentimental inclination.

As a married woman, she was entitled to bring up the subject with her father. The following night, after dinner, she went to his room. When she explained the situation, she saw an expression of unmistakable weariness cross his face, and she began to wonder if she might be asking too much of him.

"His older brother owes me money," he said, of Deng Xiansheng. "That is why he tutors Yinan without pay."

"If she is engaged, she won't need a tutor anymore."

Her father nodded.

"What about the Chens?" she asked.

"That boy is worse than she is. Let me think this over." But in the following days, he said nothing about Yinan, and Junan began to wonder if she would have to take the matter into her own hands.

She was surprised a few weeks later when he handed her a letter he had received from Nanjing.

21st Year of the Republic
13 December
Cousin and brother,

My belated greetings to you in this season of falling frost.

I am writing to you in response to your recent letter regarding your younger daughter Yinan. Since then I have made inquiries, but nothing promising emerged until today. Lo Dun of Ningpo recently decided to marry, and I have taken the liberty of mentioning Yinan.

As you know, Lo Dun is from a good family and over the years he has made a decent and steady income. He lives with his mother, and I thought that perhaps an older woman might provide a kind of maternal figure for your daughter. Moreover, Lo Dun is a steady, well-settled man. His intentions are most responsible. Please write to me and let me know what you would like to do.

Your brother-cousin,
Baoding

Her father told Junan that Lo Dun was a decent man, and so he had gone to town and telegrammed his cousin to proceed. But his cousin had wired back that the match was not entirely certain. Lo Dun's mother wanted a face-to-face meeting. Eventually it was agreed that Lo Dun and his aged mother would come to the house for tea the following week. It would be Junan's job to coach Yinan.

At the evening meal, Junan peered thoughtfully at her sister. Yinan was eating spareribs, two slim fingertips placed at each end of the bone, her long neck bent gracefully as she leaned forward. She had never been beautiful, but that slender neck, vanishing into her limp collar, brought to mind a kind of innocence that went beyond mere youthfulness. Her shuidou scar, a shallow blemish high on her forehead, could be fixed, perhaps with powder, when she and Lo Dun met formally.

On the afternoon when Lo Dun and his mother were scheduled to visit, Junan made Yinan struggle into her new pink qipao an hour early. She spent the hour instructing her sister. "Don't let him know what you are feeling. He will like you better if he can't tell. Don't hold your collar away from your neck; you shouldn't fidget with your clothes."

"This collar is so stiff."

"I'm not sure what kind of family they are—they're merchants, but probably not bookworms like you, so they can't have too many modern ideas. Bow a little, be respectful. Try to look old-fashioned. And if you smile, don't show your teeth. It's vulgar."

Precisely on the hour, Lo Dun arrived along with his mother.

He was a slender man about fifteen years older than Yinan, with a long, serious face and a patch of gray in the left corner of his high forehead. Lo Taitai appeared to be a fierce crone, but Junan was pleased to see that she found it hard to walk. Soon she would be dead. Yinan wouldn't long suffer under her torment.

When introduced, Yinan bowed carefully and fixed her gaze upon the floor. Watching her, Junan felt a mixture of emotions. She wished that Yinan wouldn't feel so miserable and timid, but she thought perhaps her sister's shyness might be pleasing to the old woman. Lo Taitai had withered until the tendons stood out on her neck, but she behaved in the manner of a person used to getting her way.

Lo Taitai looked Yinan up and down, letting her eyes rest on the face, the clothing, feet, and hands. Junan waited, confident, for she had personally seen to every detail of her sister's appearance. She had fixed a bit of powder into the shuidou scar and it was almost invisible.

Lo Taitai cleared her throat and spoke. "She was born in the Year of the Sheep," she announced to no one in particular.

"The Snake," Yinan corrected her.

The stiff lips closed in a line.

Junan gave Yinan a warning glance, but her sister was studying the grain of the wood floor. She offered the guests tea, and was relieved when Yinan excused herself to fetch it.

LO DUN PARTED on courteous terms. Her father was optimistic. But a week after the visit, Baoding wrote even more courteously that Lo Dun had withdrawn his interest. He had nothing against the family, but his old mother had objected to the match. She didn't want her son to marry a woman born in the Year of the Snake; she believed a Snake woman would be too tricky for him. She would never have agreed to the meeting if she had known that Yinan was a Snake.

When Junan read the letter, she knew that Yinan had displeased Lo Taitai by speaking.

She told her father to shrug off this failure and continue the search, but he felt they had lost face. All of his friends had known of this attempt.

He sent for Yinan. "Lo Taitai has decided she would like a bride born in the Sheep year," he said.

"Yes, Baba." Yinan looked unmistakably relieved.

Watching her, Junan was secretly pleased the marriage hadn't worked out. Perhaps someone more to Yinan's liking, a less intimidating person, might be considered. But Lo Dun had been a solid, well-connected man, in many ways a suitable match for both the family and Yinan.

Junan felt obliged to speak. "You must become more pliant, Meimei," she told Yinan. "Remember the pliant reed that bends in the wind."

"Yes."

For several seconds the two sisters stood looking at one another. Junan felt suddenly afraid. The still, pale image of her sister's face rippled and blurred before her eyes, and it seemed that an unbearable sorrow hovered over them. She hurried out of the room.

A few weeks later, her father showed Junan another letter.

22nd Year of the Republic
17 March
Cousin and brother,

You have been once acquainted with Mao Gao, in the silk business in Nanjing. It has been many years since his young first wife died of meningitis. He has recently decided to remarry, and I have taken the liberty of mentioning Yinan.

I will offer my opinion that I do not consider it a bad thing for your daughter to marry a man in his late fifties, such as Mao Gao. An older man cherishes a girl and provides a steadying influence.

Moreover, it is your situation that I am also thinking about. I am not unaware that there have been some recent instabilities in the cotton market. I believe Mao Gao is protected and can provide not only loans for your business aspirations to the north, but a crucial connection into the industry at a time when you will surely need it. Please reply immediately, as they are in some hurry.

My best wishes to you for luck and prosperity in the coming Rooster year.

Your brother-cousin,
Baoding

"He is too old," Junan told her father.
"You're only a child. You don't understand these things."

He explained that Mao Gao was a merchant of high caliber. He could hardly turn down a connection to this man. He had already telegramed his cousin and instructed him to proceed.

Junan knew she shouldn't openly disagree with him. She went to Mma's room and mentioned the match. Surely Mma would cancel the plan.

But Mma only shrugged. She had grown so old that when she shrugged, her puny shoulders seemed to part from her body. "All men are dogs," she muttered. "An older dog will jump at the chance for something fresh."

This reply, not being a dissent, amounted to approval. If Mma approved, Junan could not gracefully object. She bowed her head and went to talk to Hu Mudan. She suspected that Yinan had somehow convinced the laundry woman not to starch or iron her clothes. This problem must be remedied, if Yinan was to marry.

She fought against another bout of sorrow so fierce it squeezed her breath. Could it be that her father and grandmother knew best? Certainly, this marriage would be, in many ways, better than her own. Mao Gao would provide a generous living, and if she bore a son, Yinan would be cherished. Would Yinan become a youthful sacrifice to save the family finances? She tried to put the thought out of her mind.

HER FATHER WROTE to his cousin, who wrote back that Mao Gao leaned in favor of the marriage, but wanted to see a photograph. This brought on a troublesome sequence of events. Yinan's pink qipao had mysteriously vanished. Junan questioned her sister, the laundry woman, and the maid. None of them had seen it. She fumed at the new problem: Mao Gao was an older man who would want his future bride to wear traditional clothing. Yinan, who wandered around the house in a rumpled blouse and trousers, had only this one good traditional dress. Junan made Yinan try on a qipao of her own, but it didn't fit properly.

After a discussion with Hu Mudan, Junan decided that Yinan could have her picture taken in the dress she had planned to wear to Junan's wedding. It was a Western dress, but feminine and expensive. Junan fussed over the shuidou scar on Yinan's forehead, and in the end, her skin was smooth, although Junan knew all along what the photograph would reveal: an ordinary girl, awkward in a fancy dress, her features made plain by misery and embarrassment.

The photographer asked Yinan to hold a long-stemmed paper rose. Halfway through the sitting, Yinan began to shiver. When the photographer was finished, she tugged Junan's sleeve, and together they went to Yinan's room, where she shed her dress and pulled on the same things she'd worn two hours before. Junan looked away from Yinan's thin, childish body as it emerged from the shimmering yellow silk, then disappeared again under the shabby pants, undershirt, blouse, and vest.

"You need to stop wearing these rags," she said. "How will you get your husband to want you?"

Yinan said something she couldn't hear.

"What is it?"

Yinan lowered her gaze. For a moment Junan thought the conversation was over, but then Yinan persisted. "What is that like?"

"I don't understand."

"To be wanted in that way."

Fitting two fingers under Yinan's chin, she raised her sister's face and frowned, stalling for time. "Why on earth do you want to know a thing like that?"

Yinan shook her head.

Junan felt she'd caught a bird in her hands. Yinan's long lashes beat against her cheeks. "It is all right," she said. "It's fine. You'll see, when it happens to you, I suppose."

"Maybe I won't."

Junan smiled kindly. "That's not true." She thought about Yinan's question. "It's good," she said. She paused again. "It makes him belong to you."

"Do you belong to Li Ang, then?" Yinan sounded frightened.

"No," Junan answered. "Don't be ridiculous." But she wondered if her sister might have guessed her secret. Inside her chest of drawers, under a pile clothes, she'd hidden the fancy box of candies confiscated from Yinan. She was saving them for Li Ang's New Year's visit. She reminded herself there was no way Yinan could know.

The first few times that she and Li Ang had made love, she had felt a moment of fear when he left behind his initial caution and began to work himself into her, forgetting who she was. Her own slender arms and legs were only a pittance against his strength. He had launched himself into her, like a boat into the waves, while in her mind she stood and watched from shore. But after a moment, she'd begun to feel pleased with the way that he thrashed and flailed, gasping against her, as if she were the answer for some desperate need. This physical need had given her a sense of power.

She looked forward to his New Year's visit. She wouldn't admit it to Yinan, but she wanted him to come to her. Their last time together, she had begun to relish the weight of his body on her own, the warm, smooth skin over his muscles and bones, the movement of his body when he breathed. That time, when he made love to her, she had begun to have the physical sensation of going deep inside herself. Afterward, she lay awake and considered this feeling. It could not be love. But it was unlike anything she'd known. And she knew that this urge would be impossible to explore further without involving Li Ang: that she must ask something from him, however silently. She steeled herself against this request, this possible indebtedness. She took on her desire with clenched teeth. She could not imagine how it might end, or what it might be like to give in to this hunger, to yield.

THE HOUSEHOLD BEGAN preparations for the Year of the Rooster. It was the first time Junan had been in charge of New Year, and she was abashed to learn how little money there was to spend. She compensated for the short funds by choosing the brightest, noisiest red azaleas and the largest lanterns. She piled the few dozen tangerines in such a way that the stack appeared larger than it actually was. She made Gu Taitai save money by buying the pig at the market and roasting it herself. The traditional chicken would be prepared by Gu Taitai. Hu Mudan said she had a source for chickens, promising Yinan that Guagua would be spared.

A week before the holiday, she set three dozen eggs to steep in tea leaves, salt, and anise. She bought red paper and set Yinan to work with her calligraphy brush. Later, when she walked past Yinan's door, she caught sight of her sister sitting on the floor folding a paper bird, surrounded by finished banners she had spread out to dry.

On New Year's Eve, their father called the sisters into Mma's room.

"Mao Gao has approved the photograph," he said.

From her bed, Mma muttered, "An older dog will jump at the chance."

Junan found herself unable to speak. She opened her mouth and closed it. Despite her preparations, the news had taken her by surprise. Finally, she thought of a question. "When will the wedding be?"

"After the Harvest Festival."

Junan realized how soon Yinan would leave. She turned to her father and grandmother. Mma stared straight ahead with her clouded, almost unseeing eyes. Her father averted his gaze. She turned to Yinan. Yinan was pumping her head back and forth, back and forth, violently and soundlessly, as if she had swallowed something and could not breathe. Then she ran from the room.

Somewhere in the house, the infant Hu Ran was crying.

Junan excused herself and followed her sister. She struggled to collect her thoughts. It was a warm day and the air was filled with the odor of melting earth. She felt intoxicated, floating, and beneath this queer feeling there was an undertow of helpless grief.

The door to Yinan's room was closed. She knocked, but there was no answer. "Meimei," she said. "Meimei, it's me."

She bent toward the door. "Meimei," she said, "It's me, Jiejie."

She pushed the door open.

Yinan sat at her desk, head bent onto a pile of red New Year signs. Her shoulders shook.

"Meimei, let me help you move these signs. You don't want to get them all wet."

Still shaking, Yinan nodded. "Yes—Jiejie—"

"Meimei, don't cry. You still have almost nine months at home. Nine months is a long time."

"Don't—make me—leave—"

The room blurred for one dizzying wing beat. Junan struggled to collect herself. "I—will miss you too, Meimei, but Nanjing isn't terribly far. You need to get married, you must be married—"

"But Jiejie—"

There was a knock on the door.

Junan looked up. There was something familiar in the knock, peremptory, and loud. Both sisters straightened, turning toward the door, and in the next moment it opened, revealing a tall, lithe, handsome man wearing a khaki uniform. He stood there, holding back a little to assess the situation. Junan started. It was her husband. She hadn't seen him since his visit in the fall. Now he looked very much like a stranger, and yet somehow alarmingly familiar and welcome. She felt her fingertips pulse and her cheeks begin to glow. She had a sudden, fierce desire to run to him and throw her arms around him with relief.

Instead, she nodded and asked if he had eaten.

THAT NIGHT, WHEN they were alone, Li Ang put his hands on Junan's shoulders. In the dark she couldn't see his body, nor did she reach for it, but she knew it by its shape and weight: his torso long, his shoulders strong and sleek like those of the man who pulled the ice wagon. She turned her face away. Although his skin was very warm, she suddenly shivered—she didn't know whether it was from fear or desire, or perhaps from anticipation of this avenue to forgetfulness. She could smell their evening meal on his breath: chicken and ginger, sulfurous eggs, fish, and sesame oil. Beneath it all, there was his scent, familiar now, and when she detected it, she felt an involuntary loosening in her spine. As if he could somehow feel this, he began kissing her fervently on the mouth. She pulled away.

He stopped. "What is it?" His voice frightened her; it was so low and kind.

She couldn't answer him.

He put his hand on the back of her neck and stroked it; kindly, as one might stroke a miserable child.

"What is it?"

"Stop it—stop—don't—" She couldn't speak. If he didn't stop touching her, she would cry.

She had never thought of what her life would be like without Yinan: without the blink of her eyes, without her narrow, shuttered face, without the still gravity of her body as she sat to read or draw, without her clear voice always asking impossible or childish questions, without the smell and sound of her breathing, and the trusting beat of her heart.

"What is it?"

"It is Yinan—" She shuddered. "Yinan—"

"What about Yinan?"

His hand kept moving on her neck, gently and with patience. The touch spread through her and she found it difficult to keep herself from shaking.

"Her engagement. She will be married—and then she will be gone—"

Her voice broke. Ashamed, she looked away and fought to hide this from him. But now he was comforting her, stroking her hair. She must not give way. He was stroking her hair. He was caressing her neck and back. Now they lay close enough that nothing could have passed between them; she felt the heat under his skin, felt his ribs swell, then contract, with every breath. Around the bed, the ceiling and walls loomed darkly. *Xiaoxin*, she thought. *Xiaoxin*. Below, his knees and hands guided her legs apart. She could not see the square-cut top of his head. She searched his face for its expression, but she only saw the slice of white under his irises. She felt the mainspring of her body loosening. She fought to keep the sobs out of her breaths; she took huge shuddering gasps; she returned, again, to her sister, her sister's head moving helplessly back and forth. Asking, what is it like to be wanted?

She pressed into him, seeking his weight, wanting to be buried.

LATER SHE SLEPT, head heavy, mouth open, taking long, deep breaths. A lock of hair lay wet against her teeth. Li Ang lay next to her, watching the smoke unfurl from his cigarette. Sometimes he didn't know what to make of her: such a private woman, so unwilling to lose control. At the sound of her involuntary cry of pleasure, so raw, so unexpected, some channel had been opened within him. He was a boy again, an errand boy, light-footed, filled with energy, fighting to clear a path for Corporal Sun. He lay and remembered it all: the glimpse of the grenade, the quick knowledge of what he must do, the moment of possibility, of fate lying open. His own surety, pushing Sun out danger. The flash of dazed gray light when the grenade exploded. Then the sensation of weightlessness, of his empty back. The corporal shouting for the medic. Then the corporal's words: "That was meant for me, boy. Stay alive, and I'll always help you after this."

Now the scars in his shoulder itched but he didn't move for fear of waking her. He thought of his brother's glance, affectionate, contemptuous, on the day when he had first come home in his lieutenant's uniform. He wondered how Li Bing was getting along at the university in Beijing. He thought of Junan's ragged voice, "and then she will be gone—" It seemed to him that Li Bing had never been more far away.

"Wife," he said. Then, "Junan."

There was no answer. For a moment he waited, feeling oddly bereft. Eventually, he reached over and put out his cigarette.

Meanwhile, my mother's limp and sleeping body held a secret: in this moment of weakness I had been conceived. When she let down her guard, her womb had opened and my father's seed rushed into her. I was carried to full term and born in the early spring of 1933, the Year of the Rooster, only days after my great-grandmother Mma—sparing herself from the disappointment of the birth of yet another girl—drew her last resentful breath and let her soul depart from her body in a blur of bat-like wings. High above the house it hovered, before vanishing, with her last breath, into the other world.

BECAUSE I WAS BORN SO CLOSE TO MMA'S DEATH, MY MOTHER feared that my great-grandmother's dark and stubborn soul might bind itself to me and follow me forever. And so she gave me a name unrecognizable to Mma, a character used in neither the Li nor the Wang families. She called me Hong: a word meaning the color red, the color of life. A word to separate me from Mma and all of her concerns. A simple word to give me my own strength—so common, and so plain, that I might have been a peasant girl. My mother's naming plan succeeded. I didn't suffer from nightmares or hear echoes of Mma's crabbed voice. Moreover, I didn't take after my great-grandmother. Of Mma's most difficult qualities—such as her pettiness, constipation, and solitary anger—I inherited only her insomnia.

Even in those peaceful years, I had trouble falling asleep. Every evening, I went up to my room and began a long ritual my mother had designed to send me to my dreams. First came story time with my beloved ayi, Yinan, who read translations of Grimm's fairy tales while orange rays lit up the pages of her manuscript. Through the room's only window, which looked over the courtyard, I could see the colors of the sky deepen and fade over the wall, throwing the garden into shades of violet and indigo. I was not yet four years old, a little too young to understand her stories, but still I begged for them. I loved this time with Yinan. I loved the way she included me in everything, holding the manuscript where I could see it even though I didn't know any of the characters. She read slowly, allowing me to float inside her quiet voice and listen to the sounds of the words.

"Once there was a poor widow who lived in a cottage. In her garden stood two rosebushes, one white and one red. Her two daughters were like the rose-trees, and so one was called Snow-white and the other Rose-red. They were very good, happy girls, industrious and cheerful, although Snow-white was gentler and more quiet than Rose-red. Rose-red liked to play outdoors, picking wildflowers and catching butterflies; but Snow-white kept her mother company inside, and helped her with the housework."

Here she paused and laid her hand thoughtfully upon the page.

"Go on, Ayi," I urged her.

"Snow-white and Rose-red loved each other so much that they held hands whenever they left the house. Snow-white would say, 'We'll never leave each other,' and Rose-red would reply, 'Not as long as we live.' Then their mother would say, 'Whatever one of you has, she must share with the other.'"

There was something special about Yinan. She knew my silliest fears and my most selfish daydreams and loved them all. On these evenings I felt closer to her than to anyone in the world. By the time she finished reading it was almost dark. We sat together, safe within our tent of yellow lamplight.

We heard my mother's footsteps on the stairs before she entered the room, tall and severe.

"Xiao Hong." She frowned. "Little Hong, you're still awake?"

Yinan smiled. "I could read the sutras and she would stay awake."

In those days, Yinan and I were always trying to make my mother laugh. I had learned to amuse her by describing my observations of the servants and of my playmate Pu Li, whose father, Lieutenant Pu Sijian, was my father's best friend. Pu Li was a pleasant boy with a monotonous mind, and we all thought him funny. Yinan would egg me on. "What did Pu Li do today?" she asked me. "Did he have to tie a thread around his finger again in order to remember which hand to put his chopsticks in?"

After we had smiled at this, my mother remarked, "You're always making fun of Pu Li. Why don't you tease Hu Ran?"

"I don't want to tease Hu Ran."

She claimed to think it comical that Ran called me "young miss," when each day we played and fought together like brother and sister. But I sensed that she expected such formality. She'd once told me that he had the complexion of a peasant.

Now she glanced sideways at my aunt. "Perhaps she is in love with him?"

"Don't make fun of me!" I cried.

Then my mother did laugh. She threw back her head and laughed from deep inside herself. Despite my pique, I had the pleasure I'd been waiting for, the sight of her white throat and her lovely, straight teeth— the pleasure of knowing she was the most beautiful woman in the world. Yinan thought so as well. I could see it in her eyes. Afterwards we sat still, listening to the night. "Don't be angry, Xiao Hong," my mother said. "Not when you go to sleep. It's bad for your digestion." They tucked me into bed and sang to me.

> *I went along the wide road*
> *and took you by the sleeve—*
> *do not hate me,*
> *never spurn old friends.*

> *I went along the wide road*
> *and took you by the hand—*
> *do not hate me,*
> *never spurn a love.*

Then my aunt kissed me, and my mother kissed me, and they left me to myself. But I didn't sleep. I had already begun to lie awake for hours. Desultory sounds rose from below: the faint clucking of Guagua the chicken, my mother talking, and my aunt playing a recording of piano music. I didn't know what Yinan played, but many years later, in a department store on another continent, I would hear the melody and recognize those notes, recall their echo on a summer evening, winding off a scratchy record, drifting into sorrow. I would remember the faint voices of the servants gossiping outside, and, if I listened very closely, the sounds of them splitting salted watermelon seeds between their teeth. I would recall those evenings when I was a child, enclosed in a family and a world that felt absolutely safe.

Like all children, I was born into the middle of a story I didn't know, and I was raised to be unknowing, tranquil in its center. But glimpses of this story reached my eyes. One night, after everyone had gone to bed, I thought I heard footsteps below my window. I sat up and peered outside. For a minute I saw nothing. The courtyard was dark and still. Then I caught the vanishing white flutter of her nightgown as she climbed the stairs into the part of the house where everything had lain unchanged for a dozen years, the room that had belonged to my grandmother Chanyi.

THE NEXT MORNING I watched my mother mend a tear in my father's jacket sleeve. She made him bring home on weekends each piece of clothing that he broke or tore, so that she could mend it personally and send it back with him the following week. It was as if the pile of finished mending, waiting for him, ensured his safe return. She wouldn't allow anyone else to repair his things, and now she worked with meticulous care, putting the needle in and out of the jacket cuff so precisely that the stitches blended imperceptibly into the fabric. She kept extra bobbins of silk and cotton in the exact grasshopper-brown shade of his uniform.

"I saw Ayi outside walking in her nightgown," I said. "Ayi went upstairs into the closed-up room."

My mother's needle paused almost imperceptibly. "Never mind, Hong."

"But I did see her," I insisted. "She looked sad."

My mother shook her head, impatient. "Xiao Hong," she said, "here is one key to living a happy life: Don't take pride in how much you can see." As she bent down to knot the thread, I saw in her face a spasm of concern.

According to Hu Mudan, my grandfather had been the one to

request that Yinan's engagement ceremony be delayed. He wished to have a proper period of mourning for Mma. He proposed the delay soon after I was born, during a visit from the fiancé, Mao Gao. Mao was a solidly built man of medium height, whose flushed cheeks and small, fierce eyes made him seem younger than fifty-seven. He carried a raw energy, as rude as an odor, that revealed itself in everything he did. A large plate of crab dumplings vanished in several bites. While waiting for more food, he didn't sit still but examined the room with darting eyes; he let his eyes fall on Yinan with the same brusque interest. Hu Mudan felt a private curiosity over how odd it was that with such energy he had not already remarried. She learned the reason as she spied on the visit. Mao Gao told my grandfather that since his wife's death he had expanded his business, pouring all his waking hours into the financing, planning, and construction of new factories. He wished his family to be dominant in the industry. Now all that remained was for him to father sons.

Mao Gao agreed to the postponement. As a matter of fact, he said, while Yinan left the room to fetch more tea, it would be best if they could wait until after the following year. During that time, he planned to travel north and open two more factories.

"Gongxi, gongxi, congratulations," said my grandfather. "You're the only man I know with the courage to expand close to the Japanese."

Mao Gao only shrugged. "It's no challenge," he replied. "Of my four processing plants, I'm considering closing two and transferring the business to my more modern factories in Shanghai." He straightened in his chair, as if he were talking to a larger audience. "Those two factories using Japanese machinery turn out finer cloth than my two Chinese factories, and in half the time," he said. "The superiority of foreign work is undeniable."

In the pause that followed, Hu Mudan wondered how my grandfather would reply to this. She knew enough to recognize the voice of a collaborationist when she heard it. Mao Gao continued, "It should be, as some say, an 'Asian co-prosperity circle.' An alliance with the Japanese would be far preferable to the British or French. The British are flooding the international market with inexpensive stuff from their colonies. We must join against the white men. The Japanese, at the very least, are Asians like ourselves. They are far preferable."

My grandfather looked at his hands.

Meanwhile, as Mao Gao spoke, the snacks Gu Taitai had prepared kept vanishing between his words: another round of succulent, puckered crab dumplings, redolent of sea-smelling steam; a dish of claws; a plate of sweet rice cakes. Yinan hurried with the trays of food and tea, her tongue pushed against her teeth as she struggled to balance the plates and cups. Later, after Mao Gao had gone and Yinan had burst into tears, my mother said to her, "What an eater that man is! Two plates loaded with crabmeat dianxin came back without a shred. After you two are married, you should be careful not to let him eat so ferociously of foods with so much hot energy."

Was it wrong of her to pretend that Yinan should be anticipating this marriage with happiness? Hu Mudan couldn't say. On the other hand, it wouldn't be right to encourage Yinan's unhappiness. It was my mother's job to teach my aunt the discipline of marriage. By this time, my mother considered herself an expert on the techniques of keeping and managing a husband.

She claimed she did not love my father, but everyone could see this wasn't true. Even the laundry woman saw the tiny stitches she made in his torn jacket sleeves, the securely planted buttons. The laundry woman was chastised for the smallest stain or blemish to his uniforms, and Gu Taitai had learned to shop automatically on weekends for my father's favorite dishes. In the kitchen, Weiwei made arch remarks about my mother's moods, which came and went along with his visits.

Hu Mudan said nothing. She who'd known my mother since infancy could see much more. She saw, beneath the cool ivory features, the same possessiveness that had been Chanyi's downfall. She saw it in each thing my mother did. The meticulous, fine mending and special meals, the personal trip south of the city to wrangle precious, first-crop leaves of his favorite tea, the fierce sounds of lovemaking from their room at night—all of these betrayed her. My mother claimed these tasks were performed out of duty. But duty implied a repetitive dullness, a void, a sense of merely keeping up the quotidian requirements of her role. In reality, I believe, my mother's duties were performed as acts of magic. She spent her energy weaving spells, making invisible strands of comfort and habit designed to keep my father hurrying home to her.

AS A RESULT OF the delay, Yinan remained alone until an age long after most women were married. In my first memories my aunt was already twenty, waiting for a union with a man she didn't like. It was no wonder she grew a little odd. I now know that her fairy tale translations were unnecessary; the Brothers Grimm had already been translated into Chinese. But she spent hours on these stories, and on her calligraphy. Even as a child, I could see the eagerness with which she escaped into this other world on the page, submerging for long hours and coming up with blank eyes, her anxiety and sadness cleansed in the deep.

Yinan wanted another tutor to fill her long months of waiting. My grandfather pointed out that he could not afford another tutor; Deng Xiansheng had worked for free. But my mother, in her typical way, found a practical solution that pleased everybody. She asked Charlie Kong if she might beg the services of my father's brother, who'd been expelled from his university in Beijing and was living, as before, above his uncle's stationery shop. My mother pointed out that there was room in the house and that Li Bing might make use of his extra time by furthering his studies.

My mother parceled out a few responsibilities. He would be required to give calligraphy, history, and English lessons to Yinan. He would help with her translations and perform some bookkeeping chores for my grandfather. The rest of his time would be his own. He'd been thrown out of his university after protesting compulsory classes instituted by the Ministry of Education under pressure from the government. But here he could continue his studies; he might even enroll at Hangzhou University. In this way, my mother found a tutor for Yinan and secured another tether to my father.

She would have hired Li Bing regardless of his manner. But when he arrived, she liked him instantly. He was a skinny, awkward man. His thin neck, with its prominent Adam's apple, stretched out of the frayed collar of his jacket. He had terrible posture, and he gazed through small round spectacles with a perpetual expression of dry intelligence.

He was utterly unlike my father, but perhaps my mother and aunt found some mysterious resemblance. I remember how well they got along. They would sit around for hours, sometimes with my father, falling into comfortable observations about what they'd read, beginning with the old poems he was teaching Yinan, and moving to modern novels, then newspapers, and finally world events. My mother enjoyed Li Bing's wry wit, although this charm was tempered by what she considered an amusing moral rigidity. For example, he couldn't discuss relations between men and women without drawing abstract parallels to less personal subject matter.

One evening, when my father was visiting, they sat together in the courtyard long past my bedtime. Hu Mudan and I hovered nearby; I because no one had told me leave, and Hu Mudan in case my mother wanted anything. When my father mentioned beer, my mother shook her head emphatically. Li Bing nodded his approval. "It's a good thing," he said to her, "that Li Ang has a wife like you."

My father coughed on his cigarette. "What are you talking about?"

"It will be good for China, I think, for its soldiers to marry women whom they can't persuade into going along with them on every little thing."

"Really."

"You know what I mean. Most women give and give too much. Soon their words mean nothing. In a way, I think, they're like our country, which allows the foreigners to take and take. Most women bend so easily. They raise their sons in a tradition of softness. You, Junan: you are different. Perhaps your son will be one of a new generation: a Chinese hero."

My mother changed the subject. "Yinan, don't read at sunset. It's bad for your eyes. And Hong," she continued, "it's time for you to go upstairs." She sounded absent-minded; she didn't press the matter, so I stayed where I was. Then she turned to Li Bing. "And what about you?" she asked. "If marriage is good for your brother, what about you?"

Li Bing raised his chin. "I'm not interested in marriage," he said. "I live for other things."

"What kinds of things?"

"I live to preserve the dignity of our country."

"Perhaps you, too, should marry to help create a Chinese hero."

"Right," my father said. "China could use a spurt of his heroic seed."

At that moment, Yinan spoke. They'd forgotten she was present. She spoke without turning away from her manuscript, which she held close to her face. "Do you know what?" she said. "I often do think that some countries are like women and some are like men."

My mother and father glanced at one another.

"What do you mean?" Li Bing asked.

"Women are neiren, people of the inside, and they belong inside the house. Men are wairen. They belong outside."

My father turned to her, curious. "What about China and Japan?"

"China is a woman. Japan is a man. He is aggressive, knocking down the door of her house and attacking her, trying to rape her."

For a moment, no one replied. Li Bing blushed. Then my mother said, "I honestly don't know where she got those frightening notions. I've never told her anything of the sort."

Li Bing recovered himself. He turned his intelligent, searching gaze upon Yinan, and gently asked, "So now Japan is banging at the door. What should poor China do?"

"I don't know." Yinan considered. "She could find another strong man to be on her side and push Japan out. But if there is no other man, I think that she could let him in and learn to live with him."

My father's silent laughter made a puff of smoke.

"Yinan!" my mother exclaimed. "Meimei, you don't know what you're talking about."

"What do you mean, Meimei?" Li Bing asked. "Do you think that under such circumstances the woman should let the strange man into her house and live with her?"

Yinan stared at her manuscript. "Yes. Because what difference does it make?"

"Would you explain to us what you mean?" Li Bing pressed gently. "We want to understand."

Yinan moved her gaze to a spot on the floor. "It's something like this," she said. "The other day you were talking to Hu Mudan, Jiejie, and Weiwei asked me if she could go to town. Her friend Jing who works at Old Chen's house was going into town, and Weiwei wanted to go along."

"It was right of her to ask," said my mother.

"Well, I knew how much she wanted to go. Old Chen is planning to evacuate, you know, and Weiwei and Jing have been friends for years. They wanted to talk. But I knew that you wanted everyone to stay home and work on the garden. And I knew that they could talk that evening. So I said no. And Weiwei left the room. But at the last minute I looked up and she was going out the doorway, frowning over her shoulder at me like she really hated me."

My mother shook her head. "That girl."

"Go on," Li Bing urged Yinan.

"Well, so I've been thinking. Mma used to oversee this house and all of the servants. But after she got old it was really you, Jiejie, who ran the house."

"Yes, yes."

"But over the years, for the whole time, who has been living here and doing the work? Gu Taitai, Weiwei, Gongdi, and the others. So I wonder if it really matters to them who is the master. They are always the servants. They work for us, but how much do they care for us? I love Weiwei, but does Weiwei love me? Does it really matter to the servants who the master is?"

Li Bing raised his eyebrows. My mother offered him another cigarette.

"Thank you. You two are spoiling me. I couldn't afford to smoke this much in school."

"Of course you should share in the bounty of the general's cigarettes." She smiled at my father, but he'd retreated from the conversation, lost in thought.

Li Bing blew a tentative smoke ring at the rising moon. "Jiejie, you and your sister are both extraordinary women."

"I must admit that sometimes Meimei surprises me."

Li Bing nodded. "You and your sister are two completely different blossoms on the same branch." He spoke through a stream of smoke. In the dusk, it was difficult to see his face; there were only the two glass circles of his spectacles and the smoke rising into the path of light before them, picking up tiny flecks of light.

"Tell me, Jiejie," he said to my mother, "if Japan were a man knocking at your door, would you open the door?"

"Never."

"And if he still managed to get inside?"

My mother looked over the garden wall at the branches of the mulberry tree. "If he came inside," she said, "I would poison him to death."

THE EVACUATION OF THE wealthy Chen, along with his son Da-Huan, was overshadowed by the scandal of Chen Da-Huan's declaration of love. The object of his affections was an acquaintance of my mother's, Yang Qingwei. She was a quiet girl of about twenty-five with a sweet, pale face, who had never married because she had been ill with tuberculosis as a teenager. Chen Da-Huan declared he wished to marry Qingwei, but the elder Chen forbade his son to marry a woman with bad health. Chen Da-Huan, always an obedient son, said goodbye to his beloved and left with the Chen family for the west.

Hu Mudan wondered if my family, too, would evacuate. But my grandfather had no such plan. He wished to remain in Hangzhou and watch over his remaining cotton business. My mother didn't protest, for my father was stationed nearby. So after the Chens had left town, things went on much as before. Li Bing continued to tutor Yinan, and Yinan, at his encouragement, took up the hobby of writing poems. Scraps of paper fluttered from her pockets. My mother joked that if any more people around her started up a literary habit, she would put her foot down.

Now that the house had grown so lively, my father visited whenever he could. He always brought me a gift: a cookie, a little coin purse, or a box of sesame chews. When it was time for my dinner in the kitchen, he and my mother would go out to Lou Wai Lou, a restaurant famous for its fish and lotus chicken. They would stroll out of the front doors, my father in his pressed uniform, my mother a perfect match for him with her willowy height and graceful stride. Unlike many Chinese women, she knew how to wear the Western styles. The hats looked right on her small head; the slim, loose lines of the skirts and blouses revealed her grace and confidence. When Gongdi, the errand boy, stared at her, she pretended she didn't notice. But I knew she was aware of his admiration, and also of my father's; she watched him from the corners of her long eyes.

That spring my father joined the KMT Party, and in the summer he was promoted to captain. His promotion came along with a change of assignment: he would be put in charge of training an actual battalion under Sun Li-jen. It was the assignment he had been waiting for.

He arrived home that weekend wearing his new uniform. I remember him standing before us, very proud. The sight of him was dizzying. I ran to hug his legs, and my mother put her arms around him. "Congratulations!" she said. "Gongxi, gongxi." Then she bent down to me, her face a radiant, pale mask, and said, "Xiao Hong, you should leave now."

"I don't mind," he said. "The child can stay."

"Of course not. Hong, why don't you go see what your ayi is doing?"

Years later, Hu Mudan tried to explain. "Things were not the same between them after your father rose through the ranks." It is a part of the story I can only imagine. As a child, I ran blithely out of the room without regret, while behind closed doors, the story continued.

SHE STOOD WITH her arms around him. Under the smell of new cloth and leather, she found the rich, familiar scent of his flesh. She stood still, wanting him to lead her to the bedroom.

He whispered into her ear, "Let's go out and walk by the lake."

She bit back her disappointment. He wanted to parade his uniform before the world. She put on her best new coat and dress, and together they left the house.

They took a cab to the lake and strolled along the promenade. The spring air was chilly; the long afternoon rays glittered on the tranquil water. She watched the pale light on the faces of the passersby, and it seemed to her that they turned to her husband as if he'd been transformed. They looked at him and saw a powerful man. She understood that he had truly been transformed, that he was to all intents and purposes a different man. At this recognition, Junan felt foreboding. His promotion had brought along with it the threat of change.

At the restaurant, over the fish and vegetables, she held herself as carefully as porcelain. Although she was aware of her own strengths—her beautiful face, her throat, her iridescent nails and slender fingertips—she felt that any moment she might shatter. She poured him a second cup of wine, letting the lamp shine pale against the translucent china cup, the precise turn of her wrist, the elegant line of her white arm as it vanished into the wide sleeve of her dress. The dress, of cream silk satin embroidered with pale pink and scarlet peony blossoms, revealed the shape of her body. As they were eating, he glanced often in her direction, and she willed him to desire her.

Finally they went home. She had aired the room and made it ready for them, with the silk coverlet folded back and tucked away from the bed. He motioned for her not to turn on the lamp. The moon, bright and full, lit up the room so that they could see each other outlined in pale light and shadow. He went over to her side of the bed. He put his arms around her, fingers working at the satin frogs to unfasten her dress, and they lay down together.

After they had made love, Li Ang lit a cigarette. Junan didn't like him to smoke in the house but she permitted it in this case. As he smoked, he lounged against the pillows, his face bright and optimistic.

He explained to Junan every particular of the promotion. His salary would rise; he would have more privileges and greater responsibility. He spoke about the threat of Japanese aggression. He was so excited he sat up straight in the bed. She lay and listened, nodding.

Finally Li Ang lay back and blew smoke rings toward the lamp.

"Maybe this time," he said.

"Yes?"

"Well, maybe this time it will work." There was a new tone of purpose and forthrightness in his voice.

Junan's hands grew cold. What did he want? What had she not prepared for? The new authority in his words put her on her guard. She heard her own voice, calm. "What do you mean?"

"Well, now, after this, everything would be perfect if I had a son."

Junan knew that she should touch him, place a hand upon his arm or chest, but her palms and fingers, wet and trembling, would betray the virulence of her feelings. She stayed on her side of the bed, eyes almost closed, looking out from under her lashes at the long tunnel of her body under the comforter. Very faint, like an echo, she heard her sister's voice rough with fever, and her plaintive words, "if I had been a boy." She felt a presence hover in the room; the black wings of night beat over them.

Finally, she knew that she could speak without giving herself away. "My father wanted a son," she said.

"And your mother?"

"She—wanted one as well."

"I was just wondering: I don't mean this in any way. But—do you think it's possible that there might be some kind of infertility that runs through the women in your family?"

"What do you mean?" She was grateful for the concealment of the dark.

"Well, your parents were married for many years. But your mother bore only two children, and both girls. Not that there's anything wrong about you, and as far as your sister is concerned, she's only a little fey, but I wonder—"

"That's ridiculous," Junan said. "There is no way to prove that the sex of the children is a trait that is passed from mother to daughter."

"Probably not. But it is something I have heard."

"What you've heard is a story told by old widows and unhappy women. Since when have you taken them as your guidance?" And now, shocked into action, she forced herself to smile, so that the shape of her smile came through in her voice. She took an icy handful of her own thick hair and tickled his arm until he laughed and reached for her. But an enormous lake stone had lodged in her chest, making it difficult to speak. Soon afterward she turned over with her back to him and pulled the blankets up around her neck.

LATER, WHEN THEY spoke to me about that time, my mother and Hu Mudan always prefaced their stories with the words "Before the occupation." *That spring before the occupation, the spring your father was promoted. That was before the occupation, before they tore down the south section of the city wall: you don't remember the afternoon when your father took you to walk along the top of the wall.* They thought I'd been too young to recall those peaceful years. My mother didn't want to think I could remember them; she didn't even like me to tell my stories of the war. She'd wanted to protect me from ever knowing of it. I think my recollections also frightened her. If my memory reached as far back as the Japanese occupation, then I could also recollect, no doubt, some other things she'd rather I'd forgotten.

It is true I don't remember everything about my early childhood. I don't remember the way I used to sit on my grandfather's lap and pull myself to stand by yanking on his beard. I don't remember bawling when Hu Ran had a toothache, although Hu Mudan assures me this was true. And I am left with only stories of my father's frequent departures; for I can recall only the joy surrounding his arrivals, and one time in particular when my mother told the seamstress to sew me into a new sailor blouse because the buttonholes could not be finished prior to his visit. They say that after his departures I would scream and cry until I grew feverish, but thankfully these times are lost to me.

I don't remember how my mother worried for him in the days following July 7, 1937, when the Japanese crossed the bridge in Mukden and invaded China. I learned in history books about the Japanese bombing Nanjing and the failed attack of the Chinese Air Force upon the Japanese warships anchored off Shanghai, an attack that failed with the misery of amateurs, their bombs falling in the Shanghai streets. Hu Mudan told me my mother burned every book or newspaper in English, including Yinan's book of fairy tales. Yinan refused to come down-stairs for days, while my mother sent a barrage of telegrams imploring my father to reply that he was safe. Finally he answered with the news that his mentor, General Sun Li-jen, had absorbed thirteen pieces of shrapnel and had to have an emergency blood transfusion. Later that year, the Japanese troops launched a siege upon the capital, Nanjing. They say the cries of the women who were raped and the men who were killed filled the air and that their blood ran through the streets. But the blood didn't run as far south as Hangzhou. It was several days before we heard reports, and even they were rumors, terrified and hushed. It would be some time before the newspapers detailed the dev-astation of all those who had been unfortunate enough to remain in the city. As Nanjing fell, my mother sat at her writing table, filling out sheet after sheet of onionskin telegrams, trying to reach my father's cousin Baoding and ascertain the fate of Yinan's fiancé, Mao Gao. There was no reply.

For years, I didn't learn about the surprising final moments of my grandfather, Wang Daming. Hangzhou was taken on Christmas Eve, and one night shortly afterward he didn't come home. This wasn't unusual; he often gambled until morning. But when Charlie Kong came by and asked for him, my mother grew worried. She and Charlie went to search. It was a brilliantly sunny dawn, shortly after the New Year, when they arrived at his warehouse and discovered his remains. Japanese soldiers had requested he surrender his one remaining cotton warehouse to a forced "buyout" for Japanese fabi. The "buyers" had come armed with pistols, bayonets, and swords. My grandfather, a failed man, had stood at the warehouse door. He knew their sum was less than half the amount the cotton was worth. He asked for a higher price. They refused. My grandfather declined to sell. I like to imagine that in his final moments, he understood at last what it was that he believed, and he found solid ground to stand on. After his heart had pumped its last, the soldiers chopped off his head and hung it over the warehouse gate with a written explanation.

—

INSTEAD OF THESE EVENTS I remember things no one will talk about. One day that autumn, I saw Hu Ran unclothed. I must have been four years old and Hu Ran almost seven. He had spent the morning playing in the dusty street and went behind the house to rinse off in the pond. My aunt was reading in her room; our mothers were nowhere to be found. I saw him walk behind the house. I followed, wanting to call his name, but when I peered between the scant leaves of the cascading willow tree, my curiosity silenced me.

I knew his strange bright eyes, his ears, his dusky spider legs. But now I wanted to know more. I knew he wouldn't have wanted me to see him naked, and this made the opportunity more tantalizing. Hu Ran shrugged out of his shirt and his brown skin glinted in a bit of sun that filtered through the moving leaves. I was close enough see the layer of dust over his hands. I saw his neat shoulders emerge, and then, as he turned sideways, the dusky hollows under his left arm, and a small nipple set in a coin-sized circle. I watched his taut belly breathing as he pulled down his pants. Somewhere in the courtyard a door opened and closed, but I paid no attention, focusing instead upon his high hipbone and smooth brown thigh and, coming from somewhere between his legs, a sturdy brown thumb.

"Get away from her!"

Bright sunlight pierced my eyes. My mother had swept back the willow with one hand. Her raging shape towered over us. I screamed. With long arms she seized me and carried me off.

That night she and Hu Mudan went into her room and shut the door. From my own room I heard at first my mother shouting furiously and Hu Mudan laughing. But as my mother pelted Hu Mudan with words, a frightening silence grew. Then my mother said, "It was bad enough you chose to keep that bastard in the house. But I won't allow him to corrupt my daughter."

"All right," said Hu Mudan. "All right."

My mother's voice choked and dwindled.

The next day, Hu Ran and Hu Mudan said goodbye. They would

travel west. They would leave town on a poultry wagon and ride a steamboat up the Yangtze to Hu Mudan's village in Sichuan.

Neither Hu Ran nor I understood why we were being separated. The loss was sudden and devastating. He stood before me, serious, holding out his favorite cricket in its bamboo cage. "Goodbye, young miss," he said. "You may have my cricket."

I sobbed, "I don't want your cricket! I'll feed it to Guagua!"

"You may have my necklace," Hu Ran said. He reached into his rough cotton shirt and pulled out the brilliant jade pendant that he always wore.

But then Hu Mudan stepped between us. "No," she said. "Hu Ran, you mustn't give that to a girl unless you mean to marry her."

"Why can't I marry her?" he demanded.

She ran her hand over his short hair. "Because you are too poor for her."

Hu Ran put the necklace back inside his shirt

Hu Mudan bent down to me and squeezed my shoulder. Her small, almond eyes were kind. "Don't worry, Hong," Hu Mudan said. "It's my fate to be connected to your family. We'll see you again."

AFTER THAT I didn't sleep well for many nights. Once I overheard my parents arguing. They were discussing my father's new job for Sun Li-jen. I couldn't make out all of their words, but I knew that they were quarreling. In a low-pitched voice, my mother kept repeating the word "war." "Don't go to Hankow," she said. "You should stop fighting and avoid the war. You should stay in Hangzhou, you could join the resistance. Don't go to Hankow! Who cares about another promotion!" I heard her choke on the words, "What if you're wounded again and killed!"

My father laughed. "I won't be killed."

My mother said, "You count on luck! You should never count on luck!"

"I always count on luck," he said.

She said, "Please send a home message on Charlie's telegraph." I heard her grudging tone and knew she had no choice. But I could also hear that she was still afraid.

Later that night, a dull crash came from somewhere in the front of the house. I froze, listening, assuming that I'd perhaps fallen asleep and dreamed of it. There it was again. I hurried, in my pajamas, out of my room and down the stairs. I went across the courtyard and peered between the doors. From my vantage point, I could see down the road. I stood transfixed, bedazzled by the vision of the night. The moon shone off the whitewashed wall of the house. The dirt road itself was dark, with pale pebbles gleaming here and there. The world hung around me, dark and inviting, with the breeze washing my cheeks and stillness beckoning.

I heard a man's voice raised in a shout. After several seconds I heard more brief shouts, the shrill of a whistle, and two quick blows, so brief and short that I had barely the time to understand what I had heard. Then cursing. Footsteps beat on the earth; fast breathing sounded. Someone ran around the corner of the house, close by, so close that I could smell the odor of scallions on his breath.

He paused, breathing hard, and glanced over his shoulder to locate his pursuer. His pace was quick, his clothing dark; he might still escape them. Then he ran. I waited for him to return. I sensed that he had no idea where to go. I could already hear his light step coming, strong and steady, doubling back. Here he was. Without thinking, I opened the door.

The man pivoted from hips to shoulders with a nervous, awkward energy. His torso, bent shoulder, legs poised in the turn, seemed an illustration of surprise.

I tried to see his face under the shadow of his cap, but I caught only the faint glint of his spectacles.

"Get inside!" he hissed at me.

I obeyed that voice. He slipped past me and past the house.

I watched him vanish down the street. Then I stood and waited, overcome by curiosity. From farther up the street came a tapping sound: the pursuers. After several minutes it grew into the noise of heavy boots approaching. Tramp-tramp-tramp, in rhythm.

The next moment passed so quickly I barely had time to see what happened, much less to panic. Now I caught a glimpse of someone running: a small man, dressed in a drab uniform and cap on which was clearly visible the Japanese sun. More quick footsteps, in a dry, implacable rhythm. Two more men burst into view. They did not speak. They went about their search with brisk efficiency. They looked around the corner of the house and down the alley. They listened. I leaned against the door and closed my eyes. Were they leaving? Yes, their footsteps faded. They were gone.

I remained where I was. Something cold streamed under my arms. I dared not open my eyes, but against the back of my closed lids I could still see the red disk. I could not forget the rhythm of their boots. I had never seen a Japanese soldier before. In that moment I had my first experience of a fear that would not leave.

After several minutes, I gathered my strength to go back to my room.

Slowly, quietly, I climbed the stairs. At some point I had recognized the familiar, urgent voice. The fugitive was my uncle. This was the last that I would see of him for many years.

THEY SAID A MAN'S SEED WOULD FLOURISH IN A PLUMP woman with an accepting nature, and so Junan swallowed bowls of sweet porridge and ate the crackling skin of roasted ducks. She stuffed herself with pork fat and soft, white buns; she read novels in her room and tried not to care whether Weiwei and Gu Taitai were finishing the tasks she had set out for them. She tried to keep herself amused by playing mahjong, stopping always before it got too late, until the other women smiled knowingly and said she must be hiding good news from them. But time went by without result, and she grew tired of rich food, of holding her tongue, and pretending not to notice what the servants did.

He was dissatisfied with her. This suspicion writhed beneath her calm. She knew she was as beautiful and intelligent as ever. But she suspected now that this was not important. It was all for nothing; he would have been as happy with an uglier, less competent, more fertile woman. On bleak nights, she wondered if he might be right: if there was indeed something infertile about the women of their family. Her mother, whose death she would not allow herself to think about. Her sister, who now wandered the house like a lost soul with broken wings. Could it be that there was something wrong with her as well? Junan forbade herself to think about it.

It was December 1937. Soon he would be leaving her, following the war. Like all soldiers, he sought out unconquered territories. Hangzhou, once occupied, could no longer concern him. He might never gain reentry; Japanese troops would keep him from her. A puppet government, and its spies, would conspire to keep him from her. Or was it possible that he himself, his own desires, might keep him away?

A week before he left, she said, "Pu Taitai is moving her household to Hankow."

He nodded. His friend Pu Sijian had also been promoted and had already left for the west.

"Our family could move as well."

"Not a good idea," he said. She could hear that his mind was somewhere else. "I don't know where I'll be stationed, and Hankow may be heavily bombed."

With an effort, she made her voice as sweet and light as possible. "Here is dangerous, too. Other families are leaving."

There was a long pause. "Look," he said, "don't you worry."

She didn't reply.

He began to speak again. He pointed out that although the airfields would be bombed, Hangzhou itself would escape the worst attacks because it would be protected by its air base. The conditions in the west would be quite harsh. Unsanitary, crowded, and certainly no place for children unless there were no alternative.

"Certainly as a mother you will understand that," he said.

She said, "I am the mother of your daughter and I want to bear your son."

"But I know you would never endanger him," he said.

The air between them thickened with mutual incredulity. Junan tilted her head back and closed her eyes.

"I will visit," he said.

"You can't; you know you can't cross into the occupied territory. I mustn't even say that I know where you are. Can't you see? Can't you see that this is bound to lead to trouble?" Her voice was shaking.

"Forget about it, will you? Don't worry about it for now." He was cheerful as usual.

She did not reply, to save herself the shame of tears.

There was little time remaining, and she must act. One morning she slipped out of bed while he was still asleep and dressed in her most unobtrusive clothing. She left quietly, almost tiptoeing past the doorman and out to the street, where she hired a rickshaw and ordered the driver to take her to the commercial part of town. There she hesitated before a shop hung with red and white banners.

Inside, the large room was very orderly and the floors swept clean, but the pungent medicinal odor turned her stomach. Along the walls, their wood darkened by time, were cabinets containing tiny drawers of roots and seeds and parts of animals; jars of snakes stood in the window; a human skull watched from the shelf.

The older man who stood behind the counter wore a neat white smock. "Yes." His voice was a hoarse croak. He could hardly inspire healing. But when she looked into his minnow eyes, she saw a confidence that could come only from knowledge. She also realized, with dislike, that he had already guessed what she wanted. Still she forced herself to speak.

"I want something to bring happiness," she said, and her own voice sounded stiff and dry.

Without a word, he turned around and pulled open a drawer. There were perhaps a thousand drawers in the old cabinets. But the handle of this drawer had been used so much that the finish had worn off and the characters printed on it could no longer be read. He measured out some roots and wrapped them in white paper.

"Boil," he said.

"What is the price?"

"Seven."

"Seven coppers?"

He nodded.

"How long will it take?"

Slowly he raised his eyes. She forced herself to hold still. She fixed her eyes upon the scale and the tiny brass weights.

"You have time."

She tapped her foot. "Do you have anything faster?"

"Pills," he said. "One pill, one dollar. Silver."

"Is that the only other way?"

He smiled. "Pray to the pusa."

She recalled a bodhisattva rendered in indifferent stone. She heard her mother's voice, "Guan Yin, song zi. Guan Yin, song zi." Guan Yin, send sons.

"I'll take ten of them," she said.

She had never been able to swallow pills. Some terrified reflex always throttled her, flushed their bitterness up into her mouth. But she paid the ten silver coins without a word. She went home and ground up two pills with a mortar and pestle, hid the powder in a sweet red bean paste bun, and forced herself to eat it.

That night, while they made love, forbidden words streamed out, words that she had overheard long ago, in some dark and terrible time: "I love you. Don't you leave me. Don't you ever, ever leave me."

"I'm your husband," he said back to her, weary, patient.

Soon he departed for the west. On the morning of Christmas Eve, Japanese soldiers entered the city and Hangzhou was fallen territory.

WINTER RAINS CLOSED IN. Every day, Junan struggled to procure the offerings for her father's weekly memorial service. The curfews and sudden seizures made even a trip to the market dangerous. The flood of Japanese soldiers had depleted local supplies and driven up prices; variety was hard to find. There was nothing but overripe pears and raw grapefruits, hard pale pomelos from the south. Junan bargained for dried mushrooms, ginger, and bean threads to make steamed dumplings suitable for the monks. She helped make up a great plate of elaborately shaped, molded tofu meats. She knew that afterward the monks devoured everything, and that if they were satisfied, they would think favorably upon her and her family.

She stood next to Yinan in the temple for the sixth weekly ceremony. Behind her, the servants wailed and mourned. The smell of incense and the fusty odor of the monks sickened her. She had not been able to eat that morning, and her body quaked with emptiness. Now she swallowed hard against the low, harsh drone of chanting.

Se bu i kong
kong bu i se

se chi shi kong
Kong chi shi se
Shou xiang xing shi

Life does not differ from nothingness, and nothingness from life; the same is true for emotions, thoughts, desires, and consciousness.

Through the wavering incense smoke, she watched Yinan make her obeisances. When they had finally learned of Mao Gao's death, Yinan had taken the news quietly. Following the death of her father she grew even more subdued. It would be difficult to marry her after this sequence of bad luck. Even Chen, the neighbor boy, was now out of reach, and the most promising local men had left to build the wartime capital. Meanwhile, Yinan was growing up. Her long braids swayed gracefully as she approached the altar. She was old enough to pin them into a bun. Yinan chose three sticks of incense, waited for the sticks to flare and light, and pushed them carefully into the brass holder. What kind of woman would she become? Would she grow more odd than ever, or would this tragedy settle her, make her into a more suitable wife?

As Junan walked to the altar, she remembered the services she had attended for her mother. Then there had been three of them, plus Hu Mudan, to mourn for Chanyi. Now there were only two, herself and Yinan. Fewer and fewer people who were able to remember. Junan held the frail sticks of incense to the candle. After they took on the flame, she blew on them until each was tipped by a glowing red nub, then placed them one by one into the pile of ash. As she gazed upon the gray dust in the brass holder, the burned remains of a thousand sticks of incense, she felt fear coming over her. It was a selfish fear, she knew: an overwhelming dread that had to do not with her father, who had died respectably, but her own life. She prayed for enough courage to be responsible for the family. Her dread lingered on the slow ride home. It stayed with her even after she received a telegram from Li Ang, letting her know he had arrived in Changsha and she need not worry.

In the next few days, she was taken by an overpowering lassitude. A new queasiness, a tickle in her stomach, convinced her she had succeeded. But she could not relax. Her fear continued on for weeks, even after she knew for certain that she was pregnant.

A MONTH AFTER the temple service, Junan walked into what had been her father's office. She wore a black tunic tied with a rough hemp belt of mourning and carried a pile of business letters. She shut the door behind her quickly, impatiently.

Ever since she had grown old enough to read the newspaper fluently and long after she had mastered basic mathematics, she had desired to be alone in his office. She had watched the pleasure her father took in money and had known somehow that she would find the same. For years, she'd wanted to trace the thread of profit through the tables and figures in his accounts. She had longed to work on his black abacus.

The office was as he had left it, filled with boxes of ledgers coated with a light veil of dust. She went straight to the desk and began to wipe it off with a rag that she had brought for that purpose. But she did not move anything; she wanted to preserve whatever she could of the order in which he had left it. This order was the only map she would have to follow into the maze of his finances.

She forced her eyes to the page and sat very straight at his desk, moving only to return a ledger to its place or pick out another one. Her father's chair was large, but she was as tall as he had been. She went carefully and slowly through a page of figures. The page described, she gleaned, the expenses and profit made on cotton in his warehouse. She was familiar with his messy and occasionally inaccurate characters, but she had never tried to decipher his numbers: neat, cramped, and strangely luxurious, with knotty flourishes in the 2s and 3s, and careful commas. It was like learning to read a new language. The first page took all her energy, but she kept on, following and following, and the second was easier, and the third yet easier, until it was possible for her to run her eyes across a page and understand what she saw there.

The pale sunlight filtering through the leaves of the mulberry tree made a lacy pattern on the paper. Then it moved onto the desk before shifting away entirely. As she read she could almost hear the rhythmic clicking of the paigao tiles. A string of interest payments had come due and had to be repaid. Their household costs had eaten into the remaining income. He had sold pieces of land, steadily, until there was nothing left but that warehouse loaded with cotton that the Japanese had confiscated.

In the safe, she found only a bag filled with odds and ends of currencies once widely accepted, but now virtually useless. There were silver coins from the end of the Qing Dynasty, bowl-shaped from being endorsed repeatedly by merchants with their steel-die chops. There were Mexican eagle-serpent dollars. Silver taels from many years ago, both a standard Shanghai tael and irregular local liang. Scattered through this were innumerable pieces of the old imperial square-holed cash.

In the back of the safe was a pile of chips, scrawled with the names and numbers of debts and money owed. They were enormous, shocking sums that could have come only from gambling. Finally, a single sheet of paper, a more formal IOU, one of two copies drawn at a notary: "The deed of the house shall be given to Li Ang upon his marriage to my daughter Junan. The property shall be transferred to the Li family and its male heirs. If my daughter bears no male heir, this house becomes the property of Charlie Kong." The paper was marked with both their chops, and dated 1930.

At dinner she sat unable to speak. The ghost of a page, brightly dotted with her father's cramped figures, hovered before her eyes. Her sister and the servants left her alone. She understood that they believed her to be overcome with grief. She didn't try to talk them out of their opinions, but sat at the hushed table, turning the facts over in her mind. There was no money. There was no house. She was alone. Behind the white mask of her face, she planned. Had Li Ang known of this? She suspected he had not. He had not the guile to keep such facts from her. It would be best to say nothing. She would economize. She would call on her father's friends and demand something in payment for their IOUs. That night she asked Gu Taitai to bring the largest brass kettle from the kitchen. She placed a heap of ledgers in the bottom of the kettle, twisted one thin sheet into a taper, lit a match, and carefully touched the flame to the paper's edge.

SHE WAS ONE of many women who struggled to feed and clothe a family under occupation as the merchants' shelves grew bare. Supplies dwindled to the bottom of the bin; grains were sold mixed with mouse droppings. Yinan was no help. She was devastated by the disappearance of the pet chicken, Guagua, which Junan suspected had been stolen and sold on the black market. Charlie Kong, like most shopkeepers, was not allowed to close his store despite the lack of stock. His shack was converted into a distribution center for Japanese-made goods. There were odd excesses and shortages; there were mandatory purchases. Everyone was required to turn in their shortwave radios and purchase Japanese-made radios with limited range that rendered most stations, save those approved by the new government, inaccessible. She and the others hoarded food and clothes. They avoided holding on to paper money. They met to talk and joke and play mahjong, but when their doors were closed they were like brooding hens, moody and anxious, hiding in their rooms, clutching their jewelry and their gold and silver coins.

Most of these women were older than she, or seemed older somehow—plump and indifferent with their brows plucked into thin crescents, or bone-thin, sour, and quick. Either type missed nothing. They were the channels through which Junan learned almost everything she knew about her husband. She had heard little from Li Ang since his transfer. She should have guessed that he would be a poor correspondent. It was through talking to these women that she first learned that the government would soon move the capital farther west, to Chongqing.

That afternoon they played mahjong. Junan thought of how she should have moved the family west, over his objections. He had once mentioned the possibility of a transfer to Sun Li-jen's Tax Police in Chongqing. She should have known.

Around her, the women were discussing the way that so many men who'd left were taking concubines. This news had come gradually, trickling in by rumor. It had just happened to an acquaintance of Pu

Taitai's. The first wife had tried to strangle herself with the cord of her silk robe.

"She's a very young girl."

"She hasn't learned."

"Peng."

The lamplight, making a circle over the table, barely lit their faces. They were women whose men had long ago ceased to want them. Yao Taitai's big green mole cast a shadow over her sallow forehead. Wen Taitai slumped in her qipao, with her small, blinking, myopic eyes and flat nose reminding Junan more than ever of a reptile. But Junan could not take her eyes away from Wen Taitai's mother, with her mannish face and great, old ears, the skin a pale tissue fitting loosely over her sagging features. They said she had once beaten her husband when he had tried to take a concubine. Now a widow, she took solace in her grandsons and her mahjong. With a loud crack, she whacked her tiles into line with her stick.

THE KNOWLEDGE THAT there was no more money brought one freedom: there was no business to look after, and the family could leave. Junan paid a visit to Charlie Kong's shabby shop. Charlie maintained his cheerfulness, although he was a little thinner, as the shortage of wine was making itself known even to the most devoted. Now he made a few extra yuan by working an illegal telegraph transmitter in the back room.

DEAR HUSBAND. I WILL BRING THE FAMILY TO
CHONGQING. JUNAN.

He wrote back almost immediately.

JUNAN. STAY THERE, FOR SAKE OF OUR FAMILY.
YOUR HUSBAND.

That night, she found spots of blood in her underpants. She took a breath. She should not have moved around so much. She would have to be more careful.

She kept off her feet for days. She lay immobile, furious; although her mind was as relentless as a bamboo trap, her body had failed her once again. In the next few days, the smallest anxieties, tiny exertions—bending, angling, staircases—caused her to bleed. She had her room moved downstairs. The baby was slow to come, and by late October, when the Generalissimo relocated to Chongqing, she was still imprisoned in her room.

This forced passivity was more than she could bear. Li Ang had left behind a few things to be mended and refurbished. One afternoon, she began to work on a jacket. She thought that it might soothe her mind to focus on a task, something simple and repetitive, such as fastening on a button. She found her sewing box and took the jacket to the seat below the window, where the pear tree with its ripening fruit moved slightly in the wind. It was a bright autumn day, so clear that each veined leaf, each frost-killed vine, lay bare and etched itself upon the eye.

He had left the jacket rolled into a ball; it was rumpled and covered with dust. She put her finger into her brass thimble, shaped like a ring, and threaded her needle with the familiar grasshopper-colored silk. She found the right place, then pushed the needle through the fabric and picked up the button.

Ever since Li Ang's first promotion, she had felt a vague threat; now the uneasy feeling, so long denied, breached her calm. The promotion, although a welcome one, had brought about a change between them, a lowering of her status, and although she might continue to bear him healthy children, bear him a son, the son would only cement her present position. Soon he'd be promoted again. She could see no way of reclaiming her old status.

Now the veil was pulled from her eyes. It was like being a new bride, stepping out of the jolting, terrifying ride of the marriage palanquin and seeing, for the first time, the agent of her fate. She thought of how Li Ang had appeared to her in the early days of their marriage: charming, pleasing, the graceful span of his dark shoulders outlined against the pillows. He had seemed so easy to get along with, sleek and smiling, like a happy guest. A man to be viewed with fondness and a little disdain. She had come to see her husband as sweet and vulnerable—a little clumsy at home, somewhat under her power, and desiring her approval. Now she knew her own perceptions had eroded from misuse. She had come to factor her power into everything they did, into the way she saw herself. She had not known that her belief in her influence would backfire, that she would become so attached to the effect she had over him.

She sewed carefully, creating a shank when she was done and tying the ends of the threads in a series of strong knots. She examined the other buttons, discovered two that hung loose, snipped them off, and sewed them back on as well. She enjoyed the feeling of the needle pushing sharp against her thimble, in and out, in and out. There, the jacket was presentable again. She needed only to have it cleaned. Junan saw what looked like a tea stain on the front. She held the jacket closer. Her pregnancy had sharpened her senses. Had she smelled something? She pressed the jacket to her face. What could it be? It seemed to her that she had caught, for half an instant, a lingering scent—a stranger's perfume, the sickening fragrance of tea roses. Junan pulled her face away from the jacket and sat still for several minutes, careful not to do herself the violence of a sudden breath.

A MEMORY, a feather stroke, a few words that might have been an anecdote but for the stubborn images that lingered. It had happened years ago, when her mother was still, on happy days, a lithe and beautiful woman, throwing back her head in laughter to show her teeth and fresh, white throat.

One afternoon, Chanyi had a visit from Kao Taitai, a so-called friend who held tight to her advantages and counted others' misfortunes. Junan could still remember wishing to shield Chanyi from this visitor with her poisonous tongue. For months Kao Taitai had been watching Chanyi closely, waiting for a fragile moment to swoop down on her.

That afternoon she'd spoken casually, in front of the others.

"I know a girl. She's just the thing for him. And she is like a child, easy to control. It's better to find him one yourself than let him choose."

That evening, Chanyi had shut herself into her room. It had been late autumn, with the sun sinking fast and then a pale broth of moonlight glowing on the wall. Junan had crept to her mother's door and listened to her crying.

What had become of Kao Taitai? It was quite probable that she had not left Hangzhou. Perhaps someday Junan would run into her. This idea made her curiously afraid. She had not thought of the woman in years—she hated her. But would Kao Taitai remember her? Junan thought with some relief that she had grown very tall and might not be recognized. Everyone remarked on her height and shoulders. "My strong one," Chanyi had called her. To her horror, now, tears were in her eyes.

Her body heaved with an anxiety so rank it soured her breath. Her vigilance had failed her. Now, without warning, she felt herself being swept into the danger she had always known was there but had so far been able to avoid. It had lain in wait: a cave, a mouth of darkness. It was as if suddenly she had woken up and found herself on a raft, swirling down an inexorable river toward that darkness.

Whom could she trust?

She was on her feet and near the open door. Where to go? The house was filled with people. She couldn't escape; she couldn't hide. The pregnancy had made her body slow with rich blood. For all the working of her heart, her hands and feet tingled. Her breath came in gasps. She couldn't bear to sit or stand. She leaned against the wall and closed her eyes, seeking darkness in midday. This desire was intolerable. It recalled the scent of her mother's skin, a pale curve of cheek, a gentle hand upon the back of her neck; it was like a longing for death.

She forced open her eyes. She stood facing the window to the back garden. The jacket lay where she had dropped it on the window seat. Just beyond it, through the glass, stood the old pear tree, its long boughs drooping like hands, laden with late fruit. For a long moment its remaining leaves shone in the autumn light, and not a breath of rustling wind disturbed the sight of it. She could not bear to take her eyes away, to hear the sound of a rotten pear splitting against the stone path.

Someone was speaking her name. "Junan."

Then once again, more quietly. "Junan."

She pulled her dazzled eyes away from the window. A blue frame danced into her vision.

"Junan, what is it?"

Gradually the blue subsided. Yinan stood inside her room. She had closed the door and stood with folded hands.

She wore the rough black pinafore she put on for practicing her brushstrokes. She had tied her hair away from her face so that it would not fall onto the page, and the cotton scarf exposed her naked ears. Junan squinted. "What do you want?"

"The door was open. You looked so strange. Are you sick?"

"I have a headache," Junan said. "I strained my eyes."

"You dropped your thimble."

The thimble lay in the middle of the room. Yinan picked it up. When Junan didn't reach for it, she set it on the window seat and stood before Junan uncertainly. "It's time for supper."

"I'm not hungry."

"I will bring you a bowl of broth."

"I told you, I'm not hungry."

At the sharp sound of Junan's voice, Yinan's gaze flickered, once. Junan knew she was about to turn and go. But no, she mustn't leave. It was time for Junan to speak. "Meimei," she said finally. "There is something I want you to do for me."

"Yes, Jicjic."

Junan took a deep breath.

"What is it, Jiejie?"

"I have decided to move the family to Chongqing."

Yinan's mouth opened but she said nothing.

Junan listened to her own dry words. "Before I can go," she said, "I'll have to wait until this child is old enough to travel safely. And there are arrangements to make." She took another breath. "Meimei, I want you to go to the new capital this spring and keep your brother's house for him. I'll find a way to get you out. Help keep him preoccupied until I'm able to come after you."

"By myself?"

"I promise I'll come as soon as I can."

Yinan did not answer.

"You will fly," Junan said, "to reach Chongqing as comfortably as possible."

"In an airplane?"

Junan sat down, put on her thimble. She didn't look up when Yinan left the room. She recalled the summer evening only the year before when they'd discussed Yinan's idea that some countries were like men and some like women. She had seen Li Ang's amusement, his silent laugh issuing a puff of smoke. Yinan was growing up. She would preoccupy Li Ang, or occupy him, well enough. For a moment Junan wished to call her back, but she found that she had lost her ability to speak. She reassured herself: Now, at least, I know what will happen. It will be under my control.

She refused to cry. She braced herself and felt her body wracked with every breath. It would be under her control. Her shoulders shook. She held fast to both knees to still the quiver in her hands, but then her arms began to tremble, harder, shaking deep inside her elbows: first her arms and then her knees, until her fingertips were numb. She sat alone in her room, late into the evening, letting the darkness close over her like a promise.

Chongqing 1938–40

CAPTAIN PU HAD WARNED LI ANG: CHONGQING WAS A BLACK heart of smuggling and corruption. Everyone he met would ask for bribes. Li Ang had another way of looking at it. To him, a bribe was like a little soup sloshing out of a bowl. If some of the soup was lost, it didn't change the fact that most of it went where it belonged. His new job was to help General Sun supply his eight divisions. If a few items disappeared along the way, Sun wouldn't notice. It was like a game. Like concealing one's intentions in poker or mahjong. Perhaps Li Ang's gift with games was the reason Sun had wanted him for this job.

Captain Pu had especially warned him of General Hsiao Jun, who even in those early days controlled the wartime capital through smuggling and blackmail. Li Ang wasn't concerned. Hsiao was the head of the military supply headquarters, and Li Ang's work required that he ingratiate himself with this man. He had no doubt they would get along; he'd never met a man or woman whom he could not persuade to like him. He set about befriending Hsiao. When he played cards with him, he made sure to lose half of the time by a close margin; when he arranged delivery of supplies, he brought Hsiao the odds and ends. He saved painkillers for Hsiao's bad back and nylon stockings for Hsiao's wife. When General Hsiao personally asked him if he might join a few other officers in a small dormitory raid upon some student radicals, Li Ang said yes.

—

THE RAID TOOK place near dawn on a Saturday morning. Members of the outlawed student union had been overheard at a teahouse and tailed to their rooms, where their lit windows had identified them. The officers would stake out and enter the dormitory, trap the radicals in their rooms, and take them to the Army prison. It was a simple plan, and the operation would be finished before morning classes. The radicals would vanish in the night.

Li Ang was told to wait at the back door. He could tell from the odor of flung dishwater that this door led to the pantry and the kitchen. The students seldom used this back way, and it was through the kitchen, he suspected, that they might try to escape. Li Ang stood at his post. Soon it was close to dawn. The dormitory blocked the eastern sky from view, but all had slipped from black to gray, lightening the world in even tones, so that the leaves and bark of the nearby camphor tree, the slate gray of the tiled eave, and his own brass buttons were defined in shades of dust. A few neglected, stiffened potted plants sat on the stoop. A dozen cracked clay roofing tiles were piled neatly on the stairs. Li Ang heard the somber clang of the missionary bell, and from the street, the creak of a cart and the faint voice of a man talking to his water buffalo. The rumors of attack had dissipated and the farmers were making their way back in despite the heat. Li Ang had been standing for so long that the blood had thickened in his feet, but he didn't falter. This trick of standing was a game to him. Other soldiers, unsupervised, would begin to clench their muscles; sometimes a man would wobble or even fall. To Li Ang, the standing clarified his mind, so that he saw the sharp edge of a broken tile, or the path and corners of an alley, with unusual clarity and detail. At times like these, he felt within himself a keen physical intelligence. It came into his feet and hands and shoulders. Now, waiting, he felt as if he were a hawk hovering high up in the luminous sky; he saw each shape upon the ground, and he could mark each shadow, each movement of the mouse below.

He heard one muffled creak and then a few quick bangs—the door being swung open—and the quick, heavy steps of men in boots, entering the building. He could hear their steps diverging. Good: they'd encountered nothing unexpected; they were following the plan. Some would fan into the downstairs rooms, seizing any suspect books and materials as they went. Several would head upstairs and trap the radicals in their bedrooms on the second floor. There were several shouts, some surprised questions, and, once, the sound of a falling chair. He listened for a full minute until he heard what he'd been waiting for.

A faster tread, alone, close. A single person on the stairs. The sound of the doorknob turning. Quicker than thought he moved to the door and pulled it open before the young man, emerging, had taken his own hand from the knob. Li Ang seized him as he hurtled down the steps.

"You're under arrest," Li Ang barked. He pushed the man into the wall; he twisted both arms behind his back and held him there, still listening. He could hear no more escapees forthcoming.

For a moment they stood. Li Ang could see only the back of his captive's head, the lobe of his ear. He couldn't see the face, pushed with the cheek flat against the wall, but he could sense a contemplative cast upon the man, as if he were listening. His glasses had been knocked loose. Li Ang wondered where the other students had gone. Inside, the footsteps clumped back and forth. He heard the light crash of a cot and the sudden thunder of a desk. He turned toward his captive, who had remained with his cheek against the wall, his glasses hanging by one ear. For a moment the thick, round lenses glowed white, reflecting the morning sky and the boughs of the camphor tree.

As Li Ang stood holding the young man against the building, he grew convinced that he had experienced all of this before. The smell of unwashed hair; the shape of the head, the shape of the ear. It seemed to him the moment passed so very slowly, or was this slow wonderment only the way that he recalled it afterward? He only knew there was an absolute silence. Above them, the pale sky glowed like the inside of a shell.

"You're under arrest," he said, more evenly this time.

The captive turned his head. Nearsighted eyes squinted into his face. "Gege," he said.

The voice was quiet, its tones familiar.

"What?" Li Ang exclaimed. "What are you doing here? What do you think you're doing?"

"What are you doing, Gege?"

"Shh," Li Ang said, regaining his wits. There was still enough time for his brother to escape. "If you hurry—"

Footsteps came around the corner.

"What's this?" It was Pu Sijian.

Li Ang began, "There's been a mis—"

"Good. You've got one." And for some inexplicable reason, Pu removed the spectacles from Li Bing's startled face and tossed them into the shadow of the camphor tree.

"What did you do that for?" Li Ang exclaimed. He half turned toward the tree, thinking to find the spectacles, but remembered his position. He turned back to his brother. What he saw made him forget what he had been thinking. Li Bing had put both hands against the wall. He stood, exposing his thin back, ear to the wall and eyes shut, whether in an instinctive gesture of protection or in a fear of what would happen next, Li Ang never knew. But he was stunned by the raised hands.

The door pushed open and two other men burst out of it.

"Hey!" Pu shouted. He moved toward the men.

Just as quickly, Li Bing broke free of the wall and darted toward Pu, tackling him at the knees, a move from childhood so familiar to Li Ang that he almost cried out.

Pu, a sturdy man, threw Li Bing like a water buffalo calf and pinned him face down on the ground. "I'll take this one," he said. He put his pistol to the back of Li Bing's head.

For a moment, Li Ang stood frozen in place. The air rang with the unsaid cry, "My didi! This is my didi!" But in the same instant, he understood what his brother had just done. Li Bing had taken advantage of his own surprise. He had turned his head to the wall and listened for his friends. He had allowed the other two men to get away. He was resigned to being captured. Li Ang understood that his brother was a Communist.

AT THE END of the day, although it was so hot that he desired nothing more than a cold bath, Li Ang hired a rickshaw and asked the man to let him off on the main road, a slight distance from the dormitory. He

walked the rest of the way and went around to the back. There stood
the familiar wall, pale in the evening light. Despite the turmoil and the
seizure of their books, many of the students had returned. There was
steam coming from the kitchen, and he could smell rice porridge. An
older man, a servant, sweated as he hauled his creaking water buckets
through the kitchen door. Li Ang spat on the ground. He felt reluctant
to go near the place again. He tried to remember where the captain had
been standing when he had tossed away the glasses. He returned to the
old camphor tree, with its drooping and indifferent leaves. He searched
along its base, then in the dirt, but found nothing.

At the jail, he asked to speak to the warden.

"There's been an error," he said. "The man caught in the dormitory
raid wasn't a radical. He wasn't one of the troublemakers. He was only
on kitchen duty. I was about to let him go when I was ordered to give
pursuit to the others." There was an expectant silence. Li Ang knew
then how silly this was. The warden needed no excuses, only money. Li
Ang pulled out what he had, three silver dollars. The warden took the
coins and went back to his newspaper.

Li Bing squinted, his eyes curled like dry shrimp. This time he said
nothing.

"I went to search for your glasses, no luck," Li Ang said. "Is there
anything else you need?"

"How about a cigarette?"

Li Ang took a deep breath. "Tell me," he said. "Were you one of
them—the radicals, I mean?"

Li Bing smiled. "I don't think I'm supposed to tell you."

Li Ang tried again. "Listen," he said. "I can probably get you out of
here. But what I want to know—"

"Who asked you to get me out of here?"

"When did you change? When did you become like this?"

"I'm not aware of having changed."

Li Ang couldn't think of a reply. After a few more minutes, he left
the prison.

———

THE NEWSPAPER HEADLINES described the latest negotiations with the West; once again, Chiang Kai-shek declared the need for money and supplies. An article claimed the latest Japanese attack on Changsha had been met with stiff resistance. On the bottom of the page, Li Ang found a small story about a successful raid upon a student dormitory the day before. Many pounds of subversive materials had been destroyed, and the head of a gang of dangerous student radicals had been arrested. He was being held on bail of eight hundred silver dollars.

For a moment he thought with hope of his uncle, sitting in his little shop gazing at his favorite poster of a sexy woman smoking a cigarette. But Li Ang knew Charlie no longer had that kind of cash. There was almost no profit in the distribution work. Li Ang could have arranged to sell some goods on the black market. But he lacked the time to do it properly. There was only one alternative. He went to Army headquarters.

DEAR WIFE. MUST HAVE 800. POSSIBLE TO WIRE.
LI ANG.

He hadn't seen Junan in eleven months. He'd been disappointed at the sex of the child—a second daughter—but now he found himself truly missing his wife, and the nature of his longing was specific and surprising. It was not passion or love he thought about, but the clarity and order that surrounded her like a serene climate. She had a way of being able to see straight into a situation. He wished she were there with him so that he could tell her what had happened and ask casually, "What do you think?" She would've had shrewd advice.

Her reply came back immediately.

HUSBAND. FINANCES COMPLICATED. CAN ONLY
SEND 200. JUNAN.

This wouldn't do. She could easily raise the sum. He wired back.

POSSIBLE TO RAISE CASH? NEED ALL 800. LI ANG.

All afternoon he waited at the headquarters. Finally, the answer came.

WHAT IS THE MONEY FOR? JUNAN.

He straightened, threw his shoulders back. How could she possibly refuse? Who did she think she was? It occurred to him that he might have gotten his way by telling the truth—appealing to her sympathy and belief in family—or by adopting an attitude of submission. But he was not that kind of man. And he didn't want Junan to see how little he had, with his own brother in prison, and he himself requesting money like a beggar.

He wired back.

FORGET IT. MATTER SOLVED.

He left the headquarters and walked into the city. He didn't hire a rickshaw. He wasn't sure where he was going, and he didn't want to betray his agitation to any human soul. He strode quickly through the heat, the houses on either side of him shimmering as he moved farther into the city: ornate walls giving way to the shabbier bricks of smaller houses, more frequent streets and alleys. In the last few months, the population of Chongqing had doubled. All around him was evidence of overpopulation. crumbled buildings inhabited, beggars moaning, fami lies camped by the road. He heard a cacophony of dialects; singsong local voices taunted belligerent newcomers. The stink of cooking cabbage assailed him, mingled with the darker stink of sewage. Now the street grew more crowded: a group of women flinging their sweaty net of gossip into the well; small gangs of boys, let out of school and holding kites; old men, whose lives were over, sitting and watching from the edges. The call of a traveling tea seller rang out, followed by the wailing flute of a blind fortune-teller, a high, mournful sound that pierced the air. The man sat beneath an eave, exposing plaintively the worn, dusty soles of his shoes.

Why hadn't he simply told Junan that Li Bing was in trouble?

He couldn't explain to her his shock at the recognition of his brother's face. He couldn't explain it to himself. He thought of the early gray light, the shadowed doorway with cracked tiles on the steps. The sound of feet against the stairs, the leap toward the fugitive, pushing him against the wall, his raised hands. The quiet voice, "Gege." The way his brother said "gege" different from ten thousand other younger brothers.

It could hurt his position for Junan to know that Li Bing was in trouble. What if she let the information slip, as women did, over the mahjong table? Those women told each other everything, and later they shared the information with their men. The Communists and Nationalists had joined to fight the Japanese. Now that the enemy had stalled, old animosities were breaking the alliance. Li Ang had heard rumors of civil war behind enemy lines.

But most importantly, it was the principle of the thing: a wife should obey her husband.

After seven years of marriage, he knew that he'd been lucky in his match. Other women were often foolish, unable to run a household, squandering their husbands' income on extravagance or opium. Other women aged badly and threw shameless scenes. They couldn't leave a man alone. Junan had none of these flaws. She was pragmatic and self-contained, yet beautiful and loyal. She must have known that he occasionally went to chaweis and had slept with other women. He had been so long away from her, away from home. But she wasn't possessive. She rarely tried to hold him back.

She had submitted to him physically, but was it enough? The image rose to his mind of Junan satisfied, lying against the pillows with her breath coming fast and a quick pulse still gleaming in her long white neck. Now she had revealed the truth: she was holding back on him. He didn't have the power to get what he wanted. Or perhaps he'd never had a need; he'd simply taken whatever she had wished to give. It disturbed him that he was married to a woman to whom every action, every observation, was so entirely strategic. This was not the way that she had first appeared to be.

He went back to his office. His clerk from Canton spoke garbled Mandarin and his local assistant Sichuanese. The two men could communicate only by spitting, gesturing, and throwing wild notes at one another. They attempted to describe to him a nightmare of inefficiency in the supply lines from Burma. The Burma Road had just been opened, but it was already a quagmire of delays: substation managers needing bribes, papers to be filled out, equipment breaking down, the necessity for confirmation of pointless details. Again and again he went over the lists of supplies that Sun required, and found that he could not get most of them. They had been counting on the Burma Road.

As he sorted through the mess, he felt his anger circling around some dangerous point. He tried to push it away. But he recalled the way her upper lip sometimes drew tight during their conversations. She had never before told him that she was dissatisfied or critical of him. But now he knew. She did not trust a single thing that she could not control by her own hand.

For the first time, he saw how entirely different they were. From his earliest memories, back in a time when he still wore split pants, he had understood the benefit of holding many options open, keeping his wishes loose and easy like a fisherman's net, waiting for whatever might swim into it. By this method, he had gained much. He had gone into the Army; he had been promoted; he had married Junan. It had never occurred to him that his method might be seen, by someone else, to be undeserving or unreliable. Nor had it ever occurred to him that there might be a contradiction between any two desires that he held.

Junan didn't operate this way. He had never given much thought to the nature of a woman's mind, but he had grown to understand a certain level, stubborn look of hers that meant she wanted something. Once she really wanted something, nothing else would do. He began to comprehend that she practiced the art of holding one desire, that she chose a pattern and made her wish and flung it into the sky like a great kite, teasing it, testing it out in the world's winds, using more rope, more rope, until it hung over her like a star. There she stood on the earth, holding one thought in her mind with all her will.

Was it possible that he himself might simply be another thing that she had made up her mind about? He'd always considered it a sign of his own strength and luck that he had married her; it hadn't occurred to him that the glue between them might have been her desire and her strength. She might have cast her eyes upon him and decided; and from that moment on there was no hope for him. Now they were husband and wife. She had gotten what she wanted. And yet, he knew, she was unhappy with him. Not because he was any worse-looking, or more ill-tempered, or less promising than he had been a few years ago, but because he was bent on going against her will.

HE WOULD TURN TO General Hsiao. He wondered how on earth he might explain the situation. It was clear that the truth—and only the truth—would be accepted. He reminded himself again that the Communists and the Nationalists were no longer officially at logger-heads; the truce had been reached three years ago and it still held. It would not be seen as unpardonable to have a Communist brother. Still, he must ask the general not to tell anyone. The next morning, he hurried to headquarters.

"I am deeply sorry to have to trouble you for this favor," he began. At the sound of these words, he saw Hsaio's little eyes flicker. The rest of his face—round bones and pale cheeks flecked with smallpox scars—split into a grin. The general assured him there would be no problem with releasing Li Bing. No problem whatsoever. As for the favor, he was certain that someday Li Ang himself would be in a position to grant him some little thing or another. Li Ang recalled Pu's warning, but he felt better immediately. He left the room in good spirits.

Later that week, he received a message from Hsiao Taitai, requesting that he escort her youngest daughter, Baoyu, and her friends, to the National Opera.

GENERAL HSIAO, INDIFFERENT TO DAUGHTERS, HAD LEFT THE naming of each girl to the authority of his old mother, who had grown up in the countryside and favored flowers. And so it was Juyu (Chrysanthemum Jade), Meiyu (Rose Jade), and Baoyu (Jade Bud) who had combed their grandmother's thinning hair and spooned her porridge. The old woman had been failing for half her life, and had surprised the family by dying suddenly the year before; her stern, wrinkled face still watched the household from a black and white portrait over the incense table. In the season when Li Ang moved to Chongqing, the Hsiao daughters had recently begun to wear colors again, and there hung over the entire household a glaze of relief.

The power in that family rested in the wife; Li Ang had heard this from a few local women, who, upon learning that he was married, had confided in him. Hsiao Taitai held the reigns despite the fact that she had borne no sons, despite the general's hot temper. He had not taken a concubine; they said that Hsiao Taitai would have made his life too difficult. Hsiao Taitai held social power in the capital. She had attended a missionary school and befriended key Americans. She spoke fluent English and held frequent dinner parties, hosting her American friends and other foreigners. The more ambitious men all wanted to attend these dinners. The evening he arrived to pick up Baoyu for the concert was the first time Li Ang had been to their house.

General Hsiao lived on the safer side of a hill; in its base he was excavating a personal bomb shelter. Li Ang climbed up the steps onto a spacious porch, where the doorman met him and directed him into a front room. Hsiao Taitai greeted him. She was a short, plump woman with small features, powdered pale. When she smiled, her eyes widening with delight and sympathy, Li Ang saw that she must once have been extremely beautiful.

"My apologies, my daughter is very slow. She'll be ready in a moment."

Hsiao Taitai introduced Li Ang to her two older daughters. The eldest, Juyu, had recently been matched to one of her father's favorites. Colonel Tang had waited patiently throughout the mourning period, although, Li Ang considered, he'd had a powerful incentive. He had in the meantime been promoted to the rank of brigadier general. Now at last the couple was to be married. Juyu was rather tall, and there was something of her father's masculinity in her attitude and in her round cheeks, but everyone spoke of her beauty.

Her sister Meiyu was small and slender, with exquisite alabaster features. Meiyu had learned to read and write both English and classical Chinese poetry. She sang in the Methodist choir and played the piano. She was the most intelligent and beautiful of the three sisters, and for several years she had been quietly winning the attention of most of her father's junior officers. But Li Ang disliked Meiyu on sight; she had a way of pursing her full lips that he thought prudish and judgmental.

He was pleased to find young Baoyu lively and daring, nothing like her sisters. Her cheeks dimpled, her red lips curved, her small eyes sparkled. The government had declared permanent waves immoral and illegal, but Baoyu's hair was cut and crimped like a Western movie actress's. Li Ang wondered if it was stiff to the touch. Baoyu's round breasts and hips hinted at a pleasure in the senses. When they walked out to meet her friends, he turned toward her to say something and caught the strong, sweet smell of flowers.

Later, he told his brother that Baoyu was, in comparison to Junan, a more common sort of girl, but very friendly, easy to talk to.

"Stay away from her," Li Bing said. "I haven't even met her, but I don't understand your General Hsiao. He knows you're married, and an outsider, so why would he wish to connect you with his own daughter?"

"She's quite attractive," Li Ang said. "She likes going to the opera and her friends are rather fast. It's safer that she be escorted by a married man."

Li Bing shook his head. The brothers were sitting at a local teahouse, where the servers poured tea from a long, thin spout, Sichuan style, standing back three feet from the table and dropping the tea into the cups from high above as if it were a lethal substance. Li Ang was in high spirits. His night out with Baoyu and her young friends had buoyed his mood, and he was happy to see Li Bing out of prison.

Li Bing had been released immediately upon General Hsiao's request. Although Li Ang had been obliged to tell General Hsiao that the prisoner was his brother, he now felt unable to reveal to his brother his own role in the release. He wished, instead, to find out what Li Bing had been doing there; how could he have gotten mixed up in a radical action? Li Ang was the gege, responsible, and he had finagled Li Bing's release. He had the right to know what was on Li Bing's mind. But now Li Ang suspected that his hopes for an easy conversation with his brother had been too optimistic. Li Bing sat, thin shoulders drawn up, looking cold and surly, stuffing his cheeks with peanuts.

Li Ang began. "What exactly were you doing in the student dormitory?"

At this question, Li Bing stopped chewing as if he had bitten a bad nut. "Of course, I wasn't working with anyone you'd be interested in meeting. No bullies, rich Americans, bureaucrats, or smugglers."

"Hmm," Li Ang said. "So," he tried again, trying to keep his voice light, "how are the family? How is Junan?"

"How should I know? I haven't seen her in almost a year."

"I've been away for longer."

"She was doing very well, I thought. Managing brilliantly, considering the circumstances. I feel bad for leaving them. I had to go, or get them into trouble."

Li Ang felt uncomfortable at this allusion to politics. Moreover, his recent exchange of telegrams with Junan had wounded him. "Well, I wouldn't say brilliant."

"The little you know," Li Bing said, scrabbling through the dish of peanut shells.

"She is very competent."

Li Bing set down the dish of peanuts. "And she's very brave. I'm sure she wants to come out here to Chongqing."

"She's better off where she is. Soon we'll beat the Japanese, and then—"

"How you will beat them? By holing up in this dump and turning on the Communists? By turning the common people against you, acting like a bully? You have no idea how your clique of generals is viewed by the people. And your Generalissimo—"

"I suppose you think that you can go out and beat the Japanese yourself—"

"Your Generalissimo's a common warlord."

"No," Li Ang heard himself say with surprising firmness. "We have no right to judge a man until after we see the manner of his death and how he is remembered."

They sat still for a moment.

"Listen," Li Bing seized the silence. "Listen to me, Gege. You don't understand why I am so suspicious of power. It is because once you've seen cruelty and known it, you can never be the same."

"Ah, don't be melodramatic. We had the same upbringing."

"No. You were always stronger. You got involved; you never had to watch. These men running the government. That General Hsiao of yours, he's another Sun Chuan-fang. And do you remember, back in Hangzhou, right after we had moved there, that neighborhood boy, Chang? He used to bully me after school . . ."

A shadow passed over Li Ang's mind. He saw, briefly, a heavyset boy whose doughy face and small eyes held a disturbing coldness, no refuge there.

"Lots of boys bullied you after school," he said. "You were such a scrawny bookworm. Do you expect me to remember every scrape I had to get you out of?"

Li Bing didn't answer. At that moment the server passed by and Li Ang gestured him over for the tea. It was time to bring the conversation back on subject. He wryly regarded the enormous tea spout and, when the boy had left, he said, "This city is crowded, all right. You can tell there are too many workers and not enough work when even the job of pouring tea is a special skill that requires training."

A moment of silence followed this. Li Ang tried again. "I heard that the liaison office is looking for a supplies clerk who can speak decent Mandarin." No sooner did the words leave his mouth than he knew he'd put his foot in it.

"Thank you," Li Bing said. "For all of my life, I have longed to be a supplies clerk."

"Shut up," Li Ang said. "What's wrong with a decent government job?"

Li Bing spat. "I'd rather starve."

"Sometimes I think you would!" Li Ang heard the heat in his own voice, but he pressed ahead. "Well, let me see what I can do. I'll make some inquiries with the Bureau of Moral Superiority."

Now he knew he'd gone too far. There was no color in Li Bing's face. It was as humorless as it had ever been, more gaunt and wooden than ever, planes and angles. For a moment Li Ang felt uneasy, almost frightened. "Ah, come on," he burst out. "After all, even you aren't made of ideals. You need to eat and sleep like any other man."

"If you're referring to the fact that I'm not staying at your flat, don't try to change my mind. I won't presume to move in and disturb your social life."

"You know you're welcome to move in." Li Ang's large apartment was a point of pride.

"I won't take your support."

"You know our sides are technically at peace."

"I need to get out of here," said Li Bing. He reached into his pocket.

"Forget it."

"I said I want to leave. Am I not allowed?"

"You're free to go wherever you like. I mean forget it if you think I'm going to let you pay the bill. Between the two of us, I'm employed."

"Exactly."

"What do you mean?"

"I mean that I don't need what is essentially T. V. Soong's private army, however fat its purses, paying for my tea."

Li Ang forgot to answer. He could not take his eyes from his brother's face. There it was—a dart, a gleam, of physical aggression. Suddenly Li Bing leaned across the table and thrust his hand over Li Ang's shoulder. Li Ang turned to see what he was gesturing at. Right in front of his nose, Li Bing was holding out a handful of coins to the server.

Li Ang couldn't resist. He butted into his brother's arm. Coins went flying in all directions. Li Ang nodded once and turned back to the table just in time to see Li Bing, his glasses askew, lunge over the empty dishes straight in his direction. Li Ang felt the world tip. His chair crashed backward to the floor. Li Bing leaped off the table and landed on top of him.

Li Ang looked straight into his brother's eyes and found them fixed, stubborn. He grinned. Li Bing was as light as a fly and Li Ang knew that as soon as he got his wind back he would easily throw him off. Servers came at them from all directions. The brothers pushed them away. Li Bing fought back with surprising force and focus. But their childhood pattern had not changed. Soon enough, Li Ang overpowered his brother. Sitting on Li Bing's back, he paid the bill. Li Bing picked himself up, gaunt and angry.

"Use half your brains!" he shouted. "Your generals aren't truly trying to fight the Japanese! They're just waiting for help from abroad. And your government is a parasite on the Chinese people!"

The room went suddenly silent. "Now be polite," Li Ang said. "That parasite is paying for these broken dishes."

Li Bing stalked away. As he watched his brother leave the room, Li Ang became aware of someone watching him from a round table in the corner. It was General Hsiao, seated with several officers. He expected some sort of reprimand, but when he approached them to apologize, the general only remarked that his wife was having a few people to dinner that evening, and Li Ang was welcome to come.

———

AS HE PREPARED for dinner, Li Ang was filled with energy and high expectations. He paced his apartment. He checked his scars in the mirror. They were fading, flat and colorless in the evening light. He spent too long brushing his uniform; it was time he had a maid. He had the room for one; and he liked the idea of a young woman, one of these wasp-wasted, slang-tongued Sichuanese girls.

His anticipation mounted when he learned that he'd been seated next to Hsiao Taitai. Surely everyone in the room had noticed this sign of favor. As he took his seat he found it difficult to suppress his excitement. He went to work on his dinner. Shortly after arriving in Chongqing, he had discovered that in order to fit in, he must learn to eat the fiery cuisine. This evening's meal contained even more huajiao than usual. This was a sign of the Hsiaos' influence, since the best peppers, like everything else, were scarce and expensive.

He praised Hsiao Taitai for the meal. "My wife never cooked like that."

"So you're married," she said.

"Yes."

"In the church?"

"Pardon?"

"Was it a Christian marriage?"

"No," he said. "It was a traditional marriage." He felt somewhat apologetic that he knew so little about Christianity. Many high-ranking men, including Sun Li-jen himself, had had some education in the United States or at American missionary schools.

"It must be hard on your wife to be behind the front."

"She is a self-sufficient woman," he said.

"Oh, well, that is fortunate."

He did not know how to reply to this. He was again reminded of his exchange of telegrams with Junan.

After he had been visiting the Hsiaos for several weeks, Li Ang noticed that the youngest daughter was always nearby. When he came for dinner, she was seated next to him. When he spoke to her, she kept her lively eyes upon his face. This was so different from Junan, who often greeted his words with indecipherable calm.

"You don't talk very much about your wife," she said one day, after dinner.

"Well, my wife—" Li Ang made a gesture halfway between affirmation and dismissal.

"Was the marriage arranged?"

"Well, yes—"

She nodded, and swiftly turned the topic of conversation. "How do you like Sichuan?"

"It's a fine place," Li Ang said.

She wrinkled her nose. "Oh, please, the summers are a steam cauldron; winter is drippy and rainy."

"Perhaps I haven't been here long enough to know," Li Ang said gallantly.

"Tell me, do you ever consider living here for good?"

"I haven't thought about it."

One day, he described the conversation to Pu Sijian.

Pu was a man of marked guilelessness, a Christian convert who carried the Bible in his pocket and said the Lord's Prayer before every meal. But when Li Ang finished, Pu shook his head slowly. "There's something strange about this," he said.

"What do you mean?"

"They know you're married, so why would they push their daughter at you? And if she's pure, then she shouldn't be with men at all."

"They're certainly not 'pushing' Baoyu. She and I enjoy each other's company. Is there anything wrong with my having pleasant conversations over dinner with a young woman?"

"She should be with her sisters."

"Well, it so happens that I'm married, and they want a man who can keep their daughter safe," he faltered, "but—"

"But there's something strange about it."

Li Ang frowned. Why shouldn't Baoyu talk to him? But when he thought it over he knew Pu Sijian was right. He remembered Li Bing's skepticism. His fingers itched for a cigarette, but Pu didn't smoke. "Do you think I'm getting into some kind of trouble?"

"I don't know. As long as the two of you keep your interactions on the public conversational level, then you've done nothing wrong."

"Sounds right," Li Ang said. He rose and clapped Pu's shoulder. "I'm heading off. Hsiao asked me to go drinking with him tonight. Thanks for the advice."

Pu nodded. He remained seated, looking at his stubby hands. "Listen, Li Ang," he said. "I wanted to ask you for a favor."

"Sure."

"I've always had the feeling I would die away from home. Now that I've been reassigned to Changsha, I wonder if I might be chosen to die there."

"Nonsense," said Li Ang. "You're going to be fine."

"Maybe. It's difficult to know what God has in store. I've been given so much. I hope that when my time comes, I'll accept my end with grace. But I wanted to ask of you: if anything happens to me, will you look after Neibu and my son? Neibu's not as clever as your Junan. She'll need help."

In the light Pu's eyes seemed drained of color. Li Ang clapped his shoulder again; it was wooden, hunched. "Of course," he said. "Of course I will."

"Thank you."

"Don't worry, Pu Sijian. We will meet again soon, and we'll complain about the weather."

Pu nodded absently. Li Ang left him and went out to drink with Hsiao.

OVER BAIJIU, General Hsiao joked that Baoyu was more trouble than she was worth. He had his hands full with his work; his back injury was making him feel old; Baoyu was too much for him. He would like to marry her off to a willing man. Li Ang didn't know what to make of it. Recently she had spent most of her dinners at his side. Undoubtedly the general might be considering him as possible material for his daughter.

Now that the idea had been put into his mind, it was difficult to shake. The officers knew that he had a wife back home, but they knew it was an arranged marriage. Was it so very terrible for a man, far away from home for many months, in a time of war, to find support and solace in a second marriage to a worthy woman? The Generalissimo had done it, and so had many of the others. As everybody said, it was better than being alone. And certainly it couldn't matter, couldn't change much for Junan. She had been always self-sufficient. He and Junan had shared a life of peace, a life that he might never return to. Now luck had presented him with another option that would more than satisfy his needs during the present as well as the coming years of war. It was fortunate that the family would even consider him, given his married status. This was an advantageous pairing and it would take him far.

He pushed against a sudden memory of Junan's calm, lovely face, her graceful figure welcoming him at the door. There was no point in sentimentality a thousand miles away. Junan was a beautiful woman, an honorable woman, and, he would admit, an admirable woman, but he had never truly chosen her. Marrying her had seemed a fine and convenient thing to do; it had been an opportunity of sorts, but it had not been his decision. He had been so young, really a boy. He hadn't known whom he would become or the kind of life he would lead. Would he ever have guessed that he would have flourished working for the Tax Police? That he would be twice promoted, and later, if he was lucky, might be promoted again? Would he have known, at that point, that the Japanese would press so far into the country, that the capital would be moved? Who knew what the future would bring?

He had yet another problem, as useless and baffling as sentimental love. There were times—he couldn't explain them to himself any more than he could tell Junan—when he had the idea that he and Junan were heading into a trap. During their most pleasurable moments, while he was out walking with her for the world to admire, he had sometimes felt that at any moment the earth might give way beneath their feet. They would fall and find themselves lost in an unknown world. Now, as he turned to Hsiao Baoyu, he pushed away this foreboding. It was as illogical as the worrying of Pu Sijian. It was cowardly; it was unnecessary; it had no more to do with Baoyu than it had to do with his wife.

ONE DAY, AS HE left the office for his noon meal, he was surprised to find Li Bing outside waiting for him.

"Hey, Gege. I need to talk to you."

"What?" Li Ang was startled.

"Shh—let's go somewhere more private."

They went to Li Ang's rooms. He was suddenly embarrassed at the size of his apartment.

"Some lunch?" he offered.

Li Bing shook his head. He was clearly preoccupied. "Something hot to drink," he said. "This rain is depressing me."

Li Ang picked up a package of the general's Lucky Strikes. "Cigarette?"

Li Bing shook his head.

Li Ang spoke to Mary, the young maid, whom Hsiao Taitai had recently arranged to keep his house. Mary didn't live in the house, but came by each day to see if he needed anything. She was an orphan who had been named and raised by the missionaries at Hsiao Taitai's church. She was a small, plump girl with a mole near her full lips and another in the middle of her forehead that made her seem exotic and yet also perversely religious.

"I'll get my own tea, thank you."

"Don't be ridiculous."

Mary returned with two cups of tea. Li Bing frowned, then thanked her and guzzled his gratefully, but Li Ang could only sip at his, waiting. His brother had surprised him once, and since then he had regarded him with wariness. Now there was something in Li Bing's face—a certain colorlessness about the mouth—that warned him.

Finally, Li Bing spoke. "Your young woman was the center of quite a scandal."

"What are you talking about?"

"I've been asking around. They say that this third daughter of

Hsiao's was in trouble with men before she learned to braid her hair. But that's nothing. The real story, which not everybody knows, is that a few years ago, this girl had a child by a common foot soldier. The affair took place while her own grandmother was on her deathbed. It's the reason why the family was in mourning for so long, so that they could hide the pregnancy from everyone. The child is being raised in the country."

"I've never heard that story."

"Why would anyone have the slightest interest in telling you, an outsider? With that mother busy hushing things up. Now, she's a capable one. If the generals were half as capable as she, they'd have that Burma Road paved and defended day and night."

Li Ang opened his mouth and shut it. "That's ridiculous," he said finally. "Why would she bother?"

"The Tax Police is a fat and underworked division. You're a protégé of General Sun—everybody knows it. And this war could go on forever before America finally comes in on our side."

"I'm a married man." He was aware, even as he spoke, of sounding pompous.

"To these people, a non-Christian wedding does not count. Look at Chiang Kai-shek."

Li Ang didn't answer.

Li Bing picked up the package of Lucky Strikes. He caught the lighter from his brother and struck the flame, which glowed orange behind his long fingers. "I have other news," he said. "I've been assigned by Zhou En-lai to a northern village. I'll be helping to develop the revolutionary potential of the countryside."

"What do you mean?

"I'm leaving town," he said. "I've been thinking of it for quite some time, and I no longer have a reason not to. There are changes happening in this country. The people are beginning to learn that they need not be bullied."

"You're leaving."

"Yes. At least until next year."

Later that evening, as Li Ang walked home from dinner at General

Hsiao's house, he reviewed the conversation and wondered if there was anything he might have said to dissuade Li Bing from his plans. He didn't know.

Around him he could hear the humble, restless noises of a nighttime city overflowing with several hundred thousand extra people. The crack of a hammer striking a wooden stake into the ground. The sounds of thousands of small fires spitting small sparks, heating thousands of kettles or tin cans filled with water for tea. A thousand quiet conversations. Li Bing was leaving town. Li Ang remembered his brother's words. He had called Hsiao a bully, another Sun Chuan-fang. "You were always stronger . . . you never had to watch . . . Do you remember, back in Hangzhou, right after we had moved there, that neighborhood boy, Chang?"

He remembered again the square, doughy face and pitiless eyes. The fight had happened perhaps a year after their parents' death. They had just been sent to Hangzhou and moved into their uncle's house. At that time, it happened Hangzhou was under control of the warlord Sun Chuan-fang, and on the streets, the neighborhood bullies copied him.

On the evening of the fight, Chang arrived with two other boys. Li Ang remembered Li Bing's frightened voice from high up in his uncle's loft. "Gege, run!" But Li Ang took them on. Li Bing clattered down to help. Of course, Li Bing was nothing, one of the big boys held his puny arms as he bawled.

"Submit!" Their rough voices summoned Li Ang. "Submit!" But he did not. He knew that holding out would earn him their respect. He remembered the odd and distant sense of his own hand bruising, his own rib cracking in his chest. He watched his good fist colliding into Chang's big, hard nose. The bright, triumphant spurt of blood. The sound of Chang breathing hard through his mouth. Then finally the honorable release of his brother. Li Bing's eyes were squinched red; his face was streaked with snot and tears. "You fool! You should have stopped!" he cried. "You could have been killed!" Li Ang hadn't thought of how it might have felt to watch. Now the memory of Li Bing's high voice rang in his ears.

Li Ang turned up his own dark, deserted street. The moonlight cast the bleak shadow of his building on the road. For some days now, he had envisioned a future with the Hsiao family. The powerful general, his patron, would have been his father-in-law, and Hsiao Taitai his mother-in-law; it would have been like having an entirely new family. The idea that they were pulling the wool over his eyes—that he would be, essentially, considered a dupe and a fool by all—changed things. But he had grown accustomed to his fantasy. The world seemed less open, less grand, his life less assured, without it.

In the dark entrance, on the table, lay an envelope.

12 February 1938
My Dear Husband,

In the past few months, I have been thinking about the way in which you must seek food and company in the homes of others. I would not want you to do without these things, and yet I want to obey your desire that I remain with the children in Hangzhou, so I am sending my sister to Chongqing to keep your household. I have asked her if she would kindly run the house in my absence. She has always been very obedient to me and is more than willing to oblige; furthermore, I think that the current state of affairs is bad for her health. I think that a quiet, domestic, provincial life is what she has always needed. In order to absolve your difficulties as soon as possible, I have sent her to you via airplane. She should arrive shortly after you receive this.

Your obedient wife,
Junan

TWO DAYS LATER, LI ANG ENTERED THE FLAT AND SENSED immediately that Yinan had arrived. When Mary opened the door, the new scent inside filled him with dread.

Yinan sat in the front room, waiting beside her trunk as if she were a parcel that had been delivered and left near the entrance to be inspected.

His spirits failed him. "Welcome, Meimei," he said. "Thank you for coming. I hope your journey wasn't difficult."

"Gege." She wouldn't meet his eyes. He found himself wondering, as he always did, how it could be that the polished, poised Junan could have such an inarticulate sparrow of a sister.

"She arrived this morning," Mary said with a trace of weariness. "I showed her the room, but she said that she would wait until you told her what to do."

Mary was clearly disappointed with their visitor, who had not shown herself to be an impressive woman in style, authority, or conversation.

"Would you like anything to eat?"

Yinan shook her head.

"She hasn't eaten all day," said Mary. "She took a bath but she said she would wait to eat until you arrived."

"It's all right," Li Ang told the maid. "You can go now." She vanished into the kitchen. Li Ang arranged a polite expression onto his face and approached his guest.

When he came closer, he could smell fresh soap and see the grooves from the comb that pulled the hair tightly away from her face.

"Junan wrote to me that you might feel better here," he said. "I didn't realize you were coming so soon. I'm sorry I wasn't here to welcome you when you arrived."

"I'm all right. Thank you for having me."

"I thought that you could stay in the extra room. Would you like to see it?" She nodded. He picked up her metal trunk, unfortunately heavy. Silently she followed him; he opened the door and showed her in. He hadn't remembered how small it was. He was relieved to notice, outside the narrow window, a ragged scrap of camphor tree. He smiled, nodded, and backed out of the door.

A few days later, he returned home to a strong burning smell in the house. He found Yinan in the kitchen, wandering among the dishes, wok, and earthenware steamer.

"Where is Mary?"

"Her friend is sick. I told her I could cook."

"Don't bother," he said. "My business takes me away from home most evenings. When I am due for dinner, I'll tell Mary. You shouldn't cook anything."

"Junan told me to be useful." Still she kept her eyes down.

"Your sister wouldn't want you to tax yourself."

"She told me you would eat at home if I were here."

"That's ridiculous," he said. "I rarely eat at home." He felt angry with Junan, who had no right, from such a distance, to decide what he would and would not do for dinner. He glanced warily at the table. There was a bowl containing chunks of rice—clearly she had failed to do something to the rice that would make it steam evenly—and some green beans that appeared to be charred and falling apart. Near the stove sat a small bowl of unrecognizable raw meat.

"I forgot I had to make everything be ready to eat at the same time," she said.

"Don't worry. You don't have to do anything," he told her. "Your sister's concern was well-meaning, but ill-founded. I'm happy here, and it is pleasant to have your company, but there isn't any need for you to keep house."

As he sat at the table and attempted to choke down what she offered, he realized that it had been ludicrous of Junan to assume that he or any-one would want to eat what Yinan cooked. She had done nothing in Hangzhou but sit in her room, making paper birds, reading, or playing with her inks and paints.

The next morning he told Mary to prepare dinner for Yinan but not for him. He continued his socializing most nights at the Hsiaos', and the three of them settled into a routine. Yinan and Mary were like two women trying to keep house for a bachelor. Whenever he tried to speak to Yinan, out of awkward feelings of guilt and responsibility, their con-versations were filled with silences.

In the mornings, Yinan rose very early and made breakfast and he, coming downstairs to the places laid at the table, felt obliged to sit and eat it. The meal was disconcerting always. He had never thought before about the way that good food—solid and well-made home food— didn't draw attention to itself, while bad food couldn't be ignored. Her breakfast was somewhat burned and at the same time somewhat raw: she had difficulty even warming some buns from dinner the night before. A good meal companion also provided company and entertain-ment without calling attention to herself; Yinan did none of this. She spoke little and stared directly at a spot on the table as if it were embed-ded with a Buddhist prayer for enlightenment. When he set down his chopsticks she glanced up with an alarmed expression, as if she hadn't expected to see him there.

IT WAS SEVERAL weeks before he became aware that there was some-thing on her mind. In Hangzhou she had worked busily with her books and calligraphy. Now she sat idle and her silences lingered. He pur-chased some brushes and fine paper at ridiculous prices and brought them home, but she only left the soft, white rolls of paper on the table in her room; he could see them there untouched when he passed. He questioned Mary, and the maid only shrugged; there was a curl of scorn to her mouth. "How would I know what she does? All day she sits in there with the door closed."

In early summer, when the bombing raids began, he paid Mary to sleep in the apartment at night. This ensured that someone would be there to take Yinan to the bomb shelter if he was out. Still, he felt guilty for staying out late. The bombs frightened his visitor. She took to drifting about on cloudy nights, when it was safe. He sometimes sensed her footsteps near the door. Once, returning late, he saw the tail of her nightshirt vanish into her room.

Li Ang found himself missing Junan. If she were there, she might have ordered Yinan to do something, or otherwise managed Yinan into contentment. But Junan wasn't there, and Li Ang felt unwilling to let her know that he had done such a poor job of settling Yinan in.

He had only a few clear memories of Junan discussing her sister, whom she treated a bit like one might treat an affectionate and backward child. Shortly after their wedding, Junan had told him Yinan had once foreseen him in a dream, that Yinan had once had a dream about a soldier at the window. He'd made a joke of it. "You women," he'd said. He reached out and pulled a strand of Junan's hair across the pillow—lightly, because she had a low tolerance for teasing. "Have you ever noticed that the people who have these magical dreams are always women?"

"I didn't say she could tell the future. But she is sensitive. Sometimes she surprises me."

He began to suspect that it was somehow his fault that Yinan was in the house. For one thing, when he had mentioned to Hsiao Taitai that Yinan had arrived, the woman had smiled faintly and said something about Junan sending someone to keep watch over him. The idea was, of course, ridiculous, but in the weeks after Yinan's arrival he felt an impulse to hide himself. Her eyes were too clear. It was as if this sister, sitting in her room, had the ability to see through walls. He wasn't worried that she might tell tales about his activities. He was more afraid of what she might see inside of him. She would note the pattern of his days and know that they meant nothing. She would see that he was lost.

ONE EVENING LI ANG didn't go out to dinner but headed home. What would he say to her? He felt obligated to get some information.

He wouldn't force her say anything she didn't want to tell him, but he must somehow learn how things could be made better.

The apartment sweltered in the heat; he stood before her closed door for more than a minute. This would not do. He knocked on her door.

"Come in."

She was sitting near the window, where there was most hope of a breeze, slowly working with a pair of scissors on white paper. Her gentle profile was outlined in the clear light. He grew aware of himself, grotesquely large and sweating. He backed toward the doorway.

"Meimei, you're unhappy. What is it?"

"I'm fine."

"Is there anything I can do? Would you like to come out with me and meet some of the people here?"

"No, please, Gege. I'd rather sit and think."

"I'm sure that more sitting and thinking is the last thing that your sister would want for you."

She turned her face toward the window. "And what do you think my sister wants for me?"

"Well," he fumbled, "I'm sure she wants you to relax here and be comfortable."

"She doesn't understand."

"I will tell Junan you want to go back home."

She replied gently, as if he were the one who needed comforting, "Don't worry, Gege. I'm all right here."

"I don't want you to be unhappy."

She put down the scissors. For a long moment he feared that she might actually tell him what was on her mind. Then she looked down at the white paper in her hands. "Take this," she said, thrusting the paper at him. "Please go away."

Puzzled, he left. Clearly, she missed her sister, but there was something wistful and charged in the way that she had looked out of the window—some other emotion in her face that he could almost define. He, too, had felt it when he left Junan—a feeling similar to loneliness, yet similar to freedom.

Halfway down the hall, he looked at the object in his hand. It was a folded triangle, cut and slashed through with intricate designs. Clumsily, he unfolded the paper. It was cut in a hundred tiny lines almost as fine as eyelashes. The white six-sided flake lay in his palm, looking fragile enough to melt away, so much effort spent on a trifle. As Li Ang stared at it, it made him think of cold: a cold he had heard about from men who'd grown up in the north, a cold deeper than a thousand Yangtze winters.

THE NEXT DAY, he sent a telegram.

JUNAN. POSSIBLE TO SEND YINAN HOME? LI ANG.

Every hour he checked for her response. But he couldn't even be certain that Charlie Kong had managed to hold on to his telegraph. All afternoon he waited; the silence was unbearable. He imagined simply putting Yinan on an empty supplies plane, but it would be risky, not to mention unkind, to send her away. That evening, arriving home, he saw an envelope and seized it up, expecting Junan's neat and flowing handwriting. But it was not from Junan. The script was even more viscerally familiar. He had to squint in order to make out some of the characters, as the letter had been written in ink, and had gotten wet along the way. It was seared with water, the characters drifting on the page.

Dragon Boat Festival 1940
Gege,

I have now been living in the village for two months. I planned to write to you as soon as I settled down, and I apologize for taking so long. Believe me: writing to you is the first personal thing I have done since recovering from the journey. I have time to write only because today is a holiday. But there are no boats and no dragons here; the villagers form a parade and push each other into the water. It is as if they think that if one of them were drowned, the gods might be appeased and might give us some relief from the continuing scarcity.

After much hardship, we arrived here. Some of us, myself included, were hoping for rest, but the conditions are more destitute than any I have experienced. As a consequence of this, I have become a different person.

When you are truly hungry, when you have worked your day so hard that you barely have the strength to piss, you don't find it in your head to think about poems, or literature, or what we consider the higher things in life. After living here, I understand it is no wonder that the countryside is backward. I used to believe that it was populated by ignorant people, almost animals, and indeed this could be said to be true, but the larger story is more significant. I still pity these people, for existing for centuries, living their lives with no hope—but I know that they have been taught to see themselves this way. Despite the poverty and difficulty in scratching out even the slightest living from this land, the indifferent KMT taxes these farmers in the food, taking it from their own mouths and draining them of the strength to make more. In this way, I have found myself beginning to think of the Communist revolution as a battle against the fatalism forced upon the people by their rulers over thousands of years. Now we will stand up, and unite, and take our lives into our own hands.

It is happening already. There are several women here with us, and they are treated the same as anyone else, and called Comrade like all of us; truly the conditions force everyone to work and it is clear how deserving women are. Believe me, there are changes taking place in this country, changes that you would never dream of. I hope that someday, when we have thrown off the terrible oppression of the Brown Dwarfs, you will have the opportunity to understand the meaning of what it is I am describing here.

I work in as much poverty as they do, although because of

my ability to read and write, and my experience with figures, my chores are different: I do not do as much backbreaking toil, and although our rations are the same, it is this absence of physical labor that is enabling me to have the energy to do a few other things, such as write this letter, and help to set the writings of Comrade Mao Zedong onto the page. Sometimes I get less sleep than the others, but I do the work willingly. It is only now, I think, that I truly understand the need in this country for the changes and ideas that inspire my comrades.

I wish you all the best.

Li Bing

Li Ang weighed the frail letter in his hand. The plain wall of his temporary home loomed far away. He felt that he did not know anyone in the world.

That night, he couldn't find a comfortable sleeping position. He lay stiff and weary; an ache in his throat brought him close to despair. He thought with longing of his uncle's stationery shop, where he and Li Bing had spent so many hours arguing and playing go. How had he let his brother leave? At least he should have forced him to accept something when he left town—money, perhaps, or a good warm coat. He wondered when his brother would return, and whether they would meet again.

In the morning, early, he walked among the market stalls. The heat had barely receded in the night, and now the sun rose, enormous, the color of a blood orange. He had not noticed how few supplies were being sold. Dry beans were scarce; the vegetables were scanty. He stood before a tub of rice; the tub was less than half full, and the old woman seated next to it watched him with a suspicion that made him uncomfortable, conscious of his broad chest and the slight belly that filled out his uniform. "Hello, auntie," he greeted her, and her expression turned sour. It was the pout of a younger woman, and he realized that she was no crone, as he had first assumed, but a woman grown to look much older than her years. He turned hastily away. Near the entrance to the market were men reselling the furniture of the newly arrived who had exchanged their goods for rice: useless finery, precious heirlooms, carved rosewood chests, and lavishly embroidered tapestries, their silk tassels dragging in the dust.

By the time he left the marketplace, the sun had become a bright, delirious yellow.

Later in the afternoon, the sky darkened with thunderclouds; the sun periodically emerged, brassy and strange. Halfway home, it began to rain; the first drops fizzled on the hot stones of the stairs, but by the time he reached the house the stones were slick and dark. He was thinking of his brother, alone in the north, and the telegram on the table surprised him.

Rain had darkened the window; he could barely read the type. Absently, he opened the front door to let in light.

HUSBAND. SHE CAN MANAGE. JUNAN.

From the corner of his eye he glimpsed someone standing there, and he glanced away from the letter to see Yinan in the yard. For years, she had been wearing mourning colors for her father; under the dark sky the bow in her hair looked like a white moth. The sight of her disturbed him. Perhaps the death of her mother in childhood had made her melancholy. He had once heard his neighbors whispering, on the day his own mother had died, that some children did not recover from such loss.

When he left the house a few minutes later for the officers' club, she was still standing by the miserable camphor tree. As he stepped down from the stairs, he felt the drops splash his forehead.

He gestured toward the house. "I'm sorry," he said. "I wrote your sister to see if you might go back to Hangzhou, but she wants you to stay here."

Almost imperceptibly, she shifted her gaze down, hiding her thoughts. How ridiculous. Junan had no right to browbeat the two of them like this. He thought that perhaps he should command Junan to accept her sister home, but he imagined that Yinan's life would then become even more difficult. He felt somehow at fault. But there was nothing to do, no consolation he could give. He wished he could leave her standing there.

"Meimei," he said finally, "come inside."

"Thank you, Gege, but I'll stay here right now," she said. "The air is fresh and it smells sweet."

"Your dress is damp."

"Jiejie has made me receive the latest vaccinations."

Li Ang smiled. "And me as well," he said. "With Junan around," he said to her, "you must have never been sick a day in your life."

For a moment he thought she might return his smile. "Only once," she said. "I was sick once. I couldn't go to the wedding. Do you remember? But that wasn't her fault. It was the shuidou. You see, I have a scar."

Then she turned and pointed to her brow. He leaned closer, thinking for the thousandth time that Junan had been right, that her sister was a little too sensitive, a problem, and he wondered what on earth would become of her. Then he forgot why he was leaning toward her. He was not so very close, but he had become acutely aware of the clear gray light, the texture of her eyelids, the curve of her forehead, and, hovering in her breath, the scent of the pressed tofu with garlic sprouts that they had both eaten the evening before at dinner and that she must have eaten again at lunch. Yinan pointed again and he followed her narrow finger with its bitten nail to the faint mark on her forehead, a shallow crater, barely visible. As he stood there, gazing at the frail scar, it seemed to him that he was recalling the visage of a long-forgotten place, a geography he hadn't traveled for a hundred years, but that had once been imprinted deep into his mind. He seized her by the shoulders, felt the shock of her warmth through his fingers. Then he let go her and hurried away.

HE LEFT THE HOUSE early, before the women had awakened, but in the evening he came home, drawn back by the feeling he'd forgotten where he had put something and needed to search for it. In the kitchen, Mary was eating her own dinner. She peered at him over the rim of the bowl, surprised. She jumped up and brought him food, which he took into his room. On the way, he glanced into Yinan's open doorway. She had forgotten all about the evening meal and was seated at her table, reading and chewing the end of her long braid. She didn't notice him, and after a minute or two he walked away. After he had finished eating he stayed resolutely in his room, at the desk, and took out a sheet of paper to write to Junan. Perhaps a letter, detailing his reasons, would convince her. But he sat without writing for several minutes, staring at his pen and hand.

"Dear Wife," he finally wrote. "Yinan must leave." With these characters, his heart beat so violently that his hand shook and he splattered ink onto the paper. He stood up then, still holding the pen, and backed out of his room.

He went to the officers' club, and returned several hours later. He lay unable to sleep, afraid to close his eyes. He fixed his gaze upon the blowing curtain at the window, until he grew tired. But the moment he closed his eyes, he was overtaken by the vision of the girl standing below him in the courtyard, the white bow in her heavy hair. It was an unusually quiet night. There were no sirens, nothing to distract him from this image that silently returned to him.

The next night, he went to the officers' club for dinner. He sought eagerly the noise and companionship of his colleagues. But even as he joked with General Hsiao and sparred with the others, he could not help keeping one ear open, listening.

"What is it?" they asked, and he told them that he thought he had heard an airplane—a common enough answer, but everyone knew the skies were clear; the enemy was at that moment bombing Changsha. They joked with him that he was becoming a nervous wreck and should go to the front. He could not stop listening. Over the sound of the men, over the clink of dishes and the laughter and banter with the maids, he could hear it: the silence, swelling from her room, stretching out into the air and drifting toward him. He would go home eventually. It was where he lived. But he stayed until the last minute possible, until after all of his friends had gone and only the most drunken and incapacitated men remained. Then he took one look around him, shivered, and followed the call of that grave silence.

It was almost dawn when he came to the house. He circled the building, once, twice, staking it out, and he remembered for an instant the morning before dawn when he had lain in wait on the dormitory where Li Bing was inside. Thinking about his brother, he felt suddenly overpowered by a new and frightening belief that his own life had been a mistake, that all of the opportunities he had taken and considered to be his own good luck were nothing but a series of foolish errors, terrible choices made in moments of weakness.

Inside the flat he felt again the expectant silence pressing him into the hallway. Her closed door drew him as if he were a metal filing. He felt like an intruder. And yet nobody had asked him to keep away. The flat lay open to him; it was his. There wasn't the slightest reason for him to stay apart from it. He walked back and forth, trying to be quiet at first and finally wishing she would wake. He stopped abruptly in front of her door. He flushed; again he felt he had forgotten something. Suddenly he seized the doorknob. It turned easily in his hand.

All day he had felt swollen between the legs. It was not the fierce, strong lust he felt toward strangers, or the proprietary lust he had felt toward his wife, but a desire filled with pain, like the pain of an old injury.

He entered the room. She stood in front of her desk, and he came in and faced her.

"How are you?" he asked, and he could hear his voice was strange, out of breath, as if he had been running.

She held still for a moment, then abruptly turned away. Her hair was tucked behind her ears, and he wanted to trace a finger along that delicate line where it pulled away from the nape of her neck. As if she could sense his thoughts, her hand rose slowly.

"Do you miss home?" he asked. "Do you want to go home?" His words came forward in a rush. "I stopped by to see—You don't seem happy here. You seem—lonely." He took her hand. "Hush. It's all right. Really, I can send you home, if that would make you happier. It doesn't matter what your sister says." Now he was unable to let go of her hand.

Then, at last, she tilted up her face and raised her eyes to his. They were the eyes of a stranger, dark and altered by desire. He jerked toward her. The smooth cloth of her dress was warm against his palm. He braced himself against her shoulder, shaking a little, and began to undo the three fastenings at her shoulder. She had turned her head away from him, and he could see the tips of her lashes against the cheek; her breath came fast. The last fastener came open in his hand, and he stopped. Then the scent of her flesh rose—a little salty, a little sweet— and he slid the tips of his fingers through the opening, beneath her undershirt, around the curve of her small breast. The skin there was almost liquid, but he could not be certain. For some reason he had lost the feeling in his hands; they were huge and numb. Cautiously, he slid his palm against her chest; he could trace the shape of her bones beneath it, the ribs coming together in a sort of wishbone, and her heart fluttering so violently that he felt a little frightened. With his other hand, very slowly, he let go of her shoulder and grasped her chin, bringing her face to his. Her face was flushed, her ears pink. Her eyes were pressed closed, her lips drawn tight, set against some feeling— was it fear? No; she was simply concentrating on the movement of his hand.

Years later, when he remembered that night, pondering it as if it were the story of another man's life, it seemed to him that there had been a brief moment when he was present, separate from her. But then, when he tried to recall what happened next, he felt that he had been drawn into the silent world of a dream, as deep and smooth and all-encompassing as water.

No sound, no comprehension, only water.

THE NEXT MORNING, LI ANG WASHED HIMSELF METICULOUSLY and left the flat with high hopes that in the evening, when he returned, everything would be put back into its place and he and Yinan would once again be like brother and sister. Surely she would tell no one. Soon she would be married off and it would be as if nothing had happened.

But as the hours passed, he felt his concentration thinning. At noon meal with Pu Sijian, he sat and laughed and nodded, but all the while he could feel himself leaving the scene, his mind little by little stealing away. In the afternoon he went through a stack of letters. He was unable to focus on more than two or three words in a sentence without his mind's eye flashing back to that vision of her door. A few minutes later it would happen again. It was as if the sun were burning the haze off of his mind and revealing its true subject. Over and over again, he saw himself walking toward her door. He knew she would be there, reading, chewing the end of her braid. When he put his hand upon the doorknob, the metal would be smooth beneath his fingers. Inside, there would be cool and dark. There would be solace. By the end of the day he was unable to keep still. He left the instant it was excusable and hurried back, impatient to run up the stairs and open the door and soothe himself against her skin.

—

A FEW WEEKS LATER, he received another telegram.

HUSBAND. PLEASE CONFIRM SAFETY AFTER
THE LAST ATTACKS. JUNAN.

He did not answer.

Soon he sent Mary back to Hsiao Taitai. "She's no longer needed," he said. "My sister-in-law will find someone she knows." Hsiao Taitai raised her eyebrows, thin as inked lines, and said that this was no doubt a better thing for his sister. That night, he was assigned to the same dinner table as Baoyu. She greeted him; for a moment he couldn't remember who she was. Then he recognized her. He nodded and showed his teeth. She smiled also, but all of the expression left her eyes. She wasn't seated next to him again. A few weeks later he heard she was engaged to a new colonel from out of town.

HUSBAND. HAVE NOT HEARD FROM YOU.
PLEASE REPLY. JUNAN

He felt as if he'd fallen into a well. Above him, all around, he could hear the voices of other people. He had lived among them for many years, but now they were unreachable. Later he would recall the events of their nights together as a series of jumbled images. Her thick braid across the pillow. Her face shining in the faint light from the window, grave and unguarded. In the evenings, when he walked into the room, she would sometimes turn to him and hold out her arms. When had he felt this way before? What was it she recalled in him that felt so precious? Sometimes, when he lay with her, there came over him a sudden and terrible need to get away from her, to leave the rumpled bed, their unkempt rooms, and walk out in the world. But when he thought of the street outside their house he remembered the steps clustered over with debris, the sound of planes, the cries of merchants, and the moans of beggars. Only inside, with Yinan, did he feel safe.

He shared with her the dreary details of his job. They spoke about Hangzhou, about the occupation and before. He had never thought about what Yinan had experienced during those years. Now she told him about her match, about her fear of marriage to Mao Gao, and the way his death had made her even more afraid. She hadn't wanted to be married, but without that end point, without that destination, the future now stretched before her like an empty road.

"Of course that's not true," he said. "It might be a peaceful life, not to be married."

She understood him instantly. "But what else can I do? I'm too old for the university. I'm no intellectual."

"You read. You're always reading."

"It's sheer laziness."

"Would you like to be a poet?" he asked.

"Of course. But poetry has never solved anybody's problems. And sometimes I feel that all of the greatest poems have been written. Although I think about these times we're living through—and I know that someday, someone must attempt to capture them. They must be transformed into beauty—and ugliness, and terror. It would require a brave person, and I'm not that strong."

"What are you writing now?"

"Stories, poems, fairy tales. I'm a specialist at taking on useless projects."

At this he had to laugh. In a moment, Yinan joined him in a light peal that rang against the walls.

ONE NIGHT, SHE wouldn't let him into her room. "You mustn't," she said, holding on to the door with both hands.

"What's the matter?"

She looked away. "My period has come again."

"But I only want to chat. Women are allowed to talk every month, you know."

"You're not supposed to want me now."

"I do want you."

Finally he was allowed to lie in bed with her, but no more. He lit a cigarette. Together they watched the moon sail up the sky like a fiery lantern. Yinan began to speak, slow and wondering at first. There was a pause before each phrase, as if her thoughts were traveling up from some deep cave.

"Once, I dreamed about you," she said. "It was when we were living in Hangzhou, before Junan was married. I dreamed there was a soldier trying to get into our garden." A dim memory seized him—of walking through a dark courtyard on his wedding night, with a bit of light escaping from a solitary window. Now he lay and stared at the round moon like an enormous eye trained down at them.

"Did you want me to come in?" he asked.

"No."

He turned to look at her. She lay on her back, with the summer coverlet folded down against the heat to cool her small breasts, casual, as if they were two young brothers sharing a room on a summer evening. He hadn't expected her to be so matter-of-fact about nakedness; certainly, her sister was much more careful. He smiled. "Now, why didn't you want me to come in?"

Yinan's gaze strained at some imperceptible presence in the dark spaces near the ceiling. "In my dream," she said, "the moon was shining on you as if you were a hero, but your shadow on the ground looked bent, as if you were a broken man."

Li Ang reached for a cigarette. He had seen her through the window, her face in her hands. It had been the posture of a person filled with dread.

"But you still wanted the poor, broken man?" He kept his voice light.

"Yes."

There could be no reply. With his free hand, he gently yanked the tangled braid that lay on the pillow. She smiled, and then she gave a little sob. "It is gone now—gone beyond repair."

"Your sister loves you very much."

"She won't love me now."

July 18, 1940
Dear Husband,

Please pardon me for having made this decision without having consulted you, but our communication channels seem to be disrupted. I have not received replies to several telegrams.

I have decided to close the house and bring the children to you. It is less and less safe here for us living alone, and your second daughter longs to be with the father she has never met. She has learned to say "Baba" and it is time that she met you.

I will be arriving in a few weeks. Please do not make any special arrangements for me. I am certain that your current rooms will satisfy me. As for the Hangzhou house, your uncle is looking after it. I am selling some of my father's possessions, and you may trust that I have put most of our other important things into safe hands.

Your children and I look forward to being with you.

Your wife,

Junan

He sat holding Junan's letter in his hand. The black ink characters marched up and down before his eyes. He went to Yinan's bedroom, where she was reading at her desk. The light from the lamp fell on her profile and outlined her forehead, eyelashes, and nose. The sight of her was so familiar and so charged he didn't dare go any closer.

"Why don't you come in?" she asked. She looked up. "What's wrong?"

"It's a letter from Junan."

She set down the book and turned to face him. He understood that somehow she was ready for this, more than he had been.

There could be no avoiding it. When he spoke, his voice cracked and he was forced to stop. "Something must be done."

"I must go away."

"You can't do that, Yinan."

"I can't live with her anymore. I won't. She doesn't know it yet."

"I don't want to see your life ruined because of what we've done."

"You don't understand. It doesn't matter. I love you."

She held his gaze quietly and looked into him. He had the sensation he was falling. He cleared his throat and said again, "Something must be done."

ON THEIR LAST NIGHT together, they ate as usual in the kitchen. With the sirens their meals had grown haphazard. Li Ang didn't want Yinan to go to the market by herself, so he usually picked up something on the way home. When there was fruit in the market, they ate fruit. Sometimes they feasted on roasted sweet potatoes he had bought on the street. Although Li Ang missed his savory meals and often made up for them at lunch, Yinan ate whatever was set in front of her. On this night, it was plums. He watched as she peeled the loose skins and ate the soggy fruit, which had ripened almost to rot. He had not bothered to light the gas lamps. Soon it was dusk. Her face, pale and narrow with juice-stained lips, floated before him like a specter.

He had believed each morning would bring a change. Every night he closed his eyes believing that when he opened them what they had done would be undone. Living with Junan had been that easy. She had straightened out his life for him, so that he only had to step into the order as if it were a clean set of clothes. When he did something to make her angry, she quickly made her face smooth again. So powerful was she that she could swallow her own anger; likewise she took on all their problems and made them disappear. But her sister, it seemed, had not that talent. Or perhaps it was more that the two of them, he and Yinan, were unable to undo what they had done together. No word, no act, no breath they breathed in sleep together could ever be taken back. He should have known this about her. He should have known it from the mess she had always left around her room: the paper clippings, the inkblots, and scattered piles of paper. He should have known it from the spills and dirty dishes in her messy kitchen. She was unable to forget, and this inability had rubbed off on him.

Yinan rose and opened the drawer for the box of matches.

"What are you doing?" he asked.

"Wouldn't it be more pleasant with light?"

The flame shook in her hand. He leaned over and blew it out, then took her hand and led her to bed.

The siren began a moment later. He pulled at her arm. "Come, come on. We need to go."

"No," she said. "I want to stay here."

It would be a local bombing; this was lunacy. "All right," he said. He put his arms around her and tried to lose himself in the touch of her skin.

Later he became aware of the dark flutter of an engine. The flutter grew louder and louder until it was unbearable. There was a pause while this awful sound hung in the air; then a boom shook the house and everything inside.

"Oh!" she cried.

He held her and she struggled away. Her terror lent fierce strength to her thin arms.

"Come down!" she cried. "Come down!" He understood that she was calling to the bombs. Her cries were muffled by a second boom that seemed to come from all around them, enclosing them. His ears rang and he could not tell if there were more bombs, or only echoes. The room shook. Somewhere nearby, there came the shrieking sounds of wood tearing apart, nails bending, glass breaking in a sudden breathless wind. He smelled the stink of his own fear and bent his head into her neck to seek his customary solace. It was there.

Hours later, he awoke amid damp sheets to find the house miraculously standing. He wanted to go outside and see what else had survived. Yinan lay sleeping under him. He raised his head and looked at her, the column of her throat, the gentle bones and tendons in her arms and shoulders. She slept exhausted, with her head tipped back and her mouth open. Watching her, he grew afraid. He peeled his body away and laid her back against the bed. There was a mark on her bare shoulder, the imprint of his hand.

LATER HE STOOD high over the river fork, watching as the China National plane descended past eye level, past the huts and stairs and stony streets, down through the shroud of fog that hid the narrow island runway. He peered into the haze below, waiting for the passengers to leave the plane, to board the sampan that would ferry them to the river bank, where they would collect their luggage and ride sedan chairs up the steep path to the gate. It was some time before Junan's small figure emerged from the fog. He recognized her instantly. She sat upright in the bucking sedan chair. She didn't lean back to gaze at the city atop the cliff; she didn't seem to notice when the forward bearer leaped quickly upward, jouncing her; she didn't go to pieces at the steepness of the path, although their daughters in the following chair cringed to see the frightening drop. Behind them struggled six or seven coolies under her boxes, trunks, and bundles. The wail of their work song floated to his ears. Junan was like a civilized woman from a faraway land, traveling into savagery to save him. For this reason, she had bribed her way, and their daughters' way, out of occupied territory, past the front, through gorges, over the mountains, to land on that narrow island.

As her chair drew closer, he waited for her to show she suspected or even knew what he had done. But her perfect features held the confidence of old. Eyes level, chin raised, she rode toward him as pure as if she were seated in a bridal palanquin. She reached the gate. There was an expectant pause before he jumped forward to help her from the chair. Standing, they faced each other at a proper distance. The sunlight broke against her black hair and ivory face. A wave of terror prompted him, and he pushed toward her as if against a wind.

Flight

Chongqing 1940

EARLY ONE EVENING, JUST AT THE HOUR WHEN THE TERRIBLE heat of the late summer day was at its worst, Hu Mudan stepped off the ferry over the Jialingjiang and began the long climb up the steps of the city toward the streets where the Nationalist officials lived. A native to the province, she had dressed against the heat, wearing a broad straw hat and loose cotton clothes that hid her body. Since the birth of her son, she had grown thinner. With her narrow hips and casual stride, she could have been a small man, moving up the stairs with a certain wary lightness to avoid prolonged contact between his cloth-soled sandals and the sharp heat of the stones. But Hu Mudan was on a woman's errand. Despite the steepness of her path, despite the baking heat, she felt compelled—by curiosity, anxiety, and another emotion that hovered between love and duty—to find the house that she was searching for.

The day before, while marketing, she had become aware of someone near the string beans watching her. She looked up into a woman's face, weary and no longer young. She'd known this woman before. She knew those eyes, which had a pleasing shape but a somewhat petty and ill-tempered expression. The woman wasn't thin as much as slack, and Hu Mudan recalled the bones when they had carried flesh sweetly. She remembered the glazed green tiles and the mulberry tree; and for a moment she could almost see the delicate, slightly crumbling lines of the Wang house, and smell the overblown roses in Chanyi's garden.

"Weiwei."

"You recognized me," said the woman, and a coquettish curl flickered in the corner of her mouth.

"I would recognize you anywhere," Hu Mudan assured her.

"I haven't changed much." Then she added, with less confidence, "These have been hard years."

"Do you still work for the family? Where are they living?"

"On the hill."

There was a shade of caution in Weiwei's voice. Hu Mudan felt the sun grow cold at her back. "And the others?" she asked.

"Gongdi started off with me, but he died in the gorges."

The skin of Weiwei's face strained into tiny lines. What had happened? Hu Mudan took a deep breath. "And the young miss? How is Yinan?"

Weiwei glanced down at the pile of beans. "She's no longer with us."

"Yinan married?"

"No. She's left the house."

"Where is she? How is she getting by?"

Weiwei shrugged.

Hu Mudan moved closer. She wanted to shake Weiwei with both hands until she gave up information, but she was holding a basket. In the years since she had left the family, she had worried about Junan, but especially about Yinan. And now here was Weiwei telling her this shocking news, but carefully, as if she felt the truth would be a loss of face. Hu Mudan was an outsider now. She had been sent away. Hu Mudan sensed Weiwei backing off from her. She smiled, backing off herself, and asked Weiwei where on the hill the family was living. This question seemed innocuous enough. Then she said that she would visit soon, and described how much, and in what way, Weiwei resembled the girl she had once been. She said goodbye to Weiwei and watched her disappear into the crowd.

That evening, her thoughts returned over and over to Chanyi's daughters. She remembered the long nights after Chanyi's death, when she had paced through the house and come upon them asleep in Yinan's room, their dark heads close together, their hair strewn across the pillow like lines of ink. Yinan suffered the worst; she was frail, like their mother. In the months following Chanyi's death, Hu Mudan spent hours rocking her, sheltering and soothing her. But Junan was unwilling to ask for help. Even as a child she'd held Hu Mudan at arm's length, wanting her mother only, as if the solace of any other person was beneath her dignity. After her mother was gone, she strengthened herself against the death and did without.

On Junan's wedding day, she was tall and pale, with her high-arched nose and pomegranate mouth, so cool toward her handsome husband that a casual observer would have assumed that she cared nothing. But Hu Mudan knew better. She had long known that beneath Junan's aloof exterior lay a susceptibility to obsession. And now, hearing that Yinan lived apart, Hu Mudan was seized by the need to know what had come between them.

Hu Mudan considered herself a skeptic of Li Ang. When she had first met him, she was pregnant, needing nothing he could give. She sensed that what he could give would best be given in bed. She had looked over his body, hard and lithe, his blunt, dark face and gleaming eyes, and sensed a prodigious vitality. Oh, he was generous to women, and often kind, but his kindness was the worst sort, based as it was on thoughtlessness rather than calculation or even lust. Now, as she made her way up the steps toward the military neighborhood, Hu Mudan expected he would suffer for his thoughtlessness. Careless kindness had its price, and careless generosity.

The stench of those suffering in hot weather thickened the air. In these past three years the city had bloated like a tumor with the new people, their soldiers, their bureaucrats, and their refugees. It was almost unrecognizable. At night more bombs fell and more buildings were destroyed, more people sent into the streets. Now the city was filled with the hungry, sitting and lying on the steps, sleeping, begging, wasting away. A girl clutched a child with flies in its eyes. Hu Mudan placed a copper in her hand. She couldn't help them all. Fate had abandoned them. She picked her way into the military neighborhood and asked the women at the well for directions to the house of the officer Li Ang.

Yes, Junan had sent her away. But Hu Mudan's responsibility to the family reached to the days when Junan had been only a ball in Chanyi's belly. She was still responsible, a witness to Chanyi's daughters' lives on the earth.

FROM MY WINDOW on the hill, I could see her coming. I watched her climb the stairs, moving wearily and resolutely through the heat. At the gate, she stopped and faced the house, her face unreadable in the shadow of her hat. She let herself in. I left my room and hurried to the door. I was so excited that I almost ran into my mother and my sister. My mother stood as straight as a porcelain vase. Every part of her—the long, straight body, the slender hands, the vivid smile—was absolutely under control.

"Hu Mudan. Welcome."

"I came to check on you," said Hu Mudan.

"Of course," my mother said. "Thank you for doing that."

Her magnamimous smile sought to hide a juggling of emotions— irritation and confusion and, just possibly, gratitude. She held herself like a queen, albeit a queen struggling to live in an impossible flat, cramped and ugly—and beneath her, although she wouldn't admit to it.

"Xiao Hong," my mother said, and put her hand upon my shoulder, "say hello to Hu Mudan. You remember Hu Mudan?"

I said nothing, stopped by sudden happiness and shame.

"Hello, Xiao Hong. You've grown so tall! You know, Hu Ran is here in Chongqing. I'm sure he'd like to see you." Hu Mudan examined me. "She looks just like you," she said to my mother. This remark was wrong, I knew even then. Everyone said I took after my father.

"Here is Hwa," I managed to say.

"Hello, Meimei."

Hwa scowled. She turned her face away and backed into my mother's legs. "You can't call me by that name," she said.

"What should I call you?"

"You're not my family and you have no right to call me by that name."

Hu Mudan laughed. "This one is even more like you," she said. Then it was my mother's turn to frown.

"So, where is your meimei, Junan?"

Her question fell into the room like a stone. My mother shifted in her chair. "Yinan is no longer living with us."

"Why not?"

My mother sighed, lifting one long, white hand in a vague gesture. "She was here alone for a few months," she said, "keeping house for the colonel. She says it's something she did. Poor Yinan. She's very young. I told her not to worry, it's not important, but she insists on taking herself so seriously." She smiled as if surely Hu Mudan would understand.

But Hu Mudan didn't return her smile. "Where is Yinan?" she asked again.

"She says she doesn't want visitors."

"What a shame," said Hu Mudan. "I've been thinking of her all this time. It's too bad if she keeps herself from seeing old friends. It's really a shame, the two of you living apart. Your mother would not have wanted it."

"I wish Yinan could hear you." My mother leaned toward Hu Mudan as if confiding. "She's worked herself into a state, and over nothing."

"Maybe she needs someone to hear her side of the story."

My mother smiled again. "Thank you for coming by," she said. "Let me know if there's anything I can do for you."

"Maybe I should go to see her."

"Thank you for stopping by." The silence thickened. Hu Mudan leaned toward my sister and made a clucking noise; Hwa averted her eyes. My mother stiffened, willing Hu Mudan out of the house. I wished that Hu Mudan would resist. I needed her to stay and help me understand the nature of the confusion that surrounded us. But my mother had made up her mind.

HU MUDAN WALKED toward the setting sun. She felt so tense she couldn't raise a hand to shield her eyes.

It wasn't until she turned down the stairs that she let her joints loosen. She descended slowly, suddenly weary. Around her wheeled the city: beneath her feet, the steep staircase; and down below, the Jialingjiang in shadow. Long orange and red rays glowed against the dusty tiles and patched, stilted houses. It was all that Hu Mudan could do to concentrate upon her walking: resolutely and self-protectively, she minded her feet. She didn't notice the people sitting on the steps, and she didn't raise a hand against the mosquito on her arm.

She had descended a quarter of a mile toward the river when she heard someone running after her. No one hurried in that weather; and not many would risk their safety by running down those crowded stairs. Hu Mudan turned. Above, she glimpsed Weiwei, frightened, her face streaming with sweat.

"Hu Mudan—" Weiwei fought to catch her breath. "She just sent me to the market—"

Hu Mudan stood and waited.

"—and I thought you might have come this way."

Weiwei ran out of breath. She pulled at Hu Mudan's sleeve, wordlessly, and Hu Mudan felt overcome with sadness. She had never been fond of Weiwei, but now she nodded, fixing her eyes upon the woman's aging face. Weiwei leaned closer and said, "I know where she is. She's living with Rodale Taitai, an American woman, on the old Well Square Road, near the Dragon Watching Gate. Please visit her. It would make her feel so much better to see someone she knows."

THE DRAGON WATCHING GATE was farther down the river. When Hu Mudan reached the square, she asked around for the American, Rodale Taitai. Although no one knew her personally, everyone knew where she lived. They explained that she was a missionary who had married a Chinese man. Although she never caused a fuss, aside from walking arm in arm with her husband on the street, she was notorious in the neighborhood, where she was still known as "Rodale Taitai" because of her maiden name, Kate Rodale. Because she wasn't a Chinese, she stood apart from the others, and because she'd married a Chinese, she was never quite accepted by the wives of Americans. She lived apart from everyone, although stubbornly among them, a large, somber woman, somewhat stiff and seeming always a little startled.

Certainly, she couldn't ever look a part of the place. She had white skin—it was really white, not ruddy, like the British faces Hu Mudan had sometimes seen in Hangzhou—and startling gray, almost colorless eyes. Hu Mudan couldn't believe that a Chinese man had married this woman. She was curious to meet this man and find out what he was like.

Rodale Taitai spoke Chinese slowly and clearly. Hu Mudan watched her thin, pale mouth forming the Mandarin words and listened, fascinated; it was like watching a stone talk. With her shape and coloring, she resembled a stone, and she had the slow, logical language that a stone might have. She was saying that Yinan wasn't at home. Yinan had gone to run an errand, but Hu Mudan was welcome to stay and speak to her when she returned.

Beneath Rodale Taitai's solemn manner, Hu Mudan detected a certain spirit. She must have a sense of adventure to live so far away from home. Moreover, she cared about Yinan and seemed eager to talk about her.

"She's been here less than a month. I have asked her a thousand questions, but she doesn't like to talk, and when she does talk, she can't always explain things in a way that I can understand."

Hu Mudan met the gray eyes and compelled her to continue.

"Madame Hsiao asked me to take her in. Yinan wouldn't stay here unless I agreed to hire her as my companion, so she can earn her living."

"You must be patient with her."

"I understand what you mean. She is tentative around the house. But she's intelligent, and interesting. The company is good for me. My husband has been so busy these days. Much as I wish to help him, much as I don't want to be another one of those Chinese women who sits in the house—and I know you're not of that nature yourself, I can see it—it does seem to be true that in a time like this, the duty of a woman is to stay out of trouble and not be a burden on the men."

Hu Mudan brushed these words aside. She didn't understand the necessity for these endless debates about the difference between Western and Chinese ideas on the place of women. The entire topic was idle chatter among people who had too much time to think and not enough work on their hands. She was too busy making her own life to bother about such issues. "What happened?"

"It was Madame Hsiao who told me what I know. She explained that Yinan is from a very good family and that what has befallen them all is not her fault. It seems that Yinan's sister—is it her older sister?—is Li Ang's wife, and the only family Yinan has left in the world. They were very close. To be honest, I'm relieved that you've arrived. Yinan needs comfort from a friend."

"But what happened?"

"I'm not entirely sure myself. I know she was—involved with the colonel. Now she's punishing herself—she's sent herself away. But the sister has forgiven her. She's punishing herself for some other reason."

"What does he want? Does he want them both?"

The American woman regarded her somberly with colorless eyes. But when she spoke, it was with a note of pain and understanding in her voice. "Yes, it's true. We know that he could have them both. Many of the military men are taking concubines. They're claiming that their marriages were arranged, that they had no actual love for their first wives. It is legal. It was decided in court. But I don't think that is the problem here. It is something between her and her sister."

"She loves her sister."

"Her sister wants her to come back."

Hu Mudan shook her head. Junan's assumptions, with their impossible simplicity, would not so easily fix this problem. Something was seriously wrong. Aloud, she said, "I'll try to talk to her."

They heard a sound on the stairs. Hu Mudan recognized the footsteps. Tentative, with the soft old shoes. Familiar, but not quite the same.

The door opened and Yinan walked into the room. When she saw Hu Mudan, she cried out with pleasure. Then her face fell.

Hu Mudan went over to Yinan and took her into her arms. Yinan shook. Hu Mudan felt her own face wrinkle with tears. "There, there," Hu Mudan said, patting her on the shoulder. "Don't cry. Why are you crying? A reunion between two old friends is supposed to be a good thing."

"Have you seen Jiejie?"

"I have."

"I'm so glad she told you how to find me! She is—upset with me for being here, but I knew that if you ever came by, she would want you to see me! Tell me how she is."

"She seems to be in good health."

"Does she miss me?"

"I think she does."

Yinan cried harder.

"Well, that's not a bad thing," Hu Mudan said, dryly, but Yinan didn't pay attention. She leaned into Hu Mudan. Hu Mudan closed her eyes. Yinan was as familiar as a child of her own. Then she reminded herself that Yinan was no longer a child. Something had altered Yinan's scent, changed the molecules of her blood. The narrow face, purple under her eyes, shadowy at the temples, held the look of one who had known passion.

Rodale Taitai hovered over them. "I didn't know she felt as bad as this—"

"She'll be all right," said Hu Mudan. She sat Yinan down on the chair where she'd been sitting. "When are you going to talk to your jiejie?"

"I did try, once. She doesn't understand."

"You must try again."

Rodale Taitai spoke. "Are you hungry? Have something to eat; it always makes you feel better."

This remark surprised Hu Mudan. Since childhood, Yinan had lost her appetite whenever she felt emotional.

"Oh, no," protested Yinan. "I couldn't." She glanced at Hu Mudan.

"I've eaten already," Hu Mudan lied. Rodale Taitai brought a dish from the cupboard, leftover beggars' chicken. A savory scent rose from the wrapped lotus leaves.

"Ming is always getting gifts in exchange for favors," Rodale Taitai explained. "He works for Colonel Jiang and because he has access, people are always giving us things."

Hu Mudan nodded. Even she had heard of this colonel; he was the man who ran errands for Madame Chiang Kai-shek. Yinan unwrapped the lotus leaves and the smell of chicken filled the room.

"Your husband works on the hill?" Hu Mudan asked, to stall for time while she observed Yinan. "Does he see the Generalissimo?"

"Not often. Although once, in a pinch, he was allowed to take refuge in the bomb shelter behind the Generalissimo's office with the family and a few secretaries, and he did have a pleasant conversation with Madame Chiang."

Hu Mudan watched Yinan eat. She held the chicken thigh in both hands, working the leg away from the joint with slender fingers, stripping off every shred of meat and sucking the bones. She ate steadily, with concentration, and as she chewed, her face grew smooth and dreamy. Her pinched expression eased away; she occasionally shut her eyes with pleasure, licking the grease off her lips. When she had finished every particle, she wiped her hands, folded them in her lap, and attended to the conversation with a private, watchful look that Hu Mudan remembered from another time. Rodale Taitai was asking Hu Mudan where she was born and how she came to Chongqing. Hu Mudan could barely reply. She was stunned and worried by what she had just seen. The girl was pregnant.

EVEN IN ITS BLEAKEST DAYS, THE WARTIME CAPITAL WAS A city of reunions. From its fog-filled valleys to the hilltop lanterns lit to warn of imminent attack; from mud huts near the river to mansions on the heights; all over the city, there were meetings between people who'd been separated. Owners of factories and mills that had been carried piece by piece away from occupied cities reassembled their machinery and reopened their doors to those workers who had followed. Former neighbors found each other in new restaurants named after provinces departed. Classmates, brothers, friends, and lovers, sundered by the enemy, sought each other in this last, great stronghold in the west.

And so we reunited with my father. I still remember my first sight of him after two years. Seated next to Hwa, I leaned forward in the jouncing chair and glimpsed him on the hill. He stood waiting in his uniform, lit up by light and fog. He looked like pure qi, poised to leave the ground, and in that moment I believed that with his energy and courage he could keep our family—and the entire country—safe from the confusion that besieged us. I was filled with gratitude for his lightness and his strength. I knew he wouldn't fail me when I placed so much hope in him. He couldn't fail to love me when I loved him so much.

But everywhere we went we saw the signs posted by those who hadn't been so lucky.

LOST ON 9/14 NEAR THE OLD ELEPHANT ROAD:
HUANG DAI, MALE CHILD, 7 YRS. ONE METER, 20 CM,
TWO LARGE MOLES ON LEFT ANKLE. REWARD.

SEARCHING FOR MY MOTHER, HWA NEIBU OF JIANGSU
PROVINCE, LOST IN 2ND ATTACK ON CHANGSHA. REWARD.

MEIMEI, MEIMEI, WHERE ARE YOU? I AM WAITING AT THE
GATE CONNECTING WITH DISTANT PLACES.

Chongqing was also a place of chaos and separation. From my high window I could see the steps below filled with survivors of wartime dislocation: men and women sagging under the weight of ragged bundles holding everything they owned; filthy, hungry children and stray dogs. The swollen city was divided into factions. The waves of refugees had flowed beyond its walls, but the original residents remained, contemptuous of the newcomers. At first my mother thought the street signs were being rendered unintelligible in the local dialect. Then she learned the native residents called the streets by their former names, creating an unnavigable palimpsest of the geography.

Soon after our arrival, a jagged crack split the newly whitewashed mud wall of the kitchen. An earthenware steamer threw itself against the floor. Weiwei patched and swept, but the breakage couldn't be repaired. Too much had been lost. Hu Mudan and Hu Ran were somewhere in the city, but my mother wouldn't speak of them. Also, something was the matter between my mother and my father. They were together once again, but I missed the palpable joy that had surrounded my mother upon every past reunion. The two of them had never been talkative but they now conversed in disconnected phrases, pausing often, waiting for a third person to speak.

"I miss Ayi," I said one evening at dinner.

"I miss her, too," my mother replied. "But she's not well right now, and she needs to live in peace and quiet for a while."

"She used to read to us," I said to Hwa. "Do you remember Ayi?"

"No."

"Hwa!" my mother scolded her, but she put another piece of chicken in Hwa's bowl. She turned to my father. "Poor Yinan," she said.

My father didn't answer. But one evening around that time, when my mother was putting Hwa to bed, he gestured to me and pulled a brown paper package from his bag.

"I found this for you, Hong," he said.

It was a slender collection of Grimm's fairy tales in English, printed on thick glossy paper and illustrated with color pictures.

"You'll learn the English soon," he said. "You're growing up."

We were alone. I peered into his eyes, searching for the father I remembered in his expression mysteriously changed and softened in two years. I saw him looking sadly back and knew that he still loved me. "Thank you, Baba," I said.

He touched the top of my head. "Now go up to bed."

Later my mother cautioned me against reading too many fairy tales. She said they were like opium and I would grow up into a useless woman. I tried to show the book to Hwa, but she was furious at being left out and wouldn't look at it. I knew only a few English words, but I spent hours studying the stories and looking at the pictures. I hid the book under my pillow and in late spring, when the bombing began, it was the one item I brought with me into the shelter.

We'd been together only a few months when my father suddenly left Chongqing. He'd been ordered to the south, my mother said. That explanation was enough for Hwa, who'd known him only those short months. But my memory was longer. I had waited for the return of his teasing buoyancy and the embrace of his strong arms. I had waited, like my mother, to be with him once again. He was the reason we had come all the way to Chongqing. His new departure hurt me. Caught in my own disappointment, I didn't consider how much it must have hurt my mother.

SHE WOULD NEVER desert us. She kept us safe even from the Japanese bombers. In cloudy weather, when visibility was low, we spent our time the way we had in Hangzhou. We sang songs, learned poems, and played games. On clear days, we lay open to the enemy. We watched the signal lanterns, listened for the sirens, and when the lanterns turned red we hurried to the bomb shelter. There we ate supplies our mother hoarded: salted eggs, hard buns, and dried fruit. We took turns doing our business in a community pot. Our mother struggled to keep us clean, wiping us with cloths that had been dipped in precious water.

She taught us how to close our eyes, as if the darkness were our choice, and as time wore on we grew accustomed to it. Then bombs came, like great gods that worked a powerful unmaking. They were huge and cruel, but when we stayed absolutely still, hidden with our mother, they did not harm us. Hwa and I learned to listen for the sound of her pulse. We grew familiar with her heartbeat and the courage of her body, recovering the knowledge we had once held long ago, when we had been enfolded in its pounding darkness. We clung to her, Hwa asleep and I awake. I could feel her lithe and watchful under many layers of clothes, light, thick layers that muffled and softened the strings of beads and pearls around her neck. When I nestled up to her, I felt the hard, heavy whorls pressed into my face, but I said nothing. I knew that I was never to speak of them. They were what she held in trust against a disaster greater than we had known.

One midsummer afternoon, Hwa and I were working on Hwa's shoes. Before this, our mother had paid a country girl to help her with the soles, which were created from many layers of cloth stuck together with paste. The hardened layers were then pierced with an awl and stitched with thick linen thread. The arrangement with the local girl had worked out until one day when my mother returned from a brief errand and discovered her eating the paste. My mother's disgust and pity at this made it impossible for her to bear the presence of the girl. She sent her home with a few yams and resolved that we would do the work ourselves.

"It's about time you learned to sew," she told me. "You need practice in the home arts. You have no idea how lucky you are; your grandmother had to learn to walk with bells sewn to the hem of her dress. If the bells rang, she was punished."

On my own shoes, I'd stitched the character for "victory" with rough cotton. They were finished, and I wore them on that day. But my mother insisted that I embroider on Hwa's shoes chrysanthemums for autumn—an intricate flower requiring hundreds of small stitches. I'd been working for an hour when there came a knock on the door. There was something familiar in the knock, yet carefully polite.

Hwa and I ran to the door. I threw it open and backed away, surprised. Before me stood my aunt Yinan wearing a loose dress. Hu Mudan was at her side holding a basket with some paper parcels. Behind her stood a tall boy with thick hair in a wild brush.

Hu Ran spoke first. "Hello, young miss."

"Ayi!" I shouted. Yinan smiled her old smile, the one I'd always felt was meant for me alone. For a moment she looked ready to gather me into her arms. Then her smile dropped away and her gaze shifted behind me. My mother had entered.

"Li Taitai." Hu Mudan spoke over my shoulder. She held out her package, fragrant peppers and a box of sesame cakes.

In that brief instant I feared my mother might tell them to leave. We hadn't seen Hu Mudan since the day my mother had willed her from the room. But my mother beckoned, triumphantly, and I began to see that she was pleased Yinan had come to her. Yinan's eyes filled with tears. Hu Mudan handed the packages to my mother.

"I'll put these in the kitchen," my mother said. She gestured to the others and they walked after her. Hwa went to use the toilet and Weiwei followed.

I stole a glance at Hu Ran. He'd entered adolescence, and his adult features had emerged: prominent cheekbones, a high-bridged nose, and long, Mongolian eyes that held a watchful expression. He looked around the room, taking in the radio, the scattered sewing project, the furniture and curtains my mother had brought from Hangzhou. Then he turned his curious, bright eyes onto my face. Our gazes locked. He looked at the door and without thinking I went toward it.

Hu Ran moved fluidly down the city steps. I followed more slowly, keeping my new shoes out of the dust, watching his square, brown elbows sticking out of his shirtsleeves. His pants rose halfway up his sturdy calves. He had no new things, he explained, because his mother was sending him to school. He was much larger than the other children, but he didn't care. He wanted to learn to read. After school, he rented a bicycle to run errands for money. Two coppers for the bicycle brought in as much as seven coppers in payment. He could buy his own ink and school supplies, and he was saving for a bicycle of his own.

His manner was entirely natural and friendly. But as he spoke of all these things—his school, his coppers, and his bicycle—I held back. I felt left out of his new life. And clearly, he knew more about Yinan than I did. How did he have the right to know about my aunt, when I, her favorite, had been kept in the dark?

Then there were physical changes. In the past, Hu Ran had smelled only salty, like a boy, but now he gave off a puzzling scent that made me look away. There it was again—the mystery of the afternoon behind the willow tree—but this time I was old enough to know there was no proper place to put my curiosity.

"You've changed," I blurted.

Hu Ran nodded. "It's extra food, from the Americans. I grew six inches in one year." He turned toward the river. "We all miss you. Especially your ayi."

"She seems different." I wanted to say more, but something stopped my throat.

Hu Ran stared out at an empty rice junk, high in the water. "She's all right," he said. "She has a job. At night sometimes she still writes poems."

Tears stung my eyes. "What else do you know?" I asked.

"What haven't you been told?"

"I don't know anything."

"She's going to have a baby."

I stopped and stared. "How is that possible?"

"I can't tell you!" Hu Ran blushed.

"Let's go back," I said, seized by a panic I couldn't express.

We climbed the stairs in silence. Hu Ran reached the house a few paces ahead of me and paused on the doorstep, listening. Then he waved me away. But I couldn't bear to be protected any longer. I walked through the mud up to the open window.

Yinan and my mother sat facing one another. My mother had brought out the good teapot, and she smiled graciously at Yinan as if she were an honored guest. But as I watched, I sensed they were engaged in a curious struggle. My mother stayed behind a wall of friendliness and ease. Yinan, seated opposite, clenched the arms of her chair. She leaned toward my mother, frowning with sorrow and determination. Hu Mudan remained apart, eyes closed tightly as if she had a headache, listening and rocking in her chair.

"I can't stay," Yinan apologized. "Rodale Taitai needs me. But I must talk to you and tell you what happened. After I confess, you must decide whether you still find it in your heart to forgive me."

"Of course you are forgiven. You know this happens all the time, Meimei."

"No, I don't think it does."

"Oh, yes, it does. It's all right, Yinan. You may think I'm upset, but you needn't worry. You think I haven't seen or heard of this before? You couldn't help what happened; it was just proximity."

"No."

"The confusion afterward is natural; the feelings will pass," my mother said. "It's like having a bad cold."

"Please, Jiejie."

"You can live here with me until the baby comes. Then we'll find you a good man. No one will blame you in these mixed-up times. You can forget this episode and put it all behind you."

"I can't live here."

My mother shrugged her graceful shoulders. "I've told you again and again. I've already forgiven you."

"Please let me tell you what happened."

"I can guess."

"It's not what you think. Things—changed when I was there."

"No, Meimei. You are too innocent to understand." She tipped her head back, more beautiful than ever, and examined my aunt through her lashes. "Are you worried he'll be in the house? He's not even in the country."

"No," Yinan cried. "It's not him I'm thinking about. That was my fate and now my life is ruined. But I don't care about that, not in the way you think. It's you who matter, Jiejie. Please hear what I'm asking you to forgive. You asked me to preoccupy him. I didn't understand. But when I got there and I saw him, then I knew. I knew what you expected. And things changed, he changed. I changed."

"I told you it doesn't matter now."

"I became a person."

"Nonsense."

"I'm not your meimei anymore."

"That's ridiculous. We're family."

Yinan's voice was barely audible. "And Li Ang is your husband."

At the sound of Yinan's voice speaking his name, a queer expression came over my mother's face. She said nothing, but she raised her head slightly as if listening for a visitation from a force that she had always feared but did not want to name.

Their eyes met. Yinan, too, was waiting. Yinan took a deep breath. "Jiejie," she said, "why do you think he decided to leave Chongqing and go to Burma?"

My mother's face closed over like the surface of a pond. She shut her eyes for one second, two seconds. When she spoke, her voice was toneless, harsh. "He was ordered. By the general."

Yinan sat back, exhausted.

In a moment there was no evidence of the wound: no surprise, no lines of anguish, but rather a visage rendered utterly smooth and unrevealing. It was as if my mother's face had been frozen shut. Her voice was hard. "I don't need you to tell me what his motives are," she said. "You go 'become a person' with some other man. I'll get you another soldier, if that's what you prefer."

"No, Jiejie. Goodbye, Jiejie." I could barely hear the words. Then Yinan stood with blind dignity and went to the door. I heard the front door click shut and her slow, dazed footsteps on the path. Too late, I remembered my shoes. The muddy spots under the eaves had ruined them.

Inside the house, Hu Mudan gathered up her basket.

"Get out of here," my mother said. "Stop meddling in my affairs and take that brat with you."

Hu Mudan obeyed. When she reached the door, she turned calmly toward my mother. "I've known you since you were in split pants," she said, her dry voice falling into the spent air. "You are afraid the child will be a boy."

THEN THERE WERE no more visits from and no more mention of my aunt. The mahjong women were our only company. Hwa watched the games. My mother told me to piece together a replacement pair of shoes, and I sat in the bedroom accompanied by the relentless clicking of the tiles. I was seven years old, trying to sort through the layers of the conversation I had overheard. *You asked me to preoccupy him.* Click. *It's like having a bad cold.* Click-click. *I became a person.* Click. *He was ordered. By the general.* Now my mother was afraid of Yinan. How could this be?

One night in late summer I awakened in the bomb shelter. First there was the brief disorientation of coming to consciousness in darkness. Then I searched for my mother and for Hwa. Hwa lay sleeping next to me, but my mother was up; she was standing nearby, speaking to a strange woman. I reached out to touch her ankle. I could feel her muscles taut, all attention, in the dark.

"Wait," my mother said. "I must talk to the child." She bent down and slid her long arms around me. "Be still," she said, "and listen to me carefully. You must stay here and be good."

"Can't I come with you?"

"No."

"What about Meimei?"

"Hwa is sleeping. You must stay here and be good and wait for me to come back. I have asked Pu Taitai to watch you. You be good and stay with Pu Taitai."

"Where are you going?"

"Not far." She put her hand on my shoulder. "Stay here with Hwa." She turned and told Pu Taitai she was leaving.

"Hao," Pu Taitai said.

As they walked away, I heard my mother ask, "Where is she?"

"Farther, the left tunnel."

Then they were gone. Next to me, Hwa slept. I touched her shoulder. "Hwa," I whispered. "Wake up. Hwa, wake up." But she merely yawned, turned over, and swam back into sleep.

"You let her be," said Pu Taitai. She pulled me onto her lap. I felt smothered by the smell of her sandalwood perfume. "Come and sit with me for a while," she said. "Don't worry. God will protect us."

"Hello, Hong," whispered Pu Li. "Don't be frightened." Long ago, my aunt and I had mocked him for not knowing his left from his right.

Pu Taitai put both arms around my waist. "I have to watch you carefully," she said. "Your mother is my close friend, you know."

I sometimes watched while Pu Taitai and the other women played mahjong with my mother. Pu Taitai was always worrying about her husband, and the other women were always trying to soothe her. My mother was different from the others, more beautiful, with her calm, oval face and her white throat. And she was stronger. She did not confide. I knew Pu Taitai thought my mother was her friend because my mother lent her gambling money. But I didn't think my mother considered Pu Taitai her friend.

Pu Taitai went on. "Some of the women in our group believe that your mother in a past life was a man," she said. "She gambles like a man. I admire her, even when she does beat me. Before he went south, my husband used to say, 'What, I need to give you more money? Have you been playing with Li Taitai again?' But I told him, she is smarter than the rest of us."

She paused and listened nervously. "Your father was in charge of supplies," she continued, "and your mother could have anything she wanted, but I saw the food on your table and it was as simple as what we had." I said nothing. Pu Taitai didn't know the truth of it. My mother was too smart to draw attention to herself by living in extravagance. The black market flourished in the war—for cigarettes, for stockings, for penicillin—and occasionally, these items had come my father's way. With a canny alchemy, my mother had transformed these goods into gold.

Pu Taitai had just lapsed into silence when we heard what was unmistakably an airplane.

"God will protect us," Pu Taitai whispered. But I could feel how afraid she was. I tried to squirm out of her hold.

"Don't be afraid, Hong," echoed Pu Li. Even in the bomb shelter, he was a calm, stolid boy. At recess he spoke as slowly as he did in the classroom, and now, underground, he spoke exactly the way he did at recess.

There was rumbling, closer now. Pu Li whispered, "Don't worry, Hong. I'm here."

I liked Pu Li but didn't want his reassurance. I tried to pull away from him, but couldn't see where to move.

"I'll protect you, Hong."

I shrugged.

"It is proper. One day we'll be husband and wife."

"No, we won't." He had succeeded in getting my attention.

"Oh, yes, Hong. Your mother has told my mother we will."

How could this be? And yet something in his voice told me he wasn't lying. Next to us, Hwa snored lightly. I wrenched myself away from Pu Li and darted off in the direction my mother had gone.

"Hong!" I heard Pu Taitai cry. "Where are you going? Come back here with us!"

The others hissed at her. Through the darkness, I made my way, stumbling over people and their belongings. Nobody stopped me or even noticed me. I turned left as my mother had turned; I could feel or smell her presence, somewhere beyond. There she was. Her long white hand shone in the dim light of a shaded lantern. I squatted down, strained to see into the thick forest of people's legs.

From that hidden place, there came an unearthly sound. Was it sirens? I stood alert, half expecting my mother to find me and explain. Then the sound came again, like a keening in the dark. It was some time before I understood that I was listening to a human being, a woman's voice rising to unintelligible cries of pain. The shrieked words, blurred and twisted, rang off the walls.

Then the voice began to speak. It was a quavering voice, other-worldly and yet familiar to my ears. I didn't recognize the speaker.

"I'm afraid," said the voice.

"Shhh," I heard an old woman say. "It will all be over soon."

Then she said something in the local dialect. I saw her reach out and pick up a bare arm, push the sleeve away from the wrist, and hold the wrist between her finger and thumb. A slender wrist, like the stamen of a flower.

"Her pulse is wild and too strong."

"What does that mean, Cho Puopuo? Can you stop it?"

"We need to take away the extra blood. We'll need leeches."

"Impossible."

"Hot water, then."

"We can't risk smoke."

Cho Puopuo squatted, a tiny woman with her lip thrust out. "Bring the crockery," she said. "The cord must be cut with freshly broken crockery, to make sure the cut is clean." She felt the wrist again. "Rip some cotton into strips."

I wedged myself behind a suitcase, where nobody could see me. For a time I must have fallen asleep, for when I could see again, the crowd of women had shifted and I had a clear sight line. My mother and another woman were standing over the patient. Between their legs, I caught a glimpse of a human face, a woman's face seized with pain, eyes staring, all whites.

"Jiejie, please, I am sorry."

It was my ayi. Yinan—gentle Yinan—was here, she was in pain, perhaps she was dying. I wanted to help her but I hung back, afraid. And my mother kept her face as white and fine as dust.

"Please, will you forgive me?"

"Push," said Cho Puopuo.

"Please," Yinan said, almost whispering. "You forgave him, so will you not find it in yourself to forgive me, too?"

In the depth of silence, my mother's voice was cold as iron. "You are my sister," she said. "He is only a man."

"*Push.*"

There came a long, terrible shudder, and the cries began again. But this time, I could make out the words. "Jiejie! Jiejie! Jiejie! Jiejie—" It was the sound of someone who had lost all hope. The darkness seethed with hissing from all corners, "Stop! Make her stop!" Then all sounds were ended by an enormous boom. It was as if we were in the middle of a great drum.

The enemy was over us.

"Ayi!" I screamed. "Ayi!" But Yinan could not hear me.

Since that time, I've come to recognize a certain expression on someone's face: it is the look of a person who lives in fear of a particular experience, a dark lake of memory opening, swallowing them up. There are times we can't forget, much as we long to lose them in sleep, or love, or wisdom. So many years later, when I am swallowed back into that time, I can't remember the bombing coming to an end. I don't think about emerging, after days underground, into the gray, shattering light. Instead, I see the darkness, only darkness, and the shaking of the walls. And I remember in the very depth, in the core of that exploding force, my mother's will. No solace and no comfort, no yielding, no forgiveness.

During a pause, somebody said, "It is a boy."

MY MOTHER BELIEVED HWA'S VIOLENT HEART HAD COME FROM Chun, her wet nurse. According to her story, she had chosen Chun in haste. She had been looking for a girl in the turmoil of occupied Hangzhou; it wouldn't do to have the baby living on rice porridge, and upper-class women didn't nurse their children. Even in her rush, she chose with care—mindful that a child grows to resemble the woman whose milk it drinks—but in selecting for intelligence, she overlooked the girl's fierce eyes. Chun, who came from a remote corner of Hunan, at first appeared to be a shy young thing. But in time, without the heat of spice, she languished and complained, and my mother, distracted, let Chun cook her own meals and little Hwa take Chun's wild milk. By the time Chun's temper revealed itself, Hwa had flourished on her strong drink and would not have any other. She grew into a watchful child, perfectly obedient unless she held a grudge, when she would scream and cry until we did her bidding. Hwa's tantrums tested even my mother, who lamented that the tumult of war had caused her to over-look the household peace. It was one of the few mistakes she would confess to.

But Hu Mudan had seen the truth. The cause of Hwa's ferocity lay more close at hand; her temperament was a replica of my mother's. Like my mother, Hwa wielded her anger to protect a sensitive heart. As a child, she couldn't bear to be ridiculed or forgotten. It was as if she sensed she wasn't wanted. I cannot say how she knew, because our mother never mentioned wishing Hwa had been a boy. She had bitten down her wishes and accepted Hwa the moment she was born, laying claim to this new daughter with her own fierce sense of loyalty.

So Hwa's defensiveness ran in her blood, as did her desire for answers, her cool poise, and her hesitance to trust. Over time, she learned to manage herself. She didn't lose control; she didn't confide. She barely knew our father, and her belief in our mother's love was absolute. Later, when we were settled in America at a safe remove from the tumult of our childhoods, Hwa would remain devoted and invite our mother to live with her in California. She would believe exactly what our mother chose to tell her. And she would stand staunchly in favor of our mother's attitude toward our past—she wouldn't care to contemplate the family story, nor would she support my efforts to do so.

"You seem to think," Hwa told me once over the telephone, "that if you dwell on all this long enough, it will make sense. But even if it does, what difference does it make? In the end, everything has worked out for you. Your life is no worse than anyone else's."

"That's true," I said. "And since it's true, what's wrong with the idea that I go back to visit China?"

"It would be trying to reclaim the past," she said. "And that's impossible."

"But there's a certain point when we must think about our lives. We must consider those we've loved, and how that love has changed us."

"You talk to Hu Mudan too much."

"I think about who they were and how that influenced the choices that they made. I think about the times in which they lived—in which we lived. The Communist idea of overturning power. Ma was always older and she had the power. So she didn't clearly see Yinan, couldn't predict what she would do or feel."

"Or maybe Yinan didn't want to reveal herself," Hwa said. "Maybe she had plans for herself, from the beginning. You said she'd been engaged and that fell through. She was getting old. What else could she have done?"

I shook my head. "She wasn't that kind of person."

"How do you know?"

"I knew Yinan. I remember her. Anyway, the point is that they were surprised."

"What's that have to do with it?"

"They were surprised by their emotions. All three of them, and especially Ma. You know how much she hates that. If she hadn't been so taken by surprise, how do you think they could have ended up the way they did?"

There was a silence over the line. "What you really mean," Hwa finally said, "is that you wouldn't have ended up the way you did."

MY MOTHER ONCE warned me not to be too proud of how much I could see. I believe it wasn't pride but righteous curiosity that made me strive to notice things. Curiosity mingled with a need to uncover what flowed beneath our household calm, a hidden source of pain that wasn't mentioned. I had seen it in my grandfather, his hair a shock of white, his gaze sliding away as if the sunlight hurt his eyes. I had seen it in my solitary aunt. Now, in the aftermath of Yao's birth, I could see it in my mother. It was like living with another presence. This presence wasn't human and it wasn't a ghost. My mother worked to keep it hidden, yet it didn't disappear. Nothing could vanquish it: not Hwa's devotion nor my good grades in school; not even my mother's growing stash of jewelry and gold.

She had planned for Yinan to preoccupy him. But then something happened that she hadn't planned. How could she have known? She who had refused to see the strength of her own passion, she who'd loved him for so many years without telling him about her love or knowing his desires. She must have retraced each telegram and each event, driven to know exactly how her plan had slipped from her control. Yet the central mystery of those months in Chongqing could never be uncovered. There was an elusive, stubborn element she couldn't have predicted. It was untidy, it went beyond her preconceptions. It had crept up on her, the way a hidden tree root can destroy the foundation of a house. Now, slowly, she began to see what Yinan had tried to tell her, what she'd refused to see. She had lost Li Ang. Yinan was no longer the sister she had known. Yinan had betrayed her.

It was their love that betrayed her, more than anything, more than even their child. It was their love that couldn't be forgiven.

I REMEMBER THE sun-hazed afternoon in those chaotic days after the end of the war, when I saw my brother and cousin Yao on an infrequent visit.

Yao was then a boy of five. Like my father, he moved with an athletic grace; like my father, he possessed a cheerful openness. He charmed everyone who knew him, especially my mother. During his infrequent visits she had developed a bond with him. She sent a present to Yao for every holiday or festival, always beautifully wrapped and addressed to him by name. In the midst of the war, she sent him fine, machine-made clothes and handsome toys. That particular afternoon, she gave Yao a "victory"suit with a tiny Nationalist flag sewn on the jacket pocket. She coaxed him to put it on. It was too hot for such clothing, but he obliged her graciously, strutting back and forth before stopping proudly next to his mother.

"He's a picture of strength," my mother said. "Strong as a warrior, and good-tempered, too." She turned to Yinan. "You're doing a good job."

"You are too flattering, Jiejie," said my aunt. But her hand closed protectively over Yao's brown wrist.

"He's five years old. Surely soon, when he is ready for school, you'll need help getting him a good education."

Yinan shook her head. "The missionary schools are excellent. And since I work for Rodale Taitai, we don't have to worry."

My mother persisted. "Surely you don't want him to have a foreigner's education. He must grow into a patriotic man."

Yinan didn't reply.

"Look how handsome and how smart! A future hero of China, shining like a star. He must have every opportunity." My mother straightened in her chair. "Of course, I'll pay for his schooling. Our boy must have the best." My mother held her arms out for Yao and he burrowed into them. She stroked his smooth hair and he returned her attention with a smile. It was my father's thoughtless charm. My mother didn't understand. She responded to Yao's smile with an expression I'd never seen: proud, adoring, and filled with yearning. I was shaken by the hunger in her glance. I told myself it didn't matter: it had nothing to do with me. But as the dimple deepened in Yao's cheek, I grew furious with him. If it is possible to hate a child, I hated him for his boyishness, his ease, the way he basked in her attention without a thought of what it might lead her to feel or to believe.

Yinan's face was pale. She stood, stammered goodbye to us, and led Yao out the door.

Soon afterward, my mother sent a man to Yinan with the money for Yao. The messenger knocked on the door, but no one answered. He looked through the window and discovered the apartment empty. Yinan had fled. My mother asked around, discreetly, until somehow she learned that Yinan and Yao had left Chongqing. They had returned to Hangzhou with Katherine Rodale, and Hu Mudan and Hu Ran had gone with them.

Soon afterward, in the kitchen garbage bin half covered by yam peelings, I found a pile of black and white images. Some were whole, while others had been sliced away from larger photographs. Each of them held a picture of my aunt. One showed my aunt as a toddler, with a single pigtail standing straight up on her head. In another, I saw my aunt as a child, with someone's arm—my mother's?—curled protectively around her shoulders. One photograph with scalloped edges showed my aunt in a loose, pale dress, holding a half-bloomed rose. Her familiar eyes looked out at me, gentle and unhappy. I put this picture in my pocket. I went to the room I shared with Hwa and scrutinized it for a hiding place, but found nowhere suitable. In the end, I hid the photograph behind another photograph. I slipped it into a frame, behind the picture from my parents' wedding.

A week after Yinan departed, my mother announced that we were moving east as well, to Shanghai. By now I knew my mother's mind and guessed the reason for her decision. Shanghai was close to Yinan, but not too close. In the next few weeks, there was a flurry of activity as my mother's friends unloaded old furniture and finery in payment for their mahjong debts. We gained a cache of scrolls, a set of tables, and even a cello. Then, in the spring of 1946, when I was thirteen years old, we moved into an elegant Shanghai house close to the former French concession.

OVER THE NEXT few years I grew the way a grass stem grows, long and slender, bending at the neck. My mother cautioned me, "You'll be a striking woman, not a classical beauty. You've inherited too mixed a combination of our features." I had her long eyes but his heavy brows; her oval face and his dark complexion. He claimed some northern ancestry, and he had given me the height and ochre skin of the Mongolian marauders. "But you must not forget," my mother said, "to carry yourself with grace. Your father is a general, and so your beauty must come from knowing this."

She frequently reminded me my father was a general. If I was sour with Pu Taitai or raised my voice, she said, "Remember who your father is." I led a limited existence, shuttled between school and home, but somehow she managed to find reasons to remind me. These admonitions filled me with confusion. Why did she insist I be so proud—so proud of my father—when her relationship with him filled her with pain? I couldn't tolerate her pain. Even worse, I didn't trust my own feelings toward my father. I missed him with a ferocity that shamed me.

In the chaos of postwar Shanghai, Hwa and I lived the lives of wealthy girls. We were awakened by a maid, and dressed in clothes she had laid out for us. My mother enrolled us in a private school with intensive English classes, as well as history, literature, and mathematics. On weekdays, Hwa and I put on starched uniforms and rode the school bus; on weekends, we went window-shopping on the Bund. Hwa took to the change with admirable ease. A full head shorter than I, she was demure and chaste in her white blouse, plaid shirt, and polished loafers. She made friends easily with our classmates and their brothers, all except for Willy Chang, a slender, lively boy who wrote beautiful characters. Whenever he was near, Hwa would frown and hold quite still, as if struggling with something.

I had a more difficult time of it. I had no interest in a social life; I spent my time reading novels, fairy tales, and scandalous newspaper serials I snuck into my room at night. I grew so tall my mother had to order my shoes from a specialty store and buy extra fabric to lengthen my school uniform. Thanks to her and Hwa, I had the proper haircut, coat, and socks, but they had no control over my mind, which continued to run wild with dangerous and troubled thoughts. Surrounded by propriety, safe under my mother's care, I began to see my place within a troubling design.

In Yinan's book of fairy tales, a wild and ragged stranger was transformed into a handsome man. Chimney sweeps were revealed to be kings. And mysterious beggars held the enlightenment of holy figures. In "Snow-white and Rose-red," two sisters answered a knock on the cottage door. There stood a fierce black bear, but when the girls befriended him, he became a comely prince. I had come to understand that there was passion in the darkness. I knew that as a woman I would fall into that darkness.

I was going on sixteen, and would soon be old enough to marry. My mother rarely spoke of Chanyi, but I could sense the tragic nature of my grandmother's death. Suicide had not been my mother's fate—she was too strong—and yet the unhappiness of womanhood had challenged her and changed her. I wondered for myself. What would be my fate? When would I face the test that had overcome my grandmother and hardened my mother? When would I experience the seemingly genetic terror that possessed the women of our family? Would I find it on my own, or be cornered into a marriage with a man my mother chose for me? I recalled my aunt's unhappiness, the sorrowful music on her phonograph. I could remember how we had all whispered when she'd lost her fiancé. Was it this misfortune that had sent her on her path? Or would she have been equally ill-fated as the wife of Mao Gao?

It was our bodies, I knew, that brought us to such a desperate place. Passion and desire, the dark tug at our feet. Passion had put my mother in my father's power. Passion had conquered Yinan, caused her to succumb and to betray us all. Passion had taken my father, though I couldn't bear to think of it. It was beyond my control. My nipples grew pointed and brown, my breasts round, and my underarms sour with the smell of womanhood. As my body changed I was afraid that my desires might overtake me.

SHORTLY BEFORE I turned sixteen, my mother and I took a taxi into the old British concession to order a new pair of school shoes.

Our cab moved slowly through the crowded street. We were surrounded on all sides by people Hu Mudan would have described as those whom fate had abandoned. A woman from the countryside squatted behind a cup, so malnourished that her brittle hair had been leached of nutrients and was now a reddish brown. A man of thirty with no teeth stood at the intersection, begging. My mother looked straight ahead, seeing none of this. She had once said it was impossible for her to feed the world. I sat next to her, wondering how their hunger and destitution could fail to reach her heart. How could she clutch to herself her house, her possessions, and her gold?

We rode past a group of street-side acrobats, two men balancing a third man easily on their hands. I noticed one of the standing troupe members, a muscular, crew-headed man, whose face was set into a faraway smile. I couldn't take my eyes away from this man, safely unapproachable on the other side of the glass.

He turned his gaze to me. He was older than he seemed. He measured me with eyes encircled in shadows. *Young rich girl in the automobile*, they seemed to say, amused. *What is weighing on your thoughts?*

"Stop staring," my mother hissed. "You are your father's child!"

A mutinous impulse split my tongue.

"So what?" I spat. "There are a lot of us."

Her open palm stung my cheek. She ordered the cab to turn around. Back home she sent me to my room, where I held a glass of cold water against my face, suffering triumph and uneasiness, the natural consequence of revealing what I knew.

SOON AFTERWARD, Pu Taitai brought Hwa and me to see a matinee of an American movie, *Joan of Arc*. There were men selling peanuts and American chocolates. I struggled with the dialogue. My mother had ordered me not to read the subtitles because she wanted me to practice my English. And so I strained to follow the story line. Joan of Arc was a brave girl with stern Caucasian features, who dressed as a man and led her troops into battle.

Someone reached for my fingers, fit his hand around my palm. Pu Li was holding my hand. I stole a look at Pu Taitai; she didn't seem to notice. I thought that Hwa had seen, but then her eyes flicked back up to the movie.

I felt terribly sorry for Pu Li. His father had died crossing the mountains out of Burma—he had perished from malaria despite my father's efforts to carry him out—and I had been in a hushed awe of him ever since. My own father was wounded, but alive. His father's death made Pu Li sacred, a boy whose status as bereaved must be protected at all costs. Pu Li had ridden ahead of me and into battle. He had somehow taken the blow that had been meant for me. If anything happened to Pu Li, if I hurt him in any way, what was to keep me from taking his place and my own father from dying?

I looked straight ahead demurely, but the screened images vanished. Instead I saw my aunt Yinan, her features pale and sad, telling my mother that she couldn't live with us. I saw my mother's rigid face. I gripped Pu Li's hand fiercely, wanting something that I couldn't say in words. But his touch on mine was a mere pleasantry, like that of a polite ambassador from another country. Nothing happened. When the movie ended, I let go.

IN THAT VERY SAME week, I found under my pillow a sealed envelope with my name on it. It could only have been put there by my sister or Weiwei. For a moment, I wondered if it was from Pu Li—I even hoped that it might be. But I knew him far too well to believe he would resort to secrecy. He was a practical boy. He didn't need to keep his interest private; he could probably discuss it with our mothers and get their permission to see me alone. The note must be a message from an anonymous admirer—this often happened to the heroine of my favorite serial novel. My fingers perspired on the envelope; I was too excited to open it. In the morning, I slipped it into my history book and carried it to school. There I asked to use the bathroom, where I slit open the envelope and unfolded the paper. I felt a moment of confusion at the unfamiliar handwriting before the rough characters jumped off the page.

Young Miss,

   I am in Shanghai this week on business. Can you meet me around four o'clock tomorrow (Wednesday) at the GG Coffeeshop?

Hu Ran

The plan to meet Hu Ran required Hwa's complicity. "What about Pu Li?" she asked.

"What about him?" I replied.

Hwa shook her head, but she promised to tell my mother I'd stayed after school to play basketball. This lie worked on account of my height, although anyone who knew a thing about athletics would have seen I was too tentative and vague to do more than defend myself against a flying ball. My mother didn't know. She thought basketball might teach me not to be so odd.

I let Hwa ride the school bus home alone. I took a city bus for half a mile, then got off and walked the last few blocks toward the French concession. My legs shook with terror at every step. I took deep breaths of cold air spiced with burning coal and cooking odors. For so long I'd wished to be out in the city on my own, away from my mother and everything that held me back. Yet now that I was in the street, submersed in it, I felt invisible or removed, as if I were apart from it, still looking through a glass. The street was alive and filled with cruel beauty. Beggars sat under bright banners announcing the Year of the Ox. An older rickshaw runner, his muscles thinned to rope, pulled a cart laden with a rich man whose belly bulged out from his embroidered vest. Everywhere people transported goods, bent under their bags and baskets full of precious items such as rice, peppers, and peanut oil. Above, lines of laundry fluttered like banners.

The GG Coffeehouse turned out to be a large, square, richly smoky room with shaded lamps, ceiling fans, and framed French posters on the walls. It catered to a youngish, international, and somewhat bohemian clientele, and payment was accepted in yuan, francs, pounds, and dollars. I waited fifteen minutes, watching the vague, bright shapes that moved beyond the glass. A crone in a yellow headscarf squatted behind a dozen shabby cornhusk dolls. Two men passed by in rich, smooth wool coats, warm and indifferent. The taller man reached out and flicked away his cigarette butt, and, when the glowing end fell to the ground, the old crone reached out to pick it up.

A good-looking boy walked up the street, wearing a worker's rough jacket and thick shoes. His hair stood up in a cowlick on his forehead; it was cropped short, revealing strong bones, thick eyebrows, and a high-bridged nose. Only a common boy, but one with surety in every move. An alert intelligence shone in his face, raised upward, reading the business signs and awnings. He saw what he was looking for. He walked toward the coffee shop and reached for the doorknob.

Then the door swung open. It was Hu Ran.

"Young miss," he said, in the Hangzhou dialect of our childhood. His voice was a husky tenor. I couldn't stop looking at him. It was as if he'd stepped out of the street and made the whole world real.

"Hu Ran," I said. I raised my hand to him and let him take it. "I'm fine. What are you doing these days?"

"Living with my mother, in Hangzhou."

"I don't like coffee," I said.

His smile revealed even teeth. "I don't, either. I've never been here before. But I wanted to meet where nobody would know us."

As we drank our tea, I tried to overcome my fear. I watched him warily, trying to put him back behind the glass: his generous mouth, his eyes alert with energy. He was nervous. He was showing off, talking about the war. I listened to his voice, the voice of childhood made new and deep in the cadences of a familiar stranger, overlaid with the faint singsong accent of Chongqing. He told me about his own adventures in Chongqing, how he'd once carried a message on his bicycle during the blackout, in the middle of the night. He'd seen the KMT police shoot a man for smoking a cigarette during the blackout. As the man writhed and screamed, the tiny glowing tip of red light lay on the ground. Another night, he'd seen a whole truckload of men executed by the KMT for committing petty crimes.

Beneath my nods and responses, a strategy was churning in my mind. Keeping my eyes on his, I made my lips into an O and blew over its shining surface. His face wavered in the steam that rose from my cup.

"When we moved to Hangzhou," he said, "my mother had me write a letter to your mother explaining she was watching over Yinan and Yao. She hoped that it would bring your mother solace."

My mother had said nothing of this. "She has a big house," I said, defending her. "She doesn't need solace."

"That's not what my mother thinks."

I placed my hands around my teacup, seeking reassurance in its warmth. "What does your mother think?"

He raised his chin, watching me. "That true value in life comes from knowing that you've been generous to others. That possessions have no meaning when you cut yourself off from others."

"Is that what you think?"

"I don't know. I do know that I'm not interested in being rich."

What was the nature of this battle? Somehow during our conversation, the air between us had thickened and begun to glitter. I recalled the autumn sun shining through willow leaves, letting in sparkles of bright autumn sky. We had been children then.

"How is Yao?" I asked.

"He's growing. His face is changing; he looks like your mother. Sometimes he looks a little like your sister."

This remark took me by surprise. "Do you even remember Hwa?"

"I've seen her in Shanghai." Hu Ran looked into his cup. "I saw her with Weiwei, once—maybe she was on the way to a friend's house. That's how I thought to find Weiwei and give her a note for you."

"You've been to Shanghai before?"

"Dozens of times."

"Have you seen me before?"

He looked away. "Well—" He paused. "I went by the house. After I saw Weiwei and Hwa. I saw your lamp once. At least I think it was yours, in the left upstairs window. Everyone else had gone to bed. I thought you might be reading, the way Yinan does—or studying for school. You remind me of her, somehow. Not in the face."

I said nothing in reply, drawn into this notion. A tremor spread down my spine; the terror had been dormant, waiting in my blood.

I wanted to run. Instead I kept my face polite. We conversed a little more, in a desultory way, until I said that it was time for me to go.

Hu Ran took a breath. "Do you want to meet again next week?"

"Sure."

"What will you tell your mother?"

This question brought me up short. I looked into his dark eyes not revealing their color.

"I'll say I'm going for a walk with Pu Li," I said. "She approves of Pu Li."

I knew that I had won.

Hu Ran insisted on paying the bill. Due to steep inflation, he had brought his money in a heavy shoulder bag. Together we left the coffee shop. It was that time of evening when the sun seems to pause in its trail across the sky before pushing in one last quick pulse to end the day. This moment never seems as terribly still as at that time of year, with the last red embers of the winter sky disappearing into dusk. We walked for some time. My fingertips were cold, and I knew that I should find a bus. I saw it coming up the street, but moved toward it reluctantly. I did not want to go home. I didn't want to see my mother's starved face and stony eyes when I felt so powerful, so alive.

THAT NIGHT WHILE I sat brushing my hair, Hwa knocked on my door. Before Shanghai, we'd always shared a room, but now my mother said we must get used to living the way that we were meant to live. Now we had separate rooms, necessitating formal visits. It was a curious business. Hwa stood in the doorway, slender and insistent. I let her in; she closed the door, another curious business. I told her I was going to see Hu Ran again the following week. She sat firmly on the bed.

"Are you in love?" she demanded. "Do you love him?"

I hadn't expected her question and couldn't answer it immediately. "I don't think so."

Hwa shifted to one slender foot. "How do you know?"

"Know what?"

"Know when you love someone."

I might have said the truth: that I didn't know myself. I could have turned away and waited for her to leave. But there was tautness in her voice, as in a stretched rope. It made me wish to comfort her. "Of course you know," I said. "You've seen Mama, the way she feels for Baba."

Hwa said nothing.

"You know what you feel for Willy Chang," I tried again.

Hwa's lips tightened. "Don't talk about Willy."

I turned toward the mirror. I saw a slender girl with a face of oval gold, wearing loose white pajamas lit like wings in the glow of the light. I was not beautiful in the way of my mother, whose face, even in aging, held the delicate, still symmetry of intricately folded rice paper. But I was vivid and alive. Behind me stood Hwa, prim, her mouth pinched shut. She was fair, tensile, alert; soon she would also be pretty.

"No," Hwa said suddenly. "I don't want to be under anyone's power." Her eyes burned.

IT WOULD NOT happen to me, either. I wouldn't be like my grandmother, my mother, or my aunt. I could run from it, as Hwa was doing, or I could control it. If I kept hold of my own power, then no one could ever hurt me.

Hu Ran was staying in the Y, in a tiny room with a small window and unpainted walls. There was nowhere to sit but on his mattress. I sat down. He stood awkwardly. I took his wrist and pulled until he sat next to me.

Since my time in the bomb shelter, I had been reluctant to touch. I couldn't forgive my mother's silent fury, nor the ruthlessness and suffering that lay beneath it. Now Hu Ran and I were close enough to smell each other's breath. His nearness affected me like an illness. There, in the airless little room, a physical emotion was invading my senses like a rolling fog. I had a sudden need to put my hand on his bare throat. I reached through the fog and felt his solid pulse through my fingertips.

"Make love to me."

"No," he said. "I should keep you out of trouble."

I shrugged. "I want to do it."

"I feel responsible."

"That's xingyi," I said. "The loyalty of servants."

He winced. I smiled. "Young miss——"

"Stop calling me 'young miss.'"

"Hong," he said, angry. Then, more quietly, "Hong."

Once more, I reached through the fog and put my hand on his face. "Kiss me."

"Hong, this is a bad idea."

"Don't you want to?"

He looked away. "Of course I do."

I felt a tingling in my hands. "Do it," I said, "or I'll tell my mother you've done it anyway."

He reached for me angrily. His lips were very soft.

I slid my hand between the buttons of his shirt and felt the pounding of his furious heart. We held each other hard but couldn't bring each other close enough; we struggled with some unseen thing inside of us, between us. I pushed myself against him, harder and harder. I wanted to forget the terror in my blood; I wanted to journey into darkness. But it seemed to me, as we embarked upon this trip that had been waiting since we were children, that I grew more radiant and powerful than any woman had been before me. My fingertips could feel the finest differences of touch; my eyes could see through his skin; and some other sense more powerful than vision echoed through me. I could sense around our room the city in flames. The streets were turning upside down. China burned. Rulers fell away and towers crumbled. Rolling water swirled in from the sea. Through this chaos, I followed those who'd gone ahead of me: my grandmother, my mother, my father, and Yinan. I followed them hoping to belong inside the world they had made.

HE HAD BEEN TRAVELING IN DELIRIUM THROUGH AN INDETER-minate time, and he struggled out on frail legs, squinting in the light. He was aware of having escaped something, of having survived.

As soon as Junan arrived, he knew that he must leave Chongqing. He asked for an assignment, hoping to be gone long enough for everyone to forget what he had done. He didn't know how it might end. He only knew he wished to act, to finally see combat and put to rest a sense of uselessness, of shame.

But as he prepared to leave the city he could not shake the suspicion he'd forgotten something. Soon he would fly over the mountains lacking some crucial item, something that might save him, something he would miss. He asked Junan to check over her list. She went through his luggage, including vitamins and quinine pills, and assured him that not a thing was missing. As his departure neared, he knew what it was that lay unfinished. On his last day in Chongqing he went to the American woman's house.

It was that time of winter when the cold deepens but the days grow longer. The smell of burning coal flavored the air. Yinan opened the door wearing a heavy sweater, her body obscured and muffled in the bulky gray wool. At least her skin was clear, her hair was clean. She appeared well and even plump, although it seemed to him, observing her shuttered gaze, that she wasn't happy to see him. Without a word, she led him into the front room. There were heavy cushioned chairs and walnut furniture. Bookshelves sagged beneath countless English and

Chinese volumes held into place with elephant bookends. The room smelled of books, furniture polish, and an indefinable Caucasian scent.

Yinan sat with her heels together, plain and proper as a girl who'd been sent to a nunnery. He had forgotten her silences. He didn't want to stare at her, and so he looked away, but it seemed to him that the mere glimpse of her had brought him back into the dark. It was as if they sat in a lightless room where he could only sense her body in the chair and know by touch her narrow face with the faint scar on the forehead. He could almost feel between his fingertips the heavy strands of hair against her neck.

"I'm leaving," he said finally. "I'm going off to the war. I wanted to say goodbye."

She nodded.

"What happened—it was all my fault. I was lonely, I had been alone for so long. Nobody will blame you."

She sat as still as one waiting for an answer from Guan Yin.

"If you would come back to your family this would all be well again—your sister would understand. I am sure she would forgive you."

"Please, Li Ang," she said, "please consider what you feel."

She was also searching in the dark, feeling for his heart with gentle fingers. He couldn't bear to know what she might find.

He said, "You belong with them for now. Later, you can still be married."

At this, she gazed at him sadly as if she were indeed his sister and knew him truly as a sister might. She saw through his haze of activity and plans. He could tell from her expression that she knew, without judgment or doubt, that he was lost.

"I can't go back," she said. "I love you."

"Stop." Li Ang held up his hand.

"We mustn't see each other anymore," she said.

HE LEFT CHONGQING and abandoned himself to the soundless, rushing wind of luck. The following years have been left out of his stories.

I know only that his luck held out as he struggled to adapt. Pu Sijian helped him. Many times he regretted his decision to go to the front, but soon his own troubles were engulfed by a much larger and more desperate battle.

In December 1941, when the enemy at last attacked America, people celebrated in the streets, believing the Americans would crush Japan and bring the war to a quick end. But the U.S. needed to prepare, and as the long winter wore on, it grew clear that Chongqing was now vulnerable from the south. The British empire was failing. Singapore fell. Japan then assaulted Burma, perilously close to the supply line of the Burma Road. My father's division was one of many sent to Burma under the American General Joseph Stilwell. The early spring of 1942 found his regiment holding down the city of Toungoo, almost surrounded by the Japanese advance.

Over the years I've often tried to envision it: the line of Chinese soldiers stretched over the central country's hills and forests, in the midst of gunfire and of villages in flames. Japanese planes flew overhead. My father was a tiny dot on this map, smaller than a stone on a go board. And perhaps my father saw himself as a playing piece on an enormous game, under mountains crouching over them like huge men.

My father walked and slept and fought. He shot at shadows, bushes, animals, and men. More than once he killed a man. And yet every skirmish they were pushed back, they ran for cover from the planes that strafed them. They woke, pissing in their pants, to gunfire; they vomited with exhaustion and fear. The enemy used tanks and superior rifle power. Over the weeks they lost a mile, twenty miles, forty miles. Where were their reinforcements? He heard the rumor that three more divisions, including the 38th with Sun Li-jen, were behind him, but his old commander was a hundred miles away, awaiting confirmation of orders from the Generalissimo. They might have been as far away as the moon. Chiang was unwilling to sacrifice more of his best troops. My father's regiment had been given up for lost, and soon the few who remained would be run up into the hills.

The Burmese, angry after years of British rule, were not sorry to see them go. Some of them led the Japanese convoys along dirt roads, secret roads, and attacked the regiment from the rear. And so they lost Toungoo; around that time they heard the British had left Prone to their west. They lost Pyinmana. By early April, Mandalay was burning. Only the palace of kings was standing, glowing in the firelight. By mid-April, the British were in retreat, destroying precious oil fields as they went. The sky was filled with smoke and flames, the chattering of frightened monkeys. Li Ang's hair was permeated with the stink of oil and corpses.

Once he was shocked awake by engines whining overhead. He bolted from his tent in his bare feet and took shelter in the trees. There he saw General Chou Gaoyao running toward him. Not twenty feet away, Chou jerked suddenly and thumped to the ground like a sack of rice. That night, Chou was burned and his cremated remains were given to his cousin, Chou Tuyao, to carry back the family. Colonel Kwang was promoted in Chou's place. Kwang was the upright man who'd married Hsiao Meiyu; he was now the father of an infant daughter. He showed remarkable courage, leading the remains of their brigade against a Japanese brigade of twice their number. But soon it was over. To their east, the Japanese broke through the Allied line. Enemy troops cut off retreating Allied soldiers, and Li Ang's regiment was scattered to the winds.

Those who still remained began the long retreat to China. They loaded everything they could onto the few discarded British jeeps. They brought weapons and water. Behind them, the Japanese pressed on.

ONE BRIGHT, WARM morning in early spring they reached a bridge. The enemy was behind them; and before them, all around them, fled the refugees: peasants, farmers, shopkeepers. The two lanes of the bridge were dark with them.

General Mao was in command of the retreat. Li Ang went with him to view the scene, and they stood wordless for some time. They saw two empty cars abandoned in the middle of the bridge, hindering the steady flow of human traffic. The refugees walked slowly toward safety with their precious burdens: an old tin trunk; a wooden duck; an enormous bundle of dirty muslin. The warm air clung, motionless and thick with the odor of human bodies. Li Ang turned and looked toward Burma. As he stood against the moving crowd, bumping shoulder after shoulder, meeting face after face, some weeping, some intent, some expressionless, Li Ang began to feel a restlessness akin to claustrophobia. It was the density of the crowd and its silence. No one had the strength to speak. There was an unnatural absence of conversation; only exhortations— "Faster," "Over here," or sudden shouts, orders.

He turned back to face the bridge. His thigh was met by a taut rope. He stumbled and would have fallen but for the refugees surrounding him.

He realized he'd walked into a rope that stretched between a mother and her son who were heading in the opposite direction, toward Burma.

"Watch it!" said the boy. His voice rang out, a bright note of ferocity in that unnatural hush.

Li Ang met his gaze. The boy was wiry and undersized, perhaps ten years old, with a skinny face and triangular, observant eyes. He wore his hair cut short, exposing his greenish scalp. The tired mother wore a pink headscarf. He noted their empty bags and understood that they traveled across the river each day to sell items to the hordes of people who had made it to the other side. Then they would return, only to cross again with more goods, tied together at the waist to keep from losing each other in the crowd.

"What's this?" said Mao, behind him. "Keep going."

Li Ang turned sideways to make a path around the mother and son.

"Over there," Mao shouted. He pointed to their right, where the crowd had eddied. Li Ang struggled toward the pocket of empty space.

"We have to blow it up," Mao shouted. He spat and waited for Li Ang's reply. "We have to wait until the enemy has arrived—perhaps even while they're crossing—and dynamite it: blow it up."

Li Ang said, "But the bridge will still be crowded with civilians."

"You think we can invite them to cross first? Send for Chang."

Chang was a very small man—Li Ang could barely see him approaching in the crowd—but he was quick and good with guns and explosives. He sent his men to dynamite the bridge, putting the trigger at the checkpoint on the Chinese side.

Time passed. The crowd moved slowly, hushed and anxious. He watched Chang's men rigging the supports with dynamite from the Burma side. Then, when all was finished, they made their way over the bridge. The two of them— Li Ang and General Mao—were among the last in their group to cross.

Safe on the China side, Li Ang heard the faraway sound of gunfire. He stood at the checkpoint with Chang and stared at the sun-brightened cliffs, at the dark river that moved below in shadow. He couldn't stop thinking about the boy and his mother. The boy's thin lips, long chin, and big ears had been uncannily familiar; he resembled Li Ang's brother at that age.

"Hey," said Chang, "look at that guy over there."

"What guy?" Li Ang took Chang's binoculars.

"That guy in the blue smock."

Li Ang searched the crowd. Then it stood out to him: a small man crossing the bridge. It was something in the walk, he thought, that had alerted Chang. Within the peasant's clothing, he made out the stiff, implacable rhythm of the enemy.

"Japanese dressed as peasants," Chang said. "They're crossing. They're already here."

Without another word, he plunged the lever. Later, Li Ang remembered a sort of pause—a moment when nothing happened—and then a sharp explosion. For a moment the bridge appeared to float, weightless in the air. Then the middle section buckled—wood swaying, breaking, falling sideways—and a thousand screams filled their ears. Through Chang's binoculars, Li Ang watched the blue-clad man take one more stiff step, then tilt, fall to his knees, and slide off of the bridge. Around him, flailing, men and women dropped, some headfirst and others at odd angles. A woman in an indigo blouse, clinging to a sliding timber, dropped her bundle—a child—and jumped after it into the water.

Near the Chinese side and close to safety, the small figure of the woman in a pink kerchief slipped, fell back, dangled over the edge. Her full bag, harnessed to her waist and shoulders, dragged her down. But she was tied to something on the bridge—another figure, straining, holding to the wooden railing. Then slowly, as Li Ang watched, the son's grip failed. He slipped and hurtled after his mother.

On the Chinese side, the crowd surged off the road. Shouts rang out as people were trampled, separated.

Li Ang stayed where he was. He was one of the few who'd been protected by the knowledge of what was about to happen. This fact weighed upon him, rendering him unable to take a step. He understood that there was nothing lucky about him. There had never been. He would survive to old age, and he would remember everything that he had ever done.

LATER, ONE OF the men picked up a straggling dog and refused to let it go. He fed it scraps of food, gave it precious water, petted it. Li Ang and Pu Sijian argued privately about whether General Kwang should leave the dog behind. There were twenty-eight survivors, including four wounded, all of them suffering in various degrees from exhaustion, terror, and malarial fever. They had shed all but the essentials. How could they be wasting precious food upon a dog?

The roads were terrible. Around him Li Ang saw the detritus of an empire: washbasins, clothing, birdcages still containing expired cockatoos and parrots. Empty marmite jars. A teddy bear face down in the dust. Discarded, bloodstained bandages. Dust. Abandoned shells of vehicles lying like fossils in the road, burned out by those who'd reached this place before them and were trying to ensure that they stayed ahead of the enemy. Behind them were the Japanese, moving, someone said, more than twenty miles a day. Li Ang and Pu Sijian were assigned rearguard duty and the care of stragglers. Two of the wounded men died after a few days. Two more held on, limping. Li Ang went back repeatedly to round them up. He couldn't bear to let them go. But apathy, fright, and disappointment humbled him. Somehow he had cut his left foot. The toes were red and swollen and would not bend.

Mao had been trampled by the crowd rushing off the bridge. Pu Sijian was thin and shaking from malaria. Then General Kwang was bitten by a snake. Li Ang was the only officer fit enough to take his place. He struggled to hold on to the remaining men, but almost every morning someone was dead or missing. Men died of chills, bundled in rags despite the balmy weather. Or men wandered off in search of privacy, only to find themselves surrendering amid the dripping trees, the elephants and monkeys, flies, mosquitoes, termites, and ants. They gave in to swollen, dripping, pus-filled wounds, scabies, dysentery, and beriberi. One evening, the dog's caretaker disappeared. Another soldier shot the dog and roasted it.

Red streaks ran up Li Ang's foot. He scanned the corpses as they passed, searching for a larger boot. Meanwhile, Pu Sijian sank deeper into fever. He fell and lay with his Bible tucked into his jacket, his thin hands twitching in delirium. Before the fever took his mind, he reminded Li Ang to look after his wife and son, and Li Ang promised that he would. He tried to keep his friend alive, taking turns with the twelve remaining men to carry him on the makeshift pallet of bamboo and rags. The fever stammered Pu's bones, shaking him so hard the bamboo pallet poles rattled in their hands.

In his last days, waves of delirium overwhelmed Pu's orderly mind. He believed he had been captured and was being hauled away by the enemy. He believed he would soon be ransomed, traded for an airplane. He stopped quoting the Bible and began to cry out for Li Ang to rescue him, struggling powerfully against his captors. However there came a time when this manic power faded. He shrank tight against his bones, and he grew tiny in his pallet.

"Li Ang!" he called, hoarse and high and haunted.

"I'm here."

Pu gave no sign of having heard him. "Li Ang! Come after me!" Then he took one last great shiver and departed.

LI ANG WAS brought to a hospital in Kunming where he knew nobody. There, four of his toes were amputated and the nurses treated him as if he'd had his testicles removed, chanting silly rhymes as they spooned gruel into his mouth and turned him over on the cot. His friend had died; his brother was lost. He couldn't sleep. His missing toes throbbed, then itched, then throbbed again. Although he was given quinine, his malaria lingered, and he floated in his bed like a leaf on water, wobbling around a spout of images. He saw a child's crying face. A snaggle-haired woman nursed a baby at her breast. A mother and son, roped together, fell over a bridge.

"Li Ang!"

It was Hu Mudan. Her small face floated in front of his.

"Go away," he said.

"Li Ang! I know you're awake."

"Leave me alone. I'm taking quinine. "

"Listen to me, you fool—"

She didn't like him. Never had.

"Do you hear me, Li Ang? You must see Yinan when you come back to Chongqing."

The whirling stopped upon her name. "Yinan," he said.

"It is important."

"I can't do that," he said. "We have an agreement."

Finally she left. She did not return, and he grew sorry he had wished her gone.

His feet ached and itched. His fever broke and receded, leaving him light-headed and glazed with weakness. Echoes sounded in his mind. Every night he dreamed. He and Li Bing stood on the bridge. Around them, the world was shattering. Then the bridge cracked open between them and Li Bing vanished.

Junan came to visit him in Kunming. She set a framed photograph of his daughters beside the bed. She refused to bring the newspaper, but read him poetry and kung fu novels. Whenever his fever returned, she was always sitting by the bed, calm and strong, wiping his forehead with a damp cloth.

One afternoon, he tried to tell her. "It's as if something is missing."

"Your foot will heal soon. They'll put a cushion in your shoe and you should walk quite normally."

He didn't mention it again.

The winds of history passed over him. The American general Joseph

Stilwell took command of the regiments that had escaped to India. There, he and General Sun planned a new push through the Japanese line in a startling offensive from the west. Meanwhile, the Japanese approached from the east. Once again they had tanks, artillery, and supplies. The Chinese foot soldiers had no vehicles and a mishmash of weapons of indeterminate age and origin. Each soldier marched with a rice ration tied around his neck. Refugees crowded the trains; they clung to cowcatchers and slept upon the roofs of cars. When Guilin fell, the boarded doors of empty buildings were pasted with black and red strips of paper calling for resistance.

He was training troops in Kunming when the Americans bombed Hiroshima and Nagasaki. Following the Japanese surrender, he was promoted to general and rewarded for extraordinary valor. But there was little time to celebrate. With the defeat of the Japanese, a new war had begun. Li Bing and his comrades had done well in the countryside, and the country lay on the verge of falling to the Communists. Li Ang was given a job training Nationalist troops. They would try to hold the country for as long as they could. But the possibility of defeat, of flight, became inevitable. In the spring of 1948, Li Ang was transferred, "temporarily," to Taiwan. There he had regular messages from Junan and sometimes from his daughters. There was no word from Yinan or from his brother.

IT WAS WHILE STATIONED IN TAIWAN THAT HE GREW CERTAIN some part of him was missing. No crisis brought on this clarity. It was more like a calming period, with the world growing clear and light, his perceptions gradually more lucid. He became aware once more of his singular dilemma. He didn't miss his old belief that he would escape the world unscathed. This had gone away with his sure step and unthinking vigor. Those gifts had never belonged to him. Something else, something more essential, had been stolen.

When he remembered Chongqing, with its heat and its steep, crowded steps, the houses and streets so quickly built and rapidly destroyed, those memories were more distinct and vivid than the world outside his door. In that time he had been present and alive, in the possession of some understanding that was now withheld from him. He remembered Chongqing day and night; his memories were like an illness that caused everything around him to fade into the world of a dream.

She had said she was in love with him. He had known that this was true, but her artlessness, her candor, had unsettled him. Once she had made her declaration, there was no way to disregard what had happened.

"You mustn't come to see me," she had said, and he had not gone after her; and yet his soul had followed her, somehow faithful to a bond he hadn't recognized. He didn't know exactly when she had begun to haunt his mind. It was simply that he'd come, over the years, to think of the time following his affair with Wang Yinan—when he'd left

Chongqing and gone into the field and everything that followed—as a kind of aftermath. Nothing of those years was worth his interest, not even his promotion to general. Only a certain time held power: those months when he and Yinan had been together in Chongqing.

He wrote to Junan, "Have you had word from your sister?" It was as far as he dared go. Her replies were blithe and filled with news—news of her house, of their two growing daughters, of Pu's widow—but there was no mention of Yinan. There had been no reconciliation.

Most likely Yinan had found another man. He hoped she'd done so. Even so, he wondered, and his wondering was like a phantom pain. He was a boy again, marked proudly with his shallow scars, anticipating some quick cash at the paigao game of a local merchant. He was a young man on his wedding night, with his watertight confidence and high hopes, his heart beating rapidly, peering in at windows. In the next room awaited his fate dressed in a shimmering bridal robe. Instead, he found himself looking through the window at a young girl wearing moth-colored pajamas.

She had taken something from him. She held in her hands a piece of his desire. Without it he was crippled.

JUNAN WROTE THAT the family would soon join him in Taiwan. From this calm message he understood that the situation in Shanghai had grown acute. The city would soon fall. They would be together at last, she said.

He drank too much to celebrate the Lunar New Year. He lay adrift in his room, entertaining the cacophony of voices, young men carousing outside his window. Perhaps they were his own men, who might not suspect that they had been uprooted from their homes for good and that they had already embarked upon the lives of emigrants.

"Li Ang! Li Ang!" Once again, Hu Mudan's small face floated before his.

"What is it?"

"You drunken fool, you need to hurry. You still have this chance to find her."

"Yinan is on the mainland. Far away now."

"You know your side will lose the country. If you don't go see her now, the Communists will cut you off."

Hu Mudan had aged in the last few years. Her small, almond eyes had sunk into her face; there were deeper lines in the corners of her mouth. Time had worn her down, as it would wear them all down.

THE FOLLOWING WEEK he flew to Shanghai. An American he knew from Kunming, a pilot for the old National airline, was flying in to get some friends out of the country. Li Ang arranged to fly with him. He wouldn't tell Junan. He planned to send a telegram to the Hangzhou Methodist Church. Then he would take the train to Hangzhou, where he would go to the church and ask for the American woman. She would know where Yinan was. He did not rehearse what he would say to Yinan when he saw her. He wasn't even certain as to the purpose of his visit. He wished to see her, that was all, and his need to do this superseded any message.

The plane approached the Yangtze, following the wide delta inland. Below he could see the Communist Eighth Army gathering. There were thousands massing on the north bank, waiting. The land was black with them. In the river itself a few dozen junks and barges gathered. South of the river, he saw nothing.

As he watched the collection of the army that would bring down the city, Li Ang recalled, from years before, the story of Wu Shao, the boy who had stolen Wang Baoding's lunch in the fourth grade. He remembered Baoding leaning toward him, his pinched face marbled with wine, his long, shrewd eyes and pale lips. "This was a boy with no decent family, no education, no property, no money . . . He was hungry." Li Ang knew now that Baoding had been speaking of him. Li Ang wondered what Baoding would have thought now. But Baoding was long vanished, killed, or scattered by the Japanese he had discounted.

Li Ang's foot throbbed. The blood vessels had been injured and it was painful to sit still. The ghost toes tingled and he longed to wiggle them, to scratch them. The air was thin; his eyelids twitched; he drifted into sleep. Again he saw, this time from above, the banquet table. He saw his brother listening and watching. "Young man. Do you know what makes me so curious about your Army's arrangements with the Communist Party? It's that you don't seem to know that as soon as the Japanese threat diminishes, the Communists will not hesitate to turn and stab you in the back."

And then he was no longer at the wedding. Or perhaps his thoughts simply abandoned him, following a wandering path that had been made by the malaria. To the north, the Communist foot soldiers were still gathering in orderly groups, the junks and barges collecting on the river. Closer to Shanghai, the land was terraced into painstaking paddies green and lush. He saw below him rows of peasants in their blue and brown rags, digging trenches and erecting bamboo palisades around the city. Within the city itself, he saw department stores; the embassies, besieged islands in the turbulence. He saw the smoke from small coal fires as people warmed their hands; he saw beleaguered banks assailed by throngs clamoring for gold.

The peril in return was that it made you think. Watching from above, Li Ang wondered at the path his life had taken. If he'd remained in the countryside where he was born, would he have joined the Nationalists? Or would he be on the other side, clustering north of the river, waiting to rush into the city and reclaim it for the countryside that fed it? He recalled his brother pressed against the wall of the student dormitory, the curve of his ear, the shape of his head barely visible in the morning light.

HOURS LATER, on the ground, Shanghai flew before his eyes in vivid splinters—tragic and absurd, half familiar, half strange. He saw a young woman—slender and familiar, dressed in an old pair of trousers and a loose blouse. He hurried closer, but when the woman turned, her face was that of a stranger. "Got anything to sell?" she cawed. He exchanged his gold coin for a stack of soapy dollars. They had been washed and ironed in order to fetch more money at the exchange. He passed a small stationery stand and entered it. Inside, the familiar smell of paper and ink made his hands tremble.

"Where can I send a telegram?"

But the man only frowned; perhaps he spoke another dialect.

He left the store and wandered back into the street. The city was filled with trouble: broken people, broken faces. He considered his next move.

It was then when he thought he heard someone call out to him by name. "Li Ang! Li Ang!" He shivered and walked faster.

"Li Ang!" Closer now. Slowly, Li Ang turned.

A small, middle-aged man flew toward him, ignoring traffic signs and dodging other pedestrians. Not a military man; this much was clear from his excited face and his open manner. He seized Li Ang's hand in his. "Chen Da-Huan," he said. "It's me, Chen Da-Huan, from Hangzhou, long ago, before the Occupation. It's a small wonder you don't remember me. It's been over ten years."

Gradually the name rose through the layers of years past. The Chens had been neighbors of Junan's family in Hangzhou. The father, Old Chen, had been at the paigao game and he had also been the witness at the wedding. Staring now at Chen Da-Huan, Li Ang recalled the father, a small man in a perfectly pressed British double-breasted suit, waving a pigeon's egg in his chopsticks.

"Chen Da-Huan," Li Ang said.

"Too much has happened. I had heard that you were wounded. You seem like you have been through something. But you're still healthy, still alive."

"I can get around well enough."

"From what I've heard that means that you're a lucky one."

Li Ang nodded, looking closely at Chen. He had suffered something—this was clear enough from his prematurely aged eyes, similar to soldiers' eyes, but without the weariness of soul that came from seeing and from causing violent death.

Chen spoke in the familiar Hangzhou dialect, ". . . brother and I went to the Lianda University. After this, during the war, I finally sent for Yang Qingwei and married her in Kunming."

Yes, Li Ang recalled: Chen Da-Huan had fallen in love with a friend of Junan's, Yang Qingwei, and they'd been separated during the Occupation. "That's good news," he said. "What are you doing in Shanghai?"

"We've been visiting a specialist." He paused. "She is pregnant. But she has suffered a relapse of her tuberculosis. I'm afraid that she will die."

Li Ang shook his head. He dimly remembered Yang Qingwei, a gentle girl with a wistful smile. He would never have expected her to survive the Occupation, the journey to Kunming, and the war.

"I'm surprised to see you here. I'd heard you were in Taiwan," Chen Da-Huan said.

"I am back—briefly."

"A strange time to return, my friend."

Li Ang said, "Business."

Chen Da-Huan nodded. He looked exhausted—gray-faced, and with those haunted eyes.

"How long have you been traveling?" Li Ang asked. "You should rest."

Chen Da-Huan shook his head. "I have an appointment. I'm going to see a man—it has to do with money to help Qingwei."

"Who is he?"

"A man of influence—I'm trying to buy gold at the official rate and sell it on the black market. Over the years, with all the troubles, we lost the house in Hangzhou and the house in the countryside. The place in Shanghai we sold after the war. It had been ravaged and we couldn't keep it up. Plus the prices were down—and still dropping. We had property to the north, in the countryside. But the people of the countryside—" He stopped speaking. "A darkness is coming, a darkness I would never have imagined. We are nobody now, we have nothing. Soon we will be lost. And Qingwei—she began to cough up blood . . . There were doctors—one I know of here—that might still be of help. But with this inflation . . . When we left for Shanghai, I had four million yuan. I thought that this would see us through to Hong Kong. But during our journey, prices have gone up many times—" he broke off and looked away. "I don't have enough," he said. "We got as far as Shanghai. I took her to the specialist. He said the only help for her is in Hong Kong."

Li Ang thought of his travel funds. He had been warned of the inflation and had brought, in case of trouble, an extra wallet of gold coins. He had scarcely thought about Chen Da-Huan since his marriage. But the man's own story—his faithfulness, persisting love, their union, and now her death—had played out in that space of time. He reached into his bag and brought out the coins.

"Please," he said. "Take this."

"I can't accept."

"My father-in-law was a good friend of your father's. He would certainly want me to give you this."

He wanted Chen to go away. He held out the wallet, pushed it into Chen's hands. Would it be enough? He found his monogramed, gold cigarette case, opened it, shook out the cigarettes, and put them in his pocket. He held out the case.

"Li Ang, this is too much."

"But not the cigarettes! Now, those are precious. Save the case and wait for a good time to barter it. I have to leave now. Please. I have to go." He swallowed. "Let me know what happens."

Chen Da-Huan nodded. His eyes shone with a painful light.

Li Ang said, "Be careful."

"Yes. Yes." He bowed, dazed. "Our family will show our thanks somehow, someday. We will be grateful to you forever." Clutching the gold, he stood on the sidewalk staring as Li Ang hurried away.

Li Ang found himself favoring his foot. Would he make it to Hangzhou? He must wire money to Yinan and tell her to leave. It had been right to give the purse to Chen, but if he was going to help Yinan, he must save the rest of his gold.

He was thirsty. He felt out of his element in Shanghai, especially in this newer part of the city. A strong smell of salt water and a stiff breeze told him he was getting closer to the warehouses and docks. Someone told him of a telegraph transmitter near a certain teahouse. But after that, each man he asked would gaze at him from head to toe and say that he did not know where such a teahouse was. No one else had heard of it. After several minutes he began to suspect that he had misunderstood his instructions. Finally, he bumbled around a corner and through a courtyard, where he heard the dishes clinking and the welcome sound of voices.

He followed the sounds, through the courtyard and along a balustrade until he came upon a teahouse with an old sign over the door. It was a large, well-built room, with dark woodwork framing airy latticed windows. The place was busy. He stopped in the doorway. Several of the men glanced up, and he heard someone behind him.

The proprietor approached him. "What can I do for you?" he asked. He sounded friendly enough, but he spoke as if something were on his mind. Li Ang looked over the room again. Two men near the window were playing go, and white was nearly surrounded.

"I'd like to send a telegram," he said.

"I am sorry," the man replied. "I don't think that we can help you."

"What's this about?" Li Ang wanted to leave. These people were irritating, without manners. Someone had moved behind him, just a little too close.

"I am sorry," the man said again. He shifted almost imperceptibly closer to the doorway, glancing at the entrance. The hair rose on the back of Li Ang's neck. Cold metal pressed against his ear.

"Don't move."

All around him, men stopped watching and turned back to their business.

Someone else entered the room, this time from the kitchen. He was an older man, with a military crewcut and a blunt face from which two shrewd eyes looked out.

"That's him. That is Major General Li Ang."

They seized him and bound his hands.

WHEN SHE WAS AN OLD WOMAN AND THE PAST BEGAN TO HOLD her interest more than ordinary time, Hu Mudan spent afternoons revisiting her memories. She said she felt the recollections moving in her bones. She spoke of her childhood in Sichuan, of working in the fields under a fiery yolk that soaked the world in sweat and heat. She described the years after she left our house and returned with Hu Ran to the village of her childhood. And she told me stories about Chanyi, her best friend. She spoke of Chanyi's gentleness, her generosity and frail heart. She described Chanyi's love for Junan and the way old Mma had finally forbidden Chanyi to spend so much time playing with her daughter.

When Junan had first learned to stand, Chanyi had even worried that the child might feel cramping in her toes—as if she might have passed the misery on somehow, as if there were a memory of the body, handed down from mother to daughter along with the texture of her hair or the shape of her face. Junan had showed no sign of trouble. But as she learned to walk and run, her blithe energy had filled Chanyi with a secret apprehension. Without the crushing pain, the shame of immobility, what would teach her daughter the inevitable grief of womanhood? Chanyi would not, could not bear to do it. That was how my mother came to move with such casual grace. Her confidence sprang from her feet and her ambition followed. It was her mother who grew weary. When Junan was only twelve, Chanyi sought the peace of West Lake, leaving Junan alone to learn her grief.

—

IF I COULD transmit my own memories, transfuse them through the blood, I would have my daughters know what happened between me and Hu Ran.

But my daughters would find my memories hard to understand. They were raised with the modern certainty that love must overcome all boundaries. Their faith in love and in the power of their own lives is so strong that both of them have put off happy romances to pursue their ambitions in education, travel, or work. On occasion they have also happily put off these interests for the sake of romance. They wouldn't truly understand how difficult it was for me to accept my feelings for Hu Ran. They would be puzzled. And of course I can't expect them to know what I went through. We can never understand our children or our parents. Perhaps it is this ignorance that gives each young generation the confidence to live.

Hu Ran and I had nothing to guide us. In the space of an hour, I pushed us recklessly beyond the borders of friendship, decency, and class. Years before, I'd spied him naked behind the willow tree, and my curiosity had led to our separation. Now these impulses, blocked by our parents, had rediscovered us, and although this time they led to our reunion, we had both grown old enough to know that what we were doing was unthinkable. And so we loved each other with the cruelty of frightened people. Our love was not tranquil and not always kind. I hurt him with information and he wounded me with secrecy. He thought I took my wealth for granted, and I thought that he was oversensitive about his poverty. I didn't know it at the time, but we were mirroring the struggle all around us. It was the country's struggle living through our actions and our words.

I had fulfilled my wish: I had burst forth into the world of Yinan and my father. But my terror didn't leave. It could be temporarily dispelled by the presence of Hu Ran, but with every parting it returned, as fierce as ever. I might be sitting in school, staring at a page of English, or out walking with Pu Li with our mothers' full permission, when the shadow of my anxiety would fall over my eyes.

And so I told my mother I played basketball, and when that time was not enough, I told her I was seeing Pu Li. I told her Pu Li and I went out walking in the city gardens. This was not a lie. Pu Li and I did go out walking. I made sure of it, and I made sure to tell Hu Ran about it. I told Hu Ran it was necessary to go to the movies now and then with Pu Li and his mother. I told him it was necessary for me to be seen holding Pu Li's hand. But I didn't tell Pu Li I was seeing Hu Ran. I clung to a few placid visits with Pu Li against the swirling current of the more passionate relationship. It was a way to remind myself that my old life, my proper self, was still within my reach.

ON THE NARROW bed in his small room, we talked more than I'd ever talked to anyone except my sister. Hu Ran was old enough to remember things that Hwa could not. He remembered Hangzhou, while Hwa had left the city when she was barely three. He could recall the days when my parents had dressed up to eat at Lou Wai Lou. He remembered Charlie Kong; he told me Charlie Kong had died of apoplexy after a celebration on the evening of the Japanese surrender. Hu Ran had other news. Hu Mudan was working for a rich Methodist convert. Yinan was growing fluent in English and helped the church as a translator. The old family residence was occupied by soldiers.

I told Hu Ran what it was like to live inside my mother's cold house. I described the money she had harvested from keeping supplies my father had gotten and selling them on the black market. She was now hoarding the old furniture and other odds and ends of her mahjong winnings. And she kept her money in gold bars, hidden in a place so secret that even Hwa, with her observant eye, couldn't discern it.

"She once told Hwa and me," I told him, "that in the modern world, three things give power to a woman. Houses, money, and jewelry."

Hu Ran stretched his mouth into a wry grimace. "What do you think?"

I looked away. "I think what matters is love."

After a moment he answered, "Yes. But say you have the love. Let's say that love is something you deserve as a fundamental right. Is there something else you'd want? Something you'd like to do?"

The words came quickly. "I always thought . . ." What had I begun to say? "I always wanted to be some kind of writer, a poet, or even a journalist."

"That sounds like a good idea."

Such reckless talk. "Here's what I want," I said, and traced my hand along his collarbone. He turned to me, and I lost myself in the new, inchoate powers of freedom and passion.

For all our sharing, there were certain subjects that Hu Ran and I did not discuss. We didn't talk about the civil war, the struggle for the fate and heart of China. And we didn't dare bring up the subject of our future.

Whenever I mentioned the civil war, Hu Ran tried to change the subject. He said he didn't want to worry me. Slowly I began to see that the Nationalists, my father's kind, were a part of Hu Ran's geography in the way of a close friend, or, I thought once, idly watching a chess game at the coffeehouse, in the same way a black pawn might be aware of every white piece on the board. I grew more careful, matching his canniness with my own, reaching for as many tricks as I could find in order to get him to reveal bits of information. Hu Ran was a part of the Communist underground, the underground so influential and so large that it had become an open secret.

Since childhood, I had assumed that he and I would find each other. Even when we were apart, I had assumed we had a life together, perhaps imaginary, but always existing, always constant. But now that our meetings were dependent on desire, I saw more clearly everything we didn't share. I went to my expensive school; I lived in a beautiful house. One of my mother's necklaces was worth more than Hu Ran had ever earned. Sometimes I hated her for owning them, hated her wealth. But even as his body came together with mine, even as I tried to hurt my mother with each act I did, I heard an echo of her voice, telling me that what Hu Ran and I shared was nothing.

—

ONE SATURDAY DURING the New Year holidays I received a note that read: "Hong, please see me at the regular place as soon as possible. IMPORTANT."

I went to find Hwa. "I need to leave the house," I said. "Will you tell Ma that you think I'm out with Pu Li?"

"Jiejie," she said, "don't you think you're being disloyal to Pu Li?"

"What about it?"

"He really likes you."

"Look, Hwa," I said, "I think Pu Li is a nice person, but I can't imagine what kind of girl would be romantically interested in him."

Hwa would understand; she was smitten with the charismatic Willy Chang. But to my surprise, Hwa didn't answer. She stood quite still for a moment. I turned around, picked up my jacket, and walked out of the door.

The sky had just descended; soon there would be rain. As I hurried toward the coffeehouse, I spied Hu Ran in the window. I waved at him. He saw me but did not wave back. Instead he rose immediately from his chair.

"Ran," I said. I slid into the seat opposite and tapped the table. "Ran? What's going on?"

"You have to come with me," he said.

"I just got here. I'd like a cup of tea."

"Your father has been captured, here in Shanghai."

I stood up. My mind had slowed to a crawl. I tried to find a question, the right question, but there were too many. Was he all right? How had he been captured? Why was he in Shanghai and not Taiwan? But before I could speak, Hu Ran broke in.

"Come on."

We hurried along the street, searching for an empty bicycle cab. Hu Ran told me that the rumor of my father's capture had reached Hangzhou the night before.

"What should we do now?"

"I asked my mother what to do. She told me to come up here to

Shanghai and find your father's brother, Li Bing. He's a colonel now, and she said that only he would have the power to free your father. If you come with me, your uncle will know that I'm not lying."

Hu Ran paused, gazing at the street; his arm shot up and an empty cab came toward us. The seats were flecked with raindrops. Hu Ran gave an address and the driver grunted as if they shared an understanding. We rode for some time without a word. The rain grew heavier. Along the street, the men in shirts and vests began to roll up their display clothes, bundling up their nylon stockings, medicines, and gadgets. A man adjusted the currency exchange on a sign outside a booth: the yuan had been devalued a dozen times that day. One house had boarded windows and padlocks on the doors. A classmate had lived there; his father worked for the government and the family had left for Taiwan in late January.

I thought about my mother's frequent words, *when we return.* It seemed to me that the refrain had been put into use without any one person being responsible for deciding we would leave. *When we return, I'll plant a peach tree. When we return, I'll have an iron fence put up around the house.* When had she begun to bend her plans toward our escape? No wonder she had missed my sneaking around. Every day, more of our things were packed away. Recently I'd come upon Weiwei standing still with a broom in her hand and I had sensed she didn't see me. She had told my mother that she wished to stay on the mainland. Certain books and papers had vanished from the shelves and I suspected, from the smell of burning, where they'd gone. I could see the disappearing words from books and magazines that were no longer wise to keep, rising from our chimney in a thin stream of smoke.

I HADN'T SEEN my uncle since the night when I had glimpsed him fleeing Japanese soldiers. I had stood behind the door and he had told me to go back inside. Since that time, I had grown taller than my mother. As Hu Ran and I rode through the crowded street, I wondered, how would Li Bing know me? How did I know myself? In the last few weeks, my mind and body had gone through so many changes that those years in Hangzhou had taken place in another life. *My name is Li Hong*, I recited to myself. *I am your brother's daughter, and we once all lived together in the house on Haizi Street, in Hangzhou. I was your favorite and only niece, who sat and played upon your lap. Have you forgotten?*

Yet when we arrived at the teahouse, he took one look and hurried toward me. Had he not done so, I might not have recognized him.

My uncle had become a soldier. He stood before me, a slight, sun-stained man in uniform. He wore a cap with the red star recently adopted by the New Fourth Army; his stark cheekbones under his spectacles threw a triangle of shadow beneath.

"Xiao Hong," he said. "You're a grown woman now." His teeth were stained with cigarettes. He looked from me to Hu Ran and back again. "What are you doing here?"

"This is Hu Ran," I said. "We need your help."

My uncle bent toward us, his face lined and grave. Hu Ran relayed the information he had heard from Cheng, a man in Hangzhou, whom Li Bing had heard about but never met.

Li Bing also knew about the place where my father had been captured. The name of the teahouse had barely left Hu Ran's mouth when Li Bing seized me by the arm and hurried us out the door.

He was silent in the cab, seeming not to notice the crowded street or the raindrops on his face. I imagined he was thinking of his memories of my father, of their boyhood together in Hangzhou. Perhaps he felt regret that they had come to this end. It was impossible to tell.

At last, he collected himself. He turned to me and, in the light, ironic voice I remembered, he asked, "You were startled at the sight of me, Hong. Surely I'm not a stranger now?"

"No," I said. "But I haven't seen you in more than ten years. It seems—" I frowned. "It seems that you've changed." I found it difficult to put my observation into words: an economy and purpose to my uncle's very movements. I finally blurted, "You seem to be living with some idea in mind."

He relaxed in a faint smile.

"You share with the women of your family a rare perceptiveness. But I'm not living for an idea. It is more that the idea is living through me. There is the great purpose: there are plans and expectations. It is as if I'm not a person but a piece of an immense design. Sometimes, when I'm with my comrades, even in the middle of an important discussion, I get a sense that I'm not even in the room. I watch myself: I'm speaking, but I don't know who is putting words into me. It seems to me that we are like a boat in an enormous wind. Our sails are stretched high and taut; we have only the most arrogant illusion of our own control. And the wind could change—I keep expecting it to change. Sometimes I can feel it, tricky, ready to smash us up."

He kept speaking, in a torrent of words. Once my father had come to his aid; now my father needed his help. My father—so generous, so blinded by optimism, had been always so soft-headed beneath his seeming strength. He wasn't surprised that my father, for all his quick intelligence, had been seized at random by a small cadre of activists. He had always been like that, so sure of himself that he was always blundering into traps, never knowing when he was under the power of another: man or woman. With that statement, Li Bing stopped himself. For a moment he didn't speak. Then he turned to me. They had captured my father, it was true, but did we blame them for what they did? Was it such a bad thing to hold the ideals of Communism, to give to poor men and women some power of their own, a sense of something at stake? Was it such a surprise that, if they were given freedom from the men who stood over them, they would take up arms to defend this freedom, make a move against the fate that bound them to such suffering?

I listened and said nothing, for I sensed he was not speaking to me. Next to me, Hu Ran nodded, to comfort him.

An hour later, when my father stepped out of the back room, the light spilled behind him, his tall shape traced by the silver rays, his face thrown into shadow. For a moment he was the image I had so long treasured, pure qi poised to leave the ground. I felt that he was somehow different from every other human being: brighter, with his strengths outlined against the light of heaven. Then he came toward me and this image vanished. I saw his shadowed face, his wrinkled clothes, and, in each step, the injury that had destroyed his walk, the moment of hesitation after he put his right foot down.

"Hong," he said. His words came to me softly, as if he were speaking from a distance. "Daughter. And Hu Ran."

Hu Ran said, "General Li."

When my father saw his brother standing with us, he could not find words of greeting. For a long moment, they stood before each other, looking.

Li Bing moved toward him. "Gege."

"Didi." Most of the room was watching, but my father and uncle didn't see.

"Gege," Li Bing repeated. He took my father's arm. "Please sit." He led my father to a table. "Please sit with me for a moment. This has all been an error. I apologize for what happened. I didn't know that it was you until Hu Ran found me. I would have come right away."

Li Bing turned to Hu Ran. "Thank you, thank you so much," he said. My father grinned at Hu Ran and saluted him.

Then my uncle turned to me. "Hong, go home and wait for your father. We have some catching up to do. He should be there in an hour or two." He gestured for tea. Hu Ran and I left the room. I saw them leaning toward each other, my father's features hidden by the steam rising from his cup. Years afterward, when he told this story, my father never revealed what they said to one another.

HU RAN HAILED another bicycle cab and gave the driver the address of the Y. For several blocks, we jounced under the awning without speaking. It was cold and wet. I trained my eyes out on the shabby shops with their colored paper signs and advertisements fluttering bravely in the rain.

Finally, Hu Ran said, "So I hear your marriage has been promised to Pu Li."

"No, that isn't true," I made haste to explain. "You know my mother is friends with his mother." His expression didn't change. "Well, I don't think my mother really likes his mother. But I think," I tried to explain, "that our fathers were friends."

"A perfect match."

"No," I insisted. The cab wheel dipped into a puddle, and I clutched the side. "Pu Li and I aren't engaged," I said. "That's just something my mother told Pu Taitai, many years ago. I'm sure that she's forgotten it."

"Why are you sure?"

His gaze was too intense. "I never thought about it," I said.

"Do you really think your mother would forget about anything?"

My mind moved slowly. "Why would she promise Pu Taitai?"

He shrugged. "They say Pu Taitai is a generous woman," he said. "Maybe she has done your mother a favor of some kind."

"My mother needs no favors."

"Do you like Pu Li?"

I watched the cabbie's churning legs. I thought of Pu Li, small and solid—not quite my height—with his head of thick, soft hair and a fair, round face. He had a good-natured calm that I found comforting.

"Why do you want to know?"

"I heard you're all but married to Pu Li."

I said nothing. I remembered Pu Li's words years before, under the bombs, in the shelter. "Your mother promised my mother," he'd said.

"I don't understand," I said. "What if it is true? I still can't imagine it happening."

"Well, it will happen unless you object."

We listened to the rain hitting the awning.

"Why don't you stand up to your mother? Do you want to be under her heel for your whole life?"

I remembered my mother's words to Hu Mudan, ". . . and take that brat with you." I wanted to explain to Hu Ran that it was not so simple.

I struggled to control my voice. "Why do you care?" I asked. "You won't have to leave. This country will be yours."

He sat still for a moment. His gaze moved out past the cabbie's laboring back. "Or you could stay here, Hong. Stay with me."

"Do you want me to?"

"This country could be ours."

So suddenly it had opened up: the chance for me to choose my fate. My mother had tried to keep me safe as if behind a glass. Now I could be out in the world with Hu Ran, his mother, and my aunt. I could leave my mother behind and live a life of passion. I could stay and live out China's future.

Hu Ran reached out and took my hand. We sat together in the cab like well-behaved children, resting in the eye of a great storm. In a moment, the ride would stop. The world would come whirling back and we would find it altered past imagining.

"I'll stay with you," I said.

Hu Ran's voice was gentle. "Are you sure, Hong?"

"I'm sure."

He reached under his jacket. When he opened his palm he held the pendant of green jade that he'd tried to give to me when we were only children.

"My mother was given this pendant by your grandmother Chanyi," he said. "She said it was a sign of friendship and love, and that it would connect the giver to the receiver, always, no matter what happened. I am older now. I'm sure my mother and your grandmother would understand."

I bent my head, and he put the pendant over it. The chain was cool against my throat, but the jade was warm.

LATER, WHEN WE left his room, the soft light was dazzling, and from the cab it seemed to me that we were all underwater. We moved slowly, as if submerged, and all around us the drenched colors were more vivid than before. It was as if my decision had finally dissolved the boundary that separated me from the world. Now I was in the middle of a vast sea, bobbing alongside every person in the city. Thousands floated past, clutching bundles and belongings. A woman with a brilliant red umbrella flicked a shimmering raindrop at my window. A rickshaw runner moved alongside. I could smell cauliflower and soy sauce in his low, heavy breath.

It was some time before we reached my street. The lofty elms stretched over us; I'd never seen their leaves so green, their trunks so black. They dripped on the timid mansions, many boarded up against the flood of change. Soon, soldiers would tear the boards away. Soon, the houses and everything inside them would be reclaimed. Soon. But my mother's house was brightly lit as if by her strength and will, radiating from within, and as we walked up the path, I felt an odd tremor of fear.

Hu Ran and I went through the door.

My father and uncle were there. I could hear them from the foyer, and as I came toward the front room, I could also hear my mother's voice. Nearby sat Hwa, watchful, knowing always when she must behave. She'd been getting ready for a New Year's party when the men had come, and she still wore her bright red blouse, pressed perfectly until the silk was flat as paper.

". . . need your help with a few things," my mother was saying.

"I owe you so much, Jiejie. Of course the men can overlook a shipment or two."

"Thank you," my mother said. "It's only furniture. I am terribly attached to it. Leaving will be hard enough—" In that moment she saw Hu Ran and me in the doorway. I'd let go of his hand, but my fingertips were warm with the knowledge of his presence. My mother's gaze moved over me: my hair, my eyes, my cheeks and mouth. For a long moment I felt exposed. Then she, too, looked vulnerable.

It was my father who spoke. "Junan, do you remember Hu Ran?"

"Oh, yes," she said politely, recovering herself. "How are you, Hu Ran?"

"I'm fine."

"If it hadn't been for this young man," my father said, "I would be dead."

My mother smiled coolly. "Thank you for helping bring the general home," she said. "You deserve some compensation."

"Oh no," said Hu Ran.

"Well, then, thank you for your xingli."

"Young man," my uncle said, "I think it's time that you and I were going. We have plenty to talk about." He gestured toward the door. "See you again," he told my mother.

"Thank you for your help, Li Bing."

"Goodbye," he said, looking at my father, "and consider my advice."

"I will."

Hu Ran winked at me. I looked around to see if anyone had noticed.

I went to the window and watched them leave the house. They walked down the front path, Hu Ran's head bent toward my uncle's, listening.

AND SO WE SAT: my mother and father, Hwa and I, on the four uncovered chairs, under bright lights reflected in the rain-streaked windows. Sheets were draped on the remaining furniture: a couch, two armchairs, and a divan.

Now that my father was suddenly returned, now that he had been in danger and was saved, my mother sat shaking. Her love for him went through her; it straightened her back; it glittered in her eyes. It shamed her beyond anything else.

She said, "I've packed everything that we can take. I'm ready to leave, and with your brother's help, the furniture and other things will safely reach Taiwan."

My father didn't answer. "We're leaving in two days," she said.

Still he didn't speak. He sat staring at his hands.

"What is it, Li Ang?"

"Junan," my father said, "you are a generous woman."

"What do you want?"

"Junan," he said again, "let's talk about this by ourselves."

But my mother gestured toward Hwa and me not to move. "Surely there's nothing you have to say that your two daughters can't hear."

He turned to me and then to Hwa, helplessly, before turning back to our mother.

"I've sent a telegram to your sister."

I heard a sharp intake of breath. I stole a glance at Hwa, but she sat unmoving in her red shirt, her back straight like a young soldier's.

My mother asked, "And what did you tell her?"

"That she will be in danger." My father's voice rose. I heard emotion in it, building, as well as anticipation. He was discovering what he'd wished to say for a long time. "You know as well as I do," he said. "Yinan won't be safe. She has no family, no influence. She has the

Americans, but when the Republic goes . . . under the Communists, the Americans will leave. She'll be vulnerable."

"What does that have to do with me?"

My father took a deep breath. "I want her to come with us."

In the long minute that followed, the sound of rain lightened and moved away. Outside the window I saw the headlights of a car approaching slowly, then pulling into the drive before our house. The driver opened the door, and two women stepped out.

It was Hu Mudan, and with her stood a woman, unfamiliar, although I had the feeling that I must know her.

She was slender, smaller than my mother, with a pale, careworn face and short hair pushed behind her ears. She was dressed very simply in a long, gray skirt edged with rain, a long-sleeved white blouse, and loafers. Her skirt and blouse were wrinkled and appeared to be deliberately plain and deliberately Western—they were, in fact, donations from the missionary woman Katherine Rodale—and it was perhaps these clothes that made me so slow to recognize her. I remembered my aunt as a very young woman, a little plain, a little lacking in grace, with the girlhood softness in her. This woman was older, certainly, but she'd grown older in an unexpected way. For one, she was no longer plain; she wasn't pretty so much as pleasing to look upon, striking in her simplicity. It was as if the years had whittled away at who she'd been, allowing this new person to emerge. Only after a long moment did I find in her eyes the old watchfulness, the gentleness, transformed into an expression of quiet understanding.

"Ayi," I blurted. Hwa shot me a fierce glance. I struggled to speak properly. "Ayi." It came out sounding flat with a bright and uncontrollable happiness and sorrow at its edges.

Yinan tried to smile. My mother didn't move.

"Li Taitai," said Hu Mudan.

My mother didn't answer.

Hu Mudan offered to wait in the car and left.

When she left the room, my mother spoke. "Hello, Yinan."

"Jiejie."

My father stood. He took one quick step forward, but something stopped him.

My mother's precise voice broke the silence. "Go ahead. Say hello to Yinan."

He stumbled forward with heavy, clumsy footsteps. It was at that moment, watching my aunt and father, that I understood. Her entire body spoke of it, although she didn't move. She only looked at him, but I could see it in her eyes. My father was still and dumb. His eyes, his knees, the slope of his shoulders, the gestures of his hands, were all aware of her nearness.

"Yinan."

She raised her gaze, slowly, from his feet up the length of his body, to his face. Slowly her face lit up. Her eyes filled with tears. I saw her happiness, and grief, and something I could now recognize—now that I had been with Hu Ran—a current of feeling that couldn't be ignored.

I had never felt in anything this kind of power, a power that would render a room of people to such helplessness, such silence.

"You're well, then," said my father, finally.

"Your foot—"

"It's not that bad."

She said, "I received your telegram, Li Ang. I was going to stay away. But when Hu Mudan said you'd been captured, I had to come."

"I was captured, but they let me go. How are you?"

"I'm well."

"You must leave the mainland," he said. "You won't be safe here."

"Katherine—the American woman—persuaded the church to offer me sanctuary, in Hong Kong."

"No," my mother said.

In my mother's face, I saw a new formidable strength that could only have arisen out of pain.

"Junan?" my father asked.

She replied to my aunt. "I said no. Even if Li Ang wants you to leave, I won't allow it."

Yinan stared at her hands. "I won't go against your wishes."

After a moment, my father spoke. "Those are unforgiving terms," he said.

"Those are my terms."

"I'd hoped that after all of these years——"

"You thought I would forget." My mother smiled. "Meimei, do you remember once in Hangzhou, years ago, when we were chatting with Li Bing? He asked what you would do if the enemy came to the door, and you said that you would learn to live with him. I was foolish. I thought you were only a child."

"Jiejie, it was not that way——"

"You wanted it to happen," my father said.

His cheeks were flushed. His gaze was fixed upon my mother. "There is nothing you can do now. Please understand. You began this, you put it into motion. It is true I was at fault. But you can't tell me that my weakness wasn't part of your design."

My mother met his eyes. Her face was gray, implacable. "You would break apart our family." She spoke carefully, then looked away. "You mean to stay here, too."

"After they captured me, I had to face the truth. I——"

"You know that you must leave! You are a Nationalist general!"

"No, no longer. I'm not truly a Nationalist—I never was—nor am I a Communist. I am only a man. I am Chinese and I will suffer as China suffers."

We all sat without a word. It had grown dark outside and our blurred reflections floated in the rain-streaked windows: Hwa's shirt a splash of red, and, hovering around us, the white-draped furniture.

My mother sat very straight. Her fair skin, her long bones remained, but sometime during the war, her beauty had been stripped away.

"You think Li Bing will hide you. But you listen to these words. You'll come begging to me." She stood. "Goodbye, Li Ang. Goodbye, Meimei."

"Jiejie."

"Junan——" My father raised his hand wearily to his forehead.

"You will come begging," my mother said. She looked at him with an unreasonable smile. Her pain was hardly to be borne. We sat frozen as if the slightest movement might shatter us. Then my mother stood. She wanted them gone.

I couldn't meet their eyes. I turned to watch their reflections in the window, surrounded by the darkness. My father, weary, leaning on his cane; Yinan, pale and tearful. They were abandoning us. They were leaving me and my mother, from whom everything had been stripped away. Only her bare will remained, fused into her long, white bones, bones as familiar to me as a lover's.

I knew I couldn't stay in China. How could I—letting my mother leave in such pain? How could I stay with the people who would hurt us so? Sorrow and darkness tore at me. I wished to run to my father and ayi and clasp their knees, and I wanted to cry, "I will stay here with you!" But as I looked at my mother's desolate reflection in the glass, I knew that I would not.

Taipei 1949—55

WE ARRIVED IN TAIWAN SUFFERING FROM DEFEAT. THE WHOLE island was awash in it, a fever that had been carried across the water from the mainland by those of us who had fled our homes, abandoned our lives, and brought what we could salvage to this unfamiliar ground. This malady—taking the form of a contagious blindness, a seductive forgetfulness—had overcome the most unimaginative among us, so that certain women who had once led responsible and earnest lives would hunch over their mahjong, not talking, cracking tiles and sliding stacks of chips across the stark white tablecloth, playing relentless games to hold back thought, until their eyes burned and their arms ached and the lamplight faded in the dawn. And courageous men, previously determined to return and recapture the mainland by force, instead retreated, outnumbered and pummeled by exhaustion, to this last island. There they spent their strength struggling to defend themselves, subduing its inhabitants and building up a life in that new place, rocky, steaming, and cleansed with rain.

I can still recall the lush odor of spring growth mingled with the turbulence of hope and loss. In the first few weeks, I sat for hours by myself, wearing the pendant Hu Ran had given me, composing letter after letter to the mainland. Now and then I put down my pen and looked out of the window, where somewhere across the crowded island and the tumbling brown water the old country remained, its beaches vast, its streets dark with people. For centuries, the water between the mainland and the island had been a permeable membrane, easily crossed by sailing ships and steamships, and finally in our century by planes. Over thousands of years the dialects had grown apart and woven themselves back together. There were many families with relatives on both sides, exchanging care packages filled with canisters of tea and other sundry local items nestled in dried mushrooms. So much had made the journey between these two places. Certainly there would be a way to erase what I had done. Hu Ran and I must meet again, as we always had, against all possibility and expectation.

"I am sorry," I wrote again and again. "I could not abandon my mother." I invited him to Taiwan, giving instructions to our house in Taipei. I made wild promises to return to the mainland. My words seemed hollow, even to me. I had no way of getting back to the mainland and no way to support him in Taiwan.

Two weeks passed, then three. I saved the letters and slipped out every few days, hurrying through the crowded streets until I reached the post office. On one of these clandestine trips I ran into Pu Taitai. She was tired and gray, but overjoyed to see me. She had just posted a letter to Pu Li. She had managed to scrape together enough money to send him to Macao, where he was waiting for a student visa to America. I nodded, smiled, all the while thinking of my own letters. Where were they going? Certainly it was not possible for them to simply vanish, drop into the widening expanse between two worlds.

THAT AFTERNOON THERE WAS a knock on the door. I flew out of my room with my heart pounding. I flung open the door, smiling, my eyes filling with tears—and caught the familiar scent of sandalwood perfume. The visitor was Pu Taitai; our chance meeting at the post office had led her back to our mother. Hwa, too, was disappointed. But I saw my mother awaken from her malaise and smile as if the reappearance of this woman with her loud voice and in her shapeless gray and lavender blouse were a lucky sign.

"Li Taitai!" Pu Taitai cried. Behind my mother's back, Hwa raised her eyebrows. Pu Taitai entered, praising my mother's abilities: She had found a decent house! In this crowded city! She remarked on how well we looked despite the difficult times. Not a word about my father's absence. Not a question or aside. Nor did my mother ask her, How do you manage here? How do you get by? Instead, she told our maid to prepare dianxin.

"Sit, sit," my mother said. And she recruited Hwa and me to make up a mahjong game.

Pu Taitai ate. She ate a dozen salted plums and several bowls of green bean porridge. She ate peanuts in the shell and watermelon seeds. She ate enough dumplings and fishballs for three people. Her cheeks took on a healthy color; her eyes lost their hollow quality and began to glow. We pretended not to notice. The evening dimmed into a comfortable dark. The night lay over our house like soothing gauze and we relaxed into its stillness. The electricity was out again. We kept the candles low and let the room darken around us until we could barely see the playing pieces.

Pu Taitai did not stop talking. She bragged about Pu Li, who had received an engineering scholarship to a school in California. She told heroic stories of the Nationalist generals defending the islands, about the pockets of resistance on the mainland. She spoke with sorrow of my father, whom she believed had been trapped—captured, perhaps—and left behind, possibly killed. I don't know where she got this idea. I assume my mother had lied in order to save face. Then Pu Taitai chanted the slogan of that time:

Year one: prepare
Year two: counterattack
Year three: saodang (sweeps)
Year five: success

Over and over Pu Taitai counted our victories: General Hu Lian's brave island defense, the latest capture of a Communist spy. She said nothing of defeat, nothing of the weariness, surrenders, loss, or death. My mother smiled and gestured toward a dish of sesame candies; Pu Taitai picked one out and ate it. At last they two were truly friends. I felt happy for my mother; she hadn't had a real friend before. But something in this sympathy brought Hu Ran to my mind, and as Pu Taitai rolled the dice to begin, I felt that I was watching the game from far away.

"We must breed a new generation of Chinese patriots," Pu Taitai said. "When Pu Li marries your daughter Hong, we will mix the blood of two great generals, and this mingling will create a Chinese hero."

She beamed at me. And in that moment my mother also turned to me and smiled: an ironic, knowing smile that took my breath away.

I sat in stunned silence. Pu Taitai mixed and turned; the tiles clicked relentlessly. My mother's smile told me what I hadn't allowed myself to know. I should have known, I could have known, but I had been too preoccupied to notice. It is true the signs were small, and similar to the signs of dislocation. The queasiness, exhaustion, the tears and inexplicable hunger had felt natural in a new place. But some other force had taken hold over my body, swelling my feet and stomach, spreading to the very roots of my hair, which had indeed grown thick and luxuriant in the way of some pregnant women.

Of course my mother would have recognized, identified the change. She had seen these physical changes in Hu Mudan, in herself, and in her sister. She knew these signs as well as she knew grief.

Now she set up her new tiles, daintily. "Ai, no good. Pass." A tiny line appeared between her brows and then vanished. I suspected that she'd deliberately underplayed her hand. Pu Taitai was contented with her resulting win, and the evening ended with our guest unaware that anything had happened.

LATE THAT NIGHT, long after Pu Taitai had left, I went to find my mother. She was in her bedroom, standing before her closet, reaching for its rich contents as if for solace. I stood behind her, waiting, but she didn't acknowledge me. "I am sorry," I said. "I know this brings a loss of face."

She continued stroking the dark fur on the collar of a jacket.

"He was—is—good. You know it. If it hadn't been for him—"

"You must go to the apothecary."

I had last heard this tone in Shanghai, the night my father had abandoned her. Then I had been softened by her pain. But this time I felt in my fingertips an answering coldness. I took a deep breath.

"No," I said.

She turned and looked into my eyes. Tight muscles slid beneath her bones. Then she turned back to her closet. And with that decision I left her, as surely as if I had stayed on the mainland.

My news must have been hard for her. All her life, she'd had to live down the weaknesses of the few people she loved: my grandmother, my father, my aunt, and now me. She loved us, and we returned her love with betrayal and humiliation.

I HAD LET Hu Ran go so easily, assuming that I could return or he would come to me, as if our bodies were parcels that could be dropped into a mailbox at any time and would emerge, regardless of all politics, across the ocean.

But in the following months, I began to understand there was no way for him to make the trip. I heard rumors of the remaining Nationalist ranks surrounded, struggling, falling. Crowds of refugees hurried to board the ships to the island. Some of the ships had been prepared for the trip; others were old, waterlogged boats less seaworthy than the ferries on West Lake. The mail had ceased. The vital pathways were controlled by the Communist blockade. Gunboats patrolled the water, seeking anyone who tried to leave. Travel dwindled between Taiwan and the mainland. Only Hong Kong remained accessible, and with each week this crossing grew more challenging and filled with danger. The bamboo curtain encircled more and more tightly until the narrow strait grew wide.

At night I struggled with my inheritance from old Mma. I could hear through the wall my mother tossing in her own bed. During the day, we spoke as little as we could, although it was impossible to avoid each other in that small house. Once, during that time, she even called me by her sister's name. *Yinan*, she said to the back of my head. And I turned, and answered casually, so that she wouldn't know what she had done.

18 July 1949

Dear Hong,

   Thank you for your letter. It has only just reached me after
several months, having been forwarded to Hong Kong where I
have been waiting to return to the United States.

   I write with unfortunate news. Hu Ran is lost. Apparently,
he decided to try to leave the mainland, via the strait. At night,
while it was docked waiting to leave, the ship came under attack.
They said that someone on the ship provided a signal to the
Communist gunboats. In the ensuing battle, Hu Ran fell over-
board and drowned. Hu Mudan found out from someone who
made it back to shore. She paid someone leaving for Hong Kong
to write to me, telling me what happened and begging me to find
you, but for these months I was unable to learn your where-
abouts.

   I can't begin to imagine how difficult it must be to hear such
terrible news from a stranger. But please do not consider me a
stranger, Hong. Hu Mudan, Hu Ran, and your aunt Yinan were
like family to me, and I hope that you will consider me a friend.
Please let me know when you receive this letter. Write and tell
me how you are.

                              Sincerely,
                              Katherine Rodale

It was Hwa who braved the silence and knocked on my door. She
was polite, subdued, holding herself apart from me. Or was it I who
kept my distance? The events of the past year had split us entirely apart.
We would never be two girls together again. Hwa knew this. She didn't
try to pretend nothing had happened. But we were still sisters, and she
sat upon my bed and gave me the news. She said my mother had told
her not to mention my secret. Eventually, my condition would be
unmistakable, and at that time, my mother would handle things.

   "What else did she say?" I asked.

   Hwa shook her head. "What will you do?" she asked. "Can you get
rid of it, somehow? Perhaps then you could still be married—"

I did not want to get rid of it. "I don't want to marry."

"—if you could give the baby away? I know it would be hard, but eventually, you might forget —"

"I don't want to give it away."

"I know it's hard to see, but eventually, after a few years—the only way to move ahead will be to forget all of this."

I listened quietly until she stopped, and when I did not reply, she said goodbye and left the room, closing the door.

I put Katherine Rodale's letter in my box of things that were not meant to be remembered. There was a framed image of my mother and father at their wedding and, hidden behind it, a photograph of my aunt holding a half-blown rose, the print I had stolen from the waste bin of our Chongqing kitchen. There was a book my father had given me, Grimm's fairy tales in English. And between the pages of this book, I had pressed the slips of paper on which Hu Ran had written his notes to me. MEET ME AT THE PARK. 4 PM AT COFFEE SHOP. The ink had already begun to fade. The park and perhaps even the coffee shop might still exist, somewhere across the sea, but it seemed to me, as I remembered them, that my memories were in sepia tones, like relics drifting, gently and implacably, into the past.

I wrote back to Katherine Rodale and thanked her for her letter. I had never met the woman, had no clear picture of her in my mind, but her kind words gave me the boldness to write back. In my reply, I told this American, this stranger, about Hu Ran and myself. I explained that I had been the cause of Hu Ran's death. I had left the mainland after promising to stay, and he'd died trying to follow me. I told her that I was pregnant, that I wished to keep the baby, and that I did not know what would become of us.

Katherine Rodale wrote back with questions. She was personally concerned, she said, about my fate. She wished to know more. What did I want? What were my plans? I wrote, "I do not know about me. I have no wants. I have no plans. I will try to think." And with these awkward English sentences, I knew that I had stated the truth. Who was I? I couldn't say. For my whole life, except with Hu Ran, I'd never been a person, but rather a piece of something else—of my family, of my country, and now a scattered piece of its defeat. I was a child who'd been shuttled back and forth over the continent. I was a pair of eyes, a pair of ears, a witness of terrible things that I had concealed in my mind, awaiting study, like forbidden photographs sealed into a box. I had seen my uncle chased down the streets, pursued by Japanese soldiers. I had seen a snaggle-haired woman dry-nursing a hungry baby, and a woman hang herself from a tree along the steep and crowded stairs of a war-torn city. I was an obedient daughter, a jiejie, and a faithful student. If it hadn't been for Hu Ran, I would undoubtedly have gone on to marry Pu Li. But my fierce hours with Hu Ran had changed all that. I had been cruel to him; I had used him to separate me from my mother; and in the end I had betrayed both of them. Moreover, I had betrayed myself. I knew now what had lain at the source of my terror. I knew now that I had loved Hu Ran with all my heart.

In the next several months, waiting, I thought about all these things, writing some of them to Katherine Rodale and keeping some of them to myself. She was the first adult since Hu Mudan to be my friend. If I had to reach her in another language, I would do it. Over long hours I struggled to put my thoughts and feelings into English. "I was coward," I wrote. "I wish I stay behind," I wrote. Then, "I want to know how are my father and my aunt. I hope they are safe. "Months later, I wrote, "Soon the baby will be born. Hu Ran will never see the baby."

As I wrote, scratched out, and rewrote at the table in my room, I began to feel as if each word fortified me, gave me ground to stand on. I didn't know where this would lead. But as I wrote to my new friend in English sentences and paragraphs, I began to see an outline of myself, barely visible; it was like tracing a constellation in the night sky. My mother's and Hwa's concern faded in the light from those faraway stars.

I DREAMED THAT I was lying in a cave. The dark was my protector, my shelter, my cocoon. I felt myself reshaping there, developing hidden eyes and ears, delicate senses, even wings, like the tiny furred creatures that made pockets in the edges of stones.

Light and pain. My mother's face hovered. "Push *now*, Xiao Hong.

Push *now*." She would not let me rest. She commanded me to try. I hated her, my mother who was so unforgiving, who had in her soul this dark, cold iron. But she was my mother. She had given birth to me. I reached deep into myself and did what she commanded.

I became aware that the darkness held many shapes. Some of them were familiar, some were people I had heard about in my mother's stories. There was a sad, pale woman with her hands outstretched, waiting in silence with empty arms. There was Hu Mudan, crouched in the room fiercely alone and waiting for her own child to arrive. I thought I felt Hu Ran nearby—his bright face, his hope, his soul shining. Then I remembered Yinan, surrounded but alone in the bomb shelter, and I cried out for her, and for my mother, and for myself. It seemed the whole world rang with cries for those who had been left behind.

And from that dark place, those people who had departed, I could sense my child, my little one, arriving.

"Ah," my mother said. "A girl." A baby's wail lifted over the room like a siren. It pulled me out of the fog. Later, when I held her, she looked right into me with eyes the color of earth at the bottom of a pond.

From the moment little Mudan was born, she banished the old curse against mothers loving daughters. From the moment she appeared, with her great wail, her strong grasp, and her utter lack of apology, she brought out in me the strength to carry two. She was born on the second of December in 1949, the Year of the Ox, and she would need all of the Ox's strong endurance to thrive in the middle of the story she had entered.

IT WAS, ALWAYS, my mother's story. It flowed ever and around our house; it was our atmosphere, our air. It cast its own light on everything we saw and touched. She had been defeated. Yinan had defeated her. My mother had left the mainland thoroughly shamed. Now, away from them, she vowed to make her own life big enough and fine enough to hold her shame. She had told Pu Taitai that my father was captured, likely killed. Then she built an unassailable fortress of his death.

She wore dark clothes to mourn his loss. With Pu Taitai's help, she

rediscovered the others who'd come across and entertained their con-
dolences. Many small deals were taking place during those visits. In a
year, she had secured what she was looking for: an antique dealer with
impeccable taste, a man who knew everyone and knew how to keep his
mouth shut. Mr. Jian was a slender, balding fellow from Beijing, with a
long, aristocratic northern nose, which he used to sniff out the money
that flooded the island.

On that fateful day months ago, in another life, my mother had
asked Li Bing to help her smuggle shipments of the furniture, art, and
other valuables she had long kept in storage. He had not forgotten
and the goods had come through the blockade. My mother hid them and
waited. She suspected that these symbols of the old world would soon
be in demand, and she was right. Everyone wanted something. Mr. Jian
charged outrageous sums and told her later who had taken what. A
wealthy woman from Hangzhou paid in gold bars for a painting of
West Lake. A museum curator in Taipei bought several pieces. Even
Hsiao Taitai paid in gold for the scrolls that she had once cast off in
Chongqing, and Mr. Jian arranged things so she never knew that my
mother did not like her enough to offer them as a gift. The refugees surrounded themselves with symbols of the past, and my mother took in
more money, which she invested for the future.

I was absorbed in a future of another kind. I had little interest in
anyone except my daughter. We spent our days together in my bedroom. I nursed Mudan myself, and in the afternoons, while she napped,
I read kung fu novels or looked out the window or answered a letter
from Katherine Rodale. Because we were so close Mudan almost never
cried. My mother's visitors would often come and go without remembering there was a baby in the house. We spent our time wrapped in our
private world—me loving and mourning, and Mudan in a private world
of her own baby dreams. She was too young to know that her father
was gone and that I, her mother, had betrayed everyone else whom I
had ever loved.

She had the strength of both our families in her straight back and
fine sober energy. She quickly learned to pull herself to her feet, and I
took pleasure in the ease with which she learned to walk and run. My

mother, too, noticed all of these things. But she looked at little Mudan with a certain resistance in her gaze. It seemed to me that she was seeing in little Mudan the remnants of a time that she would rather not recall. Or perhaps she thought of Mudan as proof of my own shame. She never said a word, but as time went on, I began to see that others were not as careful. Even Pu Taitai avoided Mudan, and as time went on, I kept my daughter away from my mother's friends. I didn't want her to be harmed by such judgment and dismissiveness.

One day, when Mudan was almost three years old, my mother called me to her room.

"I have something for you, Hong." She brought out a wooden box. It was very plain, the size of a shoe box. She placed it upon the table and opened it with a small key.

She began to show me, one by one, the necklaces that she had hoarded over the years. There were strings of bright green jade and red jade. There were freshwater pearls shaped like silk cocoons and tiny round wax candles. I could remember nestling up to her, feeling the strings of them around her neck. The last three strands were perfectly round. There was a long rope of large, flawless silvery orbs and one of creamy white. Finally she pulled out a set of matched pink pearls, perfect, long enough to loop twice around the throat.

"I want to give some of my jewelry to you and Mudan," my mother said.

Surprised, I kept my gaze low.

"I've been watching her. She is a certain kind of person. Her wings will carry her far, if she has any opportunity. If she is caged, she won't forgive you. You know, Hong, that this is not a good place for—a child with no father. You must look for a safe place, a safe place for you and Mudan."

"Where should I go?"

"To a place where no one knows you, a place where no one will hold your past against you. Someplace where you can hold your head up high and face the future. You'll need money. You should sell the jade and freshwater pearls and keep the matched pearls for your daughter and yourself."

She was telling me to leave. Her voice was determined, her lips set.

"You come from a line of women born into bad luck. Each of us has been constrained by circumstances. Your grandmother, by an unforgiving society. I myself was forced to struggle through the war. And you—you have been trapped into a net of your own choosing, Hong. Try to understand. You must try to keep your own choices from damaging your daughter."

I took a pearl between my fingers. It was a lustrous silver-white, smooth, a violation hidden in a glowing shell.

"And Hwa?" I asked.

"Hwa will be married."

She picked out the rope of pink pearls and laid them aside. "Hwa will be married."

FOR YEARS I HAD withdrawn into the urgency of motherhood, leaving Hwa to her own devices. She pouted for me, but, finding no support, turned her focus and attention toward her friends. She grew sociable, confident, lively, and ambitious. At some point in those years, she also fell in love with Willy Chang. He had matured into a lithe, dark young man with a handsome face and a sensitive temperament. Before they left the mainland, Willy's father had put all the family money into gold, and as a result Willy was highly eligible.

To all appearances Willy and Hwa's shared interests were academic. He had a passion for writing poetry and my sister majored in literature to keep him company. They shared class notes at the library and rarely met in private. Hwa claimed she wasn't in love. But her words betrayed her feelings. "He can be a difficult boy," she told me once. "He is as sensitive and prickly as a pineapple, but just as sweet inside." She delighted in his poetry and his playfulness; she was as proud of his good looks as a lover.

Many of the other girls liked Willy as well. Fighting off their interest took all of the perseverance and strategy that Hwa had once learned watching my mother's mahjong games. She was particularly concerned about Yun-yi, the granddaughter of Hsiao Taitai, and Hsiao Meiyu's only child. When I think back, I know I should have told my mother about all of this, but in those days it mattered more to me that Hwa valued loyalty and secrets.

"A good boy," my mother said to me around that time. "A boy with a solid reputation—a good reputation—from a good family, with a profession to make an income."

I knew she wasn't thinking of Willy Chang. "You think that Hwa will need someone with money?" I asked.

"No," she said, "we have the money. In this modern world, it will be more important for him to have a profession than a fortune."

"But I think that Hwa might want to choose a man for herself," I said.

My mother shook her head. "Do you think I notice nothing? You wait."

Hwa's problems began the summer before her senior year. I remember it very clearly. I had left Mudan with my mother for a few hours. Hwa and I were in a department store, shopping for an outfit to wear to a graduation party, an outfit that Willy would like. She had grown her hair long and pulled it into a stylish chignon, and had already begun to favor American skirts and sweaters. Hwa found a pale pink cardigan sweater that suited her quite well, but nothing to go with it. She wanted a flowered summer skirt, she thought—she could wear the combination with her favorite white blouse that had embroidery on the collar.

Approaching the plate-glass doors, we saw Hsiao Meiyu and her daughter Yun-yi on the sidewalk, about to enter the store.

Here in Taiwan my mother knew Hsiao Meiyu socially; she and my mother sometimes went to the same dinner parties. Now that their mother was gone, Meiyu had outshone her sisters. She had become a notoriously snobbish, difficult woman, associating only with the families of generals. I would rather have avoided her, but even I knew we must be friendly.

What happened next took only a moment. Meiyu and Yun-yi came through the doors. We smiled at and waved. Meiyu glanced in our direction—I believe she almost met my eye. Then she and Yun-yi walked away. We came toward Meiyu and Yun-yi—smiling, eyes open, hands extended—and they walked past. We continued moving through the revolving door and a minute later were standing on the windy street.

"Did she see us?" Hwa wanted to know.

"Who cares?" I scoffed, although the encounter had left me shaken. "I don't think she did."

"I think she did. I know she did."

We went on to the next store, but seeing Meiyu and Yun-yi had cast a pall over the trip, and we soon returned home. Hwa would talk of nothing else. I soothed her, telling her the pink sweater she'd bought looked good on her, that no one else at the party would have such a sweater—but she was troubled.

"Did you notice," she said, "that Mama didn't attend Hsiao Taitai's party last weekend?"

The following week, our mother socialized as much as ever. We said nothing to her about the incident. But a few days later it happened again, this time with another mahjong friend of my mother's whom Hwa bumped into on the way home from the bus stop. Still, it was days before we knew what was going on. Naturally it was Hwa who pieced it together.

"Hsiao Taitai and Willy's parents are talking about a marriage to Yun-yi," she said. "Hsiao Taitai heard that he and I were special friends and told his mother. Now Willy's parents are demanding that he tell them what is going on between us."

"What did he say?"

"He said he didn't know."

"That's all?"

"That's what he said." Hwa hid her face in her hands.

"But Hwa," I said, "how could he know what's going on, when you will never talk about it? If he knows the truth, he might object to the marriage."

"But I don't know if he will."

"You must let him know how you feel."

"No!"

"Hwa, he won't know if you love him back unless you tell him how you feel. Show him. Tell him. Look him in the eye."

For a long moment, Hwa struggled to speak. Then she burst out, "I won't!"

"What do you mean?"

"I just can't."

"But Hwa, if you don't talk to him, then he'll be gone."

At this, Hwa straightened her back and smoothed her skirt over her knees. In her face I saw a look of sorrow and determination. It was not until later that night, lying awake, when I remembered where else I had seen that look of forceful deprivation and I knew that Hwa would never tell Willy. She did not want to be under anyone's power.

Shortly afterward, we heard the news of his engagement.

Hwa was broken-hearted. Her collarbones stood out. Her periods wracked her. She had no interest in the graduation parties. My mother watched all this, her lips tight. Surely she knew what was going on. But when I spoke to her about it, she merely said, "She must keep trying. She must move on. She must learn to give things up."

"I hear her crying through the wall at night."

"She will find a new man."

"I don't think that's what she wants."

My mother's lips grew tight. "A new man will make her safe," she said. "A woman is never safe until she understands that any one man is just as good as another."

I said nothing. Such silences were necessary between two adult women living in one house.

January 2, 1954
Dear Hong,

I write with great excitement. Because of immigration laws, it has taken Ming and me more time than we expected to get established in America, but I am happy to say that I am at last able to offer you good news. My church is offering a scholarship to a worthy Chinese student. I am writing on its behalf to offer you a scholarship at if you are able to pass the Taiwan govern-

ment's examination and gain admission to an American school.
The American government also requires that every scholarship
student have at least $2000 a year.

I'm sure that with your intelligence and thoughtfulness you
will have no problem passing the examination or excelling at an
American school. It will be difficult to be separated from Mudan,
but she could stay in Taiwan, with your mother, while you are
completing your education. You will be able to see her in the
summers. This is a wonderful opportunity and I hope that you
will take it. Please tell me if there is anything I can do to help.

Best wishes,
Katherine

The government examination was given to all students in Taiwan
who wished to study in the United States. Anyone who scored high
enough and found a sponsoring university would be granted a student
visa. It would be no small task, to score among the top students in
Taiwan at that time. But I had my daughter's fate to push me on. I didn't
want her to grow up in a place where she would be surrounded by the
judgment of women like Hsiao Meiyu. I didn't want her to live in the
shadow of what I had done. Thanks to my mother, I had the money to
go to the U.S., the jewelry my mother had worn under her clothes as we
were bombed.

And so I studied more English, beginning with Yinan's old book of
English fairy tales and moving on to more complicated grammar. I
reviewed my mathematics, calling on the friendliness with numbers that
was in my blood. Finally, I studied the history of the country we had
left behind. I had learned this as a child—every Chinese schoolchild
did—and now I read it all again, sitting at my desk on the island off the
continent, pushing against sleep and grief. I pored over the lists of the
great emperors, who had unified the country from its yellow northern
plains to the wild southwest and the rich seacoasts of the southeast. I
read of the triumphant openings and the eventual dissolutions of their
dynasties. Over thousands of years, they rose, and fell, and when they
fell, each left behind a group of refugees who fled into the corners and

sometimes to the island where my family had come to live. I found myself reading more and more slowly, dreading the end of it, for I missed Hu Ran and my uncle, my father and Yinan, and Yao, my brother and cousin. And when the time came and I boarded the plane for San Francisco, I believed that I was leaving all of them behind.

MY MOTHER WROTE me once a week, clear, crisp letters filled with straightforward descriptions of little Mudan's activities. If they'd been written in a more sympathetic tone, I might have written back confessing my sheer misery at being parted from my daughter. But my mother's words left no room for such openness. "She misses you," she wrote. "But then I show her your photograph, and explain that you are going away because you want to make a new home for her. She's a reasonable child and looks forward to seeing you in the summer."

Hwa wrote frequently at first. She was very lonely, and her autumn was long and hard. Most difficult of all was the day of Willy Chang's wedding to Yun-yi. Hwa was invited to the wedding, but she stayed at home. She wrote a letter pouring out her thoughts. "Although it seems impossible right now," she wrote, "I know someday I must be married. Secretly, I have always wished to marry someone I truly loved. It would somehow make up for everything that has happened to us. But perhaps that dream of love was only a little girl's dream."

I tried to think of helpful words for her. She so rarely reached out to me.

"You could take the test and come to the United States," I wrote back. "It's very interesting to live here, and you would probably meet somebody new. Or you might be able to go to Hong Kong," I added. "Ma must have a friend, or someone, who would be able to look out for you if you were to transfer to Hong Kong University. Then you could learn to live on your own, and have an independent life."

She did not reply for some time. It was more than a month before her familiar blue envelope arrived in my mailbox.

22 February 1956

Jiejie,

I am writing to let you know that Pu Li and I will be married, in Taipei, on June 3. Immediately afterward, I will fly to the U.S. to set up house in California and Pu Li will start the second year of his master's degree program at Stanford. Pu Taitai wants to stay in Taiwan. She still hopes that soon the Generalissimo will retake the mainland. But I hope that when we have children, Mama will come to America to live with us. Then there can be three generations of our family living in one house again.

I know this may seem like a sudden change to you. But it has been a long time since Pu Li was a little boy who wanted to hold your hand at the movies. I'm sure you understand. Thank you for the advice in your last letter, but after some thought I decided that I'd rather do things Mama's way. I had a few qualms about getting married but they are over now that everything is settled. The truth is I'm perfectly content. And Mama is very proud of me.

Meimei

My mother and Pu Taitai planned the wedding. Emboldened by my mother's money and Pu Taitai's connections, they put together an enormous celebration, inviting all of their friends, our families' friends, and the families of the men who had known Pu Li's father and my father. The chapel was Pu Taitai's idea; she had been influenced by her memories of high-class Christian weddings of the past. The wedding would be followed by a large banquet, and Hwa had brought another outfit, an elaborate red qipao, for a second ceremony which would be performed according to strict Chinese tradition, at my mother's request, with an elder and a witness and a ceremonial bow to the ancestors.

I flew home for the wedding. Taipei was wrapped within the tail end of a monsoon. The buildings dipped and rose past billowing towers of gray clouds, soaring sideways as if the city and all of its inhabitants were being turned in a pinwheel. It was raining when we reached the church, raining so hard that even at eleven A.M. the sky was the color of dusk, and at the church, in the dim lights, my mother and Pu Taitai stepped from behind the door as if emerging from the fog of time. My mother's luxuriant hair was streaked with silver and she held herself with exquisite poise. Now, approaching her fifties, she had grown very thin, but she had kept her grace and intelligence, as well as her old aura of self-possession.

Hwa, too, had lost weight. She had once had rounded breasts and curved shoulders, but while planning the wedding she had thinned into the woman she would be for the rest of her life: petite, close to the bone, sharp-eyed, with her beautiful thick hair cut short and curled into a permanent wave. The wedding preparations had consumed her. She had wrapped her dress in layers of cloth and packed it into a huge box, but still she feared the rain would get to it while it was carried into the chapel. The driver shielded her made-up face with an enormous red umbrella, but she held a raincoat over her head just the same. As it turned out, her precaution was a good idea. As Hwa stepped out of the limousine, a clap of thunder split our ears, and the driver, an emigrant like ourselves who had been a boy during the occupation of Nanjing, was so shaken by his memories that he let the umbrella tilt precariously to one side before an old friend of the late General Pu's, limping forward, rescued it.

In the vestibule, I ran into Pu Li. He stood resplendent in a full tuxedo with shining golden studs; patent leather shoes gleamed on his small feet. I wondered how he had gotten them to the church in the rain. It turned out that he had arrived before the rain, to make sure everything was exactly as Hwa and his mother wanted it.

"Congratulations," I said. "I'm glad you're going to be my brother." The moment the words left my mouth I thought about how silly, and insulting, they might sound.

But Pu Li merely smiled and said, "Jiejie."

He and Hwa would spend a week together in Taipei after the ceremony. Then he would move back to California to start his school year. Hwa would join him in a few months. Pu Li asked me about my plans, and I explained that I planned to major in psychology and English. He congratulated me on this. I congratulated him as well, and wished him happiness. I realized that I had never liked him as much as I did now. Then he moved on, to see to some detail. I stood alone in the echoing vestibule. If I hadn't met Hu Ran again—or if I'd gone to the apothecary—this might have been my wedding. Gradually, my moment of regret eased into relief.

My mother and I took our seats. Then Hwa entered the room alone. She stood as straight as a general and wore an expression of indecipherable calm. We had no family, no friends to walk her up the aisle. My parents' male friends, like many in their generation, had been lost. Slowly, Hwa stepped alone up the long aisle. Then she stood, severe and beautiful in her white dress.

The minister read, in Mandarin: "If I speak in the tongues of men and of angels, but do not have love, I am a noisy gong or a clanging cymbal. And if I have prophetic powers, and understand all mysteries and all knowledge, and if I have faith, so as to remove mountains, but I do not have love, I am nothing. If I give away all my possessions, and if I hand over my body so that I may boast, but do not have love, I gain nothing.

"Love is patient; love is kind; love is not envious or boastful or arrogant or rude. It does not insist on its own way; it is not irritable or resentful; it does not rejoice in wrongdoing, but rejoices in the truth. It bears all things, believes all things, hopes all things, endures all things.

"Love never ends."

Pu Li looked very serious; Hwa's expression was resolved. Across the aisle from me, Pu Taitai's face was raised toward the minister, ardently, as if she were drinking in his words, but a closer look at her shadowed eyes revealed her to be far away.

My mother sat as still as stone. She had turned her head and only I could see her tears.

The Lake of Dreams

WHEN I WAS A CHILD, MY AUNT ONCE TOLD ME THE STORY OF a potted orange tree given by a Chinese woman to a friend in Korea who loved its fruit. In China, the tree bore globes of pale gold, with glistening, sweet sacs enclosed in papery translucent skin. The Korean woman set the tree in a southern window. She tended the white blossoms, waiting eagerly, but as the months went on, she noticed that the new oranges were not the same. They were smaller, small as tangerines, with skin of dimpled scarlet. Finally the first ripe fruit detached into her hand. Anxiously she removed the peel: the plump sections had shrunk and darkened to carmine. They had turned in on themselves, as if conserving strength in this new place. The Korean woman discovered that the taste, while no less delicious, had become more pungent and unusual.

Now I remember Yinan's story whenever I think of what became of us, raised in one country and then moved to another.

Pu Li grew in unforeseen directions, his roots taking on new depth in foreign soil. His strengths had always lain in his thoroughness, his steadiness, and his good nature. Over the years, his ability to do his work and get along led to a promotion, and then another, until he became the head of a division in his thriving software company, considered fair and admirable by both his bosses and his subordinates. He also proved himself to be a loving, generous husband; and although Hwa never brought it up, I know she took a quiet pride in this.

Hwa wanted to make a fresh start in America. She created for her family a world of clarity and order, studying television programs and subscribing to magazines that taught her the American way of life. She converted Pu Li to steak, potatoes, and American desserts. When her first child was born, a boy, her vision was complete. She decided that Marcus would be raised in English, in a language with no words for the dilemmas we had known. She installed a white carpet that began at the edge of the foyer and stretched into all the rooms. Everyone who entered removed their shoes and wore embroidered slippers. Visitors remarked upon the carpet's richness and newness, and whenever she expected guests, Hwa would make a circle through the house, smoothing out scuff marks until it looked as if a layer of soft and brilliant snow had fallen evenly throughout.

And what of my own American life? Perhaps, Hwa said, it turned out no worse than anyone else's.

After college, I brought little Mudan to New York City, where Rodale Taitai found me a job at a church-sponsored agency for new immigrants. I introduced the newcomers to each other, helped them understand the laws and do their paperwork. After immigration bans were lowered in 1965, I learned Cantonese and became an advocate for those who wished to sponsor their close relatives. I went to night school, earned a master's degree in social work, and took a job with a city agency.

For years I found solace in the vast, indifferent city. No one knew about me and no one knew my family. Little Mudan was a graceful, volatile girl with Hu Ran's blue-black hair and mobile features. After our long separation, I found it a relief to go to sleep at night and know that she was in the other room reading Hong Kong comic books by flashlight under her quilt. It was even a relief to work out her adjustment problems to her new country. In time she acclimated, slowly learning to speak English. She and I grew very close, although she maintained a privacy about the time we'd spent apart.

I had assumed Hu Ran would be with me forever, a set of footsteps next to mine, a matching memory of all we had been through. But as time went on, the ripples of our parting widened. Each morning took me further away. I tried to hold his image in my mind, struggling to keep alive the smoky scent of his rough clothes, the color of his eyes, and the shape of his mouth. I suffered this for years; then finally, it seemed my memories grew calm as sleep, and I couldn't feel the pressure of his fingertips on mine. After several years, I could no longer recall him without focusing, imagining.

I must have appeared no different from many women in New York City—taller, perhaps, and more recently arrived, wearing an expression rather faraway. I had studied English, found a job, and learned to hold my American life together. No one who looked at me would have known my story or my family's story. But in truth I had been pulled apart by this inheritance, by the separations and betrayals of my country, my family, and myself. For years I kept myself aloof from even Hwa and my mother. I saw them only on vacations. I avoided their hints that I might find a man, perhaps a widower, who could overlook what they considered the shame of little Mudan. I told them I wasn't interested in marriage. Actually, I was afraid. How could I love another when I had made it so clear that I couldn't be relied upon? I knew too many of my weaknesses. I had no strength to try. Only my daughter was exempt from this. I was determined not to fail Mudan. Every morning I woke up for her, and every evening I hurried home to be with her.

I met Tom Marquez in graduate school. I felt safe making friends with him because he was unlike anyone I'd grown up with. He looked nothing like Pu Li, being tall and thin; he had a long, somber face with deep-set eyes in which I never saw an echo of Hu Ran's bright color. He had never even eaten a Chinese meal. At first these differences confused me, but in time I found out what we shared. Tom's parents were immigrants. He had been raised solely by his mother and so he understood Mudan. Moreover, he was faithful to me and made me laugh throughout my years of hesitancy, forgiving my stops and starts with the patience of a stubborn man. His trust and sanity convinced me to move forward. After several years, it began to feel natural that we join our lives together, and so we married, finally, at City Hall. Together we raised Mudan and had a daughter, Evita Junan, of our own.

So Hwa spoke the truth when she said things worked out for me. My daughters grew and blossomed. Mudan did well in school and took a law degree. She had a great belief in justice, held in common with her father and great-uncle. Evita Junan grew up powerful and lovely after the women she was named for. After college on the West Coast, she came back to Manhattan and took a series of curious jobs: an internship at City Hall, a stint on a weekly newspaper, and a position at a zoo. She wanted to take her time about deciding what to be. Every weekend she rushed into the park to join a soccer game. As I watched Evita pull on her T-shirt, her flushed face emerging and her strong throat breaking free, I knew that she would never be crippled or constrained. It had been many years since my grandmother had been forced to walk silently despite the bells sewn onto her skirts.

In the years after I left Taiwan, we met challenges and had plenty of American adventures. But as I think over our stories, I can't include them with the one I'm telling here. Perhaps our American lives belong in a story of their own. It is enough for now to say that after more than thirty years in the United States I'd grown content. Only once in a long while, when one of my daughters was sitting quietly, reading, would her frown of concentration or the line of her hair recall someone I had once known. On most nights, I slept easily. I rarely spoke to anyone about my years in China, not even Hwa or my mother, who had their own reasons for keeping silent.

I was comfortable with my new life, almost to forgetfulness, when one day at work I heard a story about a ninety-five-year-old woman who had fled the mainland through Hong Kong and managed to come alone to the U.S. She had bought illegal paperwork claiming she was sixty-four, and settled in Manhattan's Chinatown, a grandmother to all her neighbors although a relative to none. She was a woman who remembered the unbinding of feet, and the Revolution of 1911, and who had gone through another revolution in 1949. Afterward she'd made her living sewing trousers in a Communist factory. Long before I learned her name I suspected she might be someone I already knew.

OVER TIME HU MUDAN had grown smaller, her flesh wandering from her bones and her memories, also, drifting. On good days, she called in a girl from Fujian who wrote letters for cash, and she replied to the occasional note requesting an interview. After three years in the U.S., she had begun to receive calls and letters from journalists and researchers who wanted to speak to her. Hu Mudan did not turn down a single request. She welcomed reporters, researchers, and scholars to her tiny place on Pell Street and gave them tea. When I went downtown to see her, she proudly showed me the articles, clipped and covered in plastic, arranged in a loose-leaf binder.

I turned the pages. "'Chinese Customs Remembered: A New Year Celebration in the Days of the Qing.' 'A Memory of Invasion: Hundred-Year-Old Woman Recounts Memories of Nanjing Massacre.' But you weren't in Nanjing during the massacre," I said. "Weren't you living in Sichuan Province?"

She shrugged. "Why would they care?"

"They are trying to record the events of the world. They are searching for the truth."

"But why should they know about my life?" She looked fiercely at me. "These big-noses, these foreigners and ABCs who come knocking at my door, wanting to know all about me—why should I tell them all about myself?"

"They want to understand the past."

"But that isn't possible."

I couldn't argue with her. "Then why don't you turn them away?"

"I feel sorry for them," she said.

I showed her photographs of Mudan and Evita. She didn't ask questions. She accepted their names quietly; and I promised I would bring them both to see her very soon.

Then Hu Mudan sat back with her frail-lidded eyes calm, as if reunions after decades took place every day. She didn't say a word for several minutes and I wondered if she might be in the midst of a waking dream. She was old, too old for such surprises. But when I stirred to leave, Hu Mudan put one warm, dry hand on mine. I understood she wanted me to stay with her. We sat hand in hand, and after a while it seemed to me that I could feel the memories stirring in her bones, and she was traveling thirty, fifty, seventy years.

She said her bones had become like the oracle bones they told of in the oldest histories. Time pressed gently upon them, like fingers playing on a reed pipe, but inexorably, until she had learned to listen to the melodies that arose from her body. And it seemed to her that as she had grown older the music of her bones had risen up, each note joining to the next, making arias and then whole Beijing opera stories. First and earliest, the death of her parents in Sichuan. Then the curtain of rain as she rode down the river to the sea; her arrival in Hangzhou, the beautiful city; and her first view of my great-grandfather's beautiful shabby house with its tall, worn firewall and the glittering green of worn roof tiles within. That was where our stories came together, one early morning in October 1911.

Hu Mudan and I sat together until the daylight faded. It was time for me to go home. But I had come prepared to speak and couldn't leave until I did.

"Hu Mudan," I said, "there's something I need to talk to you about, something that happened years ago. It's about young Mudan."

"She is my granddaughter."

"Yes. Hu Ran and I were— At the time, I didn't know that we would ever be apart. We had always loved each other."

Hu Mudan nodded.

"It's my fault that Hu Ran decided to go to Taiwan. I'm sorry," I said. "What happened to him was all my fault."

She took my hand again in her own warm, light hand. "Xiao Hong," she said. "I knew that about young Mudan. I knew the minute I saw her photograph. And it is I who was at fault, Hong. I knew how much you loved each other. It was I who told Hu Ran to go to Taiwan after you."

AFTER SEEING HU MUDAN, my mind began to wander past the boundaries of time. I would be walking along Canal Street when I would see a girl on the corner whose timid way of standing recalled the posture of my aunt when she was young. In a market on the Upper West Side, a young woman's basket of sweets brought to my mind our maid, Weiwei, who had stayed behind in China and whose fate I would never know. And one evening, when I saw a group of old men smoking their pipes, I was seized by the desire to find my father, to learn what had become of him.

At first the moments caught me by surprise. I shrugged them off as signs of age, returning with some relief to my real life. But soon I began to look forward to these glimpses of the past. I learned to hold my mind still and let them rise. They were after all the essence of my self. They were my other story, reflected just below my life. In time I understood their source was overflowing. An entire world lay shimmering in my memory. Late at night, the outlines would take shape, indistinct at first but gradually evoking more clarity, more richness, until I could see a wide and luminous picture of those years. It was like a world at the bottom of a lake, only visible on certain days but always present. The more substantial my American life became, the more vivid, powerful, and precious grew these memories of the past, held vast and dreamless underwater.

One winter evening, walking home from work, I saw a young man locking his bicycle to a signpost. The dusk had blotted out his features so I could only see the shape of his body. I knew it was not Hu Ran—Hu Ran was dead—and yet something in his movements, the set of his shoulders and the shape of his head, caused me to stop breathing. I was seized by a physical memory, an echo of a passion from long ago. I walked on, shaken. I had lost something precious, lost it before I even knew what I had, and until I could come to terms with it, I would simply ride out on the ripples from that loss.

I became convinced that I must search for those whom we had left behind. I spoke to Hu Mudan and wrote down her recollections. I paid for access to the library of a big research university, and while Evita was in school I took the train to the campus and began to look for books and articles. After Mao's death, the bamboo curtain had relaxed and slowly began to fall. It was possible to travel, but where could my father and Yinan be found? What had become of them?

I called Hwa in California. "I want to talk to Ma," I said.

"She's in the temple," Hwa said. "What do you want?"

"Do you know if she's heard anything from Baba or Yinan?"

Hwa guessed what I was thinking. "Why do you want to see him?"

she asked. "He deserted us." In my sister's voice I heard the echo of an old bitterness. "He abandoned us because we were only girls."

"That's not the true reason. He loved us. He did."

Hwa didn't answer immediately. I heard muffled instructions to Pu Li: "Turn on the oven to three-fifty, I'll be down in a few minutes." She always covered the phone when she spoke to him, as if I might divine some secret from their naked voices. Then she turned back to me. "Did you say he loved us? How can you believe that, Hong? I barely remember him. I don't remember when I ever felt at home with him."

"He and Ma were happy, once. In their own way." There came to my mind an image of my mother and Yinan, sitting on my bed, and my mother throwing back her head in laughter. "They loved each other," I said. "Ma and Ba. And Yinan. Ma and Yinan."

"Yinan didn't care."

"Of course she did. It was complicated. That's why I want to talk to them."

"Maybe it was and maybe it wasn't. But it's not your business." Hwa's voice grew determined. In a moment she would excuse herself to see about dinner. "I'm looking forward to seeing you all at Thanksgiving," she said. "But don't go digging into things that have been forgotten."

IN THE NEW COUNTRY, my mother had focused her desires on a house. She said she would live with Hwa until her children were in school, and afterward she wanted her own home. She purchased land in the foothills near Palo Alto—horse country, high enough for views, but not so high that the property would be endangered by mudslides. She had the land surveyed and examined by an expert in feng shui. Once they had ascertained the proper direction and location, my mother took her time. She planned a low, gracious house, built around a courtyard and surrounded by a wall. It wouldn't be as large as the Hangzhou compound—she didn't need so many rooms and servants. But there was a guest room for Pu Taitai, and for my family when we came to visit. There was a TV room for Hwa's children, two smaller spaces for a maid and a doorman, a temple, and also a room that went unmarked in the plans because my mother didn't want to say what it was for.

For years, she paid taxes on a hole in the ground. The foundation stood through several rainy seasons while she waited for hardwood from Malaysia and green glazed tiles from Mexico. Most of the parts were made by hand; the joists were carved by artisans in Taiwan. She hounded dealers for garden ornaments and carved rosewood lintels. Her Taiwanese architect even flew to California for several months while they perfected the interior of the temple: its mahogany benches and antique carvings and its statue of Guan Yin, goddess of mercy, reaching out indifferently with gentle hands.

In such a palace she should have settled into a fine old age, receiving friends and favormongers like a queen. She did all of these things. But she was not content. According to Hwa, she spent hours in the temple. On our Thanksgiving visit, I couldn't help noticing the restlessness that burned in her; it lit her eyes and hollowed her cheeks when they should have grown smooth and complacent. Every day she examined the house for the slightest trace of dust. She often sat in her garden, smoking one cigarette after another, staring west, over the foothills, toward the ocean.

Early Friday morning, I joined her in the garden. We sat silently for several minutes beside the fountain. It had been a dry autumn, and the winter foothills lit up silver-gold, first at their tops, then down along their length. The deepening light reflected on the still, white features of my mother's face.

She spoke first. "Where is your husband?"

"He's still in bed."

She nodded, but a slight line deepened between her brows, as if she thought I was wrong to leave him even for a moment. She treated Tom with care, always grateful and puzzled that I'd found a perfectly good man, not divorced or even widowed, who was willing to help raise a child who wasn't his.

I waited until she finished her first cigarette. "Ma," I said, "have you heard anything from Baba?"

"No."

"Sometimes I want to talk to him," I said. "I want to know if he's all right."

My mother turned to me. For a moment her face came alive around the eyes. I thought I saw hope in it, and fear, and in that moment I believed perhaps this search of mine might be something I could do to make us close again.

"As far as I know," she said, "he died long ago."

I couldn't reply.

"Hong, sometimes it's best not to think about what's gone." Her voice was gentle, almost kind. "If you can at all avoid it, you'll be happier that way."

I watched the smoke from her cigarette drift into the air. For decades now she'd held her silence, relying on Pu Taitai to spread the story of my father's death. I sat wondering at, admiring, the way my mother had held on to her marriage. She'd used her wits, her family, and finally a division caused by world events. Over the years, her feelings for my father had changed—they hadn't disappeared, but they'd been transformed through some emotional alchemy—into a desire to save face. Now she lived separated from the truth by politics and geography, safe behind a wall of unassailable widowhood.

So they were gone; more than likely, they had passed away into the tumult of change. I took Mudan and Evita shopping; Tom and I climbed in the foothills and went to visit an old mission. Then I returned to New York and found this letter waiting.

November 2, 1989

Dear Hong,

I recently received a letter from Hu Mudan that fulfilled my wildest hopes. I write to you in joy that I have found you at last. For years, I thought all chance of news was at an end, and recently, when things began to change, I didn't know how to search for you. Now Hu Mudan writes that you are well and that Hwa married little Pu Li. Hu Mudan asked you to forgive her for going to me behind your back. She wanted me to contact you so that you wouldn't hold sole responsibility for any correspondence. She thinks of you, always, and is very proud of you. I'm very happy to hear that you are doing so well.

Your father and I have managed to make it through some difficult years. Your father had some trouble but is now well. Yao is returned to us after a long stay in the country. He is married and has a wonderful young son, Cai. In the hardest times we have been lucky to have the help of our old neighbor Chen Da-Huan, who is now running a publishing company in Hong Kong. He has been a dear friend and made our lives much easier.

My precious Hong, it has been years since I have seen your face. I am deeply happy to think that we are once again in the same world. I long to talk with you again. I write this in hope that you and your sister can come to visit me in China and that we can recover the friendship we cherished when we were young.

Love,
Yinan

After we finished dinner, when Evita had gone downstairs to do her homework with a classmate in our building, I translated Yinan's words for Tom.

"What should I do?" I asked.

Tom looked at me, puzzled. "Aren't you going to China?"

"I don't know."

"Are you nervous?" He pushed the hair out of his dark, somber eyes and looked at me intently. I knew that he was thinking of his own father, who had left him and his mother when he was only four.

The next day I left work early and went to see Hu Mudan. It was a gloomy, wet afternoon, fraught with the violent autumnal changes. I hurried to the subway station, stepping into puddles. I tried not to think about my mother. I was afraid that she could sense me, a determined and errant trick of fate, moving through the crowds in the station. I took the train to Chinatown and hurried through the flocks of bright, dripping umbrellas. The division of my family was about to end.

It was one of Hu Mudan's bad afternoons. The weather had filtered through the walls and seeped into her bones. I offered her aspirin from my purse but she wouldn't take them. She told me nothing could change how old her body had become. There were days, she said, when she could trace her skeleton by the throbbing in her bones and could scarcely move, each gesture of a finger sending pain through her body. On those days, Hu Mudan felt lost and vague, dozing in one time and waking in another.

Together we watched television. A group of castaways on an island were arguing about a ship that one of them could see from far away.

I told Hu Mudan about Yinan's letter.

"Of course I want to visit her," I said. "Tom and I will take vacation in the spring. But I don't know how to tell my mother. I know she wouldn't approve."

"Houses burn," Hu Mudan said. "Keepsakes disappear. What matters is that we've lived and we forgive the ones we love, forgive them for their lives." For a moment, she seemed to wander, eyelids as light as autumn leaves. "You tell your mother that. You say I said we must forgive each other."

"Do you forgive me?"

She smiled. "How can I not forgive the mother of young Mudan?"

"What about my mother?"

"Does she forgive herself?"

"She says my father is dead. And she prays," I said. "She prays for hours every day, even when Hwa's son and daughter come to visit. Hwa says that when she thinks no one will notice she goes into the temple and kneels before Guan Yin. Hwa can hear her knees against the floor."

"Hmph." This implied Hu Mudan knew more about my mother's prayers than I could guess.

I wanted to believe my mother prayed for detachment. Perhaps she wished to let go of her old grudge, release her anger.

"Hu Mudan," I asked, "are you religious?"

"No," she said. "Not now."

"Were you ever?"

"In Hangzhou, the Methodist church was such a peaceful place. I would walk by and wish that I could sit inside."

"Why didn't you go?"

She hesitated. "Well, I did go in once. They had two services, one for foreigners and one in Chinese. I stood inside the door and listened to the Chinese service. There was Western music, plain, sweet songs all worked out in harmonies. Then the man talked for a long time about some god. He said that if you just believed in this god you would be saved. After you died you would live forever in a land where you would never be hungry or cold or bothered by anything again. I thought about it for a long time afterward, but I couldn't believe it."

"Why not?"

"I don't think there is any world waiting after this one to help any one get over anything they've done."

"You think they can't recover?"

"Not necessarily. All I know is that this god has nothing to do with it."

"Then you don't believe there is an afterlife?"

"Rodale Taitai did."

"Do you think the spirit is separate from the body?"

"When I was a girl, I was once very ill. It was the same sickness that killed my mother and father. I was so ill they almost gave me up for dead. I heard them say, 'A girl without a mother or father, what does she have to live for?' Then their voices went far away. I could feel myself disappearing, my spirit and mind dissolving as my body grew weaker. When I grew strong again, my spirit returned. I think that when my body leaves this earth, then so will I."

She closed her eyes. I sat and imagined Hu Mudan's idea of death. It would come when the uncountable parts that made her work would simply wear down and stop, like the gears of an old watch.

Minutes passed. She spoke as if she hadn't drifted off. "You tell your mother: it is the only thing that matters."

Sometime later, she opened her eyes. She said, "You can't come in this door. You must come in at the kitchen door." Her voice was cool, alluring, as if I were a person whom she'd met only recently and we were caught together in some powerful enchantment.

———

THIS WAS WHEN I called Hwa and she said it was impossible to reclaim the past. Moreover, she said that if I did insist upon returning to China, I should keep my disloyalty to myself. Our mother was getting old; my news would leave her angry and shaken. She would consider any contact an alliance, and I would be her enemy.

"You don't understand," Hwa said. "Baba is dead to her. He's been forgotten."

"She never heard of his death. She lied."

"Not really," Hwa defended her. "She said, as far as she knew."

"I know she's not at peace."

"You don't even live on the same coast with her," Hwa said. "You chose to live a separate life, and so you have no right to decide what's best for her."

"And you don't want to see him, either?"

Her voice rose. "You leave me alone," she said. "You want to live your own life. I don't interfere with yours, and you have no cause to interfere with mine."

Hwa was right. I had failed. When little Mudan was born, I'd been so absorbed in my own affairs that there were years when I'd forgotten all the time Hwa and I spent together as children. Small wonder that I had lost her. Her marriage to Pu Li had built another boundary. She had vanished into that marriage and into her loyalty to my mother.

And so the following spring, Tom and I left the country without telling my mother. We flew from Kennedy Airport to San Francisco and then Hong Kong. From Hong Kong we flew low over the mountains into Chongqing, now a bustling city where many of the old neighborhoods had been built over, but where the entrances to bomb shelters still tunneled into the cliffs along the Jialingjiang. At the old dock, where they had once brought the bodies from the Japanese bombings, we boarded a pleasure cruise along the Yangtze River. Before many hours had passed, we were hidden deep in Sichuan Province. Around us rose steep banks where the farmers worked the scant cover of soil that lay over the rocks, coaxing it into patterned fields green with young pepper plants and beans, or letting it flower white and yellow with rapeseed. The water under the boat was as clear as glass, and we could see the beautiful stones that lay heaped along the riverbed, pieces of the mountains that had once been compressed and shaped under enormous weight and heat into their vivid stripes of black and white and gray, now worn into smooth ovals. It was in a place like this, I knew, where Hu Mudan had been born.

We flew to Beijing and took the crowded train. We had a double seat all to ourselves, but I couldn't relax. Like a child, I sat looking out the window, restless, anticipating my father's appearance with a child's love and childish expectations. For so many years, I'd wanted to return to China, and now I sat watching the broad fields of winter wheat flow by without seeing them.

"I wish that Hwa were here with us," I said to Tom.

He shrugged. He didn't like to fly, but his face had brightened the moment we landed in Beijing. Now he was busy making notes in a little blue book. "I bet she'd come if she could," he said. "But she has a lot invested in keeping your mother happy."

"She was always that way." I considered this. "But she got so much more that way after I left home for the United States. It's as if she's living out the life my mother wanted: devoted husband, big house. A son."

"Perfect daughters aren't allowed to travel much."

We smiled and let the matter stand. But as I looked out the window at the plowed fields and relaxed at the chatter of Mandarin around me—albeit a northern Mandarin with its own accent—I believed that I was acting on my mother's most secret desire. She had once loved Yinan and my father more than anyone on earth. Underneath her preening solitude, her cloak of status, and her power, she must harbor a deep longing to reconnect with them. Someone must reach out to them. I had disappointed her so many times that I was now uniquely qualified to go against her wishes in the interests of her happiness. Perhaps this made me no different from Hwa; I wanted her to be happy. As we rode toward the station where her enemies were waiting, I knew I wanted to please my mother and always had, no matter how unreasonable she was, no matter how unbending.

WHEN WE STEPPED DOWN FROM THE TRAIN I COULD SMELL burning coal and chestnuts. The northern sky was pale gray and the air was cold. I didn't recognize the elderly couple waiting farther down the platform, watching the passengers leaving from another section of the train. They stood together in old overcoats, a little frail, a little lost. She clung to his arm. When they turned and saw me it seemed that she might lose her balance. Holding Tom by the elbow, I walked toward them in a daze. I had imagined a Yinan to match my mother, who was trim and lightly tanned from the California sun. This Yinan was vague and faded in the winter light.

But her voice was fluid and warm. "Xiao Hong," she said. "Thank you so much for finding us!"

"Ayi," I said.

She squeezed my hands, and in her eyes I could see something of the luminosity that had glowed in my mother's ghost-sheeted house.

My father's wool coat hung off his shoulders. Time and trouble had burned his strength away, wasting his body and washing the color from his face. Only his outline remained, faintly flickering at the edges.

"Hong," he said. "You look good."

"You look good, too."

"Ha! Don't joke with me."

His voice was light with happiness. I basked in his old buoyancy, our past pains forgotten. It had all come out right in the end. We had survived our separations, betrayals, and choices. We'd lived to find each other once again, and all was forgiven.

They greeted Tom warmly. Yinan spoke to him in English.

"Should we find a taxicab?" I asked.

"In a minute." My father turned to me and smiled, revealing a surprise. "Yao is on the next train. He was so excited by your visit that he's coming in from Tianjin, just for the night. He should be here soon." He and Yinan beamed.

YAO WAS THE first one off the train. Although his arms were filled with packages, I noticed something of my father's old grace in his stride as he hurried toward us. He wore the same wide smile I remembered from the day my mother had asked him to parade in his new victory suit. But when he came closer I could see that time had worn him down. His skin had coarsened, his face was shadowed and lined, and one of his teeth was missing. There was a restless quality in his walk, his wave, and the way he put down the packages to hug me.

"Jiejie," he said. His jacket smelled of cigarette smoke and something chemical and pungent.

"Didi," I replied. The word felt unfamiliar on my tongue.

I introduced him to Tom. "I am pleased to meet you," Yao said in English. "It is a long time since I have had a chance to practice," he added. I remembered he had gone to missionary school. Then he switched into Mandarin. He mentioned his wife and son in Tianjin. They were unable to make the visit, but they sent greetings. The packages at his feet were filled with small gifts for me and Tom, Evita, and Mudan. There was even something for Hwa, her children, and my mother.

We spent a pleasant evening in the front room of my father and Yinan's shabby apartment. Yinan made a local hotpot. After dinner, we drank beer and cracked peanuts, exchanging details of our respective lives. My father and Yao smoked cigarettes. We didn't mention the history or grudges that had divided us; soon it seemed to me that I'd been gone only a few years and that I had come home again. Only Tom's presence reminded me of my American life, and he lounged easily in a folding chair, holding a bottle of beer, deciphering their English and frequently laughing. My father and Yinan glowed under the lamplight. Our presence made them young again. As they talked and gestured with their hands, I was reminded of the long-ago evenings when they had sat out in the courtyard splitting salted watermelon seeds.

My father was pleased to know that Hwa had married the son of his old friend Pu Sijian. He listened with some interest to the story of Pu Taitai's persistent faith in his old government. And he asked me to confirm what he had heard about the difficult fate of General Sun Li-jen. After moving to Taiwan, Sun had been put under house arrest for many years under accusation that he had been somehow involved in a plot against the Generalissimo.

They described Li Bing's death of lung cancer, in 1965. I told them about Hu Ran, and through their empathy I felt my words gain dignity and sorrow.

Yao showed us photographs. Xiu, his wife, was a slender woman with large eyes, her expression intelligent and somehow sorrowful. But their son Cai looked like a young version of my father. His face was open and curious; he gazed eagerly at the camera.

"He wants to be an astronaut," Yao said. "We try to tell him he's too old for such daydreaming, but then again he's quite talented in both physics and athletics."

Tom and I passed around the pictures I had brought of Hwa and her family, my daughter Mudan and her family, and Evita. I had also brought a snapshot of my daughters with Hu Mudan. It showed two grinning, vibrant women towering over a tiny figure with the wrinkled, peaceful face of an old bodhisattva.

"She wrote to us out of the blue from the United States," Yinan said, laughing. "After she went to Hong Kong, she had a job working for a rich, old woman. She took care of her the way she used to watch after old Mma—putting her on the toilet, making all her favorite dishes. But this woman was more grateful. She died and left Hu Mudan some money, so Hu Mudan decided to go and look for you."

"How did she get to the United States?" asked Tom. "She has no family. She can't read or write."

"She bought a fake family. The name is Lu. She knew that if she met enough people she would run into Hong or Hwa, and there, she did it."

Later we argued over their insistence that Tom and I sleep in their bed. Tom won by claiming that the three of us "young people" wanted to stay up talking and would need more snacks from the kitchen. They finally agreed that we might spend the night on the floor of the front room. Then my father stood and helped Yinan rise to her feet. Watching her stand, I felt the weight of years fall over us again. They vanished, bent and frail, into their room.

THE BEER HAD loosened our tongues, and we spoke easily, keeping our voices quiet so as not to disturb their sleep. Yao asked if we wanted more to drink. He smoked and laughed and tipped back his bottle with the same restlessness I had observed at the station. I didn't know what to make of him—closer than a cousin but not quite a brother; a stranger and yet one so familiar. I also tried to reconcile him with the boy I remembered. He had been so promising—alert and filled with life— and yet now he looked as if he had been used and broken from within. I learned that he worked at a paper mill—this accounted for the chemical odor of his clothes—and that he didn't often get a chance to leave his family and see his parents.

Tom listened carefully, now and then rearranging his long body in his chair. He often held himself apart from strangers, but it seemed he felt a bond with Yao. When Yao offered him a cigarette, he nodded, although he hadn't smoked since graduate school. When he had taken a few puffs, he asked, "Do you miss your parents?"

"Yes. My mother, mostly. My father and I don't always get along. He can be difficult." Yao paused. "Remote. Sometimes it is as if he isn't there. My mother understands him."

I didn't know what to say.

Tom said, "I suppose you never saw him during the years of civil war."

"He never knew me until 1949. But I thought about him all the time.

He was my father, a general and a hero. He loomed so large in my mind. Then we were united, finally, and it was all different."

He stopped abruptly. Again, Tom spoke. "Was it awkward for you to meet him when the government changed over?"

Yao frowned, leaning forward to light the cigarette. The flash of the match revealed the pure lines of his bones—my mother's bones—under his coarsened features. "There was a time when we couldn't be in the same room together." He blew out a stream of smoke. "He could be distant, moody, and then he would snap to himself and be so friendly and optimistic—as if he had forgotten. He was so sure of himself. And I suppose I was the same way. It was hard on my mother."

How had my father felt? I wondered. He had wished for so long to have a son, only to meet a stranger whose dreams of him were shattered by his actual arrival. How could any human man live up to a boy's dreams?

"He wanted to be close. I wished I had let him. But it was all so sudden, all of the changes. And I don't think he understood immediately that our reunion was—harmful for me. When Li Bing moved us north, we had to keep his identity a secret. We went by my mother's surname, Wang. And I grew ashamed—I had political training in school and I began to find it hard to accept who he was." He paused. "I suppose it was my own shame that drove me to Maoism. I did well in school but somehow in my mind it had all fallen apart. I didn't go to college. Instead I went to my uncle"—here I detected a note of pride in his voice—"and began to work for the Party."

"Li Bing was my father's brother," I explained to Tom. "He was part of the underground, before 1949." Tom nodded, not noticing that his cigarette had gone out. The conversation mattered to him in some way that I could only guess.

"I was doing well until Li Bing died. I was going to marry Xiu. But about a year after our uncle died, the party began to examine itself, and they discovered my bad blood." He paused and looked down at his hands.

"How did it happen?" Tom asked.

Yao didn't look at me. Instead, he fixed his eyes on Tom's face, as if he sensed someone who might understand.

"Later I found out that it was I who'd let it slip—not the whole truth, but something, to a school friend, years before—enough so that they were able to learn who he was. They put him into prison. He was there for over a year. He was only released after my mother and I went to Li Bing's old friends and begged, many times. Then they decided I was somehow tainted, tainted by his blood. They sent me to the countryside and told me to purify myself among the peasants."

In his voice I sensed emotions—passion, anger, bitterness—but he spoke carefully, almost hesitating, as if the words burned his tongue.

"Xiu and I promised we would wait for one another. How could we have known how long I would be gone? It was eight years. She did wait for me, but we wasted so much time." He looked at his old leather shoes. "It's all right, it doesn't matter. When I was first assigned, I was angry at him—so angry. I wanted to curse him for his stupidity, his belief that he could live here under the Communists and not get caught. What must he have been thinking? Was it true he loved the country so much that he couldn't bear to leave it? Then he had naïve, sentimental emotions. Would it have been so bad for my mother and me to go? She says that it was her fault—she says she was the one who made him stay and that she had promised Junan—but I know that if he really wished to go he would have done it."

I stared into my lap at one of Yao's gifts to me, a bright, embroidered handkerchief. I didn't know how to tell him the truth.

"Before I left, I went to see him in prison. He said that he was sorry." Yao shook his head. He sighed and the blaze of anger that had fueled his story faded into resignation. "And then I understood. Staying in China was something that he decided long ago. He couldn't have known what was going to happen."

He talked late into the night. He had been assigned to a tiny mountain village that seemed utterly desolate. The fields were stony and the villagers had suffered in the war. They had been punished by misfortune and could barely feed themselves. They were so poor that even the richest of them had used up his jar of cooking oil; in the springtime, they ate boiled leaves.

Yao didn't speak the dialect. He did not even know where he was. But he had a farmer's blood in him, through our father's father.

I imagined that the villagers were attracted to his handsome looks, his height, his physical vigor, his charisma, and his love. For he had inherited one thing, it seemed, from his mother: that openness, that sympathy, where he respected others and loved them. He also inherited her ideals. The people in his village were swept up in his visions. He organized the villages, dug deeper wells, sanitized the rivers, and founded schools. He toiled with his mother's patience and his father's strength.

"It all worked out in the end," he said. "But when they told me I could go, and my exile was over, I came back to find that I was old and that the world had changed."

His energy released, he slumped in his chair. His lined face was frozen in the pale light. I heard footsteps on the street and the low sound of a water buffalo. It was dawn and the last farmers were entering the city.

"You need to get some sleep," I said.

But Yao didn't want to sleep. "Tell me more about your mother," he said, turning to me. "I remember her from when I was a boy."

His voice was open, interested. His question caught me off guard, and I couldn't answer.

"She was always so warm and generous," Yao said.

Tom raised his eyebrows at me, but Yao didn't notice.

"My mother loved her so much. She still talks about her—I think she still misses her, regrets the war for parting them."

"They were very close as girls," I said.

"She brought me, once, a train set on tracks that took up so much space I had to open the door of the house where we were living. I had to get rid of it years later; there wasn't room for it when we moved north." For a moment he stopped speaking. From the worn shape of his face a faraway look emerged; he was thinking about the promise of that gleaming train.

"I have to tell you something secret, Jiejie. When I was younger, I sometimes used to wish that I'd been able to leave with you. I would have gone to the United States, and everything would be different."

He was silent for a moment. "But it's too late for me, I've lived my life."

THE NEXT DAY we took Yao to the station. We hugged each other and said goodbye, promising to write. Afterward, Yinan and my father returned for a nap. Tom and I stretched out in the front room, but we didn't sleep. The room seemed empty without Yao's restless, burning words.

Tom reached over and put his hand briefly on my shoulder. "I don't think it would've been right for you to tell him why your father stayed behind."

"I hope you're right." I felt grateful for the comfort of his presence. But I couldn't relax. After a moment, I said, "It sounds like they tried to tell him, but they didn't, or couldn't, explain what happened with my mother. Maybe they wanted to protect him. Or preserve his good memories. They want to keep him from being bitter."

"He has a lot to be bitter about." Tom turned onto his side, and for a while I thought that he had gone to sleep. Then he spoke. "But how many of our lives aren't wasted in some way? If Yao had come to the U.S., he might have spent years struggling to get started. He might have gotten bitter about the racism or something else. It's hard for men, in ways that women don't always imagine. Not everyone is as successful as Pu Li."

Perhaps Tom was thinking about the way his own father had struggled. I knew little about the man except that his ambitions had been thwarted by a language barrier. Tom had made a hard journey to graduate school. And what about my own life? I wondered. I liked my job, but I had once told Hu Ran I wanted to be a journalist or writer. I lay awake thinking about my brother's restless words. Later, on the verge of sleep, I realized that Yao had simply absorbed Yinan's version of the story, and since Yinan would never say a word against my mother, Yao had assumed the villain was my father.

We spent a few more peaceful days with them. My father showed us the factory and took us to the sites where decades before the locals had resisted the Japanese occupation. Tom spent hours taking notes as Yinan instructed him on how to make northern buns and noodle dishes.

Later she showed me some of her old poems. Her work was cryptic, stark. Perhaps she shared with my mother a privacy that made it hard to glean anything truly personal from her work. Several poems appeared to be about her mother's suicide.

> *She held it her cold white hands.*
> *Water gravestone, water tomb,*
> *Falling silently into the lake of dreams.*

It seemed to me that all her poems addressed a single person as their audience, the one living person who would truly understand them.

By the end of our visit, I could see that Yinan and my father had been through a great struggle, a dark time of drowning, and on the other side they had emerged lighter. Some central element had been discarded. Perhaps they had been forced to give it up in order to survive. They were not quite the people I remembered.

And yet, they said, there had been help for them. In the days when Yao was being sent away and Li Ang had just been released from prison, one person reached out to help them. The first letter from Hong Kong found them after Yao's departure. It was addressed with an elegant hand in unsimplified characters. At first they couldn't imagine who might have found from outside. My father held the envelope at arm's length—his eyesight had grown farsighted from age and distances—until he made out the name of his old acquaintance, Chen Da-Huan, to whom he had once given his cigarette case, and who had not forgotten him. When he opened the letter, a long, green hundred-dollar bill fell into his lap.

In his letter, Chen Da-Huan thanked my father for helping him. He and Qingwei had eventually reached Hong Kong. Qingwei had not lasted long—they had known she was dying—but gave birth to a son, Fengwa, and spent the last year of her life in relative comfort. Chen Da-Huan had vowed to repay my father. He'd searched assiduously for news of him—speaking to refugees who had crossed the border, and running newspaper ads until he found the information.

Wasn't it wonderful, Yinan said, that Chen Da-Huan should remember this small favor? That it was possible to be reunited after so many years? At this, Yinan turned to look at me, her eyes magnified by the lenses of her reading glasses.

"Hong, during this whole visit, you've said almost nothing about your mother. Is she well?"

My father covered her hand with his.

"I think about her every day. I've been hoping she would find us. I've been hoping"— here she paused —"that she would want to speak to us, after all these years."

"Yinan," my father said.

She shrugged off his hand. I could see this was something they'd been over before. "How is her health?" Yinan continued. "Is she happy?"

I looked at Tom, but he shook his head. Yinan wanted my answer, not his. It wasn't the first time during the visit that I had tried to avoid answering a question. For example, I had told white lies about why Hwa and Pu Li hadn't come with us. At one point, I had joked about Hwa's culinary memory lapse, her steak and mashed potatoes. In truth, I didn't know what to make of Hwa's life. She seemed happy enough, but after more than thirty years, she still refused to visit Los Angeles, where Willy Chang was living with his wife and children.

Explaining Hwa was difficult enough. I had avoided the subject of my mother, suspecting that what I had to say could only disappoint.

Yinan persisted. "Did she send any messages along with you?"

"Yinan," my father said, "don't you see that she won't speak to us, she could never do that?"

"I believe that somewhere, in her heart, she still loves us."

My father's hands tightened on the arms of his chair. "Even if she did," he said, "do you think she would admit it?"

"I've known her longer than you have. She was the first person I can remember besides our mother. She's a loyal person, a good person. She was always good to me. Who knows how she feels now, after so many years?"

"I'm thinking about your feelings." My father's voice was loud, as if he were talking in an empty room.

She lightly touched one of his clenched hands. "I can take care of myself. Let Hong speak."

Then they turned to me. They had waited for so many years. I had come all the way across the world. I had no choice but to tell them what I knew.

And so I described Hwa's instructions that I not tell my mother about our trip. I talked about my mother's money and her beautiful walled house with its contemplative garden and green roof tiles. I told them about the way she prayed for hours alone before the figure of Guan Yin. I told them everyone believed my father was dead. My father looked tired and Yinan wept, but she kept asking questions. She insisted that I give her my mother's address. Her questions were quiet and plaintive like the questions of a child. My own voice sounded cold in my ears—was it my mother's legacy in dealing with such feelings? Or was it because I knew that with each word I was betraying her? And yet I didn't feel disloyal to her. My loyalty was of another kind. Like Yinan, I believed that she could still be comforted.

ON OUR LAST DAY in China, my father and I spent a few hours alone. We walked to the park and sat together on a bench in front of a statue of revolutionary heroes. I showed my father a photocopy from a book listing the Nationalist officers. I had gone far into the university library and found a dusty, heavy volume with a copy of the same photograph my mother had framed for the wall of our house in Shanghai. Third from the left, he stood among a group of uniformed men, straight and confident in the prime of his life.

The text read,

LI ANG (1909–49)
HANGZHOU, ZHEJIANG PROVINCE

1926 INFANTRY
1928 ARMY RANK SECOND LIEUTENANT
1931 MARRIED
1932 ARMY RANK LIEUTENANT
1936 JOINED KMT
1936 ARMY RANK CAPTAIN
1937 TAX POLICE STAFF
1942 COLONEL
1945 MAJOR GENERAL
1949 CAPTURED OR DECEASED

My father smiled, a little sadly. "And when I die," he said, "this book will hold the only written evidence of my life." He shook his head. "I would never have imagined it when I was young."

"What did you want when you were young?"

"That was another era. We didn't think of what we wanted to do. We did what we thought we had to do. We acted with our heads, not with our hearts. And then I changed. I didn't understand what I had done until long after it was over. By then I'd become another man; there was no going back. I had to make a life that I could live with."

"Is that why you stayed here in China?"

"Yes," my father said.

"Was it worth it?" I asked.

He looked across the park at a group of people practicing tai chi. He knew my real question. How could you have left us?

"For all these years I've pictured the last time I saw you," he said, "in that house in Shanghai, surrounded by furniture covered in white sheets. You looked so angry and so young. I knew your mother would watch out for you, but I couldn't help worrying about whether you'd be happy, how things would turn out for you."

"It all turned out okay." I blinked against my tears.

"It is okay," he agreed. After a moment, he said, "But you've inherited my flaw. You remember too much. You, and me, and Yinan, too. It makes an unsafe life."

"My mother would have kept you safe."

"She tried," he said. "I know she tried. Look, this was a present from her." He gestured at his old overcoat. "She brought it to me in Chongqing, more than forty years ago. It's very warm and it has lasted a long time."

I took a long, shaking breath. "I missed you, Baba."

"I missed you," he said. He put one hand lightly on top of my head. "We both missed you, your sister, and your mother. We've thought of you and loved you for all that time."

LATER THAT YEAR, MY FATHER AND YINAN TRAVELED TO Hangzhou. They arrived to find the city grown beyond its walls. Uncle Charlie's street had been paved and lined with offices. The Wang family compound had been rebuilt as well. The old neighborhood was gone; they could see nothing of the old house except a cracked green tile under a potted plant on someone's windowsill. And in a dusty corner, there still survived the old mulberry tree that had once fed Yinan's pet silkworms.

Also the lake remained, wide and serene, and they could see the ugly stub of the Thunder Peak Pagoda. The scene was little changed from how it had appeared on the day when Yinan had first seen it as a child.

They stood before the lake for quite a while. Around them, children dressed in red and pink jackets ran and shouted. Tourists boarded low boats, each led by an English-speaking guide. Young couples walked arm in arm along the path. No one paid much attention to the old man and old woman gazing at the water.

YINAN HAD NEVER been strong. The long hours in the factory had hurt her eyes and her neck, and worst of all the fabric had contained a chemical irritant that boiled in her blood, thinning her bones. She suffered from repeated colds and a disturbance of the inner ear. That autumn, she was diagnosed with leukemia, which explained her frequent illnesses, the pain in her bones, and her feeling of inexorable wearing down.

One night that winter, Li Ang woke suddenly, frightened. What had startled him? Without moving, he eased his gaze toward the other side of the bed. Yinan lay on her stomach, face buried in the pillows. He listened carefully, sniffed for the familiar, faintly bitter cloud of her breath. It was a winter night so cold that the streetlight outside the window was only a glow behind the patterned ferns of frost and ice that thickened the glass. He lay for a long moment. Then there came a slow breath, and then another. Then the tick of the clock, its dim face shining slightly in the light from the window. He lay watching the needle of the second hand as it jerked slowly around the face. He knew what had awakened him. It had not been a noise at all but silence, a terrifying moment of silence that had come, he realized, from the fear her breath had stopped.

Then it was morning. Brittle, pale sun fell across the bed. He dressed and went into the kitchen, where Yinan had already risen and boiled hot water for the tea. The steam had frozen on the kitchen window, enclosing them even more completely in their small apartment. He felt relief at her nearness, at the small, familiar window glinting with pale sun. He ate his porridge.

She appeared in the kitchen doorway wearing her coat and scarf, carrying her boots in her arms the way one might hold a child.

"What is it?"

"I need to mail a letter." Now that she had Junan's address, Yinan wrote to California each month.

He was worried that she might slip and fall; they'd paved the roads and now ice lingered. He finished his tea and went to get his coat.

I imagine the way they must have looked on those rare times when they left the house together, only on fine or necessary days now, a neat, gray couple, a tall man somewhat bent about the shoulders, limping slightly; next to him a smaller figure featuring the brief and still-elegant brim of a hat given to her by Americans in the days of civil war. She tucked her gloved hand under his arm. It would have been impossible to explain to a stranger what they'd been through and what they meant to one another. Their lives had fused together like the roots of two trees planted close against the wind.

It was breathtakingly cold, and the light snowfall squeaked against their boots. They walked with their heads bent slightly to shield their faces, speaking little in an effort to keep out the cold. When they reached the post office, Yinan mailed her letter, watching the clerk's hands to make certain that the envelope went where it should.

"Before we know it," said the clerk, "it'll be the New Year."

The clerk often chatted with Yinan as he made her change. He did not address Li Ang by name. When Li Ang had returned from jail, almost everyone had behaved as though they'd never accused him, as though nothing had happened. Only this clerk remembered and was ashamed. Now he avoided looking at Li Ang.

They turned around and headed home.

In this direction the cold stung them, it drove through their clothes. Li Ang could not feel his nose or his ears under his cap. He pressed closer to Yinan, whose body was drawn into a comma, bracing stiffly against the onslaught, too clenched to shiver. Inside, they could scarcely feel the warmth. While Yinan took off her things, Li Ang put his old coat back into the closet. He came back to the entrance and found Yinan sitting on the bench there, rubbing her stiff hands.

"I can't pull off my boots," she said.

Li Ang knelt before her. He took hold of her boot and tested it, tugging against its stubbornness. She sat before him obedient and silent. Perhaps her feet had swollen slightly. He worked carefully, wiggling the heel and searching for the right angle, his nostrils filled with the smell of melting snow. Finally the boot eased away, and at the sight of her stockinged foot stuck straight out he felt sorrow pass through him.

He said, "You know she won't write back."

She did not answer. He pressed further, determined to have it out.

"Why do you insist on writing to her and letting her hurt you?"

From below, he watched with dismay as she turned her face away.

"I'm sorry," he said. "Ah, stop crying."

Presently she rubbed her eyes and said, "It's only something my mother told us once. She said that there are separations in the world, but we will all be certain to see each other in the afterlife."

Li Ang replied automatically, "Why are you thinking of the afterlife? You're still young."

She put her face into her hands. "Jiejie," she wept.

He reached out and took her hand. It was cold and dry, and he could feel the flesh slightly loose on the bones, as if whatever had been holding her together were wearing out at last. Then all of a sudden he remembered the feel and scent of her hand fresh and yielding, as it had been when he had first held it so many years ago.

HE HAD REACHED the age when many men, sensing their approaching end, revise their orientation toward the world. Some, no longer useful there, take solace in its edges, minding their newspapers and sitting by the street, watching and discussing the actions of younger people. Still others grow discontented and move hopefully toward religion and philosophy. But my father didn't follow either path. He understood that he and Yinan, and everything that they had known, were fading from the world. Their lives together were ending; and he had no desire to be anywhere else. Still, despite his efforts to be present, there were moments, as he was going about his day, when he would feel his thoughts snap and he would forget where he was. He would enter a sort of waking dream, and he would find himself lost in memory or fancy.

One of these visions came repeatedly. The dream varied in its opening, but never in its ending. Perhaps he would be in the hospital, waiting with Yinan for the results of some examination. Perhaps he would be at a meal, chewing a mouthful of the savory green called empty-heart. Whenever the time, whatever the place, what happened next was always the same. An invisible power turned him around. He would suddenly be looking in the opposite direction, as if he had been lifted by a great hand and turned in the air. Then just as suddenly and with complete naturalness, someone would walk into view, a tall, slender figure with no distinctive features. A certain quality about this visitor drew my father's attention. It was someone so familiar and yet unknowable. In the next moment, the identity of the visitor would become clear. It was my mother, changed little after this long absence. She would stretch her hand out to him, gracefully, beseeching, filled with sorrow. *Junan.* Then she would vanish, leaving an empty space.

———

AND SO THAT SPRING we made arrangements through the mail, and in his old age, my father made the journey across the world and through time to visit America. He came to see us in New York, where he stayed for several days and collected for Yinan a recorded video message from my daughters. He and I had lunch with Hu Mudan. But the true reason for his long trip would wait until its end. He had promised Yinan that he would fly home through San Francisco and stop long enough to visit my mother. Yinan said it was the only thing she wanted before she died. He asked me not to warn my mother; I think he was afraid she would refuse to see him.

After having lived a life of bold and often thoughtless action, he now wished to finish quietly. He craved a peaceful death. But there was little chance of this, he knew.

Most likely fate would hold a troubled end for any man who'd wielded more than his share of power. He often thought about the death of the warlord Sun Chuan-fang, whom Li Bing had so much reviled in Hangzhou. He had been a force of such brutality and strength. But he had killed too many people in his early years, and as a result of this he was remembered by too many of the living. After his defeat, at the hands of Chiang Kai-shek, he had repented his behavior and become a devout Buddhist. He had moved far north into a city where he hoped to fade and be forgotten. But others had not forgotten him. One day while he was praying, a young woman entered the temple. It was the daughter of a general whom he'd once ordered to be put to death. Her name was Shih Chien Ch'iao, Outstanding Sword, and she had tracked him down, determined to avenge her father. She shot Sun Chuan-fang in the back of the head.

The first time Li Ang had seen Yao, in Hangzhou, the boy had walked into the room where he and Yinan were standing close together. Li Ang couldn't breathe. He had only recently learned of his son's existence. He saw a tall, handsome boy, whose dark features revealed Li blood. At the sight of Li Ang, the boy's haughty Wang nostrils had flared, and his lips had parted—full, beautiful lips that curled in sudden angry tears. Then Yao turned and left the room, overcome. Yinan rushed after him. Li Ang did not follow them. He had brought nothing to Yao but his seed. And from that time on, it always seemed to him that he was watching his son as if through a window. How could this not have been? Should he not have been punished in some way for abandoning his daughters? He reminded himself he hadn't known of Yao when he had left them. But he had left them nevertheless, and in their place he discovered a child who did not know anything about him except that he had been a Nationalist general.

Soon Yinan would die, leaving him on his knees facing all that he had done. He had suspected, long ago, that he would continue on, his body somehow shielded, protected. As a young man, his own physical invulnerability had been his fondest assumption. Still later he'd understood that he would not escape the ravages of experience and memory. And yet his body had held on. Scars glittered on his skin; pieces were missing here and there. Now he understood that the most difficult of life's ravages were invisible. Certainly those in power had always understood this. They had erased so many men, killed them without a trace; and those they had tortured were tortured in such a way that the worst scars could not be seen.

Junan had also held a kind of power, and wielded it with no outward regrets. Certainly, he thought, she must hold somewhere the same scars, the same troubled memories. Now he would carry to her the bitter news of Yinan's illness. Perhaps his news would soften her and she would yield to his request. Didn't the most hardened, aged general feel a moment of compassion upon learning the misfortune of his former enemy?

ON THE PLANE to San Francisco, my father dozed and tried to read the newspaper, but his eyes tricked him so that certain characters looked like the characters in Junan's name. This jolted him to an awareness of what he was doing. He didn't want to see Junan, but he had promised. He was dreading the sight of her, and every minute he came closer.

He arranged for the cabdriver let him out early so he could walk and steady his nerves. Later he wrote to me that California seemed too perfect to be real, with houses so new that the trees were quite small with trunks and branches as smooth and slender as the throats of young girls, and the streets unbroken under the sun. His shadow hovered beneath him, bent and hollow on the pavement.

His eyes, grown farsighted with their years, detected the red roofs of the renowned university and the distant, glittering buildings of San Francisco. It was a windy day with little smog, good visibility. His gaze followed the road and then a turn to the right, until he glimpsed a long, pale brick wall that marked the boundary of my mother's house.

He knew about the house and still he was surprised. What he saw seemed to float in the back of his eyes, every shape and line familiar, from the squat, ornamental sculptures to the faint glitter of green tile that lay within. He felt for a moment as if he were looking at a place that had long since passed out of the real world, and even the smells of grass and flowers were as faint as the perfume of dreams. Walking slowly toward the house, he saw the foliage against the wall and then her line of rosebushes, proud and meticulously tended, lifting huge, precise ivory blossoms high against the brick.

He felt his thoughts rising lightly, borne like a scent on the wind, and he found himself standing once again in the old courtyard where he had entered, so many years ago, wearing his foot soldier's uniform, looking for Junan's father. He could almost smell the kitchen, hear the clicking as Wang Daming mixed the paigao tiles. He was a young man again, with his watertight confidence and unassailable hopes, heart beating before the elegant, worn walls, trying to guess at the opulence and mystery within. How he had wondered about the charms of Wang Daming's beautiful elder daughter who lived there.

Had he really changed? he wondered. Had love or time changed him one bit, or was he still that man who moved so thoughtlessly forward?

He expected somehow that she would be standing at the door, as she was the evening they had met. But when he knocked on the door, it was opened by a small, indifferent manservant.

With an effort of will, he announced himself.

"Please tell the madame that Li Ang has come to pay his respects."

The man turned and vanished. In a moment, he was back. This time, Li Ang detected signs of a disturbance. The man's hands trembled as he closed the door. He looked dazed and shaken by a sudden bolt of wrath, and Li Ang knew his visit was a surprise.

He was shown through a large room and into the courtyard. As he came closer to the garden, he caught a glimpse of color and knew there would be flowers of such profusion and rarity as he had not seen in sixty years. There would be a goldfish pond with a willow tree, fruit trees, and a mulberry. There was indeed all of this, and in the center of the garden were enormous black stones that she must have had brought there from towering foreign mountains, tall shapes like petrified wood, swirling with deep obsidian-colored patterns.

Near these stones, she sat alone. As he came closer, he noted the elegance of her bones, even more clear since the flesh had melted away. The throat and face and hands had grown small with age. She had conquered what emotion had seized her upon learning of his visit, and sat perfectly composed, with her hands folded in her lap, weighted down perhaps by the gold and pearl and enormous jade rings on her wrists and fingers. More jade and heavy gold lay around her throat. Her oval face was pale. Behind her, on a narrow table, three elongated statues of the bodhisattvas watched him with stone eyes.

He bowed slightly, and she nodded in return.

Even after so many years, it was a shock to come face-to-face with Junan's powerful will. Her eyes were slightly lidded over in an expression he remembered well but had never quite learned to read. Only one person might have been able to tell what she was thinking, and Yinan was far away.

He reached into his bag and produced a gift, a box of candies of a kind he recalled she had once liked, bright, hard candies twirled into many shapes.

"Well," he said, and smiled at her. "How are you, Junan?"

"I am perfectly well. Of course, my strength isn't what it used to be. And you, you're getting so old!" she said.

"But reports of my death were inaccurate, I fear."

She frowned; he hastened to make peace. "I've become an old man," he said. He added gallantly, "You, on the other hand, are very much the way I remember."

But he found the changes to her face and body unsettling. After so many years of separation he had come to imagine Junan as the woman of his youth, her skin forever white and fresh, her lips red, eyes sparkling.

"Let me pour you a cup of tea."

"No, no," he protested. "I'll do it."

"All right," she said.

Reassured, he slowly poured their cups, careful to control the movement of his hands. "A pity that you don't drink brandy before dinner," he remarked.

"It can't be helped."

"Let's drink to meetings after many years. Ganbei!"

Together they raised their cups, and in this way they arrived at conversation. Junan's body may have aged, but her mind was as quick and true as it had ever been. She provided him with gossip about their old acquaintances. Pu Taitai still insisted on living in Taiwan. There, she spent her time busily engaged in telling and retelling a kind of myth about the events of the first half of the century, a myth that acknowledged the basic events—the attempts of the Republic to hold the country together, the Japanese invasion, and the Communist takeover—but that, through ingenious shifting and careful balancing of forces and faults, managed to ignore their own defeat. For years, Pu Taitai had repeated the revised slogan,

> *Ten years of birth and gathering*
> *Ten years of teaching them*

After twenty years had come and gone, she had mentioned this less frequently, but Junan didn't think she had ever ceased believing that Taiwan would someday triumph, and the Nationalists would return to mainland China and become, once again, its rightful government.

In America, Hsiao Meiyu had disinherited two of her grandchildren for marrying "foreigners." Junan found it a pity that the son had married a blonde—the children would have such thin, light hair—but she didn't wonder about the daughter, a paragon of terrible genes—small-eyed and dull-faced, with those fat, cucumber legs. What Chinese man would have married such an ugly girl?

"'Patriotic.'" Li Ang cleared his throat. "On the mainland, a young woman isn't called 'ugly.' She is 'very patriotic.'"

He could hear in his own voice the old, flirtatious tone he had always used with her. He had missed this. It was the way they had once been together—not during the war, when each conversation had been fraught with the exhaustion of logistics and separation—but in the early days, when they had first been married. They'd barely known each other then; he had believed she couldn't truly hurt or change him. And she must have believed the same of him.

Then Junan asked, "What brings you here?"

"Me?" He stalled for time.

"I know you wouldn't come to visit me unless there was something you wanted from me. What is it?"

Li Ang took another deep breath. Suddenly the California air held no nourishment.

Years ago, Junan had said that he would come to her, begging. Now the situation was exactly as she had predicted; but knowing this didn't make it any easier. He would come begging, but if he must beg, he would present a request whose refusal he could bear. He had prepared a question secret even from Yinan, turned it over in his mind as he lay awake during the past few weeks.

"Well," he said, "it's been a long time since we have met. And I've had many years to think about you."

Still, Junan sat waiting. He might have been speaking to one of the tall cypress trees behind her.

"Yes," he continued. "Many years to think of how I've wronged both you and your sister."

Junan smiled.

"It's true. I know what I have done." He paused. He knew that what he said was true. For a moment he considered stopping here, asking for nothing. But he still cared what she thought of him. She didn't respect apologies. He needed to press on.

"You have no reason to forgive me," he said, "but will you at least take pity on Yao's boy, Li Cai? He's a very smart child, the star of his class. His father has suffered so much for my choices. Will you sponsor Li Cai to come to the United States?"

She didn't answer but sat watching him closely.

"Throughout these years," he added, "Yao has thought of you as his benevolent auntie. We have never changed his views. He would be forever grateful to you if you would help his child."

"What do you really want from me?"

"I've just said it."

"No, there is something else."

He noticed then that his hands were still clenched on the arms of the chair. He took a deep breath. She had stripped away his cover. Now, naked and vulnerable, he must put Yinan's request before her.

"I want you to put an end to this feud between you and Yinan. I want you to forgive her."

She shook her head.

"Please," he burst out, "Yinan—she is suffering. Only you, only you can put an end to this. Please, go to her. She is ill. She will die. Show her that you have forgiven her and both your spirits will rest in peace."

He paused and looked up at her hopefully. His hands trembled. He blinked, to dry his eyes. The looming shadow of all he had lost, and was still to lose, fell over him, and he waited, as if they were both young and filled with promises. For a long moment she did not respond. She had folded her hands in her lap and now she sat frowning at the gold on her wrists and fingers.

"She sent you to do this."

"She—"

"It can't be done."

Her voice was shaking, splintering apart. "Many different things bring peace to different people, and you know it." She took a deep breath and when she spoke again he knew that she had calmed herself. "But you shouldn't try to interfere in our quarrels." She put a cool hand on his. "This was something between Yinan and myself. Between sisters. Surely you understand?"

"No," he said. He realized then that he had never understood either of them. After all of these years, their bond, even in anger, had been a bond that he could not penetrate or know.

"Some things, once broken, can never be fixed."

His voice was also shaking. "You know the three of us may never see each other again alive, Junan."

With an effort she controlled herself. She stared at her hands until she could raise her calm, white face and bend her smile upon him again. "I know," she said. "I don't expect to."

There was a long silence before he stood. He left the garden and walked back through the beautiful house, where the servant showed him out. Soon he would board the plane and fly back to her sister. He had missed Yinan terribly and he had gifts for her, photographs and presents. It was best to look to the future and put these things to rest. But his conversation with Junan had been burned into his mind.

YINAN DIED EARLY THE FOLLOWING SPRING. MY FATHER WROTE to me enclosing copies of her poems. It was some consolation, he wrote, to share his memories of Yinan with someone else who'd loved her. The poems were written in complex characters on many sheets of paper, some yellowed and others fresh, some in her own handwriting and others newly copied by my father. I read them all, many times, particularly one that he'd written carefully on a thick, cream-colored sheet.

Many days I wait for you;
Fine days, frost shining days.
Clear sky, boats shake in the breeze.
Soon it will be winter.

I put the poems in my safe-deposit box, pressed between the pages of the tattered book of fairy tales. Inside the book I'd also saved Hu Ran's faded notes and the two old photographs I had brought with me all the way from Chongqing. After more than four decades of preservation these items had shrunk and faded. Only my mother's pearls seemed indestructible, uncoiling from their pouch as if alive, a rope of graduated silver orbs with the largest pearl bigger than my thumbnail. They shimmered in the light, casting a kind of radiance over the dingy papers, and for a moment I imagined what my mother might say. "Houses, money, and jewelry hold their value, Hong. All else diminishes."

Still, the photos held my interest. One was the print of Yinan as a girl, holding a single rose. She wore her hair pulled back and a pale dress that fit her awkwardly, as if someone else had just adjusted it. It was her pose that held my attention: the downcast face and lifted eyes, the expression of timidity. But there was also something else, something other than timidity, which cast her image in a haunted light.

In my parents' wedding photo, they seemed almost unbearably young. My father's face held no evidence of future suffering or wisdom. He was merely handsome in his lieutenant's uniform, his expression both cocky and oddly pure. At his side, my mother was perfect. She wore her hair in a chignon, its weight tipping her head back and lifting her chin. Even then, at nineteen, she held herself with dignity, absolute control. Her high, oval forehead shielded impenetrable thoughts. Her intelligent gaze was clear as water. The delicate curve from nose to mouth, the mouth itself, the jaw: in nothing could I see the smallest weakness. Still, it must have been there. A wayward swirl in her hair, a sunken bone, some brief mistake. A telltale fingerprint of fate. Where was it?

I studied Yinan's photo, searching for a resemblance between the beautiful sister and the plain one. In each of them, it seemed to me, there was a look of privacy, hinting at a place that couldn't be touched. I believed this was the part of themselves that they would share with no one but each other. My mother and my aunt had always been close, and even in their betrayal they drew together in a way that left out everyone else. The betrayal had made a phantom sister that could not be replaced by any other person. Through the years, they were unable to exorcise this ghost. Each sister had a hollowed soul, like a room kept waiting in expectation of an important visitor.

FOLLOWING MY FATHER'S sudden visit, my mother stopped speaking to me. She wouldn't return my calls or answer my letters. I tried to talk to Hwa. But Hwa, too, was still smarting from my mother's anger. When she'd discovered Hwa had known about my trip to visit Yinan, my mother had given Hwa a thorough tongue-lashing. Hadn't I done enough? my sister asked. Did I need to talk about what I'd done, as well?

I did need to talk about it. Not to gloat, as Hwa suspected, but because my conversations with Yinan, Yao, and my father had raised up darker feelings that I couldn't put to rest. Only my mother could release them. But my mother had made up her mind: she would speak to me only when she wished. And so, for many months, I waited to be summoned.

Hwa said my mother reacted little to the news of Yinan's death. It's quite possible she'd had some intimation of its coming, some instinctive knowledge or perhaps a dream. The day she learned the news, she kept all of her appointments. She met with her attorney. She scolded her broker for selling some stocks in Pu Li's company, threatening to fire him, and he sent a fruit basket in apology.

But in the following weeks, it seemed that my mother's old ferocity had been replaced with mere vigilance. Perhaps she knew it, too. That summer, she had a black and white photograph taken of herself. She demanded that Hwa drive her to the big temple once a week. The monks kept ashes there, near a stand of trees several hundred yards from the temple building. The ashes were kept in slots that reminded me of old apothecary cabinets. My mother donated money to make certain her own ashes would be in a prominent location. Hwa told me she'd ordered a blown-glass paperweight to be set on the shelf before her slot. Inside the clear globe shone, impeccable, a red glass flower.

Hwa called in October, after her stroke. "You'd better come now," she said. Tom was on a retreat for the school where he taught, and so I flew alone into San Francisco on a brilliant autumn day and took a taxi to my mother's house.

THE DOORMAN STOOD on a silk rug darkened and crushed from equipment wheels and foot traffic. Hwa waited, pale, behind him. We faced each other and nodded. From somewhere in the house, I heard the whirring of a machine.

"Mama's lost her vision," Hwa said. "They don't know if it's a temporary thing. But she can still talk, her mind is clear."

"It's good to see you," I told my sister.

She looked down at the rug. "Let's go."

My mother's room was quiet and in perfect order. A bit of light fell upon her beige satin coverlet, embroidered with a hundred characters for longevity. As I moved toward her, I could see that some mysterious process keeping her alive had withdrawn itself. She had become a long, pale filigree of bones covered with a waxen layer of living flesh. But when I reached the bed, her eyes opened, fierce.

"Ma," my sister said. "It's me." Her voice was high and thin.

"Who else is there?"

"Did you have a good nap? You're looking better."

My mother's eyes moved toward Hwa. She snapped, so suddenly that I flinched, "Don't lie to me, you ninny."

Hwa hurried out of the room.

My mother's gaze moved away from Hwa and stopped not quite where I was standing.

"It's me," I said. "It's Hong."

I sat down in the easy chair beside my mother's bed. For some time we were silent. I looked out of the window, where the shape of a live oak stood out against the hills that had burned through their green and bleached to a lion-colored gold. Its gnarled branches reached against the evening sky. I sensed the age of the tree, the waning of day, and an uncomfortable, crabbed power that moved toward its end.

It was true we'd become enemies, although I'd never wished to be. Soon my mother would be gone—I would no longer be at risk. Yet we were at odds. I could hear it in the churning of the machines; I could feel it in the air, in the gathering dusk. I felt the need to vanquish her, to strike, as if I couldn't believe that the black and violent center of my world would ever vanish.

"We're angry with each other," I said.

"Yes."

"I know you disapprove of me for going back to find them. But you must have thought of them so many times in all those years. Weren't you just a little glad I did it—glad that you could see him one more time before you died?"

"Our lives are none of your business."

"But your lives are all I remember. They're at the heart of what I know."

She said nothing, but her head moved, slightly, to the side, a shadow of her old gesture of impatience.

"You think you know so much," she said.

"Didn't you even want to know that they survived?" I asked. "They did survive, you know, despite all of your decisions. Even you can't have complete control over other people."

I remembered that my father had tried to hint this to her once, on that last, rainy afternoon in Shanghai. How did it feel now to her, listening in darkness? A spasm of weakness, or perhaps pain, passed over her face, but I couldn't stop. I was thinking about my father in his wool coat; of my aunt Yinan crying after forty years. I was thinking about Hu Ran, perishing in the water while my mother's furniture came straight through the blockade; I could see my brother, Yao, his life broken, his eyes burning, as he said that it was too late for him.

"I don't understand," I said. "When you treat them terribly, you're injuring yourself. You don't consider your own feelings. You loved them more than anyone else, and you still love them. You love them both, and yet you ruined them."

"Tell me," my mother said, "what would you have done? You think you know me well, but do you know yourself? How much would you have sacrificed to keep the one you wanted most?"

I opened my lips but could not speak.

She stared straight ahead, bravely, into the darkness. Then perhaps she shook her head again; her head fell to the side, a movement signaling that it was time for me to go. Her eyes closed. "You were always his daughter," she said, almost to herself. "You wouldn't understand."

She was right. We know so little about the people who have come before us. And so my mother and I reached a kind of truce. We waited in silence, listening as the wings of night swept over us. As I left the room, I handed her the string of small buddhas she kept on her night table. She couldn't move her fingers but she liked to hold the beads. Something in their regularity comforted her, as in the prayers she'd repeated for the past few decades. Now I knew she wasn't praying for release, forgiveness, or an easy end. The prayers gave her strength. They somehow deepened her resolve to live until her end without changing.

IN THE KITCHEN, Hwa's heels echoed on the spotless floor. All the lights were on, and the faucets had been shined to an almost painful gleam. Hwa let running water slop over the lip of the teakettle. When she set a glass plate of sesame candies on the table, a piece jumped off the plate. I reached out and took it so as to make her forget about it. Hwa pushed in a drawer so sharply that I jumped back. She marched to the stove and stood over the teakettle, waiting.

"I don't know why I put up with her for so many years." Her voice was stifled and shaking.

"Hwa," I tried to comfort her. "I know she seems harsh, but—"

"She is harsh." Hwa was crying. She sobbed, curled into herself, and when I put my hand upon her shoulder it felt resistant, like a shell.

"Hwa, it's not your fault. It's all mine, and she knows it. She doesn't mean to be cold to you."

Her sobbing rose higher.

"Meimei, you know she loves you. You've been so good to her for all these years. When she's had a chance to rest, she'll want to talk to you to make sure it's all right."

Hwa raised her face and looked at me. Her eye makeup was smudged and her lips were pale.

"No. That's not what happens. Do you know what's going to happen? I'll go back to her and break down in tears. Then I'll beg for her forgiveness. That's what I always do."

She waited for my response, but I didn't know what to say.

"She's still upset that I didn't tell her Baba was coming."

"You wanted to protect her," I said. "Can't you explain?"

"No, that's you. You're the one who's allowed to explain."

Hwa's words shot toward me, as if searching for a place to strike, and I braced myself.

Hwa said, "Deep down, Ma knows what she's like. She knows that anyone who stays with her gets whittled into nothing. So she's lost everyone she's ever really loved. She lost our father and Yinan. She loved you, and she let you go. She knew what you were doing, all those years ago in Shanghai. I would tell her you were with Pu Li, or playing basketball, or whatever stupid excuse you'd invented, and I don't think she ever believed me. She let you go your way, even though it almost killed you." She turned her wet, wrecked face to me. "She asked for you yesterday."

"Hwa, you're just upset."

"You never had to marry the man she picked out for you. You never had to live with her. Do you think I didn't know who Pu Li really wanted to marry? Do you think I didn't know what I was doing?"

Her eyes were glittering, absolute.

"Listen. I'm not blaming you. But do you know how they 'proposed' to me? His mother wrote him a letter, from Taiwan. I didn't even know she had done it. Then his mother asked Ma, 'Is this okay?' I was still heartbroken over Willy. I didn't have the energy to say no. The next time he came home, he knew that it was all decided. He never asked me. Never even spoke about it."

"Hwa."

"You didn't care. You were so beyond it all. Making your escape from us."

"I didn't mean to leave you, Meimei."

Hwa looked away. "At any rate, Pu Li didn't love you enough to insist on you. He did what his mother told him."

"Meimei," I said. "After all this time has passed, surely it doesn't matter."

"Of course it matters."

"Surely you love each other, after all these years."

"Yes," she said. She was crying again. "We love each other now. But it still matters."

For a few moments she seemed to take a satisfaction in my silence.

She washed her teacup and saucer and put everything away. But after some time, she grew uneasy. She glanced at her watch. Then she stood up, wiped her eyes, ran a hand through her hair, and left the kitchen. I heard her footsteps crossing the courtyard; I knew my mother could hear them, too. Hwa would go to her and close the door, and somehow, in that hollow room, the two of them would conduct the dark and necessary ritual of forgiveness.

THE DAY AFTER my mother died, her lawyer, Gary Liu, drove over to Hwa's house, bringing an envelope of rough brown silk marked over the flap with an impression of her largest, most elaborate chop. Inside the envelope was her will and the instructions for her memorial services. She would be cremated, and there would follow the traditional forty-nine days of mourning. She left everything she had to her four grandchildren, except for the house, which she gave to the temple, along with an endowment for its upkeep.

It would have been unrealistic to expect our mother to depart the earth without also leaving precise instructions. But even Hwa hadn't imagined the instructions would be so elaborate. She'd included the name and address of the tailor who'd made the sheath in which she was to be cremated, with the final alterations to be made after she was dead. Her florist would arrange her favorite flowers according to her sketches. She named two caterers for the offerings, one for fruit and one to make the many bean curd shapes. She drew a diagram of the table, labeled with the other things she wanted there: fruits and paper money, incense, decorations. She cautioned that the offerings would be considerable and that because of this her black and white photograph should be hung at a certain distance over the table so that the piles of fruit and food wouldn't dominate her image. After the ceremony everyone would attend a lavish banquet. The restaurant had been consulted and an expensive menu planned; there was a separate but equally elaborate menu for people from the temple, who didn't eat meat. Limousines would take the mourners to the restaurant. The seating in the cars had been assigned.

As my mother had planned, it all took place without any significant disturbance.

Her guests overflowed the temple parking lot. Besides our family and Pu Taitai, I think the people most affected by her death were those who'd helped her with her house and health. The man who'd redone my mother's furniture brought his Italian wife from San Francisco. The young nurse who'd brewed my mother's medicine was with her husband. The cleaning women and the gardeners stood together, somber. Then there were her former friends and rivals with their families. There were those whom even Hwa hadn't seen in years, but who'd responded to the call. Several of her old mahjong friends from Chongqing tottered to the temple with their children at their elbows. A fleet of cars arrived from the suburbs of Los Angeles. Finally, a glossy private limousine pulled up and to everyone's surprise, Hsiao Meiyu emerged, a tiny, elegant old lady wearing a severe black qipao and a hat with a little net that fluttered in the breeze.

There were two visitors my mother hadn't planned for. Hwa's son Marcus brought his girlfriend, a young woman with stand-up hair and a polite expression of blue-eyed curiosity. And Hu Mudan flew out with Tom and my daughters. Tom helped her from the car. Hu Mudan saw me immediately and broke away from him, looking small and tired from the flight, but alert. She felt obliged to watch over the proceedings. My mother wouldn't have wanted her to be there. But my mother couldn't stop her now, and Hu Mudan was old enough to do whatever she wanted.

I had tucked Yinan's poem into my mother's sheath. She wouldn't have approved. But it seemed fitting that my father and Yinan should be somehow present for this ceremony. The poem would soon burn away, and at last my mother's long sorrow and anger would be released.

EVEN HWA DIDN'T know her whole story.

My mother had let me go, but she had always kept her lips close to my ears. "Listen," she said. "Listen and watch." Since I was a child, we'd had an unspoken understanding: that I would keep her story the

way she had kept her mother's. She would silently pour into me her stories and her secrets. I would hold on to them for her, over her coldness
and her anger, over her admonition not to be too proud of what I saw.
I was allowed to be myself, to travel far away from her, as long as she
didn't have to bear them alone. I had staggered under the weight of her
stories. But now that she was gone, what would I be? I had been the witness to her life, and now that it was over, this arduous task mattered to
no one but me.

In truth: I had once sacrificed everything to be loyal to my mother.
It was my mother whom I had wanted most, and despite my sacrifice
she died without ever understanding this. I wondered what Mudan and
Evita knew. Did Mudan truly understand the story of the mute pendant
she wore in the hollow of her throat? What would Evita one day tell her
own daughter about her mother? She was a child of her generation. She
possessed their look: the hidden inwardness of people who have
learned, by necessity, to divine the mysteries of two cultures they do
not entirely inhabit. The past to her was as mysterious as her own beautiful face when she looked in the mirror, the face of her ancestors.

The low, harsh drone of chanting filled our ears.

Se bu i kong
kong bu i se
se chi shi kong
Kong chi shi se
Shou xiang xing shi

How had my mother comforted herself with these words, seeking
nothingness, and all the while holding on to the long anger that sus-
tained her?

She had taught us that the most powerful love is founded on possession. She kept us secure throughout the terrible war and through the
tumult after. In return, she asked only that we be absolutely loyal. How
is it possible to obey the contract for such love? One by one, we had all
disappointed her. Chanyi had left her, Yinan had betrayed her, my
father had proved himself to be a mere man. Hwa had withheld a secret,

and I had brought her shame. We had all failed to love her in the way she wanted to be loved.

Now the drums called our attention. We stood gathered around the coffin. I imagined her small body within as I had seen it in the morning, shrunken and unfamiliar, wound in a chrysalis of robes. The vivid violet silk was embroidered with phoenixes and unicorns and tongues of flame. The coffin slid past the group and the small door closed after her. We leaned toward her, not in curiosity but in a kind of apprehension. So it had been when she was still alive and she had made so many of us shrink at her direction, and now her body, sealed away, revealed nothing. It made me wonder if all along she had been rehearsing for this moment of ultimate withholding.

Typically the oldest son was chosen to push the button lowering the casket to the underground furnace. She had borne no sons, and so I pushed the button. There was no struggle, no evidence of an angry spirit. There was only a gasp of silence as the casket moved below, and then the roar of flames.

I waited for the world to bend, as if she were still holding on to it. I felt a long moment of slow loosening, a blooming of relief. My head grew light, as if long braids that had entangled me had lifted in the wind. She had been like a dark star, drawing all of us toward her. Soon we would be free to walk away from her, so blind and suffering, harsh, and mortal.

When we left the temple, I was startled by the daylight. The sun stood high and weak in the white clouds, a faded orb enclosed in the center of an ancient egg. Under this pale autumn sky, I walked with the others to the line of waiting limousines. I moved slowly, testing the ground, but the earth did not tremble. Only the hollow sound of drums echoed in my ears.

ACKNOWLEDGMENTS

FOR THEIR GENEROUS SUPPORT during the writing of this novel, I would like to thank the Creative Writing Program and the Council of the Humanities at Princeton University, the Radcliffe Institute for Advanced Study, the National Endowment for the Arts, and the Rona Jaffe Foundation. The MacDowell Colony, the Corporation of Yaddo, and the Ucross Foundation provided precious solitude and time.

It is also a pleasure to thank Sarah Chalfant and Jin Auh for their work and encouragement, and Jill Bialosky for her invaluable patience and unerring instincts.

I could not have conceived of or written this book without the sure counsel of my parents, Helen Chung-Hung Hsiang and Nai-Lin Chang. I am also indebted to Professor Eileen Cheng-yin Chow at Harvard University for her wit and knowledge, and to Siqin Ye for his Mandarin and hard work. For help with research on China and particularly Hangzhou in the 1920s and '30s, I would also like to acknowledge the late Wen Guangcai of Hangzhou.

I am especially grateful to the following friends for their insightful and generous readings: Eileen Bartos, Andrea Bewick, Nan Cohen, Craig Collins, Alyssa Haywoode, Ray Isle, Elizabeth Rourke, and Kris Vervaecke.

In the past seven years, I've often been grateful for the wisdom of Eavan Boland, Connie Brothers, Deborah Kwan, Margot Livesey, and Gay Pierce. I've also been kept afloat by the moral support of Augusta Rohrbach, Scott Johnston, and my beloved sisters Ling Chang, Huan Justina Chang, and Tai Chang Terry.

Finally, I want to thank Robert Caputo for his humor, insight, and unwavering belief.

INHERITANCE

Lan Samantha Chang

Your novel, Inheritance, *explores a family rift that is intensified by the split between mainland China and Taiwan. Early in the novel, two brothers are divided by their political views. One is an ardent Communist and the other a Nationalist officer. In 1949, when the Communists come to power, the family literally splits in two, with the narrator's mother leaving for Taiwan and her beloved sister staying on the mainland. The two sisters are out of touch until after Mao's death in 1978. Is the novel based on a story in your own family? Could you comment on your decision to portray this period of Chinese history?*

Both the current governments of democratic Taiwan and Communist China trace their origins to the Republican Era, the period from 1911 to 1949 when China became the world's biggest country to attempt democracy after thousands of years of dynastic rule. *Inheritance* is set during those tumultuous years of struggle against civil unrest and continuing military aggression from Japan. In those years my parents were born and raised in China. The novel is set in the world my parents knew when they were young. As a matter of fact, my father's younger brother did become a Communist as a teenager, while my father chose to leave the country for Taiwan in 1949. My father, who is apolitical, has always been pretty reticent about his family, and I didn't learn about my uncle's Communist beliefs until a few years ago, when my father went back to visit his family and put two and two together. At some point during his visit, my father saw a familiar name on a government publication, a name he remembered from his youth. He realized that this man, one of his late brother's close friends, must have converted his brother to Communism when they were teenagers. Although I know nothing more than this, the idea—of two brothers with conflicting political beliefs—worked its way into my imagination. The rest of the novel has no basis in my family history. The novel is an imaginary history, an exploration into lives that might have been.

Would you speak more of this idea of "imaginary histories"?

I often say that while growing up I found my parents, particularly my father, to be a mystery. My parents had been through a great trauma—

their fears for us and the few stories they told indicated this—but they spoke about the past so seldom that to this day I feel that I am missing some very basic facts about their lives. This silence came, I think, from a desire to protect us. They wanted to forget the past and focus on the future. *Inheritance* is in many ways an attempt to people this silence, to fill it with the voices and visions of an imaginary past. The characters, and the drama that shaped their lives, are invented. I've always been interested in the idea of two sisters who share one great love. My narrator, Hong, recalls her childhood in the turbulence of war, and seeks to uncover the great mystery of her childhood: the love triangle of her mother, her father, and her beloved aunt. I've also been intrigued by the idea of a child as a detective: collecting clues, gathering evidence, trying to fit together the lives of her parents as if there were a great, key piece of information at the heart of it all that would explain everything. Of course, the basic question—Who are these people I know and love?—remains a mystery.

Describe the research you conducted while writing the novel.

I began researching the novel with the rather idealistic notion that I'd somehow be able to recapture the world of China in the 1930s and 1940s. Like many researchers I soon became mired in the human problem of time: namely, that we live forward in time and that it's impossible to truly know the past.

I grew up with immigrant parents in whose memories that old China was still vivid. So I went to China in high hopes of finding that world, only to discover that it was no longer there. China had changed, was changing enormously every day. In the last forty years books had been burned, walls razed, records destroyed, and people encouraged to look forward. The new country was abounding with vibrancy and growth, new attitudes, new policies, new life.

I realized that I would never be able to recapture the past. This recognition was daunting but also curiously liberating: I understood that in certain ways I would be required to rely on my imagination. So I went about my research using what I could find. I went to Chongqing, Shanghai, and Hangzhou, the city where the Wang family lived. I spoke to my parents and relatives, particularly a distant cousin of my father's who lived in Hangzhou. He also did some research for me on his own. Around this time I was fortunate to receive funding from two great universities, Princeton and Harvard, and access to their libraries. I found old maps, archives of old newspapers, and many memoirs and photographs. With the aid of my parents and a brilliant Harvard undergraduate, Ye Siqin, I was able to glean details and ideas from these sources. Now that it's finished, I am grateful that I wrote the novel when I did, because so many of the people who participated in the events of the 1930s and 1940s are dying. My father's cousin, Wen Guangcai, passed away in Hangzhou just last year. I'm very glad that I was able to meet him and talk to him.

You grew up with three sisters in the town of Appleton, Wisconsin. Did your relationships with your sisters inspire this novel? Is the tumultuous relationship between Junan and Yinan anything like that between your sisters?

No one who hasn't had a sister can know precisely what it's like, and every set of sisters has a different story. In my experience, there's a tremendous intimacy—growing up as daughters of the same mother and father, and the possession of a shared emotional world—and yet a tremendous difference, a great divide, that becomes even more obvious when romantic love enters the picture. Love is the enormous gamble we all take, and regardless of how similar our upbringings are, our lives can differ greatly after we choose partners.

In my novel, two sisters fall in love with the same man, and only one of them can have him. This choice, on his part, changes their lives forever. The different destinies in store for these two women—political, personal, and financial—make up the second half of the book. And yet they are, despite years of estrangement, still closer to each other than they are to anyone else on earth.

A profile in the New York Times *once described you as struggling not to be categorized as "the next great female Asian American writer" in a literary tradition dominated by white males. As one of a generation of young writers of color now publishing their second books, how do you balance being an ethnic writer in a white world?*

I'm an American writer. I grew up reading Ernest Hemingway, James Baldwin, and Maxine Hong Kingston, and I love them. American literature is a big house with plenty of room for everyone; I believe that trying to carve it into subdivisions is a waste of the readers' time. I'm writing for the reader who's hungry for human stories that go beyond the ethnic identity of the characters. In my next big project, I'm returning to the Midwestern setting in which I grew up. This world is peopled by characters of many backgrounds, but their stories are all human stories.

What novels have influenced you in your writing of Inheritance?

Inheritance presented two challenges: the challenge of creating a narrative voice that could encompass the span of years and the changing worlds of the novel, and the challenge of adapting a story set in the past to a more contemporary narrative structure. I read and reread Henry James's *The Portrait of a Lady*, a great novel with a love triangle whose characters Isabelle, Osmond, and Madame Merle were of particular interest. I found *The Moor's Last Sigh* by Salman Rushdie very helpful in the way in which Rushdie uses the first-person narrator to tell family stories that took place before he was born. I also read and reread *The Makioka Sisters* by the great twentieth-century Japanese writer Junichiro Tanizaka, which taught me a great deal about how one great novelist melded Asian material with more European literary forms.

READER'S DISCUSSION QUESTIONS

1. *Inheritance* tracks events of loyalty and betrayal across four generations of one family. Has one factor triumphed over the other in the fractured family picture we witness at the novel's end?

2. Why is Hong compelled to revisit the past and uncover the secrets of her parents?

3. What role does chance play in the lives of the characters in *Inheritance*? What lessons can be learned from Junan's efforts to control her family members' destinies?

4. How do the sisters Junan and Yinan change over the course of the novel? What qualities of each remain constant?

5. What does the relationship of Hong and Hwa hold in common

with that of Junan and Yinan? What universal themes of sisterhood does *Inheritance* consider?

6. Despite the constant economic and political upheaval that occurs over her lifetime, Jinan shrewdly maintains her family's wealth. Yet she lacks other forms of enrichment. Describe the different forms wealth takes in the lives of the novel's various characters and how it affects the choices they make.

7. Describe how Hu Mudan represents the spiritual center of the novel.

8. What does Hong hope to prove through her relationship with Hu Ran? What does she ultimately learn?

9. In explanation of her grandfather's gambling addiction, Junan comments: "Only in paigao did he find what he desired: the dedication to uncertainty, the fellow players who shared his own need to extinguish themselves in the wild and bitter hopefulness of chance." How does this self-endangering appetite for risk manifest itself in the behavior of other characters in the novel? Is this instinct true of everyone?

10. What salves do the various characters of the novel discover to deal with their regrets?

11. How might Hwa have told the story of her family differently from Hong?

12. Junan offers "thoughtlessness" as an excuse for her father's behavior, and retains a deep affection for him. Does Li Ang deserve her sympathy?

13. Is Hong right to withhold the truth from her half-brother Yao about Yinan and Junan's last meeting?

14. How is the great flux of historical change in Chinese society over the course of the twentieth century manifest in the generational differences among the members of Hong's family, from Chanyi to Evita?

15. Lan Samantha Chang attests that her inspiration to write *Inheritance* came, in part, from her desire to know the long-buried China from which her parents emigrated. What does our desire to write or read fiction that recounts history reveal about how we choose to process the past?